HAUNTED REQUIEMS

LYRA R. SAENZ
THE NOCTURNE SYMPHONY
HAUNTED
REQUIEMS
THREE TALES
OF DARKNESS

Published By: 4 Horsemen Publications, Inc.

4 Horsemen Publications, Inc.
PO Box 417
Sylva, NC 28779
4horsemenpublications.com
info@4horsemenpublications.com

Cover & Illustration by CD Corrigan
Typesetting by Autumn Skye
Edited by Jen Paquette

Library of Congress Control Number: 2024952326

Paperback ISBN-13: 979-8-8232-0804-8
Hardcover ISBN-13: 979-8-8232-0805-5
Audiobook ISBN-13: 979-8-8232-0807-9
Ebook ISBN-13: 979-8-8232-0806-2

DEDICATION

To my own tiny star. Keep shining bright.

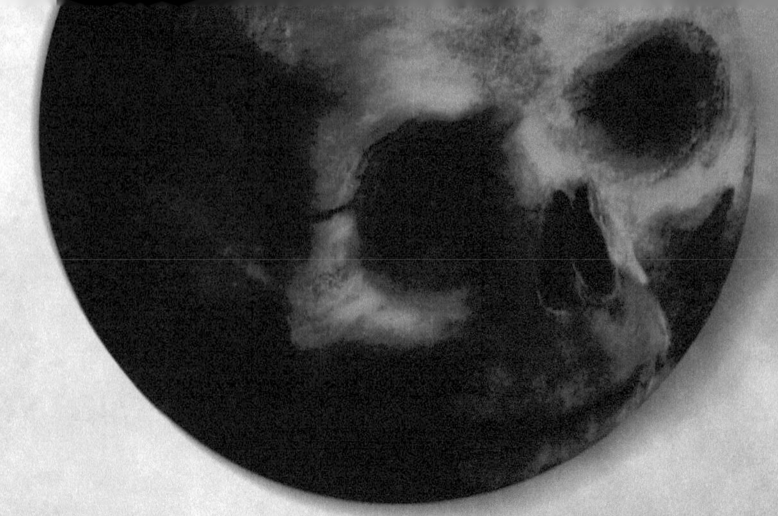

TABLE OF CONTENTS

THE DEVIL'S TRILL

FALSETTO IN THE WOODS

NURSERY RHYMES IN THE DARK

THE
DEVIL'S
TRILL

This novella contains spoilers for *Sonata*, book 2 of Lyra R. Saenz's Nocturne Symphony. Readers who have not yet read *Sonata* are advised to pause before venturing further.

Additional Warnings: Mentions of rape, torture, domestic abuse, stillbirth/infanticide, and abortion.

'Til Death Do Us Part...

There are secrets between lovers,
So very dark and ugly.
We'll take them to our graves one day,
where the dirt stinks of decay.

But secrets never die.
Not really.
Not for some.
For all your deeds come out to play
until secrets there are none.

I married my love's secrets.
I wear them on my neck,
Where fingers wound and wrapped and wrung
Until I could not speak of it.

There are secrets between lovers,
so dirty, dank, and grim.
We lay them in our marriage bed
to rest with sacred vim.

But parasites don't sleep.
They dine on us instead.
They nibble at our toes
And grow fat upon our souls.

They grow and grow and grow some more
Until there's no more left to eat.

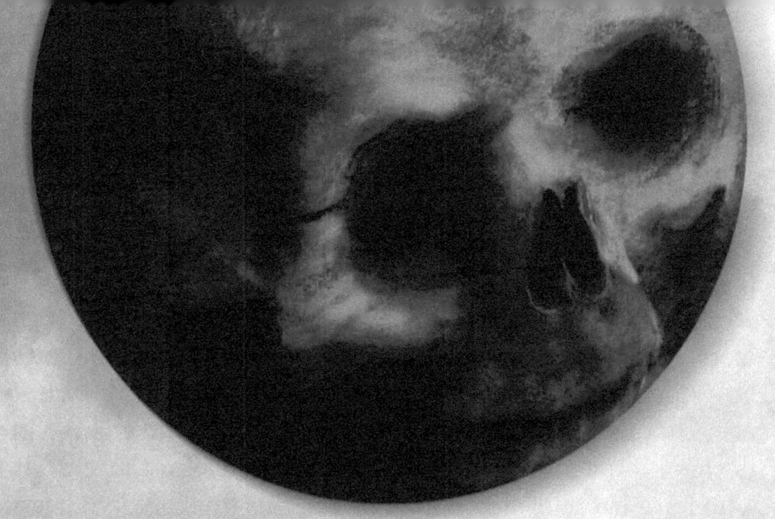

I

THE OVERTURE

I saw death in her eyes.

I saw it plainly as I see you reading this page. It was not a threat, nor even a promise. It simply was. I was going to die, and I was so sure she was going to be the cause, I lost sight of the real war instead. I fought, of course. I fought like hell, but how can you fight fate when you're blind to the future?

I was going to die, and I thought I stood before my executioner.

Turns out, the ax swung from below.

It smells like shit.

All dungeons smell like shit, even the most high-tech ones. Excuse me, prisons... All *prisons* smell like shit. Gotta be politically correct. "Dungeon" is too medieval—whatever that's supposed to account for. Not that the change in designation actually makes anything better for those of us who have been leveled with a bed in this fine facility. Clean, sterile, and shiny with its chromium-plated bars, glass doors, ID scanners, and automated security systems. You would think it would smell like a hospital in here, yet it smells like human feces left out in the heat for five days before someone scooped it up, put it in a pot, and mixed in the breast sweat of a six-ton elephant who hasn't left the stable in over a year to make stew: a *creme de la poopoo*. That's what it smells like here. Hard-boiled shit.

Not that I can say it's unexpected. I mean, what else are you supposed to write with in here? Well, that's what the lycans and vampyres use anyway.

I don't get even that luxury.

Creatures like me aren't afforded the same meager accommodations as more mundane hexen. We're too... how do you say... unpredictable.

"Put the witch in for holding. The general will decide what to do with her later."

Witch... That's me. My designation, my title, my number... the witch. To think I would be living the high life in Lorelei surrounded by my army of chimeras were it not for those infantile technomancers.

Meddlesome brats!

My cell is made of the finest titanium. Six perfectly identical sides make a pristine cube. I wouldn't be able to tell which direction was up or down were it not for gravity keeping me upright, and every panel is laced with anti-magic tech. The silver-laced wires pulse with a dull white light. (Were I to so much as look at them wrong, they'd light up and load me with enough voltage to down a water buffalo.) There is no bed, just a raised slab. At first glance, I thought it was made of the same hard steel as the walls, but the first time I sat in it, it yielded to my weight. When I sleep, it shapes itself to my body, a perfect cloud of comfy. It would be a five-star experience were it not for the fact that it radiates a disturbing field of hot/cold energy whenever I lie there. A massage with too much and too little pressure designed to subdue anyone who lays their corpse in it. It makes for a fitful sleep, hard to wake from and disturbingly easy to fall into.

One Star.

Out of curiosity, I once tried to fling myself against the wall in an effort to bash my own miserable head in, but just like the "bed," the structure yielded, and I ended up bouncing unceremoniously onto my ass like a five-year-old in a balloon house. Heh... and they say we bend the laws of reality. What have they to say for what they warp with their science? Walls shouldn't have the surface tension of a trampoline one moment only to harden to solid stone the next.

And the waste room situation... a square bowl welded to the floor. Imagine if you will, the way a dog has to squat to pee only it's wearing a short dress and heels and its front paws are tied together... That's how I feel every time I use it, regardless of my lack of proper footwear. Just something about the angle and position makes me have to lift my heels a good five inches to aim properly. Because they don't want me getting creative with my bodily fluids (witches can get a lot done with a little urine and the right array), my waste bin is monitored by several droids and emptied the moment it is soiled. I made the mistake of trying to go outside my little bowl—once. We won't talk about how that ended.

Definitely leaving a negative review on this stay.

As if merely using the cursed toilet and bed weren't difficult enough, cameras follow my every sneeze and cough. They keep me in manacles: pretty steel bracelets linked to one another with a cord of radioactive something or other. I don't know what exactly the material is, but it makes me so tired I can barely wake up more than the two or three times a day they feed me, and that's only because they turn the damn things off so I can move around without accidentally strangling myself. Speaking of... Why don't they just let me strangle myself? What could they want with a live witch? I was under the impression the League wanted us eradicated, not living the shit-scented high life in one of their resort prisons.

Without windows or clocks, I can only judge how long I've been here by the number of meals brought to me. I estimate, if they are being stingy, that it's been a little more than a week. I've never gone so long without using magic, and I can feel my powers festering.

It's an achy, uncomfortable feeling: magical atrophy.

You know how when people end up bedridden, their muscles atrophy? The muscles deteriorate, and they lose their ability to move around, so their skin builds up bedsores, and after the physical body has had enough, the mind just kind of goes a little lopsided. That's what it feels like when a witch doesn't use her magic. It festers inside like ants dying under the skin, and no matter how much you scratch, the itch only worsens until...

ACCESS GRANTED

The A.I. attached to my cell's locking mechanism chimes over the intercom in a cheery singsong voice. Why do these +ies always choose feminine voices for their artificial intelligence?

"Well, well, well... Look what we have here."

The man that walks into my cell is more machine than person: a robotic arm, half his face metal and bolted in place, the shine of silver under his shirt collar, and by the resonant echo of his right boot, he's got himself a prosthetic leg, too. The few fleshy parts I can see seem knitted together with wire cabling and scar tissue. When he looks at me with muddy green eyes, the hair at the back of my neck rises.

"What do you want?" I spit out as I find my feet. Like hell I'm going to keep lounging on my back as a technomancer invades my cozy little stink pit.

"The boys told me you were a freak, but they didn't mention how easy you were on the eyes."

His eyes... Goddess below! I've met serpents with more human eyes. Human in biology they may be, but they are monstrous in intention.

"Stay away from me."

"Just relax, witchy."

"Guards!" I call. He laughs.

"Really now? Who do you think let me in here?"

He reaches for me with his mechanical hand. On impulse, I lash out with my magic, trying with all my might to summon something to my defense, but nothing comes. Not even a puff of smoke. It merely lingers, hollow at my fingertips like cobwebs.

Pain flares in my cheek as he slaps me across the face with enough force to send me nose-first into the wall. Cold digits close around the nape of my neck, and my feet leave the floor.

"Let go of me—ah!"

The wall punches the air from my lungs. It's cold against my front. I kick backward; my bare heel hits his metal leg. Ouch! White pain zings up my leg.

"Come on, love. I promise I'll show you a good time."

Eyes closed: teeth gritted... *Is this really happening right now?*

"Montwyatte!"

Everything stops. The world grinds to a halt, and suddenly my heart isn't racing as fast anymore. The hands leave my body. My damaged foot can't hold my weight, so I slump to my knees. It's definitely broken... or at least sprained. Goddamn cyborgean arseholes.

"Well, if it isn't the flunky. What do you want, Donnie? Scared I won't leave anything for you?"

My hair is tangled in the bolts that make up the joints of his fingers.

"Miss Helsdottir will not to be treated in such a manner. She is considered an asset to the state, and I advise you to leave these premises now."

The new entrant is by the door, obstructed from my view. I can only see a pair of polished dress shoes under the hem of a pair of finely pressed black slacks, but his voice is soothing, like warmed butter over cinnamon toast. There's a gliding rhythm to it, the kind of voice that should be reciting poetry over an open campfire while bongos play on the outskirts and naturalists pass the devil's grass back and forth. Who is this man?

"Or what, Donnie-boy? You'll tell daddy on me?"

My would-be rapist huffs like a spoiled teenager caught sneaking his girlfriend into his dormitory. I'm noticing now the notches on the back of his neck: lines of ink of varying widths all in a column along his cervical spine. It reminds me of the olden days when the hexen royals used to tattoo sigils on non-magical humans as a means to keep track of them and any augmentations they undertook. The sigils would connect them to a psionic witch capable of tracking their every thought, word, and deed for disloyalty or dissent. Suffice to say, this was just one of the reasons the human+ revolted.

Maybe if the psionics had done their job right, we wouldn't be in this mess...

Only, this tattoo isn't even remotely one of those sigils, or if it is, it's been deconstructed into a series of lines tic-tac-toe-ing across the man's back. I wonder if each line represents something, like notches on a bedpost, or maybe the tattoo as a whole has a meaning of its own.

"I would ask you not to call me that."

"Or what, short stuff?"

"Last I checked, despite my lack of technomancer certification, I outrank you during wartime."

"'During wartime,' he says. Hah! What a joker! Wartime, my ass."

The man laughs his way past the other male and out the door. The air trapped in my lungs escapes, a long sigh of relief I didn't even know I was holding. The room feels so much bigger now that his mass is gone from the space. I take a moment to breathe.

In... 2... 3... 4... Out... 2... 3... 4... In... 2...

"Are you alright?"

The hand hovering before me is well-manicured. A heavy signet ring decorates his index finger. The sleeve of his shirt is held by a silver cufflink adorned with a single opal. It's a nice-looking hand. One I wouldn't mind taking.

"I'll be fine."

His palm is cool to the touch, his grip firm but not too tight.

"Good. That's very good. My name is Donarick."

Wow... As I look into his eyes, one mechanical, one human, something slides into place that I didn't even know was askew. It's jarring, being confronted by your own incompletion, your own shortcomings. Worst of all, it makes me dizzy, this new feeling.

I've never fallen up before.

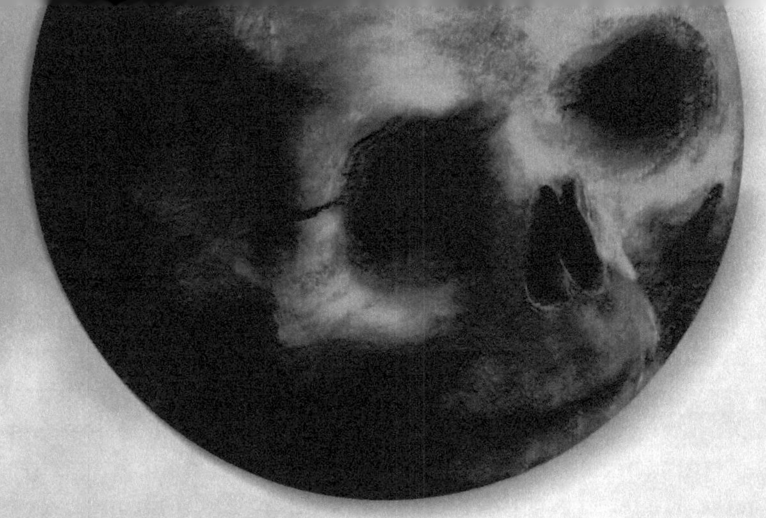

II

WAR MARCH

If there was one lesson I learned as a child that I think stands true today, it's that creatures like me either live forever or die young.

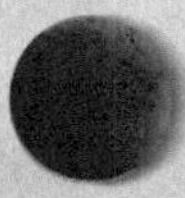

So, I join Seraphim's forces in exchange for my freedom, not that I really have much choice. Either fight or rot away in my little titanium cell. It's a sweet deal really. I get to kill as many human+ as I want, and in return, no one bothers me ever again. I'm not sure whose idea it was to recruit hexen to their cause, but I've got to hand it to them: technomancers and witches working side by side to bring down a common enemy? It's brilliant!

I don't think too highly of the Pontiflex Catalan or General Llywellyn. They're no different than any other power-hungry politician I've ever heard of. Greedy old men are greedy old men no matter their creed or color.

The Pontiflex's son, on the other hand, is a conundrum. Donarick Thames is no technomancer. He failed his examinations last year, and I don't expect he'll ever truly pass. He lacks a proper understanding of what it means to use techno-magic. Besides, he's too kind. I see him running negotiations back and forth like an eager puppy between the Pontiflex and the old Goblin King, Yggfret. Yes, I stand amid the last true hexen royalty. Yggfret Bloodfang is even more intimidating in person than his reputation gives him credit for, yet he indulges the young adept like a butcher fattening up a prize hog.

"I shall be venturing with the general's forces as they march on Deriva."

Yggfret's declaration comes as a surprise to all of us gathered in the "Special" accommodations Seraphim's military has provided us in their radiation-poisoned wilderness. (Goddess forbid, we let the witches stay within the actual city limits where radiation filters keep the masses safe from the nuclear waste their own government created.) He is the only one who is here willingly. Something about having negotiated our release in a bargain with the Pontiflex. Every one of us has been rotting on the inside of a cell for some length of time. You can tell based on the decrepit state of us all. If you ask me, the only marked improvement between this bunker and my prison cell is the added bunk beds. And I suppose the smell is slightly better, less hard-boiled and stale than *l'odeur de merde*.

"Why for? They don't need us."

While the other witches granted freedom in exchange for service are just as eager to spill +ie blood, they don't trust our newfound allies as far as they can throw them, and for some of us like Monsieur Géant, who boasts inhuman strength, that can be pretty far. I'm not sure if it's his naturally strong will or the leftover influence of giant blood (Giants are incredibly self-important. I've never met one whose head wasn't metaphorically bigger than their arse) that makes him so critical of Yggfret, but the goblin king seems just about ready to eat the half-giant witch himself.

"There is something I need to verify in Deriva. When better a time than when our allies march against it?"

"And if they fail?" inserts the bruja Xochtli. Short in stature but not in presence, the woman's voice, thick with an old Mestizo accent, echoes about the room in the voices of other witches.

"Then they fail. Their failure has no bearing on my venture."

Even if we are presently in alignment with Seraphim, we have no confidence in them or their ability to win a war against the rest of the continent. After all, why would they seek the help of witches if they were capable of making change themselves? Surely, it isn't just a neighborly show of faith.

Seraphim, as the northernmost country in Deus, is the closest neighboring country to the Wastes. The last major hexen territory, the Wastes have become something of a boogeyman to humans, a place where monsters and horrors abound. I've never been personally. I was too busy being raised in an orphanage amid a bunch of humans who would've tossed me out on the street the moment they realized what I was. Right there in New London is where I was born and allowed to grow.

That far into the center of the continent, Hexen-led territories like the Wastes were a distant dream. Well, until I met another hexen child. He used to speak of the Wastes as though they were some far-off utopia where all hexen could live a full life, free from the woes of human+ society. Whispered stories in the night long after lights out. We'd sit and fantasize about the wilds, about running away together to find the Wastes. Ah... Those were wonderful nights. He was the one who first taught me how to control my magic. He swore after he came of age and found his freedom from our little patch of hell that he would whisk me away like some knight in shining armor. I would have loved that.

Alas, a week before his coming of age, one of the overseers caught him fiddling with a spell. He disappeared the next day. Nothing was said about his absence, just that the orphanage decided to let him leave early. That's all: a quiet steal into the night. I didn't believe it, and I never saw him again.

Two years later, when I came of age, I summoned a salamander into the electrical room. We weren't allowed matches, and most buildings are fireproof anyway—at least against mundane fires. Magical flame, on the other hand... Suffice to say, the whole building burned down within minutes, and I made sure to barricade the emergency exits so the adults couldn't get out. I thought I would make my way to the Wastes after but ended up in Lorelei instead.

Now, I'm here, watching and waiting for the country who will "unify" the continent to commence with said unification. Apparently, Deriva is the initial domino that must crumble for it all to work.

"What's in Deriva, Yggfret?"

The witch king's mouth twists into a sadistic sneer.

"Let's just say I owe the Vulcana a visit."

Right. The Vulcana, the technomancer Elisabeta De Claré. She's the one who took off part of his left ear. Her quick-fire son and smart-mouthed stepdaughter are the reason I'm even part of this poor excuse for a coup. (Che! This whole thing is doomed to fail. Seraphim has the fewest technomancers on their roster. And we all know the reason for that.)

"You'd best make arrangements for your own accommodations, Yggfret," says Xochtli. "I doubt our new 'friends' will manage anything considerable."

What could motivate Seraphim to attack Deriva of all places first? Deriva is a fairly neutral island country. Did the Vulcan do something to upset the Pontiflex? I smell a vendetta, or is there some resource they want: use of their navy, access to a port and the goods kept a plenty there, or is it something else? But they couldn't. Seraphim doesn't have the muscle or the resources to go up against any of the other League nations.

"W-w-what if th-they s-s-s-succeed?" asks a mousy looking fellow in the back.

What then, indeed? Well, we go to war, obviously. It'll be the war to end all wars. Technomancers vs. technomancers. The destruction! Our ancestors vacated earth to escape a nuclear winter. Did we really go through all of that trouble just to allow Deus to fall to the same fate?

The witch who asks the question shakes under Yggfret's gaze. I would've thought him to be a shifter were it not for the indicia burning orange at his nose: a strange little mouse done in a single stroke. He must have an attunement to animals, particularly rodents if the rat seated on his shoulder is any indication. He's been whispering back and forth with it for the last hour, and this is the first time he's said anything loudly enough to be heard by human ears. This is hardly the kind of witch who should be on the front lines of a world war. What did he do to end up in a prison cell? Faint wrong in the street? Pathetic creature.

"They won't," scoffs Géant.

"They m-m-might," squeaks the rat-tamer.

"Yes, and one day a basilisk will lay a chicken egg so it can hatch into a pixie bear."

The whole room chimes with laughter at Géant's joke, including Yggfret who can't help but chuckle into his fist. Yes, we're all here enjoying fine wine and military hospitality at the behest of a country none of us feel has a chance to win. How could they? They couldn't even pass any techno-mancers at this last year's trials.

"You may yet find yourself a pixie bear, Géant, and not too long from now if my stars are right."

"What do you know, Yggfret?"

"Divination has always been my favored art."

"Divination is a load of stargazing crock. You and I both know no one can truly tell the future."

"And yet here I am, the willing guest of a League country about to stage a coup d'etat against its allies. What do you take me for? A halfwit like you who got yourself caught stealing from an airship?"

"At least I was doing something to disrupt the +ies. Meanwhile, you sit in a hovel hole on the side of a mountain—"

"Géant!" inserts Xochtli. "Have a care. You'd still be drawing sigils with your piss were it not for Yggfret!"

"If it weren't for Yggfret, I'd be ringing your neck, you worm-encrusted—"

I've no idea who throws the first spell, but a god-awful staticky sound falls from Xochtli's mouth while at the same time Géant throws his fist. This! This is the reason witches are rapidly losing the war against the League. We can't work together. We're too volatile on our own. Put too many of us in a room together, and chances are, the room won't survive. Really, if we ever want to reclaim our status as the royalty of this wretched continent, someone will have to figure out how to get us all to work together.

If only the old hexen families hadn't been completely eradicated centuries ago.

A blast of fire singes the tips of my horns. I grit my teeth and summon magic to my fingertips. Should I summon a banshee or a gorgon? The banshee would out-scream everyone and shut the whole room up while the gorgon would just turn everyone to stone, thus achieving the same result.

I could just flip a magical coin. Yes, a random magical weave sounds chaotic enough. Before I can begin the summoning, the buzzer over the doorway goes off.

"Ladies and gentlemen, please. There's no need for dissent. We are all here under the same banner."

It's Donarick. Dressed exactly as he came to me two days before, the human+ stands with his hands clasped in front of his waist in a pose reminiscent of an opera singer. Are you here to give us an aria, dear Thames?

"Well, if it isn't our generous host," sneers Géant.

"I understand the change in your circumstances might be difficult to digest," comes Donarick's response. "But I promise you full autonomy outside of these walls should you choose to vacate them."

"Full autonomy doesn't guarantee safety from your adepts, metal man," says Xochtli. "You honestly think we trust you enough to simply wander about unguarded?"

"Perhaps not, but you are in full possession of your magics. You have my full permission to act in self-defense should one of our people act in defiance of their orders. They are expected to treat you as honored allies. Our war efforts depend on our mutual trust."

"Your war efforts, more like, and what happens when your people end up running away with their tails between their legs?"

"I assure you, Monsieur Géant, we will win."

"That a fact?"

"Consider it a promise, my friend."

Donarick's mechanical eye glows a bloody red as he utters these words. I find myself wondering if he has ever actually been in battle before. Has he even shed blood before? Has he killed before? If so, how many? Someone so clean has to have killed at least once. I've never met a human+ capable of soothing a room of hexen without first firing a warning shot.

"Miss Helsdottir, could I have a moment?"

All eyes turn to me. Yggfret's mouth holds an intrigued quirk. I may not know the witch personally, but I know enough about him not to read into it. There's too much there to examine, and I'd like to keep what little sanity I have.

"Sure..."

"Outside if that is alright? I have a filtration mask for you that should fit perfectly."

Really? I think as he slides his own mask back over his face. Outside in the nuclear frost? What does he need to speak of that can't be done in the comfort of our homely little witch barracks?

Donarick's hand is extended toward me. His smile is kind even if it only reaches one eye. I don't take his hand, but I do follow him out the door.

Inside, the furnace was cranked high enough to melt the wax off a candle. Because of that, I forgot just how frigid it is outside.

It's cold, bitterly cold. My horns ache at the sudden shift in temperature. It was still hot as can be farther south when I was imprisoned. One month later and were I any farther south, winter would still be a figment of my imagination. Not here though. While winter inches forward at a drunken snail's pace for the rest of the continent, it is already in full fury here. There may not be snow on the ground, but make no mistake, this place is as chilled as a meat freezer. Icicles hang off the edges of the gutters, and the trees are as barren as can be. Even the pines have lost their needles, though I doubt that is due to any kind of chill.

Even through the safety gear, the cold bites my nose and nips at my ears. Radiation masks aren't the most insulated, and evil be blessed, I sweat like a pig whenever I wear one. Never mind that the smell of rubber and self-healing glass is absolutely abhorrent. If I focus on it too much, the nausea bubbles into my throat, and I start to retch.

"As much as I love traipsing around in a toxic wasteland, I'm rather confused as to why this conversation must take place amid the elements."

"My apologies, Miss Helsdottir," he says, his voice mechanical and synthetic through the mask, "but if this meeting goes as I hope, we will have need of the space."

Oh...

We round the side of the next complex, and a barren beachside comes into view, rocky, more mud than sand, and half-frozen. I've seen the view before. I saw it when they transported me from my prison cage to my new shared accommodations. This particular stretch of sea makes a crescent moon inlet into the land. A few guillemots poke their beaks into the sand, searching for crabs. They find litter instead: bottle caps, aluminum tins, bullet shells. My lip curls in disgust. Damned human+, thinking the earth is theirs to pollute and contaminate with no regard for how their actions will one day destroy everything worth saving in this place.

Something new to the view, however, is the large enclosure now closing off the channel which leads out to open water and framing the entirety of the beach. Dotted along the fencing are several adepts, all wearing hazmat suits and sporting electrical prongs as though awaiting the opportunity to shock some large animal into submission.

"Making new accommodations for us?" I jeer.

"To come to the point, I would like to request your might on our expedition to Deriva. I feel your unique skill set will prove quite valuable on this upcoming raid."

"My unique skill set?"

"Your ability to summon monsters."

"Netherbeasts."

Not monsters. Monsters are a different thing entirely.

"Yes, netherbeasts. There is one in particular that I feel would be very useful on this venture. You wouldn't by chance have the ability to summon and control a cipactli into this paddock?"

"A what?"

"Cipactli. The legendary sea monster whose body was used to create the Old-World continents of Latin and South America. Have you heard of it?"

"Do I look like a descendant of the Aztecs to you?" I spit, gesturing to my pale skin and too-red hair. My last name is Helsdottir, for crying out loud.

"The cipactli of legend was a part of the Aztec and Mayan creation myths. Part crocodile, fish, and toad. Tezcatlipoca used his own foot as bait to lure the creature out of the water and kill it. From its body, they made the earth. If you need an image for your imagination, by all means, take a look."

The hologram Donarick pulls up would be comical, at best—an overgrown fish with a crocodilian mouth and the hind legs of a toad—were it not for the extra jaws decorating the beast's body. Teeth... Teeth everywhere, that would be the better description for such a beast. I can only imagine what it would be like to fight such a creature. Did you manage to avoid the head? Yes... whelp, too bad! The tail took a big bite out of your arse. Oh, you avoided the tail too? No worries, not only did you get slashed by the front claw, but the gnashing jaws on its palm have eaten your spleen.

"So let me get this straight. You want me to summon a legendary netherbeast that was allegedly killed by a god? How is that supposed to help anything?"

"There's more than one," Donarick explains. "And legendary isn't so much a descriptor as it is a misnomer. You can't expect indigenous cultures to understand how dimensional travel works."

"Right," I drawl out. I've never summoned a cipa-whatever-the-damned-thing-is-called, so chances of me being able to control it are slim to none. "Well, thanks but no thanks. I don't feel like losing a foot today."

Not for you. Not for any augmented person on the face of this godforsaken planet.

"Tezcatlipoca lost more than a measly foot trying to kill that singular beast. But not to worry. I promise your safety is of the highest priority."

He has no idea what kind of consequences can arise from a misaligned summoning. I could summon the wrong thing, pull myself into a wormhole, cause a dimensional rift, or if by some miracle I am successful, I would be perfectly primed to act as the creature's next meal.

"Your promises don't amount to jack-didily-squat in the face of a netherbeast."

"Then allow me to provide you with some insurance."

There's something hidden in his statement that doesn't sit well with me. He gestures to the side, and a pair of guards step out of the vehicle. Between them, they drag along a limp-bodied woman. Judging from the scaly tail dragging the ground and the smoothed features of her face, I would imagine she is a hexen. One of the lizard folk who thrive in the abandoned sewage of radiation dampened cities.

"I realized you would be reluctant to put yourself in danger, so I thought we'd appease your summoning with some dinner ahead of time."

Ignorant fool.

"You think one measly sacrifice is going to appease an angry netherbeast known for ripping the foot off a god?"

"Perhaps not, but my men are ready to pull you out and trap the beast the moment it enters this plane."

"Where it gets its next meal from is the least of my concern. I've never summoned anything bigger than a displacer beast." And that blasted creature wouldn't obey a word I said even when I had my athame. Without it, I haven't a hope of summoning anything stronger than a forest nisse. "Perhaps you don't mind having your head ripped off by an uncontrollable netherbeast, but I would rather not venture the risk."

Oh, look, one of the buzzards found a bottle top in the sand. Two of its compatriots have decided its superior shine is deserving of a contest of will. They squawk and peck at each other until their oh-so-coveted prize goes hurtling into the water.

"Perhaps this might help."

My brow furrows as he beckons one of his men over. The guard presents to Donarick a long, thin box warded with magic suppressing tech nodes. Donarick tip-taps some sort of code into the box's side, and the nuts and bolts that make up the casing unwind like clockwork. It reminds me of a girl I used to know at the orphanage. She had one prized possession that she would never let anyone touch: a jewelry box with a swan lake ballerina nestled within. I used to love watching the ballerina spin to the rhythmic chimes of the music. I hated the way the last note never quite finished, leaving the whole composition hanging on a dissonant key. She said it was because she dropped it when the adepts rescued her from her burning home. All the jewelry spilled out, but she saved the box. It was the only thing besides her that made it out, including her parents in whose bedroom the fire began.

That girl was adopted not long after she arrived—go figure with her pretty blue eyes and skin as white as snow. I wonder if the last note ever played again.

There's no music coming out of this box though. Just dead silence.

As the lid lifts, a holographic shield pops up around the box, locking in place the outpouring of malignant energy. Settled within, nestled in the bedding of a silken cushion and leaking magic like a runny faucet, lies a carved length of wood. About as long as my forearm, the reddened wood is of simple yet elegant design, finely tapered and adorned with geometric carvings throughout the shaft. The grip is wound with cream-colored leather and bound with purple wax. But the physical attributes of the instrument, while pretty and worth taking note of, are not what beguile me so. The wand hums with power. Old power. The kind of power not even Yggfret could summon forth without some serious repercussions.

"I see I've captured your full attention. Allow me to introduce Dagslys—the Dawn Ripper."

At the mention of its name, the wand pulses a crimson red.

"Where did you get that?"

"Being the sole nuclear power in the League comes with its perks. You don't honestly think we are foolish enough to allow ancient magical artifacts to be left unaccounted for once their witches have been dealt with?"

"Whose was it?"

"The Seidr King Mørknatt."

"You're lying."

What young witch hasn't heard of Mørknatt? The last true king before Deus went to hell. The man summoned some of the greatest monsters and netherbeasts ever seen on this plane, and that's his wand. His wand! This wretched adept is holding the wand of the witch who brought dragons to Deus. I don't believe it.

Thames laughs as he shakes his head.

"Not at all. It took five full-fledged technomancers to bring him down. Of course, back in those days, we didn't have the same technologies we do now. I imagine two or three would do the trick today. No matter. He is gone, but this lovely, little trinket remains. They tried to destroy it initially, but no one could put so much as a dent in it, so it's been sitting in the Vatidome's vault for nearly 600 years."

I don't know what the more appropriate reaction is: anger or awe.

"I didn't realize you people felt the need to gloat."

"I am not showing you this to gloat, Miss Helsdottir. Think of it more as an offering. This wand's owner was a summoner, just like you."

"So?"

"So... Perhaps you can gain mastery of it."

"And why would I want to do that?"

"It might give you just the boost you need to achieve the impossible."

"You think a wand that outlived its witch will listen to me!? Ha! You're battier than a vamp on a jolly rancher's blood!"

Donarick's lips twitch, one side into a smile, the other into a frown. It's reminiscent of the time one of my caretakers had a stroke during lessons; one half of his face just stopped working. Only this doesn't seem necessarily involuntary... Could it be due to his augmentation?

"I have faith in you."

The wand pulses. Some witches experience magic like an auditory cue: humming, whining, and the like. Others have a more sensory response: it leaves an aftertaste on their tongue or builds like a stench in their noses. Others still have a physical response; it feels warm or cold or leaves goose-flesh along their arms. That's where I sit—in the physical camp. Only, mine is not so innocent.

I feel the power dripping off of the wand, and arousal flares in my belly.

Lust for power... unquenchable, inconsolable, and as deeply rooted in my magical system as the blood that flows through my heart. Most people crave skin or food or even pain. I *want* that wand.

"I can't make any promises," I tell him, "but I'll see what I can manage."

"We march on Deriva in one week. I'm hoping I can count on you to join our forces."

Hope all you want, Thames. Magical artifacts aren't computers. You can't just push a button and make them work.

"You must be joking. It takes an incredibly skilled magic user to claim the allegiance of another witch's artifact, and next to that, you want me to summon some legendary beast that I haven't even heard of. What are you playing at? Giving them an excuse to put me back in the pit?"

"Not at all. I may not fully understand the magnitude of what I am asking, but I do grasp the skill necessary to do it. That's why I pushed to have you pulled out of prison despite your youth."

I get it. So, there was a chance I would be left to rot were it not for my proven skillset. How grand!

"And what if I fail?"

His expression falters. So too does his steady grip on the wand's case, but before I can truly read into his countenance, the suave male visage is back and cranked up a few notches.

"Summer," he takes ahold of my hand, "I'm giving this to you because I believe you are the only one capable of it. I believe in you, Miss Helsdottir."

He believes in me. No one has ever told me they believe in me before. It's almost as titillating as the magic tickling my awareness. They say witches who lust over magic are the ones most likely to fall prey to magic fever and insanity. They say lunacy ferments best in the sexual organs. They say witches who claim the lost artifacts of others are damned to the finite space between Hades and Limbo. They say... well, *they* say a lot of things. Most of it is bullshit.

As I reach for the wand, both sides of Donarick's mouth curve up in a smile.

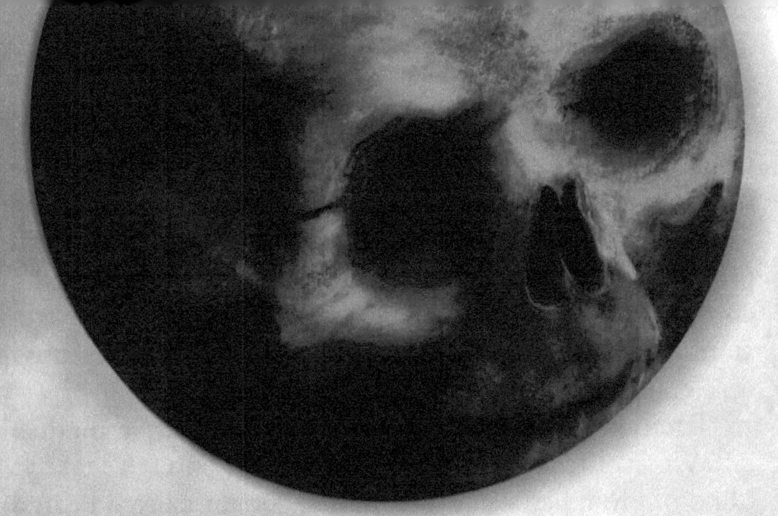

III

CON BRIO

*I'm sure you think I had it coming. Hel, I think I
had it coming.*

ONE WEEK LATER - DERIVA

Nothing burns like void fire.

"Aaaaahh!!!"

Prince Xipilli screams so nicely. It almost makes up for
the last few weeks I spent sniveling in a cage because of him.

Dagslys is quite apt at drawing blood even if it isn't quite meant for doing so yet. I've already made plans to reforge the wand into a blade. Something like my old athame, but it will probably need a longer hilt, and I'll need to make sure the core is compatible with the wood. After my first successful summoning, Donarick promised me he would begin setting up a crafting lab for me back in Vatidomus City.

"I don't know who you are, but I will make you pay for this."

Whoever trussed the poor boy up had enough sense to blindfold him before I came in here. Donarick said I could play with him all I wanted: my reward for helping bring down the capital of Deriva. There's a hissing sound behind me. Jormungandr is growing bored. The two-headed snake is no great world serpent now, barely the length of my arm, but there is enough venom in that bite to down a moose, and I'm sure I don't have to mention what happens when you look directly into the eyes of a basilisk, or rather, what happens when you look into the wrong set of eyes. His head with the deathly gaze is practically asleep while his venomous head just continues to hiss, venom dripping down the maw.

"Aww, poor baby. All alone. No one is coming to save you. No daddy. No mummy. No big sister. Just you and me until we both die of boredom."

The wand tip sparks as I bring it to his chest once again, and the screams continue. The magic burns so nicely into his skin. The brand is almost complete, something to remember me by. The same rune graces my throat, blown up and burned to his chest in a permanent scar. Every time he looks in the mirror, every time he takes a lover to bed, every time he goes to the beach, every moment he spends out in the open for anyone to see beneath that privileged royal collar will be one where they also see me. The thought fills me with so much glee, I can barely contain my laughter.

Oh, I suppose he could go and get a skin graft to cover it up, or perhaps enough laser treatments will make it fade, but magical scarifications live beneath the skin. Even if he survives this experience, he'll need to constantly reapply a masking if he wants to banish it from his sight.

"Jormy, baby, why don't you keep our friend company while I check in on Lucy?"

The basilisk slithers from my arm to curl around the prince's torso and neck before seating itself at his head. The venom continues to drip slowly from the creature's fangs onto the man's forehead. I watch as the viscous fluid ambles its way down between the crease of the man's eyebrows, past the bridge of his nose, and into the hollow points of his eyes. Once the droplet hits his tear ducts, the sizzling begins, and the prince thrashes in agony.

His screamed curses are music to my ears as I allow the door to slam shut behind me. I'll come back to collect Jormy in the morning.

Deriva really is a beautiful country. Most island countries are. There is just something about the way the sea nurtures the coast while the volcano's wrathful embers provide the impetus for new life to flourish. I've heard that the witches who once called Deriva home could manipulate lava the way others manipulate water, bending it to their will to harvest its healing and destructive properties. Those witches, contrary to the heated pool of power they controlled, were peace-loving pacifists who saw more terror in the eyes of their rage-filled goddesses than they ever would on the mortal plane. That's why they were exterminated so quickly. They didn't see any threat in the technomancers and were foolish enough to think they could live in peace with them.

They were wrong.

And did Pele or Xochitle come to their aid? No. The volcanic goddesses merely watched as their people were destroyed. After all, the volcano erupts at the behest of none.

Now, Deriva is controlled by technomancers. At least under the Moctezumo family, the islands have been kept clean, following strict legislature against pollution and waste. They even kept quotas on fishing and oil-harvesting in the oceans. Despite the "limitations," Deriva is the richest country in the League as far as oceanic resources go. It's unfortunate that Seraphim saw them as enemies: the high-browed fool of a Vulcan and his spitfire of a wife, now dead at the hands of my new allies. I shudder to think how much wildlife the nuclear pollution will kill and/or alter irrevocably. (Seraphim already destroyed its own land. Naturally, they'll destroy everyone else's.) I doubt there are enough hexen or fae left in the area to counter the effects of this war.

The sun is setting. There's something so picturesque about the way Ör shimmers red on the horizon. His reflection in the water is as bloody as the corpses that line the docks. I wonder how much of the stained water is from our great star and how much is actual blood in the water.

I didn't realize how late it was. I've been *visiting* with the young prince for over two hours.

A pair of soldiers roll another body off the edge of the dock. They laugh as the corpse makes a heavy splash against the surface. I imagine the sharks will have quite the feast tonight.

"And they call us heathens…" I hush as I make my way out of the main compound and toward the beach. Here, all is as serene as ever. The violence didn't spill into this area. You would never think looking at this view that a massacre occurred just twenty meters away.

Ör, our sun, finishes his descent. Purple overtakes the sky, and a few stars begin to twinkle. The moons aren't out. Or rather, they are, but there's a dense black spot in the sky. It must be one of those rare nights that Dei is dark, and Koi is in its new moon phase. They could be in an eclipse, but I don't care enough to look it up on the astronomy service. That would require the use of a computer or handheld, and the last time I handled anything even remotely high-tech was during a class I was forced to take at the orphanage. Three-hours a day for three weeks, I was forced to learn how to type on an old-school laptop. It was painful and annoying. The screen gave me a headache, the stress gave me indigestion, and I ended up with a rash along my hand and forearm. Needless to say, I dislike handling technology. I don't know why some witches are capable of handling tech willy-nilly while the rest of us can barely watch television for more than 30 minutes. I like to think it's because those of us who are intolerant are just more powerful than the others

That's just the way things are.

The sand is warm under my toes. I've never been to the beach before. It's kind of surreal that I stand here as a victorious raider just like my ancestors. Loki ought to be proud.

The waves crash steadily along the shore. Their constant sloshing is a calming repetition while their foamy crests glow in the darkness. Bioluminescent waves... and just beyond that watery rainbow array, my triumph.

Lucy, my cipactli, basks at the edge of the beach, letting the water rush over her scaly body. Like a great saltwater crocodile, she lies on her belly with her mouth open. Well, several of her mouths open. Her frog-like legs are extended behind her, twitching in the water. She used those limbs to jump the full length of Cresta de Corail not hours ago.

It was her great maw that felled Tlanextli long enough for Llywellyn to slice the Vulcan's throat.

"Hey, baby girl, you doing okay?"

From the satchel at my side, I pull a nice treat for her and toss it. The speed with which her hind jaws clamp down on the arm is disturbing, and the two mouths at her back ankles tear into the meat with equal gusto. Her tail thrashes, whacking the water with great damp slaps loud enough to echo across the whole of the coastline.

I toss the entirety of the satchel to her. The crunching of bones and sinew fills the beach as she chows down on her treat.

"Good girl," I praise her, and she obediently slithers her way to me. That crocodilian maw, large enough to swallow me whole, nudges my side. I take the invitation to wind my arms around her nose. I imagine if crocs could purr, she would be purring at the gentle touch of my hands on her snout. A piece of the Vulcan's sleeve is still caught between Lucy's teeth.

I wonder if Seraphim would have managed without my Lucy's might backing their nuclear weapons.

I barely met the deadline for departure.

It took me two days to attune Dagslys, another three to summon Lucy onto this plane, and another 32 hours before I fully had her under my thrall. It's no small feat to take command of a dead witch's magical artifact, but I did it. Two sleepless nights of exchanging magic with the wand, allowing it to pollute my system so my own power could in turn fuse to the instrument... It was a painful process, deliciously so.

Lucy's eyes, sunken into her head, would normally reflect a limey yellow in the low light, but under my influence, only a hollow blackness peers down at me. They are just like

Jormy's eyes. The basilisk was an accidental summon, the second failure in my attempts to summon a cipactli. (The first beast... somewhere along the route from its dimension to ours... well, let's just say it came through compromised, for lack of a better word.) Jormungandr was so small, I thought the summoning had failed entirely until one of the adepts babysitting me keeled over after a bite to his ankle. A second made the mistake of swatting the snake away with a pole and got an eyeful of death. They would have killed him had I not interfered. Now, he's mine. My little two-headed baby. He's grown since, but it will be years before he reaches Lucy's size.

"How does it feel to be the witch who brought a country to its knees?"

Wearing a smirk I wouldn't call uncomely, Donarick stands at the edge of the brush-line where the walkway gives way to sand. What is he doing out here? Dressed down with only his camouflage trousers and a plain white button down, half undone and hanging loose around his hips, the man looks like the kind of subject a renaissance era sculptor might use as a model. He's no David, too slight of frame and not tall enough, but he might pass for a Mercury or Apollo with their nimble limbs and eternal youth.

"Shouldn't you be enjoying the celebration feasts with the other +ies?"

"I've no interest in eating at a dead man's table."

Lucy bristles at the intruder, a low growl rumbling up from her belly. I shush her away, and she belly-slides into the water with a hiss. Once her tail disappears, I turn toward the cyborg at the far side of the beach. I don't quite know what to make of this man yet. He has been kind to me, not just in the moment when he kept that brute from attacking me in my cell, but ever since as well. After I acquiesced to taking Dagslys and summoning the cipactli, he had me moved into a wing of his father's private abode. He'd check in on me from time to time, make sure I was eating and sleeping alright, and there was even one memorable morning in which I woke up in the middle of the training studio where I'd accidentally fallen asleep while plotting summoning circles to find someone had moved me to the settee and thrown a blanket over me. I wonder if he moved me.

"I seem to recall you bragging at dinner the other day that the table we were eating upon once belonged to your great, great grandfather. Is that not eating at a dead man's table?"

"Yes, well... I find it distasteful to eat in a banquet hall when the corpse of the previous owner is still cooling in the rafters above my head." Distasteful is an understatement. My nose wrinkles at the thought. Barbarians, the lot of them, supping below a fresh cadaver like animals who hang their kills in the trees for later. "I guess you technomancers really aren't so different from us as you like to pretend you are."

"All is fair in war."

"You forgot love," I correct. "If you're going to quote poetry, at least do so correctly."

"Ah, my mistake. Allow me to rectify." He clears his throat. "'The rules of fair play do not apply in love and war.'"

"Hmm, I've never heard it that way before."

"Lyly's *Euphues: The Anatomy of Wit*. I found it to be a dated read, but some aspects of the text are timeless."

A snooty little literature snob, then. The sand grows cold under my feet, and with Lucy lounging in the bay, there's nothing more for me out here.

"Can't say I've had the misfortune of reading it. Enjoy the beach. Don't get too close to the water. Not sure how Lucy feels about augmented humans, but meat is meat, and I'm sure she won't mind picking wires out of her teeth."

Thames is standing along my path back to the compound. I'm hardly tired. There's been far too much excitement today for me to sleep without properly exercising some of the excess "energy" still bubbling in my core. I wonder if there are any soldiers brave enough to lie with a witch around.

As I pass him by, already plotting who I might play with for the evening, Donarick's hand catches my bare bicep.

"You didn't answer my question."

Coriander and cloves with a hint of cucumber... It's the oddest scent I have ever experienced, yet on this man, it somehow works. Perhaps it's the sea salt cutting into the freshness of the cucumber smell. Who knows?

"What question?"

"How does it feel to bring a country to its knees?"

I scoff. "I'm far more interested in finding a half-decent looking man willing to go to his knees for me, but I doubt I'll find anything even resembling that in this cesspool of toxic masculinity."

"Too few men know how to properly worship a woman of your power."

"Guess I'll have to settle for a lackluster performance as usual." I brush him off, but his other hand comes up, wrapping around my waist to grasp my other arm.

"I knew the moment I saw you that you would achieve great things, Miss Helsdottir."

The heat from his body melts into my skin, a sharp contrast to the cold metal of the ring on his finger.

"Sir?"

He isn't much taller than I am.

"Donarick. Call me Donarick, and I will be as a slave to your every desire."

Taken aback, I pivot to him, disbelief across my face.

"I mean it, Summer. You have cast an utmost powerful spell over me, and I can't find it in myself to wish it gone. So, I bid you, call me by my name, and I will do everything in my power to bring you unending happiness."

"Very well, Donarick. Prove it and turn off your augmentations."

If my demand stuns him, he doesn't show it.

He steps away and finishes unbuttoning the rest of his shirt. The fabric falls aside to reveal a lightly muscled torso. It would be hardly any different from any other man's chest I've seen were it not for the metal plate stitched into his left breast. A small monitor alights there: a little rectangle with a pulsing line through the center that spikes with the rise and fall of his chest like a heart rate monitor. I can't be sure what kind of augmentation would require such an expensive decoration or what its use might be, but the scar tissue surrounding it is ugly. Crisscrossing striations and surgical scars from where staples and stitches once pulled the flesh together. He must catch my stare because he answers my unasked question.

"Before I was even born, one of my heart valves didn't develop properly. They cut me out of my mother's belly when I was three months premature, and I had my first heart surgery just four hours later. I can't even count how many operations I've had since. My father says I need to prove myself worthy of the doctors' efforts to save my life. Otherwise, all of their time, money, and talent would have been spent on a no account better off dead in his mother's womb. Naturally, my mother disagreed, not that her opinion meant much to him. The doctors advised her to abort me, and for her stubbornness, she gave her life. I think that's why my father hates me so much."

I don't know whether to apologize or laugh. The woman who gave birth to me—whether by choice or by law, I'll never know—left me on the side of the road still covered in birth fluids without even a name. I was the product of rape, you see, and I suspect the brute who fathered me was a hexen of some sort. A babe born unwanted and left to suffer the surname Helsdottir.

"This," he taps the plate on his chest, "is a daily reminder that were I not born into a human+ society, I would have been dead before my life even began."

"What happens if you turn it off?"

"What happens when a clock stops ticking?"

"So, you're telling me you'll die if you turn off your augmentations?"

"Not exactly. A clock doesn't die just because it stops ticking. There's just no guarantee it can be fixed after the fact."

"Meaning?"

"My chances of suffering a heart attack will rise by about 25% if I were to honor your request and power down my augmentations."

"Ah, so no turning off of augmentations then. Gotcha. I guess I'll find my fun elsewhere—"

"I am telling you this not to deny you, Summer. I merely wish to be sure you understand the length to which I risk everything for you."

"You can't be serious. You might die."

He presses a button, and the ticking heart rate monitor turns black on his chest. "I am deathly serious, Miss Helsdottir."

A smirk pulls at my lips. He is powerless before me, vulnerable and foolishly naive. How titillatingly fresh! I pull the man into a kiss. I want to drink the power from his body and leave him spent in the grass.

"Alright, my lord. Let us dance under the moonless sky until that heart of yours quits itself."

I fuck the human into the ground, and every time I worry that his body has had enough, he begs me for more.

Two days later, before I am scheduled to return to Seraphim with Donarick, Yggfret asks me a favor, and it deals with Wren fucking Nocturne.

I don't know why he wants me to force a draught of false death down some technomancer bitch's throat, but who am I to question a king?

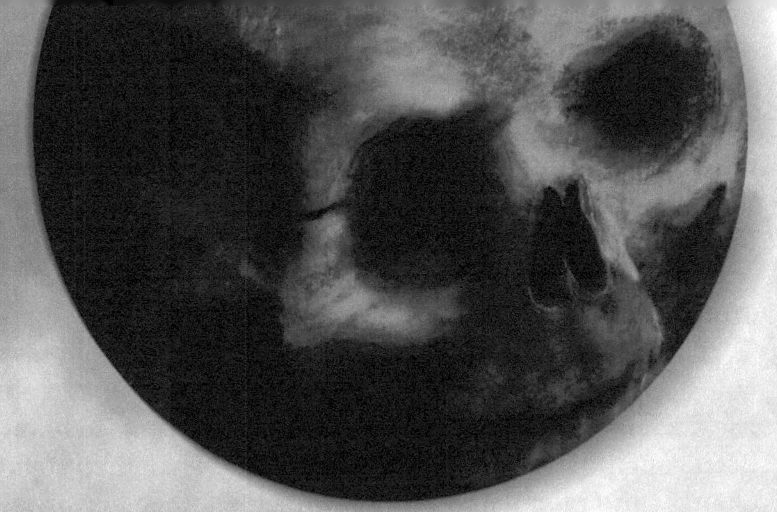

IV

CANON IN D MINOR

I thought I was the one in control. I thought I was the one with the power. But then again... every drunk thinks they are driving straight until the car flips over.

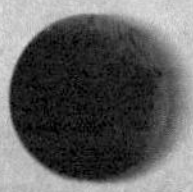

It happened at dinner.

I've been spending more and more time with Donarick. So much so that my fellow witches tease me for having moved into his quarters. I haven't moved into his quarters, but if I have a few books stacked on his shelves and a few outfits hanging in his closet, that is my own secret to keep.

"Miss Helsdottir, I finally have the honor of making your acquaintance."

The appearance of Donarick's father this far from his mansion in Vatidomus City is nigh unbelievable in and of itself. Even my lover, and yes, he is my lover, seems to have been caught by surprise. He reorganizes the kitchen staff, changes the menu, and arranges for his father's favorite tastes. Not that the man notices or expresses any iota of thanks for Donarick's efforts.

"The witch who brought down the Vulcan."

Grease shines on his chin from the strip of pork he is still chewing. For a man so supposedly pious, the Pontiflex is a glutton. Heaping plates of every course circling his placemat, he uses his fork the way some use a sword, hacking and scoring through his meat and vegetables like a medieval squire.

I smile and force myself to swallow a carrot even though the gravy clinging to the man's jowls has made me lose my appetite. "I'm afraid you give me too much credit, Your Grace."

General Llywellyn grunts, the distasteful bastard. He follows the Pontiflex around like a puppy. Even if I could reconcile his behavior in Deriva with vengeance, I'll never forget the kind of torment that man inflicted on the non-princess of the island country. I saw them bagging the corpse after the fact. Well, not the corpse, just the limp body of a woman afflicted with magical malady.

"Too much credit, indeed. If I'd known bringing a pet to battle would be all it took to bring down Tlanextli, I would have brought my parakeet ages ago."

"I hardly think your parakeet could have felled the Vulcan, Llywellyn," says Donarick, to which his father hums in affirmation.

"Yes, Archibald, I'm sure if you had only known, Miss Helsdottir's efforts would have been entirely unnecessary, but alas, she's pulled through for us." Another piece of chicken is felled by the man's chompers, quickly followed by a forkful of salad. "Honestly, when Donarick presented the idea of working with witches, I was afraid I'd have to have him committed to the sanitorium at last. Too fanciful, he's always been."

Another strip of bacon goes into his mouth. Has he even swallowed the last bite yet?

"Witches... I mean really, who could ever hope to gain any sort of traction with heathens?" Llywellyn laughs as the Pontiflex continues his insults. "I mean really, Yggfret is a conniving old bat, hardly worth any amount of trust, but I suppose witches are not unsimilar to their lycan pets. Give them a bone, and they'll kiss your hand every day until you have no more need of them. But you..." The Pontiflex points his fork at me. "You, Miss Helsdottir, I have to hand it to you. If there were any hexen whore worth her salt, it's you, and I hear my Donnie-boy has had more than a few helpings off that plate."

"Father!" shouts Donarick, slamming his fist down on the table. My wine glass trembles at the force of the punch. The Pontiflex startles, turning to his son with wide eyes.

"My son?"

His apparent shock doesn't stop him from taking another draught of wine, though.

"You may come into my home. You may drink my wine and sully my table. You may even insult me however you see fit, but you will not disrespect Miss Helsdottir in such a way."

"Don—"

"No!" Donarick's chair, flung backward by the violence with which he stood up, clatters against the ground. "Miss Helsdottir has proven herself an asset to our cause. It is through her efforts that Deriva was brought down, and I..."

Donarick looks at me, a strange expression on his face.

"You what, my son?"

Donarick turns back to his father, determination written across his brow.

"I believe she is my soulmate."

My stomach drops out of my belly, bounces off my pelvis, and lodges itself in my throat.

"Soulmate?" Llywellyn scoffs. "What sort of hexen nonsense has she been filling your head with?"

"It is not nonsense," Donarick declares. He circles around the table to stand beside my chair. "And she is not the source of my newfound knowledge. This truth I know in my heart. Summer Helsdottir." Donarick settles on the floor beside me, one knee raised and a jewelry box in his right hand. "The last few months have been a whirlwind, and I know this may seem premature, but in the wake of our rising victory and the change it will bring, I know there is no one else I would want by my side."

He unfolds the box's lid to reveal a beautiful diamond ring.

"Donarick?"

I'd forgotten he was a man of means. As the only child of the Pontiflex, he is the sole inheritor of an entire estate beyond my wildest dreams.

"Will you be my bride, Summer?"

Surely, this is a fairy tale. Surely, I've warped myself into an alternate dimension. How is this even possible? What do I even say? A witch and a cyborg?

You say, "Yes."

There it is again, the lust for power. I don't know if I love Donarick. I don't know if I'm truly even capable of love. Well, no. That's a lie. I've always loved power. Power is the only thing that has ever kept me safe in this wretched world. Maybe, the right person, someone who comes with a caboodle of inherited power, can help with that cause. Help me fall in love with something other than power.

"Yes." The word leaves my mouth before I can control it. "Yes, Donarick, I will marry you!"

Before I even realize that I've left my seat, Donarick is spinning me up and around in the air. I'm laughing. I don't think I've ever laughed like this before. It's... It's exhilarating.

"So, I will one day welcome a grandchild of mixed heritage," says the Pontiflex.

The spinning comes to a halt. Donarick places me back on my feet.

"We haven't exactly discussed that yet but—"

"Donarick, my boy, if you would have just let me finish, you would have heard me regale Miss Helsdottir with praises for her abilities. She should be lauded as a queen among the hexen."

"Yes, but Summer and I—"

"What an intriguing combination of genetic might!" the Pontiflex continues without so much as acknowledging his son. "Perhaps they'll be a true super soldier. Oh, how proud they will make me!"

He laughs. Donarick looks gob-smacked.

"Doubtful, your grace," responds Llywellyn.

"I don't doubt it," he declares. "We've already seen how magic can prove useful to science. Miss Helsdottir's might during the assault on Deriva proved extraordinary indeed. I'm sure any child she bears will grow to be the most wondrous of beings, indeed. Now, imagine if that little spaling were to be my grandson."

I say nothing and can only blink stupidly at my food. Well, it's nice to know the Pontiflex sees me as a suitable mate for his sole heir, albeit in a creepy, pervy, continuing-the-family-line kind of way. The forkful of salad I force into my mouth tastes like mowed grass. And why should it taste any different? I am apparently breeding stock.

"Well, come. Let's drink. We have much planning to do."

That's how I, an orphan abandoned on the side of the road, came to marry an aristocrat. I married Donarick just a few short weeks later. The Pontiflex himself conducted our ceremony, private and intimate, featuring the attendance of a few notable Seraphim generals and King Yggfret alongside a few other members of the coven. Monsieur Géant coiled flowers around my horns while Xochtli sewed sigils of power and good fortune into my skirts.

Dressed in white and wreathed in lace, I've never felt more like a princess.

There is much fanfare. People talking of the unification between our two races. Of how this cements the alliance better than any contract. How Seraphim will be truly unstoppable with witches on their roster.

I care not for these things.

All I care about is the way Donarick looks at me as I walk to meet him at the altar, like I am a goddess and he a slave meant only to worship at my feet.

I thought I was the one in control.

I wasn't.

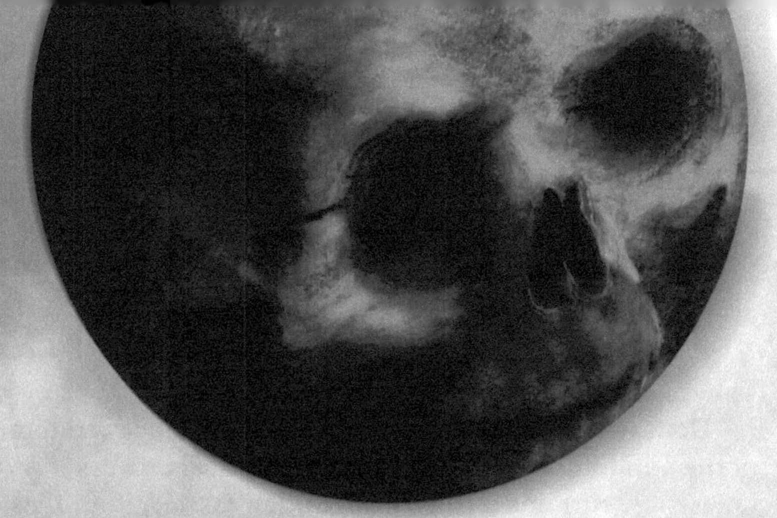

V

INTERMEZZO

I understand now why Yggfret saved this woman's life all those years ago. She was a technomancer then, a puppet to the League and unknowing of her own potential. Even after she found her magic, the League thought they could control her, and I suppose for a time they did. I wrote her off when I heard she killed herself. Just another mad witch like myself.

I was wrong. I see that now.

Seraphim never should have messed with that woman.

A YEAR AND A HALF LATER - VATIDOMUS CITY

They're outside. I hear them.

Donarick pulls me by the hand down the long corridors of the Vatidome. Centuries worth of classical artwork, fine tapestries, curtains strung with golden tassels, it all flies by unseen and unimportant compared to everything happening now. Soldiers run past us. They look at us like we're mad, running the wrong way when it is they who run to their deaths.

"Lock the doors!"

"Do not let them in!"

"Protect the Pontiflex!"

A blast sounds from outside, and the painted glass of one of the windows implodes. Rainbows of glass rain on our heads, yet Donarick doesn't stall. While the guards turn to the onslaught of firepower, he angles us down the next passage and into one of the study halls. He lets go of my hand to slam the door shut and then promptly kicks a nearby desk into the wall.

"Damnit! It's all gone to hell thanks to that cursed witch."

I know who he's talking about: Wren Nocturne, back from the dead and toting along a host of magical might as never before seen. Well, it's difficult to come back from the dead when you never really went there to begin with. Yggfret, you damned fool! That draught of false death did its job, and the former technomancer returns for her vengeance. She already got Llywellyn. Donarick saw the aftermath of that attack and heaved. Now, the damned witch has snuck through our barrier, broken the circle maintaining it, and allowed her allies to make their way to the Pontiflex's throne room.

We've been winning up until now. Seraphim was winning, all thanks to its alliance with some of the most powerful witches in Deus. Murasaki didn't know what hit them when ghouls invaded their mainframes. The Sekmetians didn't understand why their network was constantly experiencing interruptions. They certainly didn't realize their locators were being redirected to carefully constructed ambushes, and the Aighneans, they thought their equipment malfunctions were merely misfires, devastating explosions perfectly timed to occur the moment they aimed their canons at Seraphim's forces.

It was all us. The witches of Seraphim. Pulling the strings of battle without anyone ever even suspecting magic was in use.

Go figure, it would be a witch on the other side that brings it all tumbling down. We never did understand how the Alliance managed to reclaim Deriva. Now we know.

My ravens have been trying to keep her in sight, but tracking a necromancer through a forest of death is nigh impossible. After the circle went down, I knew my fellow witches had fallen to the woman's deathly touch. I wasn't one of the witches maintaining the circle, but I was crucial to its success. My job was to hold a perimeter around the coven to warn us of any oncoming danger. It's the setup we've been running for months now during every major battle. Today, we simply orchestrated it on a grander scale, trusting the technomancers to keep us safe while we kept them in a cozy little bubble of anti-tech wards. No one bothered to ask who would keep them safe from a witch on the opposite side. Why would they when no one knew she was there to begin with?

I stepped away from the circle when the signature of one of my ravens went dark. I found the poor thing pinned to a tree. His wings had been nailed to the top two corners of a triangle, the tail left to dangle down to the point. His beak was splayed open and his tongue ripped out. It was as I was pulling my raven from his dying place that a purple circle materialized on the ground. One of my compatriots fell through the reverse summon. It was Géant with a single-worded message.

"Run."

And in the next moment, he toppled over dead.

The giant witch tried to use my summoning circle in reverse. He must have wound up transporting himself through a dud plain of existence because his magical network was completely jacked up. I tried to revive him, but it was like sticking my hands in a mangled plate of leftover spaghetti.

Then, the barrier fell.

How did I know? I didn't. Not until a drone nearly blasted my head clean off.

By the time I got back to the circle chamber, they were gone. All of them. Every witch whom I had formed a bond with in the last two years, dead on the ground, and at the center, one raven-haired woman oozing necrotic power.

I did the only thing I could think of. I took Géant's advice. I ran.

Yggfret, the bastard, had to have known this would happen. He must have with his divine sight and fortune-telling nonsense. And he allowed it all to happen. Hel! He designed it.

"She's destroyed everything!"

Donarick, my love, is frightened. I smell it in his sweat. I don't know when I became so attuned to my husband. My heart aches so badly for this man, I can barely breathe, but

I suppose that's what all of us say when we fall in love with someone. And now...

"Killing Llywellyn, warning the Alliance of our pact with witches, wearing down our resources one outpost at a time, and now she's taken down your comrades. If only I'd realized sooner they had a witch on their side. Our last defense—"

Now the house of cards comes tumbling down, and we'll be going down with it. Or perhaps the more accurate way to put it would be coming down on our heads.

"Don, calm down. It isn't over yet. We can still win this."

"No, we can't. It's over, Summer. We don't have enough technomancers to stand up against the Alliance, and the coven... they're dead, and we will soon follow. It may not be today. It may not be tomorrow. But eventually the Alliance will arrange our execution for the whole world to see."

He's right. I know he's right. We've made our bed; now it's time to sleep in it. The coup is over; our forces fall one by one before our very eyes. I've never wanted to smash the surveillance monitors so much as a pair of adepts in Alliance colors shoot down the guards stationed at the front gate of the compound. Discovery at this point is unavoidable, and the fate that will follow after... I know how the League conducts their business. They've done it to hexen since the earliest days of the war.

The Pontiflex will be killed. Who will it be, I wonder, to strike down my dear father-in-law? There are any number of adepts thirsty to put an end to this war by any means necessary. As his last living child, my Donarick will be humiliated, ripped of his augmentations, and paraded before the masses as a lesson to those who would defy the League. Then, when they've had their last laugh, they'll stage his execution on a televised broadcast just as they once televised the executions of the last hexen aristocrats in their own throne rooms. It is a fate written as clearly in the stars as it will be on paper. Unless...

"What if the Alliance gains a new ally?"

"What?"

"You, my love. You will become the alliance's new ally."

Madness...

"I'm not following, Summer."

"We will declare you as an ally to the League. You will denounce the Pontiflex and save yourself from the damnation being his son will bring you."

Donarick wrings his sleeves between his fingers. It's a tick I've noticed he has when facing tense situations. He did this after Xipilli's rescue. His father berated him badly, even struck him for losing such a vital hostage. I know because I was the one who had to mend his broken ribs later.

"You want me to betray my father?"

Traitor...

"It isn't betrayal if you were never on his side to begin with."

"What do you mean?"

"We aren't on your father's side, my love. We aren't on the League's side. We aren't even on the hexen side. We are on our side."

"That's a fine sentiment, darling, but I don't think they can distinguish Seraphim from us very easily, Summer. We've been too enlaced with this side of the warfront."

"Not if you prostrate yourself as a double agent."

"A spy?"

Oh, my poor innocent Donarick.

"Yes, a spy. You can say you were acting as a spy."

"And how will we do that? It isn't like I just put my hands in the air and say I was rooting for the Alliance all along."

"Wren Nocturne, their precious hero, is alive because you made it so."

"But that's not true."

"Yes, it is. You gave her a draught of false death the night she was captured, and when Llywellyn thought her dead, you arranged to have her stowed away someplace safe. Someplace where she could heal and become the Alliance's ace."

"What are you saying?"

"I am saying that you saved Wren Nocturne's life, and whether it is true or not, it is what you are going to tell them."

"Summer, did you—"

"Does it matter?" I interrupt his question before it can fully form. That is a truth that I will never speak aloud, not even to my dearest husband. Donarick's face closes. I can't read his expression anymore.

"So, we tell them I saved her because I had an inkling she would be the key to taking down Seraphim? That's asinine, and even if they did buy it, it won't be enough to acquit us of our guilt."

"Not alone, no."

"So?"

"So, you kill the Pontiflex."

"You want me to kill my own father?"

His voice is hollow.

"He's already dead, Don. Living off borrowed time."

"He's my father." It's a weak protest. One spoken out of obligation more than fortification.

"And he killed you the moment he marched against the other nations. Please, my love, this is the only way."

There is a long silence as Don contemplates my proposal, and slowly but surely, his expression blooms open once again.

"What would you have me do?"

Donarick, my dawn, always so eager to please.

Did you know that demons are just the gods and goddesses the Christians couldn't tame? The ones they liked became saints. Like Brigid for example. No one has an issue with fertility and harvest goddesses, especially ones who welcomed all to their hearth with warm bread and strong wine.

The others... Let's just say Beelzebub wasn't a fan of the whole forgiveness of sins thing. He thought it rather trite that someone could simply beg forgiveness and receive it only to rinse and repeat the process over and over and over again.

Seems like a legit loophole to me.

I would never ask forgiveness for any of my sins. I know I don't deserve it, so why do I wish so desperately for those green eyes to offer it?

I instructed my lover to stab his father in the back in plain sight of the Alliance's top brass, and he followed my plan to a T.

Pontiflex Catalan died staring his enemy in the face while his own blood shoved a knife between his ribs. Now, my love gets to sleep in his own bed while the rest of Seraphim's forces rot away in the very dungeons he pulled me from. I've been hiding out in the woods for three weeks. Since he outgrew human-sized abodes, I've kept Jormungandr tucked away in a cave in the mountains. This is where I've been hiding, and while the magical terrarium I've set up for the serpent is a cozy temperature, I'm tired of sleeping in a bedroll made of moss and leaves, so naturally, I sneak to my husband's side.

"What are you doing? It isn't safe for you here."

The moment he sees me, he comes alive. There is a new vigor in his embrace, a shaking anticipation, and I relish the feel of his skin against mine.

"Oh, pish-posh. No one saw me."

I damn well know that sneaking into the Alliance's victory compound to see Donarick was a downright stupid idea, yet here I am. I always did think love made a person dumber. But no one looks twice at the help. I've stolen one of the maid's uniforms for this venture into enemy territory. Servants are invisible no matter what class of person they serve.

"You are absolutely insane, you know that?"

The man pulls me to him with a violent need. Our mouths slam together in a drawn-out kiss that is more blood and teeth than lips. There's no need to rush. We are in his private quarters. No one is going to disturb us. No one will even know I was here.

"I've been officially named a technomancer," he says once we come up for air, our sweaty bodies lying side by side in bed. There is a strange quality to his voice, like he is speaking more to the ceiling than to me.

"A technomancer!"

"They have also named me Seraphim's Head of State," he continues.

"But Seraphim doesn't have a Head of State."

He grunts. "They are reconstructing Seraphim into a pseudo-democracy after Aighneas and Sekhmeti, and they've decided I am the best fit to rule until such a time as elections can be held.

"Don, this is great!" I jump from the bed in excitement. Pacing about the room, I begin to ramble off my dream. "You'll have all the privileges of a world leader. You always hated the way your father ran the country, and you've always thought so highly of hexen. If it weren't for Llywellyn's foolishness and your father's greed, your plan to unite witches and technomancers in combat would have changed the entire world for the better. I can gather the few witches left, and you can sway other +ies to your cause. With you as our leader, we could make Seraphim a place where hexen can live without being hunted. A true unification of Hexen and Human+ states."

Donarick's silence draws me to a sudden pause. In all of my ranting and planning and celebrating, he hasn't said a word, hasn't so much as moved.

He doesn't seem happy. Not in the least.

"Honey..."

"They are going to use me as a figurehead, Summer."

"What—"

"Do you realize what that means? I'll be some puppet for them to control. They'll pull the strings, and I'll have no choice but to dance for them lest I want us to end up right back where we were when the Alliance tore down those barricades."

"Don—"

"This is what I killed my father for? A meaningless costume and a handler who will whip me into my place should I so much as voice an opinion?"

He hides the fleshy parts of his face in his hands. All I can see is that ever-glowing mechanical eye. He only ever turns it off when we make love; at all other times, it glows this constant red.

"Do technomancers get to choose the color of their equipment's light sources?"

His flesh eye looks at me, confusion in that pale blue gaze. He probably thinks I'm insane.

"You mean our cyber energy signatures?"

"Sure."

"No. The color we radiate is the optical translation of our inner workings. The Murasakans call it qi or ki. We just call it the magnetic synapsis."

"Cool." These human+, so desperate to differentiate themselves from us that they make up all this useless terminology. "So, your inner aura is red."

"It isn't an aura, Summer. That's a magic thing."

Sounds like the same shit to me.

"Do you know what it means to have a red energy signature?"

He frowns.

"Summer..." There is a growl in his voice, but I digress.

"Red is the color of leaders and royalty. It is the color of passion and intense base power. It roots you into the earth so that you can grow taller than those around you like a redwood in a forest of saplings."

"Summer, what are you getting at?"

"You are no puppet, Donarick J. Thames." I settle back on the bed next to his hip. "You were meant to rule."

"Tell that to the new council."

"We don't have to. We'll show them."

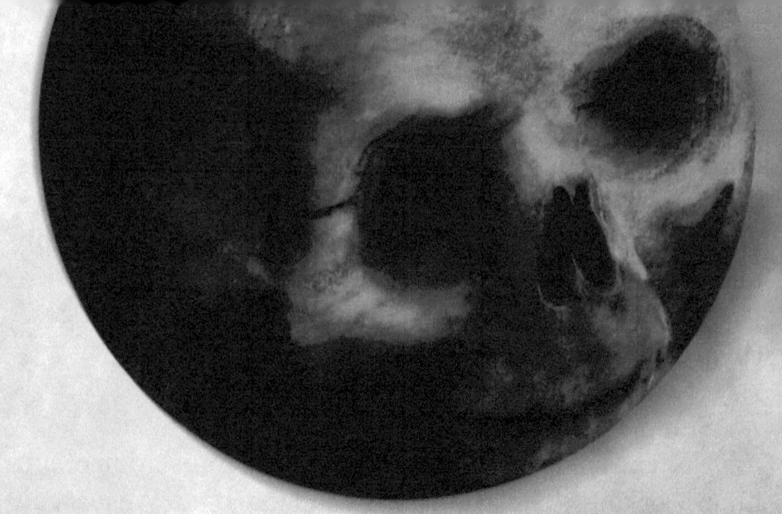

VI

OH, FORTUNA

Men are like knives, you see. You can handle a thousand of them and never suffer an injury, but if you lose sight of how dangerous they are for even a moment, you'll end up sliced open with your heart, and maybe even your body, bloody on the pavement.

Plots and schemes... Schemes and plots... Whatever is the difference? I certainly haven't a clue, but Donarick seems to have gained a knack for them since our secret promise to one another in the quiet of his rooms. I would tell you all about the series of events that led to my husband's rise to power, but that would take too long, and I've never been one to spoil a good mystery.

As Donarick recovers from the integration surgery that would grant him full status as a technomancer, I learn who our enemies are. President Gewalt can be sided with, if only temporarily. She values power over anything else. Pharaoh Rameses falls into the role of Primarch like a snake curled into an egg. He is an inconvenience. His hatred for hexen, not to mention his megalomania, makes him a dangerous leader. I don't know why the technomancers saw fit to elect him to office, but money is power. However, he is not my biggest concern. It's Ebele and Deriva, united by the marriage of Prince Chike Nagi to Princesa Atzi Moctezumo, that pose the real problem. Their young daughter represents a future unification beyond what is occurring even now. Goddess forbid the princesa's latest pregnancy results in a son. Then my Donarick will really be on the outs of a strong alliance. Not to mention the danger of that alliance growing a third leg with the ever-growing relationship between one Wren Nocturne, the heroine witch of Deriva, and Prince Kaito Miyazaki of Murasaki no Yama.

But worrisome romances are easily dealt with.

Suffice to say it was my idea to have the new Primarch meet an untimely end, but it was my husband's brilliance that shooed a second bird out of our hair at the same exact moment. It was just too much to hope Wren Nocturne would stay gone.

"What do you mean you didn't manage to kill the target?"

To say my husband is displeased would be an understatement. Donarick is livid. It's been nearly a year since Rameses' murder, and we thought it high time to continue our push to bring greatness to Seraphim. However, his plot to kill a heavily pregnant princesa and her young daughter as a means to weaken our opposition has fallen through.

The being at the foot of my husband's threshold is no technomancer. It isn't even a cyborg by any such standard. It is something more, something off the grid that shouldn't exist, yet here it is not so much in the flesh as in the metal. Man-made and designed, it looks like any other machine I might find in the League: silver enameled with copper plates and few patches of skin to mimic humanity. There are wires and bolts and the smell of oil, but this is no ordinary bot. This robot is the stuff of even a technomancer's nightmares.

"The target wasn't alone," the android reports. "They had an escort with them."

"And who was this escort that a Freed One such as yourself couldn't manage to assassinate a pregnant princess and her screaming toddler?"

The sigil on its chest glows in even the bright light of the overheads. A Freed One: the technomancers may have made its body, but the witches gave it sentience. Now, neither the hexen nor the human+ wish to have anything to do with them.

"My database shows it was the half-sister."

Wren Nocturne... I can hardly believe it. This information comes to us after a long search for the woman who murdered Pharoah Rameses, or should I say Primarch Rameses? His removal from office paved the way for Gewalt to take over. Aighneas happily fills the role of superpower with their former president leading the League. The Technomancer Council has been on the hunt for Wren Nocturne ever since, a foot race between them and her dear brother who so desperately wants to find her before they do. They'll never find her, though, neither the new Vulcan nor the council. She's disappeared from the League's surveillance. It'll take a witch to find her, and there are so few of those left to call on, yet here she is protecting her half-sister from assassination.

"Wren Nocturne has been in hiding for almost an entire year. Why would she show up now?"

"The data is inconclusive, Mr. Thames."

"Then what good are you!" shouts Donarick. The robot tilts its head a quarter of an inch to the side. There is murder in that head tilt, and I don't think my husband realizes just how much.

"Perhaps she caught wind that her sister was in danger, my love."

Donarick shoots a sharp glance in my direction. I'm not supposed to draw attention to myself, but the robot doesn't care. In fact, the head tilt of death reduces ever so slightly. I raise my eyebrows at Donarick, offer my own head tilt, and silently tell him to get himself in fucking order. He blinks at me with his mechanical eye.

"My apologies, Freed One. You should have your credits delivered as arranged, minus the portion you would have received upon the success of your mission."

The robot makes a beeping sound as it checks the status of its account. "Yes, everything seems to be in order."

"Wonderful, now leave us," commands Donarick, and the mechanical assassin pivots to march out of the room. "I didn't realize failure could be so expensive—Argh!!"

Don's hands fly to his face. He curls in on himself in pain while his tech goes on the fritz. I rush to his side. The headaches are getting worse. Ever since his operation, he has been suffering from a constant influx of migraines and low-level seizures. The doctors said it would be normal to have such instances as his body gets used to the new tech configuration, and that the effects should wear off after a few months. It's been a year, and if anything, the symptoms are getting worse, but does he go to the doctor? No. He likes the power too much, and any chance of having the privileges of a technomancer would be ripped away at a moment's notice if they found out he was suffering tech rejection. Because that is what this is—his body rejecting the augmentations.

"Don," I call, offering him a vial of potion from my breast pocket. He downs it before it even gets the chance to settle in his fingers. It might seem like hyperbole to say the effect is instantaneous, but it really is. Donarick's brow relaxes and his shoulders ease as the pain dissipates.

Did you know that Basilisk tears have properties that can paralyze cell growth if ingested? Sounds like a perfect poison, I know, but for someone suffering implant rejection or cancer, it works better than chemo or radiation. It's the only thing that makes the symptoms disperse. Well, that and head scritches. He always likes it when I card my nails over his scalp. He basks in the attention for whole minutes before finally speaking again.

"All of our planning wasted..."

"Not wasted, my love. Just a minor setback."

"Perhaps, but how could she have known? Not even my people knew of our plans."

"I suppose it's possible she was simply visiting."

"An outlaw witch visiting her aristocratic sister. Preposterous!" A clatter sounds from the back of the hall. Donarick huffs. "You'd better have something worthwhile to share, Corax, because I am not in the mood for more bad news."

Out of the shadows behind Donarick's tapestry creeps a large rodent. The oversized muskrat is the size of a small dog and twice as cute, but once the creature makes its way out of the corner, it shifts. Muscles lengthen, fur disappears, teeth shorten, and high-pitched squeaks become deep groans until a naked man stands at the center of the room. A ruffian lycan if I've ever seen one, there's nothing ratty about his human shape. More than six feet tall with a mane of thick brown hair, Corax's oversized husk dwarfs even the former Pontiflex's throne.

"I might have the answer to your question, my liege."

"Corax," sighs Donarick. "You know how much disdain I have for your habit of eavesdropping."

"You don't seem to have any problem with it when I am gathering information for you."

"Touché."

"My sources state that Lady Nocturne was visiting the princesa about some increasingly personal matters."

"What personal matters?" I ask.

"There are rumors, my lady. Rumors the witch is keeping a child with her in the forest."

"A child?"

"Yes. A young girl. Can't be more than three years old."

Donarick laces his fingers together in contemplation.

"A wartime babe. How interesting?"

I don't like the way he says that. It's too keen.

"Is it hers?" I ask. A part of me hopes it isn't. Surely, it can't be. I wasn't exactly there to watch when the woman broke her brother out of Llywellyn's makeshift prison in Deriva, but I know what happened, how she essentially sacrificed herself and her freedom for her brother, and everyone knows what happens to women who become prisoners of war. Yggfret said she was almost truly dead by the time he dropped off her body at the hospital.

"There can be no way of knowing," answers Corax. "The number of war orphans roaming the continent... she could have just picked up a stray. She frequents an orphanage in Lorelei, bringing gifts of food and money."

"Perhaps she simply adopted a street urchin," I add.

"Doubtful," mewls the lycan. "A woman like that taking in a stray. Ha! She can barely take care of herself. Why would she take care of someone else's brat?"

The lycan has a point. Not that I've ever thought much of the intelligence of lycans, but if it is hers, that would mean the child was conceived right at the beginning of the war when... My stomach tightens. That is a fate I would wish on no one, not even my worst enemy.

"I don't believe it." No woman should have to carry a fetus she doesn't want, much less one put there by an enemy. "It isn't possible." Surely, she would have gotten rid of it as quickly as she could.

But what if she didn't get the chance?

"There is a way to find out," whispers Donarick, a calculating look in his eye.

"Don?"

My love's eyes are alight with inspiration. A lightbulb has gone off in his head, and his new optical augmentation shines ever brighter for it. My spine straightens, and I hold my chin just a little higher. This is the man I married. This is a man who deserves to be king, not some no-account-brat born into royalty like the new Miyazaki Emperor or Moctezumo Vulcan.

"Can you imagine the potential, Summer? A child born of a technomancer and a witch. A super soldier indeed."

"But it's a child, my love."

"Children grow up."

"Yes, but..."

He doesn't seem to hear me. The noise of his own plots is far too loud. It's kind of sexy seeing him like this even if whatever seems to be brewing in that mind might be bitter to drink. This is the man I would follow to the ends of Deus. Donarick J. Thames, my savior who kept me from another technomancer's torment on one dark and lonely night while I sat waiting in a cold, barren cell.

"Darling, I have a new mission for you."

This kind of arousal, terrible and terrifying, shouldn't be possible.

"Of course, my love." He knows I'll do anything for him. "Whatever you would have me do, so long as you think me suitable for it."

"My beautiful Summer, you know I have full faith in you."

I can't help but smile into the kiss. After all, I've never failed him before.

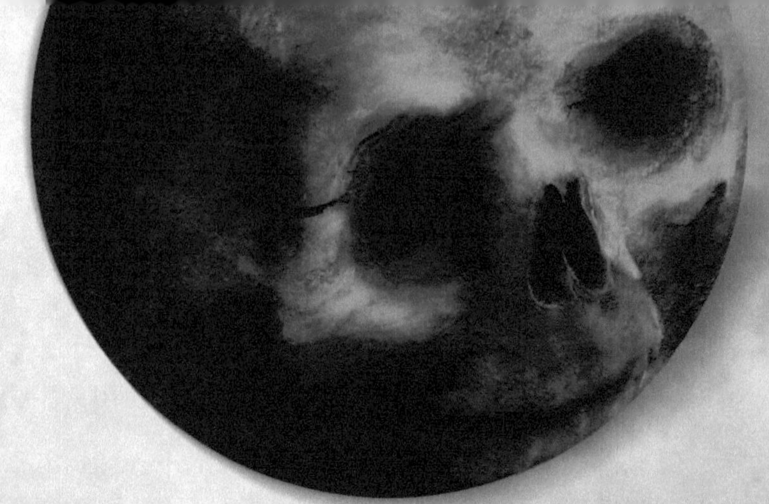

VII

MELANCHOLIA

Once upon a time, there was a fair maiden who loved a handsome knight.

One day, while the maiden was traveling, she found, in her pocket, a secret gift.

But she was on a dire mission, one which could crumble nations.

And so, the gift was kept secret and safe inside her pocket.

This gift she cherished and kept to herself to return to her handsome love.

*But when the time came to open the present, all
she found was a meek dead dove.*

I am first clued into my condition when a lycan comes up
and sniffs my pelvis. I know, rude! The creature has the
audacity to look at me like I assaulted her when I punch the
beast away with a blast of magic designed to force her out
of her wolfish skin.

"I didn't mean you no harm, witchy."

"Yeah, well keep your nose to yourself."

I had every right to sock the wolf in the nose and am
about to do so again when her eyes go canine, and she sniffs
the air again.

"I ain't never met a pregnant witch before. Smells downright deeeelicious."

The she-wolf licks her chops, and I let loose my spell.
Dark electricity zings from my fingertips into the lycan's body,
and before the beast can properly reorient itself, I summon
a steed and hurry away.

I suppose I should have known it was a possibility that
I might get pregnant way back when we started this whole
affair—the birds and the bees are an inescapable matter of
course, after all—so I do the responsible thing and take a
test. Ornery things, pregnancy tests. It takes me nearly four
days to find a halfway decent one. I'm not exactly in sophisti-
cated territory. The hexen centers between Seraphim and my
destination are controlled by vampyres and lycans, neither
of which have much need for pregnancy tests. Lycans reproduce so rapidly, it's easier for one to already be pregnant

than not, and vampyres can't get pregnant, which leaves only a small population of unaugmented humans, witches, and various sundry hexen demanding the pee-sticks, and the ones here are some diabolical mix of two unbelievably archaic methods of pregnancy prediction: injecting pee into a frog and watering a patch of barley with it. Not a fan.

By the time I finally find some counterfeit tests made to mimic the ones in the League, I am well beyond late for my cycle.

I don't know how the humans have the patience for them. Too many steps and the involvement of bodily fluids and then you have to set a timer, and after the little line turns blue, you then need to press the button to do a self-guided ultrasound. I mean, I suppose it's cool and convenient for people who are used to that kind of thing, but the ultrasound stick makes me itch at the thought of using it, yet here I am prodding my gel-slick belly with it. I'll admit it's pretty neat seeing my little witchling in the holograph. An aura reading spell would have been much easier to do, but the pregnancy test was able to tell me how far along I was: 12 weeks—just long enough for a little bundle of cells to pulse with a sure-fire strength in that tiny projection, even if the creature pic-tured looked more like one of my summons than anything remotely human.

When I perform an aura reading, I can tell it will be a boy, and my skin warms with happiness at the knowledge of my future offspring.

Shhhh...

Hush little baby, don't you cry.

Mama's gonna buy you an alibi.

And if that alibi falls flat,

Mama's hands are stained red beyond a fact.

The young prince is born on the 4th day in the Month of Light. A very auspicious day, if the stars are to be believed, but the child has been born under a false sign, for while the new parents know it not, their son is not long for this world. Not if I have anything to do with it.

They once called me the baby thief.

Baba Yaga would have been proud of my accomplishments back then, but I am not proud of that time. I do not take pride in causing harm to the innocent, but every witch knows the best results stem from the worst of deeds.

It isn't difficult stealing a baby. So many parents are taught the importance of separate sleeping arrangements. Put the baby in another room, make the baby sleep in a bassinet, and if the mother is of royal blood, have a wet nurse come in to feed the child.

I steal into the palace riding on the wings of an invisibility spell and a distraction made by some of my more virulent summons. The gremlins may not be from this area of the world, but they cause plenty of mischief. It's always fun to see how the human+ deal with their technology being turned topsy turvy.

This late at night, I was expecting him to be asleep. He is paler than his parents, but I can see the dark caramel tones of his mother's exotic complexion beneath that creamy, newborn skin. In fact, just looking at the babe, he seems to have more of his mother in him than anything else. Is there a chance he isn't really the heir to the throne? No. He has his father's eyes. The prince's child looks at me with dark chocolate eyes.

The poor little thing has no idea who I am, yet his lips quirk up into a gummy grin as I peek over the edge of his crib. It's probably just gas. I know that somewhere in my mind, yet it's still strangely endearing.

I'm supposed to kill this child. That is my mission: to kill the Nagi heir, so that Seraphim will not lose power.

I'm supposed to kill this child?

I know I'm supposed to. It's for the greater good of all of us, but for some reason, I hesitate.

The babe cries. Loud, piercing wails that will summon my trackers straight to me if I don't keep pace, and I don't know if I can keep this flight up. My insides are burning, and it's hard to draw a breath.

Jormungandr carries me as well as he can, but he is no Kukulkan or Quetzalcoatl. Those serpents were born of the sky. Basilisks, on the other hand, are born of the earth. They can't fly, and there is only so much a ground escape can do against an aerial pursuit.

"Ahh!"

A drone swoops overhead. Sharp steel claws grasp for my head and hair, but I duck away, bending forward over the wriggling bundle in my arms. The metal rips straight through my jacket and opens my shoulder all the way to the bone.

The infant cries harder, and another pang flexes through my abdomen. Is Gideon kicking? He's never struck me so hard before.

"Cease all lethal measures!" a staticky voice over the radio cries. "The witch has our newborn prince hostage. Do not take any action which might injure the baby."

"*Knuse!*" I shout, thrusting my wand in the direction of the drone. Void magic furls around its body. A moment later, the drone breaks apart into particles. All the microscopic bits of ions and protons that make the machine a physical thing disperse into much simpler, less dangerous pieces. Perfect packaging for sending something to another dimension where particles can't form bonds.

My lip quirks up in a half smile. Even the baby in my arms seems to celebrate my success, having quieted in the wake of my spell. My belly, just barely starting to round at my 23rd week of pregnancy, becomes uncomfortably tight. My knees clench together. Jormungandr swerves sideways as another drone shoots instead for the snake's seeing head.

Jormy's heads, unable to decide in which direction to evade the blast, split only to rebound into one another. If snakes could trip, this would be exactly what the nether-beast does. We tumble down the slope to land in the nearby ravine. The result is a tangled mess of serpent. At least, the dumb beast had the forethought to wind its scaly body around me and my charge. Otherwise, we would have been thrown goddess-knows how far away.

"Over here! I've got her in my scopes."

Faen! They've found me. I can hear them already scrambling down the ravine's edge.

"I hear the baby. He's alright."

"Is the witch dead?"

"No idea."

Not dead. Not dead at all, and that will not be changing anytime soon. Holding the baby in one arm, I dip my fingers in the open wound on my shoulder. Through clenched teeth, I grit out the words of the spell while drawing a reverse-summoning circle in my own life blood.

"Lous eht os, esrevinu eht sa, touhtiw os, nihtiw sa, woleb os, evoba sa."

The circle glows with anti-light. Magic falls from my being into the earth. It's like being pulled from a bucket of water fully clothed. The weight seeps into my limbs, into my core, into my heart. I am sinking into my circle. When I am knee deep in the space-time riff, pain buckles in my core, doubling me over.

What the—! Gideon?

Reverse summoning is dangerous on even the unburdened body. What will it do to an unborn?

I hesitate. My body lightens and the circle pushes me out. With the few inches that I rise, I must enter the adepts' field of vision because no sooner do I unbreech than the lasers rain down.

"No!" I duck down, screaming. Apparently, these adepts have a different interpretation of what it means not to "injure the baby." *"Esrevinu eht sa..."*

The portal draws me back down. Jormungandr's scales disappear inch by inch into the void's dry waters.

"Tuohtiw, nihtiw sa, woleb os—!"

Another pain right in the basin of my pelvis.

"Evoba sa!"

My voice sounds like a rampant animal. I don't even recognize it. The pitch is wrong. There is a roaring quality to it layered over a volatile hiss like one of the old things I make a point to avoid by summoning creatures out of the deep between dimensions.

I'll be traveling right alongside them tonight.

My body, already heavier with my growing babe, drops down into the pit, and the infant screams along with me.

Where I land, the light is dim. It is just before dawn in this part of the world. I recognize the place. It's my Jormungandr's usual cave, lined with moss and decorated with heat orbs for my darling reptile. It is a place that is normally dry and warm, yet I am cold and wet.

Water has soaked through my pants, tremors run up and down my spine, and a deep rolling pain comes and goes in the pit of my belly. Underneath me, a pool of blood begins to form.

No... It's too soon. It's way too soon. And there is no one here to help me.

When it's all said and done, I lay spent and exhausted.

To my right, one bundle of linens wriggles and cries, hungry and tired from the trauma it has just endured. To my left, another bundle of linens lies still, the babe within blue and battered from the ordeal it didn't have the strength to survive. My heart, a broken thing in my chest, bleeds as a life that never really had a chance to live fades from this world. The surviving infant writhes, his screams for food reaching a fever pitch.

He looks so little like his father...

It's because he's mine.

He's mine. He'll always be mine.

Gideon is everything I could ask for. A happy babe who giggles when he sees me and gives the cutest burps every time he finishes his bottle. It was hard going at first. He didn't want the formula—not that I blame him really. Who wants to drink a disgusting concoction of cow's milk and synthetic breast milk enzymes? But he couldn't have my breast. I was afraid I was going to lose him, too, but eventually he began accepting the bottle, and we've settled into a routine ever since.

Sore from my delivery and weak from blood loss, I haven't yet garnered the energy to return home. I still haven't introduced him to Donarick. Soon. Very soon he will meet his father. Once it's safe. Once no one is looking anymore.

Jormungandr won't stay near me. I suspect it has to do with the smell of postpartum. I can barely stand the stench myself whenever I change my pad. Gideon is sleeping in his bassinet, a cushioned rock basin I've dug out, so I have somewhere to put him while he sleeps. Next to him, I keep unsullied diapers, bottles, and a cauldron I haven't checked the contents of in days.

I am cleansing my hands of my latest mission assignment when the footsteps find me.

"Summer."

"Who's there?"

I don't know this technomancer.

"I've been looking everywhere for you."

"You're not welcome here."

Inhuman eyes trail to the infant still swaddled in his basin.

"That isn't your baby."

"Yes, he is."

"No, he isn't, Summer, and I am taking him."

"No! He's my son. You won't take him away from me."

I lunge for my baby, but the technomancer's hand slaps me away. My head snaps to the side, my shoulders and hips follow, and my head hits the wall.

By the time I come to, my Gideon is gone, and Donarick's sad human eye stares down at my prone form.

"My love, what did they do to you?"

"They took him. They took our son."

"Our son?"

"Gideon."

"We had a son..." Donarick looks from me to the bassinet and back, disbelief across his face. "Why didn't you tell me?"

"I'm so sorry, Don—"

He shakes me by the shoulders.

"How could you not tell me you were pregnant? What did you do with him?"

"They took him!"

"Who took him?"

"I don't know."

"You don't know." His fingers bruise into my shoulders. He shakes me again. My barely healed wounds from labor tear open. I gasp in pain. "You don't know!!"

"Donarick, you're hurting me."

He stops immediately.

"I'm sorry," he whispers. He lets go of my shoulders and threads his hands through my hair. "I'm sorry. I'm sorry. I'm sorry."

He mutters apologies into my temple, each word decorated with a sweet kiss. The light outside the basilisk's cave changes and then changes again until finally, Donarick's apologies cease. An eerie silence replaces them before...

"We will get him back."

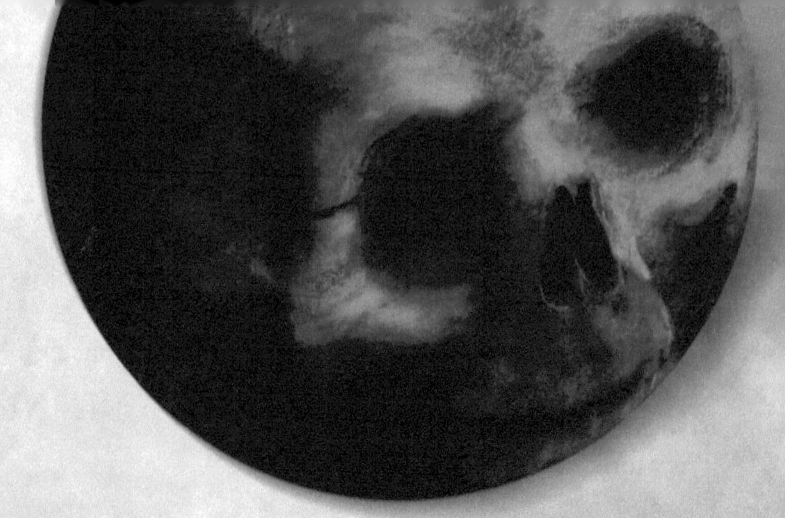

VIII

STACCATO

Donarick was my rock after Gideon. He picked me back up, put me back together, and sent me off on my revenge.

He snaps the collar round my neck.

Ding Dong! The witch is dead. Which old witch?
The wicked witch.

Ding Dong! The wicked witch is dead.

I'm dead...

TWO MONTHS LATER

Wren Nocturne is dead. By the gods! Wren Nocturne is dead but so is her young charge.

"I told you to get there first!"

It stings. The slap to my face stings. It wasn't a hard hit. Not really. Not compared to the second.

"I trusted you!"

The second strike knocks me off balance. My side collides with the banister. All this because I failed.

"I've kept you safe this whole time and this is how you repay me."

The man's chest heaves with exertion and rage. I've never seen him like this before, this unhinged, this heated, this out of control.

"Donarick," I start.

"Quiet!" The second hit is much harder. "The girl is lost because of you! Because someone beat you to the witch's hideaway."

"I did get there first. There was no one there, Don. Not a trace of a life to be found. The bombs, they—"

"Liar! You've mucked this all up, Summer. How could I have entrusted such an important task to a *hexen*!"

He spits the word out like a curse.

"But I—"

"Shut up!"

His ring cuts open my cheekbone. Blood wells at the site.

"Donarick, please. Your heart."

"Is none of your concern, witch!"

Another strike sends me rolling sideways, and the floor ends.

I've never fallen down stairs before. Never even imagined what it might be like. It happens in slow motion. First the ceiling waves at you then the carpet burns you. Painful, yes. Bruising, sure. Concussion, certainly possible. But that's only how they portray it on television or theater when the damsels hit the bottom with one shoe missing and their hair out of place only for prince charming to sweep them up and marry them.

That's not real life.

I never imagined there would be the crunching of bone, the snapping of tendons, or the head splitting agony of my skull opening.

The landing finds me like a bag of skin and pain. I can't move. I can't talk. I can't even open my eyes. And when a foot puts pressure on my head, darkness edges in.

I don't know what hurts worse: my broken body or my broken heart.

It's cold inside of my summoning circles. Void magic, while not as chilly as ice, is as bleak as the empty spaces between little known and unknown planes. I am a void magic user. It's my natural magic, gifted to me by the cursed genes that make me a witch. It's perfect for summoning creatures from said void. There's something comforting about dealing with "monsters."

Monsters are honest. Those elder things that lurk in space between the hands of time are the most honest beings I've ever come into contact with. They are living, breathing amalgamations of baser emotion: delight/delirium, desire/ despair, destruction/death, dreams and deconstructions. These are creatures who drink madness. They consume it, let it curdle in their gut, and then spew it out into the nearest vessel for re-consumption. I've eaten their aforementioned puke, and they never lied to me about what it was. I did it willingly to gain their trust.

So, yes, it's dangerous, creeping into the in-between, but at least the creatures that reside there are truthful. Here on Deus, in reality, people will lie in your face, knock you down, and leave you there to stew in your own waste. But mon- sters... monsters will keep you warm if you just give them what they want, but the process of getting them here is like dropping yourself into a tub of ice.

It's cold in the circle. I hate the cold.

I suppose the one thing my mother did right by me was give me the name "Summer." Summer like the sun. Summer like a blissful vacation to the seaside. Summer like the heat that melts the edges off the pavement. But the cold... Not only is it uncomfortable, not only does it require preparation and survival skills, but it's also a thief. Cold usually comes with darkness. It invades from the deep places of the world to suck the heat from the ground. The cold will grip you by the throat and squeeze the life out of you. Collect your life- force for itself until there is nothing left for it to syphon off. Cold is for dead things, ice for the decaying, and frost is for the unmoving skin of the lifeless.

I am not a dead thing.

*They say that witches who steal from their kin
are damned... Is this my damnation?*

Beep... buh-beep... beep... buh-beep...

There's cotton between my ears.

"Ah, you're awake. What a relief! We were afraid it would be weeks before you woke up."

Weeks? What happened?

"Where am I?"

"My name is Dr. Faust, and you are presently being treated at St. Brigid's Hospital."

"How did I get here?"

"Mr. Thames brought you in of course. Your husband was scared out of his wits when you fell down the stairs."

Is that what he told the doctors? That I fell down the stairs. What a convenient excuse... I suppose it isn't a lie. I did fall down the stairs.

"And where is my husband, now?"

"Anxiously awaiting your recovery. You've been in a coma for nearly 20 hours now."

A coma... The asshole put me in a coma!

"Well, your vitals are holding strong despite the dehydration. You were probably experiencing a bit of vertigo which is why you fell in the first place. You've got a bit of bruising and swelling, but that is to be expected for someone who's just fallen down a flight of stairs. Thankfully, there's no injury to the baby."

The world grinds to a halt.

"What?"

"The baby is perfectly healthy."

"What baby?"

"Oh, I suppose congratulations in order. You're about six weeks pregnant. That's why we needed an ultrasound. Your urine analysis showed a presence of hCG, so we had to make sure the fetus was still viable after such a nasty fall. The good news is your little one's heartbeat is strong, and everything seems to be progressing as normal."

"Oh..."

"Yes, well, I'm sure your husband will be happy to hear the news. I can let him know when he comes backif you'd like."

"No," the answer comes all too quickly. "I-I'll tell him."

"As you wish. My nurse will be back with your discharge papers. Remember lots of fluids and don't forget to take your medications. I've prescribed you an antibiotic and a pain killer that should be safe for pregnancy. I recommend a follow-up as soon as possible with your OB. The first step to a healthy baby is good prenatal care. By the way, you should get on a vitamin regiment asap."

"Right..."

The doctor turns his back on me as he walks out of the room. In my head, I am counting backward from my last period. I could've sworn I had one just two weeks ago, or was that something else? But the last time I bought a pack of tampons was over three months ago, and I bleed through a whole box every time. It can't have been that long. Could it?

Disbelief. That's what this is. Bone-deep disbelief... If only I could say it was helping with the pain. My ribs ache-from the fall.

I've never wanted children. Not until my Gideon. I suppose I had him for a while, but... Why would I want to submit another life to this wretched world? And Donarick... There's a bandage on my cheek where his ring cut me and gauze wrapping my torso. It is only by fortune his treatment of my person didn't already cause a miscarriage.

Do I really want a life like this for a child?

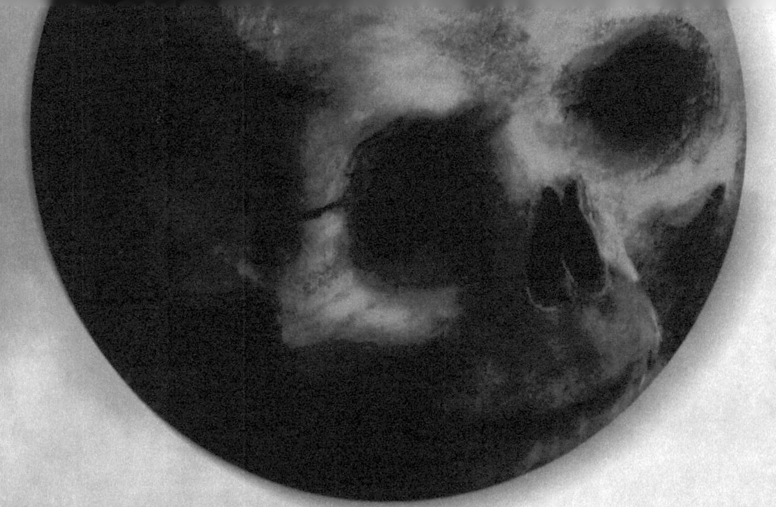

IX

LAMENTATION

Did you know that in the old-world women of limited means used to purposefully roll onto their infants in the night to smother them to death? It was during a time that abortions were the worst sin a woman could commit. They made the mistake of confessing their crimes to Catholic priests who, as a result, deemed that any woman caught sleeping in the same bed as their babies would be excommunicated. 'Cause we can't have women of low status offering their babies a swift, painless, merciful death when the better option is that they starve their way into the afterlife.

The irony of it is that babies are far more likely to die in their sleep when made to sleep away from their mothers. Just look at the spike in SIDS rates in the Victorian Era when lacey nursery cribs were all the rage.

Abortion is illegal in Seraphim, so I travel all the way to Murasaki no Yama to get the treatments that I need.

The clinic I visit is clean. The workers there are warm if not friendly. They seem to understand that these kinds of decisions are not made lightly and that it's none of their fucking business why their patients choose the way they do. I use my husband's credentials, stolen without his knowledge, and receive VIP treatment.

I'm surprised by how painless the process is.

Were I to have undertaken the task at home, it would have involved ingesting goddess-knows how many toxins, and if that didn't work, well, the hanger-method is as dangerous as it is painful, but it is effective. There are magics that could be performed. Dark magics. Magics that involve sacrificial rights and surgical accoutrements to even work. Magic capable of transferring a pregnancy from one woman to another, but that requires another participant willing to both experience pregnancy and work with a witch to do it (one of those might be easy to find... The other, well, I'm in hiding for a reason.), and my sadism stops at the idea of forcing someone to carry a pregnancy they don't want. Blood, yes. Murder, yes. Dismemberment, absolutely. But rape, no!

And forced pregnancy... Absolutely not! Thor! Even witches have morals.

This early in the process, all I have to do is swallow a couple of pills, and my body will expel the fetus naturally. If I'd waited any longer, I would have needed a D&C, but then they would have just put me under anesthesia and taken care of the business while I slept.

The nurse who brought me the medication gives me a tender smile as she tosses the pill case into the nearby bin.

"Alright, you're all done. You can get yourself dressed again."

As I redress, there is a niggling voice in the back of my head that keeps saying, "What if..." What if I kept the baby? What if I ran away and raised my child alone? What if I lived in a fairy tale world where hexen and human+ could live as one?

Tch, stop dreaming, Summer...

There's a small rustling sound from the bag I've set down on the exam table. The bag shifts, startling the nurse.

"Ma'am, I think there's something in your backpack."

"It's nothing," I say, grabbing the bag and tossing it over my shoulder. Something clatters around inside, but I pay it no heed and hurry out of the room. Once out onto the street, I duck into the nearest back alley to hide behind a dumpster. The fetid odor of the trash makes me want to gag, or maybe it's the early effects of the medicine. They did tell me nausea was a fairly common symptom. *Summoned monsters!* I didn't even think of that. How am I going to get home if I can barely keep my guts down?

The journey here has been long and taxing, not to mention filled with technomancers. The only way to enter Murasaki no Yama from Seraphim is via air passage or light rail, both incredibly risky and exceedingly dangerous for someone like me. So, I opted for another method of travel.

"You stupid animal," I curse, ripping the bag open. Inside, a pair of slitted amber eyes stare back at me, framed in angry whiskers and an enchanted muzzle. Silje hisses at me from the confines of the makeshift prison I've stuffed her in. "You could have gotten us both caught and thrown out."

Another hiss for my troubles.

I don't even grace the feline with a response; I just stick my hand in the bag, wrap my palm around the cat's throat and, through gritted teeth, pull the power I want from her directly into my synapsis.

The yowling that ushers forth from the netherbeast's throat will echo in my dreams tonight. I just know it.

I wasn't always like this, you know. I wasn't always the kind of witch who would steal another's prized accoutrements. Stealing another witch's familiar... it's like stealing a piece of their soul, yet here I am torturing this one because it's the only displacer beast on this plane of existence and my only means of getting back to the manor before Donarick realizes I'm gone.

I toss the netherbeast back into her holding pen when I arrive home just minutes before Donarick returns from his trip to congratulate the newest technomancer initiates at their graduation ceremony in Aighneas. He's in a good mood. Three of Seraphim's adepts have passed the trials, making our roster of technomancers all the stronger.

Over the course of the next week, I suffer the worst cramps and the worst bleeding I have ever experienced in my life. There's something dark and sickly about miscarriage blood, even an intentional one. It's different from my normal cycle. There is no prospect of something new taking its place as my menstrua would normally be. No, this blood is purely destructive.

They say that women who have an abortion are forever damned in the eyes of the divine. They say we will be cursed to infertility and suffering for all the rest of our non-child-bearing years. They say... well, they say a lot of things that don't really matter at the end of the day. My abortionist wouldn't agree. I only met her once, but she was a lot kinder than some midwives I've met.

There was a midwife at the orphanage who would come only when called, and oh, how I hated her, the bitter old crone. Every so often, a woman would come, heavy with child and with no means to care for her burden. Some came wanting to give their children away. Others came asking for the help they would need to care for their child themselves. But regardless of their circumstance, all of them first needed to deliver their babies. So naturally, the midwife would have to deliver her baby, and my goddess, how she bullied those women. She shamed them for getting pregnant regardless of their circumstance. She let them labor for days only to cut them open when such a call should have been made much earlier. And no sooner would these babies be pulled from their hosts' wombs then they would be whisked off into the arms of their new parents. No concern for mummy dearest. Not even for the mothers who wanted to keep their babies. They were too young, too poor, too irresponsible. How could we allow them to raise a child?

That's how the orphanage would make its money, you see.

FOR SALE: INFANT FRESH
FROM THE WOMB

Because that's how prospective parents want their children, new and unsullied. A multi-million credit black market on babies, and no one so much as batted an eye.

Donarick is as sweet as ever. He thinks I'm just having a very bad period. He wipes the sweat off my forehead, brings me my favorite chocolates, and at the end of the week when the pain has dimmed and the bleeding slowed, he takes me out on the town to my favorite restaurant and a movie, and on the way home, he makes his proposal.

"I am tired of hiding you in the shadows, my love."

"Don," I whisper, "I know it isn't safe for me—"

"I've devised a plan to bring you into the open as my true wife and soulmate."

He takes my hands in his own, and for a moment, I am seeing the man who asked me to marry him in response to his own father insulting me from across the table. It's almost as if the last four months haven't even happened. Like I haven't just flushed our baby down the toilet because I couldn't trust him to treat them like a human being rather than a lab rat.

"What do you mean?"

"Chiamaka."

Not what I was expecting.

"What about Chiamaka?"

Since the untimely death of her father and brother, Chiamaka has proven herself a fiercely protective lioness not only of her young, orphaned niece but also of her country, taking the reins until her young charge reaches the age of majority.

"She is the one we need."

"She'll never come around. Not so long as her niece draws breath."

"Who needs a willing partner when I have a willing witch?"

I raise my eyebrow.

"What does that have to do with anything?"

"My darling, are you familiar with a type of magic called a glamour?"

I wish I could say I was stabbed in the back. It would be easier that way. But I can't. My death came from right beside me.

I guess you could say I was blindsided.

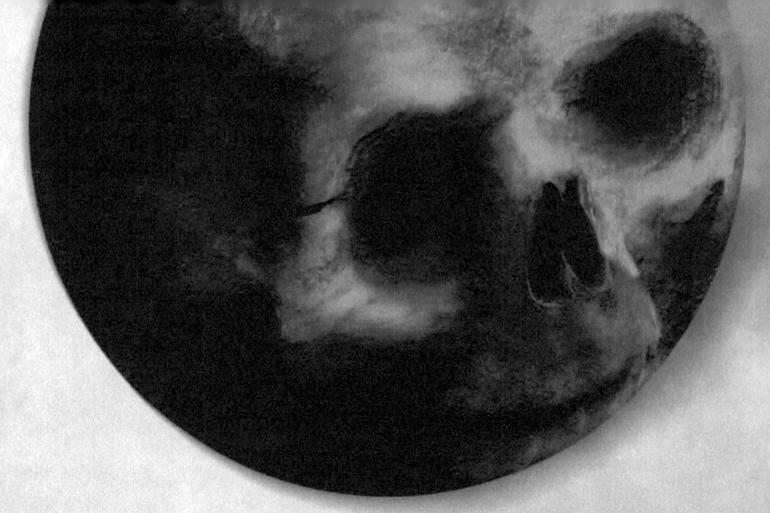

Afterword

Domestic abuse is a horrible reality of our world. If you or someone you know has suffered in an abusive relationship, silence is never the answer. Remember, we are all fighting our own battles, some more haunting than others. Kindness is always a choice.

Below is a list of help services for survivors of domestic abuse:

- **The National Domestic Violence Hotline**
  1-800-799-7233 (SAFE)
  www.ndvh.org

- **National Dating Abuse Helpline**
  1-866-331-9474
  www.loveisrespect.org

- **National Child Abuse Hotline/Childhelp**
  1-800-4-A-CHILD (1-800-422-4453)
  www.childhelp.org

- **National Sexual Assault Hotline**
  1-800-656-4673 (HOPE)
  www.rainn.org

- **National Suicide Prevention Lifeline**
  1-800-273-8255 (TALK)
  www.suicidepreventionlifeline.org

- **National Center for Victims of Crime**
  1-202-467-8700
  www.victimsofcrime.org

- **National Human Trafficking Resource Center/
  Polaris Project**
  Call: 1-888-373-7888 | Text: HELP to BeFree (233733)
  www.polarisproject.org

- **National Network for Immigrant and
  Refugee Rights**
  1-510-465-1984
  www.nnirr.org

- **National Coalition for the Homeless**
  1-202-737-6444
  www.nationalhomeless.org

- **National Resource Center on Domestic Violence**
  1-800-537-2238
  www.nrcdv.org and www.vawnet.org

- **Futures Without Violence: The National Health Resource Center on Domestic Violence**
  1-888-792-2873
  www.futureswithoutviolence.org

- **National Center on Domestic Violence, Trauma & Mental Health**
  1-312-726-7020 ext. 2011
  www.nationalcenterdvtraumamh.org

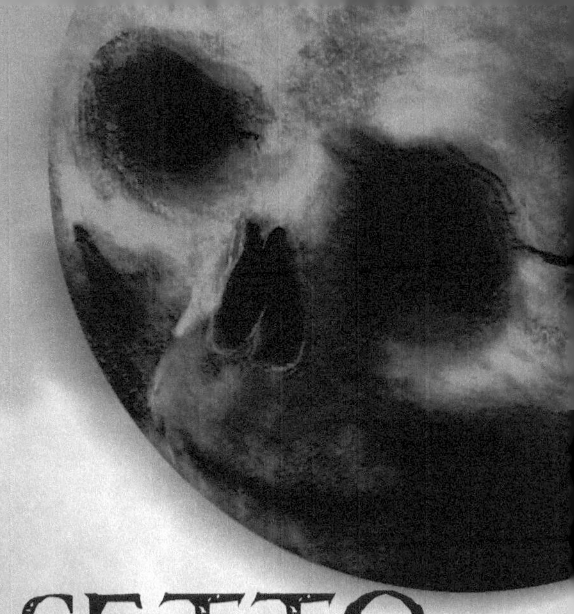

FALSETTO IN THE WOODS

This novella contains the following content: Scandinavian Folklore, Implied/Referenced chronic illness, off-screen death, reference to suicide, sexual situations, mayhem typical of Halloween adventures, and ghosts.

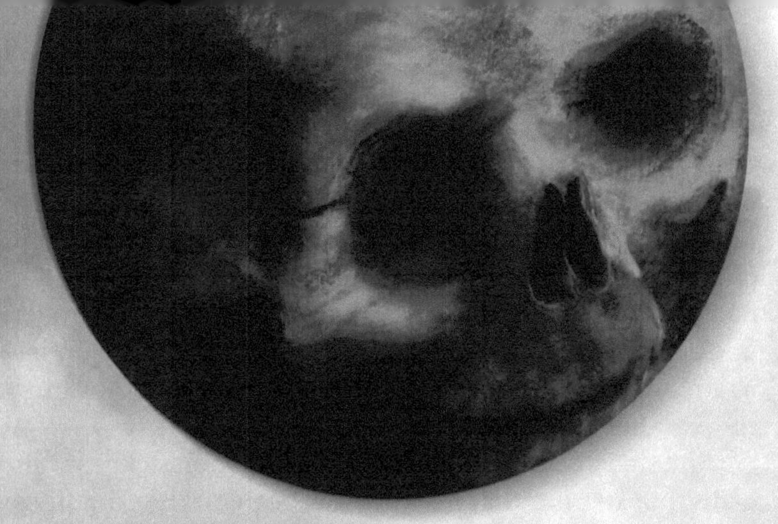

I

A WALK IN THE
BLACK FOREST

30TH DAY IN THE MONTH OF DARKNESS
(OCTOBER 30TH), 1870 A.P. – DEUS'S BACK ROADS

Lily drums her nails against the dashboard. Hanging from the rearview mirror, the pineapple air freshener swings violently back and forth, back and forth as Sebastian's truck bounces over the cracks and bumps in the beaten-down dirt road. The glass of the window is cool against her forehead, a distraction from the motion sickness bubbling in her stomach. Every time she opens her eyes, it gets worse, but closing them isn't much better. The world spins, rapidly descending spirals that make her feel like she's being flushed down a toilet.

"We're almost there, babe," says Sebastian, her boyfriend of two years, reaching over to thread his fingers through her hair. He presses his thumb into the pressure point just under one of the tech nodes at her temple. The metal plate underneath her skin throbs in response, a wave of relief washing through her synapses.

She sighs. She doesn't normally get motion sickness this badly, but her internal network has been on the fritz since the last dead zone they drove through, and she doesn't need to check her comm to know they're completely off grid.

"I cannot believe I let you convince me to go on a stupid camping trip."

"Oh, come on, city girl. Give it a chance. It'll be fun. You told me you've never been, outside of a training exercise." The wheels bolt over another uneven ridge, tossing the car wildly enough Lily's stomach jolts into her throat.

"Couldn't we have just gone to a theme park? There are plenty of haunted houses at Kosmos World. Surely, there's a ghost–themed one this year."

And this drive is getting right up there with some of the milder rollercoasters.

"*Fake* ghosts. People wearing make–up, fake blood, and plastic teeth. If it weren't for the dark lighting, they wouldn't be scary at all."

"The holoprojections are pretty realistic."

"We went to Fright Fest last year, Lil." He cranks the stick shift into park. "Besides, my brother's been scouting this place out for his next ghost tour. We'll be his first critics before he opens officially."

Now that they've stopped, her insides cease their acrobatics, and she opens her eyes to look at him, dressed in his driving leathers, plaid shirt, and blue jeans. His sun–kissed hair flops airily around his cheekbones, sunny golden bangs, ruffled from the knit beanie on his head and hanging in loose curls over his sunglasses. She envies his tan, still a bronzy honeycomb despite prime swimming season having long since passed. The evidence of what little bit of sun she managed to get has already disappeared, not that it did more than darken her freckles and dry out her strawberry blonde hair, leaving it in frizzly strings around her head.

Thank the gears for moisturizing shampoo!

"Here I thought your idea of Halloween fun was entertaining trick–or–treaters with your horrid Count Dracula accent and wearing those fake fangs that give you the most horrible slur."

He makes an affronted face at her, dimples showing through the scruff of his facial hair, the warm browns of his eyes bright in the setting sun.

"I'll show you 'horrible'!" He digs his fingers into her sides, eliciting a shrieking laugh out of her. She swats the rogue digits away, delivering two smacks to his chest for good measure. He laughs her off and gestures to the landscape past the frost–edged windows like an auction house conductor. "But babe, look at this! Can you honestly tell me this isn't one of the most beautiful sights you've ever seen?"

Lily draws herself out of the door to look, and oh, he's right. He is very right.

Beyond the portals of their humble vehicle, a boundless forest stretches, lush with orange, yellow, and red leaves. The colors are as breathtaking as the sunset, like the whole forest has gone up in flames—the kind of place that would inspire painters and musicians to create masterpieces.

Nothing like the piteous groves in New London. Their inner–city home is too far south to see true seasonal changes and too urbanized to hold a candle to this majesty. Even the largest city park, Abney Gardens—hailed as one of the most visited tourist spots in all of Aighneas—has hardly any trees in it. Well... any real trees anyway. Plenty of synthetics, hybrids bred to thrive on city pollution and clean the smog out of the air. Scattered as they are between the jogging trails and free speech zones, the small groves of synthetics are nothing like this living, breathing forest sprawled beyond the window. A wonder of the natural world. She would call it magical if she didn't know better.

Magic is anything but wonderful.

"I gotta hand it to him. Kyle did pretty damn good."

"Okay, your brother gets points for location, but I'm still not looking forward to freezing my butt off."

Another car pulls up behind them as Sebastian turns off the ignition. It's half the size of Sebastian's truck, baby blue, with rainbow bumper stickers all across the front and back. How their friends survived the long drive in Javier's tiny smart compact without killing each other is beyond her.

Sebastian leans over the center console and nuzzles her ear with his nose. "Don't worry, baby. I'll keep you warm."

"Yeah, I bet you will."

Lascivious bastard.

Giggling with delight as his breath tickles her neck, she ducks away, slipping off her seatbelt and stepping out of the car. A shiver rockets up her legs as her bare ankles meet the cool autumn air. It was a warm 75 degrees when they left the little highway hotel where they spent the night, but that was at five o'clock in the morning. They've been on the road for nearly ten hours, and while she did change into warmer jeans and a long–sleeved shirt at the last rest stop, she didn't change her shoes. A pair of knee-high stockings and her favorite pair of hiking boots are calling her name from the back of the truck.

"Didn't you used to spend weeks at a time out in the wilderness? You told me your instructors once dropped you in the middle of the desert with nothing but a backpack and a map and told you to find your way back. What's a few nights in the woods with lots of gear compared to that?"

"I was seventeen and training to be a technomancer, Sebastian. It's been nearly seven years."

Seven years since Lily tried and failed to pass the 247th Technomancer Trials. She isn't bitter about it; she flunked out on a stupid alchemical theorem! She'd even been invited to try again the following year, but then the world went to hell in a handbasket as Seraphim opened fire on pretty much every other League nation. Because of it, however, the trials were halted for two years, and by the time they started back up, well... let's just say her health disqualified her from participating.

It's fine. She doesn't miss the lifestyle. Aighneas keeps a militarized training regimen for their human+ trainees, and while she does miss wearing the uniform from time to time, not having to wake up at an ungodly 4AM every morning is utter bliss. Oh, and being able to wear make-up whenever the fuck she wants is a bonus. Besides, she's pursuing other career opportunities. Or maybe she should say other "educational" opportunities? "Career" implies she's done anything other than go to school the last six years of her life.

"You realize my thesis is due in less than a month, right?"

"And you said you didn't want to work on it this weekend because you wanted to enjoy the holiday."

Sebastian has a career.

He's a kindergarten teacher at a local elementary school. They met almost two years ago, completely by chance, when

Lily was monitoring one of her student teachers from the university. As the youngest doctoral student in the department, she'd drawn the short straw to supervise the undergrad students trying for their teaching certification.

"You said *you* didn't want to work this weekend. I merely hummed in agreement, thinking I'd be left in peace to do my work."

She doesn't even like Halloween or Hexennacht or Samhain whatever you want to call it. It's a holiday for hexen. Humans just hate missing out on an opportunity to get drunk and stupid.

"The fresh air will be good for you," continues Sebastian as he helps her into a thick thermal coat. "You've spent so much time buried in your hub, you've started growing mushrooms on your head."

"I have not!"

He catches her by the hip, dodging her slap and tugging her in close despite the hiking pack in her arms. For a normal, Sebastian is strong. He winks down at her with a twinkle in his eye. Lily's neural hub immediately goes into overdrive trying to cool her down as a blush rises to her cheeks.

"Hey," he says with his winning smile. "You remember what you told your undergrads about Hexennacht, right?"

"That it's a rip–off of some old–world holiday called Halloween, and that it's the reason so many children need dentures before their adult teeth come in."

"I don't remember that being part of Professor Albridge's curriculum," pipes up Javier, stepping out of the passenger seat of the little blue smartie. Javier is one of Lily's cohorts, and the first real friend she made after entering civie life. He swaggers his way toward the bickering couple like some varsity sportsman, though he's never played a day in his life. "I have a delicate disposition," he'd use as an excuse whenever she tried to get him to play holo ball with her at the campus gym—a sport which, by the way, is basically a virtual version of ping pong.

So yeah. Suffice to say: Sports + Javi = NO.

Unless someone was talking about a rigorous game of chess—that's an entirely different story. He's been toting around his recent championship cup the way a wrestler wears their heavyweight belts, hips cocked forward, shoulders back, and throwing elbows even though his noodly arms couldn't shove an overweight guinea pig out of his way. Despite his miraculous ability to carry around at least twenty books at a time, all of Javier's brawn is in his brains. Why he said yes to Sebastian's asinine weekend getaway is lost on her. You'd think he would much rather stay home and play video games over the weekend with his husband.

"Well, Professor Albridge isn't here to correct me, now is she? Besides, while she's on sabbatical, I'm teaching the class, and I don't teach nonsense."

Javier shakes his head at her, curly brown locks bouncing. How is it men manage to have such luscious hair without even trying?

"Hexen Anthropology, right?" Javier's tall, dark, and buff husband Derrick comes around, carrying his and Javier's tent kit.

Where Javier is the epitome of a noodle, Derrick is a perfectly cooked steak. Tall with hazel–hued, deep brown skin, Derrick is a personal trainer and a bodybuilder who enjoys his weekends LARPing with a group of cosplayers as Rahad the wizard. He even keeps a full beard, perfectly groomed to make him look like a wizened sage. "100% home grown!" He likes to crow whenever he's flexing, but she's never really sure if he's talking about his muscles or his facial hair. Not that either is something to shake a feather at. His beard is as luxurious as a lion's mane, partially braided and beaded, well–oiled, and meticulously combed, and his biceps are the size of Lily's head. But for all his ferocious appearance, he's a total sweetie, doting on Javier whenever he can.

"I remember taking that class as an elective in under-grad. My favorite unit was the one on Halloween myths and legends—how they shape the way we celebrate Hexennacht today."

"Yup. That's why she only offers the class in the fall," replies Javier as his husband folds him into an oversized coat. Javier rises onto the balls of his feet to adjust the colorful pompom–peaked knit hat atop Derrick's bald head, making sure it is centered rather than hanging over his ear. Javier slaved over his knitting needles in the grad office for a whole week, trying to finish it by Derrick's last birthday. Amidst midterms, while Lily had been slammed with students com-plaining about their grades, Javier's students gave the knit-ting man a wide berth, probably too afraid of flying needles to risk stressing the grad out any further.

"You don't understand how jealous I am that they assigned the class to you. All they gave me was Old World Anthro."

"They gave me the class because my thesis is on hexen rumors and superstitions. Yours is on the cultural shifts that took place between the A.D. and A.P. eras and how Old–World cultures evolved upon transition to Deus."

"Yeah, I know, but you could at least keep some of her traditions. The best part about being her TA was getting to wear costumes the whole Month of Darkness."

"That's because Hexennacht is your favorite holiday for some unholy reason." Jeanine, Javier's sister, steps out of the backseat wearing a fur-lined black coat with a hot pink back-pack, better suited for school textbooks than a camping trip, slung over one shoulder. Between her long sheet of black hair and powdered skin, she looks like a pre–Gomez, co–ed version of Morticia Addams.

"Like you aren't the freak who starts decorating three months early," Javier says.

"What can I say? My aesthetic is spooky and pink."

"Yes, and you keep that vibe going all the way through New Year's."

Jeanine pulls the lower lid of her right eye down and sticks her tongue out at her older brother. "It's the Night*mare* Before Yule, not the Night, and bats are so much cuter than turtle doves."

Javier just rolls his eyes, turning the topic back to Hexennacht.

"There's a myth that a lost spirit might find you, banish your soul into the underworld, and take possession of your body. That's why organics and posties are supposed to dress up on Hexennacht so the spirits don't recognize you as human."

"It's strange how most people decide to dress up as hexen or fae though. Why not just be an animal of some kind? We're supposed to be scared of witches, but they sell witch hats everywhere during the Month of Darkness."

"That's the point, Jeanine. They're scary. You want to frighten away the ghosts."

"I heard it was so doppelgangers can't steal your identity," laughs Sebastian.

Derrick holds his hands up. "Whoa, whoa, whoa. Hold the spooky stories. I didn't pack a costume."

"Oh, Derrick," teases Javier. "You overgrown chicken."

"My sorority sisters and I were planning on having a spooky movie marathon," whines Jeanine. "Yet here I am with you losers."

Javier makes a face at his sister.

"It's not like anyone made you come."

"And let you get yourself killed on a Hexennacht camping trip? Do you realize how horror movie cliché that is? If you wanted to get scared, we could have gone to a haunted house or something. There's a really spooky one held by Alpha Kappa Psi every year."

"Eew! Who wants to pay to have a bunch of horror-obsessed frat boys grope you?"

"They don't grope you, Derrick."

"Last year I got groped, and I will swear on it until the day I die."

"Yeah, whatever."

"Another one," continues Javier, "says the reason we give out candy is because vampyres won't drink your blood if there's too much sugar in it."

"You mean," inserts Sebastian, "they won't drink the blood of people dying from alcohol poisoning."

Actually, the blood–alcohol myth isn't a myth at all, and fairly practical, if Lily's reasoning is correct. If alcohol can fuck up a living person's system that badly, what do you think it'll do to someone without a fully functioning liver?

"My favorite is the one about the three old crones who came back to life only to die again at sunrise because they were outsmarted by a bunch of teenagers. There's a talking cat and everything in it."

"You're such a geek, *mi amor*," says Javier, leaning up to kiss Derrick on his whiskered cheek.

"That's a movie, not a legend," says Lily. "People coming back to life is a bunch of hocus pocus. It's not possible, and whatever stories you're thinking of, stop—95% of those stories are utter crock."

"Says Miss–I–once–trained–under–The–Morrigan," sing-songs Jeanine, one hip cocked to the side. "Of course, you're going to tell us not to put any stock in it. But you must admit, there's a granule of truth in every story."

"And usually that truth is 'it's an utter lie.' I thought I made that clear to you guys last week in class."

The undergrad is a regular to Lily's tutoring sessions, preferring hers to her brother's for some odd reason. When the twenty–one–year old isn't spending time with her sorority sisters, she is avidly studying hexen as much as anyone outside of the League's adept and technomancer program is allowed to study. She jokes about her love of the topic, saying she just wants to marry a technomancer one day by getting a research position in the government, but Lily knows she enjoys the topic.

"Yes, yes, and never forget you can't spell 'believe' without the word 'lie.' I remember."

"Correct. Real hexen tales are not jokes to be taken lightly. They aren't fairy tales you can turn into kiddy films where animals sing, and all the princess loses is a shoe. Professor Albridge's class is only allowed to be taught on the grounds that everything is framed by historical curiosity, nothing else." Not to mention, it doesn't hold a candle to the things she learned as an adept. "We read those texts to understand hexen thinking, protect ourselves against them, and for those of us capable, kill hexen. You'd be more frightened of them if you ever actually met a witch."

"Yeah, well the chance of that ever happening is pretty slim, don't 'cha think, Lil?"

Lily's shoulders sag. *Yeah... Especially now* she's *gone...*

"But you're writing your dissertation on hexen folklore?" asks Javier.

"Not exactly. I'm doing my research on the myths and rumors surrounding the Songstress of Lorelei. And even if I was, folklore is just that: folk*LORE*! None of it is real. Like the urban legend about pop rocks bursting in your stomach if you eat them with soda."

"Or hair growing on your palm if you—"

"Gross, Derrick."

"Anyway," inserts Sebastian loudly, stretching the vowels out with a long aaah, "I'm not talking about the mumbo jumbo we teach five-year-olds to get them to behave. I'm talking about what you told me last year. People used to believe the veil between the living and the dead is thinnest on Halloween. The legend says too much celebration can rouse the ghosts of recently deceased witches at the witching hour."

"Sebastian..."

"They originally wanted to jump all of the clocks forward an hour at 3AM, but with the different time zones, it didn't seem like a logical solution, so instead the League installed a mandatory curfew on All Hallow's Eve because they're afraid people will disturb the ghost of the Songstress of Lorelei."

Derrick crosses himself and Javier pales.

"Good thing we came to the middle of nowhere to party," drawls Jeanine. "That way no one can hear us screaming when we accidentally summon a vengeful witch from the dead."

"No one is summoning a witch anywhere." Lily glares at Sebastian, who holds up his hands in defense. "There is no truth to that legend. Anyone who says otherwise doesn't know what they're talking about, and we will not be looking for the opportunity to test it."

"Of course, baby. Sorry. I was just thinking about that story."

"Well, stop thinking about it before I knock it out of your brain. Ghosts and witch spirits. What a load of crock!"

This seems to quell Derrick's rising panic, and the color returns to Javier's cheeks.

"I thought you said your brother was bringing us on a ghost tour?"

Sebastian laughs, shifting from one foot to the other. "My brother just thinks this place is cool enough to attract tourists. Kyle's ghost tours are always gags and money scams. None of it is actually scary, and there are certainly never any real ghosts. This is an autumn camping trip that just so happens to fall on Hexennacht."

"Good," huffs Lily, crossing her arms. "The last thing I need is to be stuck in the middle of nowhere *and* surrounded by ghosts."

"Right, just some good, old–fashioned camping. Glad you're coming around to the idea."

His sarcasm is unamusing, so Lily shakes her head and goes to fish the rest of her gear out of the truck bed.

"I am not coming around to the idea. I thought we would be going to a lodge or something, not walking into the woods in the middle of nowhere where I can't get a connection."

"Babe, I'm sorry I wasn't clear, but that's the whole point of camping. Disconnecting and getting away from the stressors of regular life. You can't do that at a lodge where the televisions are always turned on to the news."

Lily huffs, letting her duffle plop to the ground by a tire.

He doesn't understand. He isn't augmented. Not like she is. This far away from the city, she is completely disconnected from the network. When Sebastian told her they would be going glamping, she imagined paying to sleep outside some swanky resort where the bathrooms were just a stone's throw away, the WIFI had a password, and her comm units were still a viable means of communication. Instead, she's found herself in a dead zone.

"Where are we anyway?"

"You mean you don't know with all of that high quality tech in your head?"

"Do I look like a GPS? You were driving, and you purposely went out of your way to keep this as mysterious as possible, and unfortunately, I tend to make the mistake of trusting you far more often than I should."

"Hmm, you really shouldn't do that," he teases back, winking at her good-naturedly, the man already moving past their little pseudo spat despite her lingering ire. He's lucky he has a great smile. The cleft chin gives him an unfair advantage. Otherwise, she just might've punched him. It helps that she kinda loves him, too. Just kinda.

Lily rises onto her toes as he leans down, but just as they are about to kiss, the loud roar of a 10-cylinder engine pulls up.

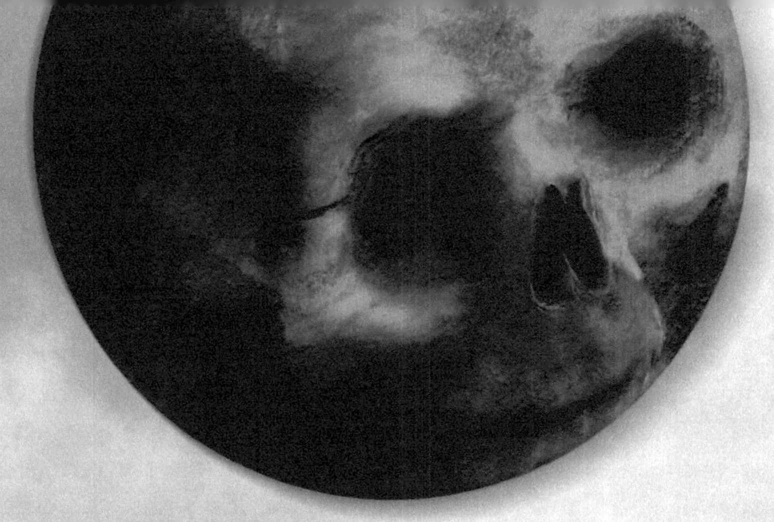

Lucy in the Sky
with Diamonds

"Seriously, Bassy. Already making it with your honey? We just got here!"

Lily bites down the groan threatening to rumble out of her throat. It's Kyle, Sebastian's older brother. Hard-assed, boot-wearing Kyle who is as dark as his brother is golden. Perpetually red-faced with dark, sunburnt auburn hair and darker brown eyes, they could pass as twins were it not for the opposing color schemes of their hair and eyes. They have the same winning dimpled smile, albeit Kyle's is marred by the ever-present bulge of chewing tobacco in his cheek.

"Lily's not my 'honey,' Ky. She's my girlfriend. There's a difference."

The heavy titanium of Kyle's mechanical arm catches the sunlight, reflecting right into Lily's eye as he shuts off the bike. The keyring makes a harsh scratchy sound as he twirls it around a steel finger. Kyle is augmented, not in the same way Lily is, but he has a mechanical right arm—the result of a chance encounter with a lycan. The bite had been high up on his arm, bisecting his bicep, and the protocol is a full amputation two to four inches proximal to the heart from the bite depending on time since attack to prevent the spread of the curse. The whole limb was lost as a result, but he makes do with his prosthesis and calls himself a cyborg even though he only has the one augmentation.

Legally, someone can only declare cyborgian status in Aighneas if they are in possession of a minimum of three augmentations necessary to sensory ability and/or mobility like hearing aids or mechanical limbs. The exception to this is if for people in possession of an augmentation they would die without.

Someone like Lily with a synthetic nervous system.

Lily may not look it, but she's got far more tech running through her body than he does: muscle enhancements, skeletal plating, a toxicity filtration system, oxygen optimizations, and most notable, her neural net, her cerebral connection to the cyberscape, indicated by the circular hub high on the back of her neck. (An implant she's had since she was eight years old.) She used to have an offensive system in her left forearm, complete with a high-density laser, but after resigning from the military, she replaced it with a basic utility system complete with a pocketknife, screwdriver, corkscrew, and flashlight.

"Not from where I'm standing." Kyle laughs, one eyebrow cocked skyward. "You two looking mighty cozy. How ya doing, Lil? My little bro been keeping all 'em hidden buttons of yours fine-tuned?"

She doesn't appreciate the lewdness of the question or the dig at her augmentations.

"What can I say? He's good with his hands," she says, aiming a winning grin at Kyle as if she was shooting a laser at a target drone. "Better than any mechanic I've ever met. Knows just how to make my motors purr. Hope you don't mind the noise. Oh wait, your arm is so noisy I can hear it creaking a mile away, so that shouldn't be a problem."

The man grunts in admiration of her come back and shoves his flesh hand in his pocket.

"Don't worry. I'll be sure to set up my tent far away from yours. Provided of course you didn't lose any of the equipment I put in your truck."

And why he couldn't drive his own shit here, Lily hasn't the slightest idea.

"Why don't you check for yourself, you rusty piece of junk?" Sebastian throws back with a smile, greeting his brother with a handshake and a chest bump.

"Jerk! I've been driving all day. You gonna make me start lugging hiking equipment around already?"

"You could've ridden with us, Kyle," calls Jeanine.

"Right... and listen to you chatter on about the latest episode of *Gossip+ Girl* while the married couple makes kissy faces at each other for more than twelve hours."

Javier and Derrick look sidelong at each other while Jeanine rolls her eyes.

"Dude, we've been married for two years, not two weeks."

"I mean, we like each other, but we're not newlyweds."

"Yeah, sure. I believe you. Hey, Bassy, give me the keys. I need to stretch my legs."

Sebastian tosses his keys to his brother.

"Right on. Let me get my shit, and we can hit the trail."

The man treks around to the back of Sebastian's truck. Lily visibly sags as he leaves. She doesn't dislike Kyle, but she doesn't particularly enjoy sharing space with him either.

"So, are you going to tell me where we are?"

"Absolutely!" Sebastian wraps an arm around her shoulder and tucks her into his side. "We are in Blackwood Forest."

"But Blackwood is a pine forest, isn't it? This is a broad-leaf forest."

"That's what Kyle told me. He showed me pictures of where we're going. There's a lake and a cabin and an amazing view of the mountains. You're gonna love it."

"Dragging me all the way out to the middle of nowhere? I had better love it."

Otherwise, she just might make him sleep outside the tent. Maybe a spider would bite him in the ass.

It's not long before Lily finds out why Kyle couldn't pack his own equipment into his truck.

"Tada!"

He pulls the tarp off to reveal a brand–new carriage droid painted in a green and blue camouflage. Round bodied with a cubicle–like sensory cam for a head, it looks a little like a turtle with a flat shell. It even has four miniature engines equidistant from each other around the body to help it hover off the ground.

"May I present the top–of–the–line KC–4M19?"

Kyle picks up a remote and flips the switch. The droid revs to life with a series of multi–tonal beeps and clicks, fancy lights flickering on in vibrant greens and blues—installed for pure aesthetic. The droid is roughly the size of a child's play wagon, and with a puff of steam, it rises off the bed of the truck and zips its way over the tailgate to hover a good foot above the dirt ground.

"Now we won't need to lug all of our shit around. We can put most of it on KC here."

"She is so cute!" Jeanine squeals, running over to put her hand on KC's "head." The little camera swivels and a scanner pans over her face.

"*He* is not cute."

"Robots are usually referred to as female, Kyle."

"Yeah, well KC is a hard–working bot. Ain't got time to be called 'cute' by nobody."

"Well, *she's* cuter than you. That's for sure."

Kyle looks at the co–ed in faux hurt before giving her a smirk. "Welp, guess he's only going to be carrying my stuff then."

"Wait, no. I take it back. KC can be a 'he.'"

Fifteen minutes later, they're trekking their way through the forest, Kyle at the helm and KC buzzing along behind them carrying Jeanine and Javier's backpacks along with a small supply of foodstuffs, a cooler, and camping equipment. It skims across the uneven ground and debris of the forest floor as easily as a hoverboard over cement. Lily has to hand it to Kyle: the little drone was a great idea for this trip. They'll be able to move faster and take more with them into the woods. Only an hour into their trek and already they are surrounded by forest. Were it not for her internal compass, Lily would have no idea which direction to go to get back to the cars.

"This place is amazing. Can you imagine hosting a tournament in these woods?"

Derrick, fantasizing about his next LARPing adventure, is not wrong.

The forest thrums with life and unfettered, wild magic, and she doesn't need her scanners to tell her as much. She can feel it in the ground under her feet, in the trees around her, the bones of the world vibrating with power, and unlike most places where magic still lives, this forest does not slumber. In the short time they've been walking, they've passed a burrow of rabbits, countless birds, and a small herd of deer with their fawns grazing in the grass. None of the animals react to their presence, entirely unconditioned to fear them, carrying on with their day as though there weren't a bunch of noisy people traipsing through their woods. A fox catches a pigeon, the birds sing their evening anthems, and a squirrel scurries up a tree with a prized acorn between its teeth.

The vitality of nature in action.

"Rahad would totally hunker down in one of these trees," Derrick says, gesturing toward a thick evergreen, "and chuck fireballs at all of the poor paladins trying to clip–clop their way to glory. What do you think, babe? Should I make a proposal to the committee? Change the venue for the next tourney?"

Lily doesn't say it aloud, but Derrick's idea may very well have him and anyone else foolish enough to try and invade this place falling asleep in a fairy ring, doomed to never wake again and dance themselves to death.

You don't go traipsing into woods like this to play foolish games. Kyle had better know what the hell he's doing bringing them to a place like this.

"I don't think so, *mi amor*. Didn't you say they were planning the next tourney for the Month of Ice? It'll be way too cold by then, and as much as I love you, I am not wearing long johns just because you want to go LARPing."

"Baby, don't worry. I'll keep you plenty warm. No long johns required."

"Gross, you two!"

Jeanine makes a gagging face as Derrick plants a wet one on Javier's cheek. Javier winks at his sister, hand thrown up in a lewd gesture.

Lily just shakes her head. Let them be as sickeningly sweet as they like. They've worked too long and too hard for their relationship—they deserve to make everyone around them puke if they want to—and Lily will tell them to go puke elsewhere if they have a problem with it.

"Speaking of sleeping in long johns, are we planning to stop soon? It's getting dark."

And the temperature is dropping. Lily rubs her hands together in a vain attempt to warm them. How could she have forgotten her damned gloves in the truck? And her toes are starting to go numb, too.

"Don't you have body temp regulators somewhere in all of those fancy tech systems?" Kyle laughs.

"No, BTRs are technomancer-grade augmentations."

"Oh, right, and you flunked out."

"She didn't flunk out, Kyle."

Sebastian mouths "Don't listen to him" to her behind Kyle's back, tacking on a cross-eyed, tongue-out, wacky face to the end that never fails to make Lily laugh. He even adds a rotating finger to his temple pointing in his big brother's direction for added insult.

"Well, she sure as hell didn't pass either. And lucky you for that misfortune. You think she'd be dating your sorry ass if she had?"

Talk about a backward compliment...

Javier separates from Derrick, turning and walking backward with his hands on his hips. "And you think you could've passed, hotshot?"

"I sure as hell have a better chance at it than you."

"I'm not going to argue that, but those trials are no joke. People die during them, and it's not Lily's fault she got sick after—Ah!"

With a sharp snap, Javier tumbles sideways.

"Javi!" Derrick cries out as his husband rolls head over heels backward down the steep slope, his limbs and body meeting various trees during his descent before he lands in a puddle of groans and bruises at the bottom of the ravine.

Derrick takes off after his husband, the others not far behind.

"Javi?"

"Ughhh..."

Derrick drops to his knees next to a wincing but awake Javier.

"Hey, booboo, what hurts? Talk to me."

"M—my ankle. Ow!" he shouts, trying to move it. "Goddamnit... Why does this always happen to me? We've only been in the woods for two hours."

Derrick wipes the tears from Javier's eyes, cleaning up the mud now caked to his face.

"That brain of yours is just too much for your body to handle. That's why you're so clumsy. It runs so fast your feet can't keep up."

"Yeah, neither can his mouth."

Kyle ambles his way down and taps Javier's ankle. Predictably, Javier whimpers like a kicked puppy.

"Great! Just great!" Kyle throws his arms in the air, then crosses them as he stands over their injured friend. "We'll have to take him back to the trucks. Cancel your little Halloween party, folks, because we're marching right back home."

Javier looks up, wide-eyed, glasses askew on his face.

"Wait, no! It's just twisted. See—I can walk. We don't need to go back."

Despite the protests of his husband and sister, Javier tries to stand up only to crumple back to the ground in a heap when his ankle fails to hold his weight.

"Fuck!"

"Yeah," gruffs Kyle. "Like I said, we'll have to carry him back. So much for a fucking camping trip."

"Can't KC carry him?" asks Jeanine. "Then we can keep on going."

"The drone can't lift more than a hundred pounds, so no. We'll have to do it ourselves. Glad you decided to lay off the cheeseburgers, babe."

"Don't be a dick, Kyle."

Lily shoulders her way past Sebastian's brother to Javier. "Here. Don't move. I have a medi–stim."

Lily drops her pack to the floor and yanks open the center zipper.

"You have a what?"

"A medi–stim. They're adept-grade first aid. It's basically an injection of nano–bots. They'll enter your bloodstream and heal you from the inside."

"Whoa, whoa, whoa—a bunch of mini-robots zooming through my insides?"

"Think of them like a bunch of micro-construction workers moving in to repair the damage to a building before it needs to be condemned."

Javier's eyes, magnified by his glasses, are round with fright. It's so adorable, Lily wants to wrap him in a hug. He clearly watches too many science fiction movies, gory things made by producers who just love to splash a bit of blood on a couple of batteries, computers, and wires and paint portraits of cyborgean horror to the terror of normals everywhere.

"Is it safe?"

"It's perfectly safe. I've used them dozens of times. The nanos'll flush out of your bloodstream in 24 hours, and it'll take less than that to fix up a twisted ankle."

Javier's eyes shift from Lily to Derrick for reassurance—"You'll be fine, booboo"—and back.

"What do you think? Yes or no?"

Javier nods, hissing when the needle goes in. The injection is barely a sting, Lily knows from experience, little more than a mosquito bite without the lingering itch; though, she supposes for a normal it might leave a bit of an uncomfortable bump.

"Umm, Lily?"

Sebastian.

"Yeah, babe?"

"You didn't tell me you brought like hi–tech stuff."

Hi–tech stuff? It's just a medical stim. They're a basic first aid item. You'd be a fool to forget bringing at least one on a mission. Technomancers are as much an investment to the League as they are weapons. As such, they're expected to keep themselves alive by any means. Even trainees were hardly allowed to leave base without at least one or two in their kits.

"I told you I brought first aid supplies."

"You consider medi–stims first aid?" asks Kyle.

Lily turns to Kyle in confusion.

"Well, yeah. You don't spend years of your life in military training and forget to implement the most basic of rules. Lionheart once got a write-up as a recruit when he forgot his stim on a training excavation."

"Baby, those things cost like five hundred a pop."

She freezes.

Oh, right. She'd forgotten. They're civilians. In Aighneas, nanotech including medi–stims are military exclusive unless you are willing to pay an arm and a leg for them as a private citizen. Lily, ex–military as she is, is not just allowed to have them but the maintenance required of her augmentations requires her usage of them lest she risk disintegration, rejection, or ultimately death due to a frayed wire.

"I have access to them because of my status as a cyborg and my contacts with the military."

To Sebastian's left, Jeanine shifts uneasily from foot to foot, casting odd glances toward Lily. With the growing darkness, the lights in her eyes must be visible. Unlike the sights of the Miyazaki family and Muraskan technomancers, hers don't turn off. They remain perpetually lit, a faint red glow at the very center of her pupil.

"I didn't realize you still had connections with the military."

"I was augmented as a child by the military. I may not be considered military personnel anymore, but I still have responsibilities, and without the various nano injections, my tech system could collapse. I've told you this."

Who does he think is paying for her degree?

"I guess I didn't realize you still received nano–tech from them."

"Well, I don't care why or how you have it because, holy shit, I feel good."

The group laughs at Javier's dreamy proclamation.

The man is on cloud 9, eyes dilated, jaw slack, head lolling to the side, and he won't be coming down anytime soon. She'd forgotten how normals respond to stims, the strange mix of high and low incited by them. Some normals become high as a kite; others drop into the deepest of despair; others still experience the most extreme swings from one end to the other, manic in their polarizations of behavior. Derrick helps Javier stand, not that he needs the help. He practically leaps up onto his feet. Once he gets there, though, he makes the mistake of putting his full weight on his injured ankle.

"Ow!!" he moans, teetering sideways into Derrick.

"Don't get too excited. That's just the painkiller talking. You'll still need a couple of hours for the nanos to repair your ankle before you can walk right again."

"So still a gimp then. Got it."

"Just for a little while."

"We should set up camp for the night," suggests Jeanine, flipping her ponytail over.

"Not here," gruffs Kyle. "This is a ravine. If it rains, we'll end up flooded out. We'll go back up the hill to higher ground."

"Whatever you say, boss." Sebastian claps Kyle on the shoulder before ducking down to slide under Javier's other arm. Then he helps trudge Javier out of the ditch with Derrick. Meanwhile, Kyle chews the dip in his mouth, spits a black globule on the ground, offers Lily's look of disgust a winning smirk, and follows.

Jeanine shrugs. "At least he doesn't carry around a gross bottle of spit."

"You'd think he would know better. Nicotine doesn't meld well with mechololaxone."

Jeanine laughs. "You know. I find it hard to believe those two are related sometimes. They're so different."

Sebastian's seen his share of struggles. He moved away from his family to go to college despite his dad busting his ass about going into the family business of swindling people for a living. Kyle, on the other hand... Lily's met a lot of men like Kyle. You meet them in the ranks of adept trainees all the time. Men with glory fever in their veins. Men looking for fresh meat to rend, men looking for a fight, men looking for a license to kill.

"Yeah, I know." Lily shoulders her pack, stepping back toward KC, hovering on the lip of the ravine and seemingly waiting for them. "Come on. Let's not let the boys leave us ladies behind."

"Oh, please. You and I both know they would die without us."

The girls' laughter rings through the trees as the sun lowers, streaking the sky through with the most brilliant shades of orange, red, and purple, and the whole forest goes up in the cool flames of a shifting of season.

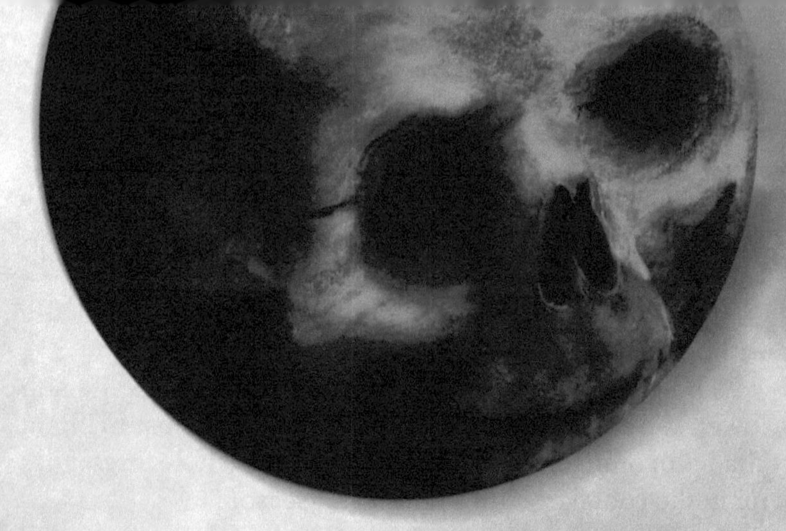

III

THE WITCHING HOUR

THWACK!

"You have an axe?"

Kyle twirls the weapon with an utterly blasé attitude, Javier flinching into Derrick despite being a good four feet out of range. The hatchet spins like a top as it leaves his robotic hand before he catches it deftly, the business end pointed toward the closest tree trunk.

"Of course, I have an axe. You think I'm going to go into the woods without a means to clear a path or chop firewood? If we were in the jungle, I'd've packed a machete."

With one mech–handed swing, he embeds the axe into the wood with a heavy thwack. The thunk reverberates in Lily's bones, and when he swings again, this time down toward the base of a thick branch, the limb collapses, splintering from its trunk. The leaves rustle and whine as they hit the ground, narrowly avoiding Derrick and Javier's freshly erected tent.

"Hey, Ky, easy with that axe. You nearly hit Derrick and Javier's tent."

"Sorry, Bassy." He throws a wink at Sebastian, not sounding repentant at all.

Javier huffs, leaning into Derrick. "Do we really want the metal man swinging an axe around?"

"Javi, don't call him metal man. He's augmented, not a robot."

"You sure? Seems to me like his skull is made of metal too and quite hollow."

"You want to take a swing, chess master?" Javier's shoulders rise in alarm as Kyle addresses him with a guffaw. "Oh wait, you can't! No thanks to that ankle of yours. Hell, you've probably got more robotics swimming around in your bloodstream than me right now thanks to Lily's little medi–stim. Hahaha. 'Metal man.' I like that, dude. Maybe it'll be my next tattoo."

The axe hits the tree with another thwack.

"Kyle," Jeanine protests, "can we not rip the forest to pieces?"

"You want a fire or not? Because I sure as fuck ain't keeping you warm tonight. Not unless you ask real nicely."

Thwack!

Another branch tumbles down.

"Yuck, you perv. I just don't think we should be cutting down trees. It seems... I don't know. Disrespectful."

"They're plants. They aren't owed respect."

Thwack! The crunch of leaves.

Thwack! The scream of bark.

"Alright!" shouts Lily. "I think we have plenty of wood."

"Aww, but I was just getting my gait right."

"I'm sure your form is fine. This is too much as it is. We can't exactly burn whole branches. You can chop up what's already on the ground."

"Spoilsport."

"Kyle," chides Sebastian.

"Alright, alright. I'm done." He whacks the axe into the thick trunk of the maple tree he just hacked up and leaves it there. "Bunch of piss–buckets."

The man marches off into the forest with a half–hearted proclamation of taking a walk around the area, telling Sebastian to get a fire going while he's gone. How Sabastian manages to understand his brother is a mystery to Lily. Every other word is a spat curse.

With a shrug and a sigh, Sebastian rises from anchoring their tent and makes his way to the axe embedded in the tree trunk. He grasps the handle with both hands and tugs. The hatchet doesn't move, it's buried so deep into the tree.

Derrick whistles lowly, impressed. "Anger management much?"

"Derrick," chides Javier.

"What? It's true. Here, mate. Let me give you a hand."

The two tug at the axe together, yet still it doesn't budge— stuck fast. After a while, they give up, Derrick turning to Javier.

"Hey baby, what was the name of the sword in the stone?"

"Excalibur?"

"More like Axe–calibur."

Lily rolls her eyes as they give up, choosing instead to break off smaller branches by hand. Before long, Derrick and Sebastian have a gently crackling fire built up in the center of their camp.

"Ooh, you know what would be perfect?" Jeanine smiles over the mug of her hot cocoa, eyes sparking in the light of the fire. "Scary stories around the campfire. Anybody know any?"

"Oh, no, no, no, no, no." Derrick waves his hands in the air in front of him, flicking his beard the way a model would her hair. "I am not about the Are–You–Afraid–of–the–Dark bullshit. No, no, no."

"Aww, baby. They're just stories." Javier winds his arms around Derrick's middle, laughing at the taller man's distress.

"And all stories are rooted in some insidious truth, and I ain't about that life."

"Oh, just one, Derrick. I promise it won't be bad."

"Are you going to tell it?"

Javier blushes. "Um, well. I don't know any."

"Exactly."

"Do you know any Hexennacht stories, Sebastian?"

Sebastian shakes his head. "Not any scary ones. Just the kind you read to five– and six– year–olds. You know, talking black cats, magical pumpkins, and friendly neighborhood sheet ghosts."

"Bummer." Jeanine wilts. "I don't know any, either."

"I know one."

They turn to Lily, Jeanine and Javier looking like eager school children while Derrick and Sebastian both look about ready to run for the hills.

"It's called—"

"Wait, wait, wait. Before you start, you need a flashlight."

Javier digs a torch out of his backpack and tosses it to Lily, who clicks the light on and dramatically tilts it under her chin. Her cheeks become gaunt and hollow, her eyes hooded and black, and her brow disappears into the shadows.

"Spooky enough for you now?"

A chorus of "Woos" comes from her friends. Even KC gives an appreciative "beep beep," the little drone resting on the ground. Sebastian takes a drink from his water canteen and nudges her hip.

"Do your worst, babe."

"You sure, honey? I might make you cry."

"So long as you promise to tuck me in when I go to bed."

Bony fingers dig into her sides again, making her howl with laughter, and she gives him back just as good.

"Ow, babe! Your nails are sharp."

"Then don't tickle me!"

He goes down laughing as she shoves him off the end of the log. Javier gives Derrick a conspiratorial glance.

"And people say we're bad?"

"Any day, you two."

Dusting the dirt off his trousers, Sebastian reclaims his spot next to Lily, tucking an arm around her waist.

"Sorry, sorry. I'll behave," he says, planting a chilly kiss on her cheek. His lips are already chapped from the frosty air, and she wonders if he brought chapstick.

"Should we wait for Kyle?"

"Nah, he wouldn't appreciate it. Go ahead. He'll come back when he comes back."

"Okay." Lily clears her throat and settles back in her seat. "I give you The Eerie Old Tale on Eerie Lane Brook."

"Nice." Despite his earlier reluctance for scary stories, Derrick rubs his hands together eagerly.

"At the edge of Eerie Lane Brook before there even was an Eerie Lane Brook, there was a wise old redwood that stood watch over the forest for decades, possibly even centuries. It was said a forest sprite lived in the tree and would grant wishes to any and all who came to find her, provided of course they brought with them an offering that brought her great pleasure, and yes, I do mean *that* kind of pleasure."

Lily grins coyly. Jeanine giggles while Javier whispers to Derrick, "Guess we won't be qualifying."

"One day, however, a businessman came sniffing about. Paul Cartridge's dream was to build the perfect home, smart and fully automated, and he just so happened to want to build the house right where the ancient tree stood erect for so long, so of course, without any regard for the old tree or the legends surrounding it, he chopped it down."

"Sound familiar to anyone?" drones Javier.

"Shh!"

"The locals warned Paul against this. They claimed the tree was a guardian spirit, magical and effervescent, and the reason they all benefited from the good fortunes of fine weather, plentiful harvest, and profitable business ventures. To cut it down would be to bring a fate worse than death upon him. Needless to say, he didn't listen, but he didn't waste the wood, either. He used it to build his house. The stairway, the banister, the floorboards, and the most essential part of his home: his computing hub. A magnificent operating desk inlaid with a high-powered motherboard and holo-projection nodes. The brain center of his home, the cerebellum and cerebrum all wrapped up in one pristine room where he could immerse himself in the cyberscape and ensure his family (Dorine, his beautiful wife, and teenage son, Jimmy) never wanted for anything."

The howl of a great wolf sings through the night. Derrick and Jeanine both tense, looking toward the sound.

Lily turns back to the group and continues her story.

"Once the house was built, he moved his family into their new home, and for a while, everything was fine. The businessman would kiss his wife goodbye before going to work every day, Jimmy started going to school, and the wife began to get to know the neighborhood housewives. A quaint perfect little existence in a house that knew their every want before they could even want for it.

"But then strange things began to happen. Nothing outright alarming. The toaster would burn Dorine's toast, the television would lose signal, the window blinds would open and close uncommanded. For the longest time, Paul chalked it up to a bug in the system, working tirelessly to solve the problem, but every time he squashed one bug, another would crop up, even worse than the last. Hot water outages during Dorine's spa days, electricity failures during the World Cup, and worst of all, the internet disconnecting during Jimmy's online games."

"Dun, dun, dun!"

The boys laugh at Sebastian's sound effects. The girls just roll their eyes

"Now, Jimmy was a very curious child. He enjoyed reading comic books and playing video games, and his favorite place to play games was on his dad's hub. The network was fast, when the internet wasn't down, and the graphics were state of the art, but his dad didn't like him playing in his office, especially with all of the strange occurrences happening. The last thing Paul needed was another firewall going down, and the last time Jimmy used his hub, one of the games he downloaded left a virus behind. Nearly lost his dad a bushel of important business files, and it cost his old man a full week's pay to get the files decrypted. One of those hacking scams where they mutilate your files and then charge you to debug everything. How they snuck through his system he was still trying to figure out."

Expressions of disgust and exasperation all around.

"Despite these seemingly mild setbacks, the house was a major success, bringing Paul a promotion at work much to the congratulations of his co-workers, so when he came home that day, he decided to treat his wife to a date night, just the two of them. Jimmy was old enough to stay home alone, and the house would look after him. So, with a reminder for the teen not to go into the cerebrum of the house, Paul and Dorine left their son to his own devices. Jimmy did his homework and his chores and cleaned up around the house like he was expected to, but when the sun went down and still his parents hadn't returned, he began to grow bored. That's when it happened."

"When what happened?"

Lily pitches her voice, purposely amping up the brightness of the neural lights in her eyes.

"'How can I keep you occupied, young master?'"

Javier shivers as Lily dims the accoutrements.

"That night, all alone, while his parents drank and ate and celebrated, the house spoke to Jimmy for the first time. He couldn't for the life of him remember if he'd ever heard the house speak to anyone. An A.I. perhaps? Curious, Jimmy went to investigate himself, sneaking down to his father's office to check the main hub and found the door ajar, a neon green glow emanating from within. 'Come on in, young master,' the A.I. said again, and just before Jimmy could respond, his parents arrived home.

"Jimmy told his father about what happened, and in a panic, the man disappeared into the hub to sort out the mysterious voice. He didn't surface again until the next day when Jimmy heard a loud shout.

"He rushed into the office to find his father on the floor with vines growing from his augmentations. They were everywhere, growing from his mechanical limb, from his cranial disks and neural nodes, even growing from the dental caps inside his mouth.

"'Ca–call your mother,' his father choked out, and Jimmy was quick to listen. His mom helped his dad to the car, taking him to the hospital, but before he left, his dad told him in no uncertain terms. 'Stay out of the office!'

"And so, they left, leaving Jimmy home alone. The hours passed, the clock tick, tick, ticking down the seconds, the minutes, the hours until…"

Lily lowers her voice again, this time to a husky, seductive timbre, and beside her, Sebastian, color seeping into his cheeks, unzips the top of his coat.

"'Jimmy,' a voice whispered through the comm system. *Jimmy.*' It was the same voice that spoke to him the night before only this time it seemed more… other, more mystic, more alluring. '*Come play with me, Jimmy.*' And Jimmy, helpless to resist the enchanting voice, snuck down to his dad's computer where the voice beckoned to him. A phantom hand gestured to him."

Lily lifts a hand making a "come hither" motion with her fingers to Sebastian, who leans closer in response.

"He crept down the stairs. Pit pat, pit pat, pit pat. To the state–of–the–art computer on the brand new, redwood desk. The door to the office stood ajar, a dull green glow emanating from its confines. Just like the night before, but this time, there were no interruptions. So, Jimmy tip–toed his way forward, put his hand on the doorknob, pulled it open, and—"

"BOO!"

Jeanine screams as Kyle glomps her from behind. Javier's mug flies through the air, and Derrick falls off his seat.

"Kyle, you jerk!"

Kyle laughs like an asthmatic hyena, doubled over and kekaw–ing as Javier dabs, crestfallen, at the cocoa now spilled down his coat.

"You bunch of noodles! I can't believe I got you so good."

"Way to interrupt just as the story was getting to the scary part." Jeanine shoves Kyle away.

"I am the scary part, sweet stuff."

Kyle pops the cap off a beer bottle taken from KC's back. The drone gives a little brreeep when the man gives her a little stroke on the head.

"Clearly." Jeanine rolls her eyes. "Finish the story, Lil. What happened to Jimmy after he opened the door?"

"No one knows."

"What?"

"No one knows what happened to Jimmy. When his parents got home, he was nowhere to be found. They searched everywhere. His bedroom, the kitchen, the attic, even the basement. It was like the kid just vanished into thin air. And when they checked the office, the computer was overgrown with moss and tree matter, like the desk had come alive again to grow around the technology. On the blinking screen was Jimmy's favorite computer game and a single flashing message.

"'Game Over.'"

Sebastian whistles.

"Jimmy Cartridge was never found, despite years of searching. In their grief, Paul and Dorine left the house where their son went missing, moving far away with their belongings. Naturally, Paul didn't leave the mainframe, setting up their system in a new smart house, and for a while everything was fine. Except, some days, when Jimmy's dad is working in his office at the hub, the last video game Jimmy ever played will open up on its own and an otherworldly voice will invite his dad to play."

Derrick shivers, culling the gooseflesh on his arms. "Oh lawd, that ending."

Jeanine, however, scoffs, shoving Kyle next to her.

"Too bad it didn't have the impact it would have if a certain somebody hadn't come barreling in in the middle of the story."

"So did the forest sprite merge with the computer?" asks Javier to Lily's responding shrug. "Creepy."

"That's why we teach the kiddos to stay as far away from magic as possible," says Sebastian. "You don't mix magic and technology, even accidentally. Too much bullshit might arise."

"Hn, sounds like a load of crock to me," laughs Kyle.

"Well, I liked it!" declares Jeanine. "Thanks for sharing, Lily."

"How's your ankle feeling, Javi?"

"The swelling's already diminished, and I think I can walk on it again. Should be good as new come morning."

Derrick runs a hand down his husband's back.

"Perhaps we should hit the sack. It's getting late, and we have even more trekking to do tomorrow."

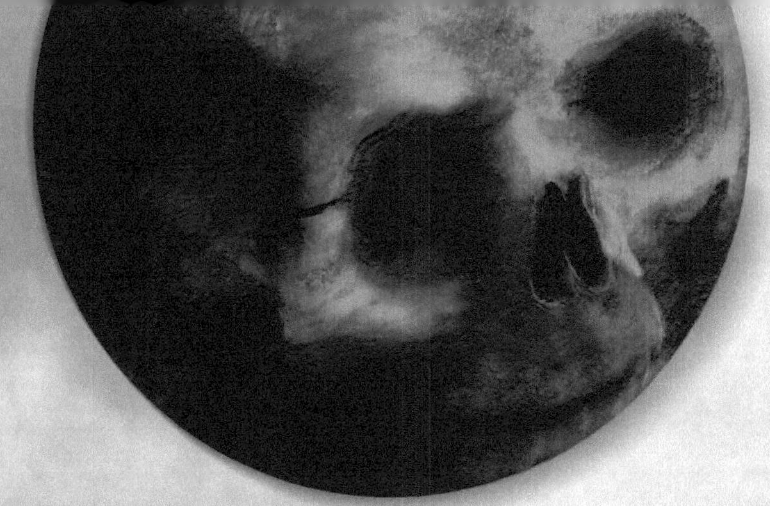

IV

ROCKY HORROR
PICTURE SHOW

"I can't believe Fumiko–sensei gave me an Inadequate on my last paper."

"Here, let me see."

Wren pulls Lily's holo over to her. She has her stylus between her teeth and a paper textbook in her lap. The other girl has been working quietly on her latest punishment paper. How she hasn't managed to get herself dismissed is beyond Lily, but she guesses if anyone knows how to write a perfect paper for Fumiko Miyazaki, it would be

Wren Nocturne. The Queen of Extracurricular Assignments.

"Well, here's your problem. You've gotten the laws of magic backward. It isn't cause and effect. It's effect without cause. Witchcraft doesn't need an incentive, just an intention."

"Yeah, I don't understand that. How can you have an effect without a cause?"

"Okay, think about it this way. How do you start a house fire?"

Lily frowns. "I don't know. Light a match or a candle and forget it's lit, I guess."

"Right, well a witch doesn't need the match or the candle. They just conjure the flame, and the house goes up in smoke."

"But isn't that the cause then? Magic caused the fire."

"According to Lockecraft's theory, a causality needs to be measurable by time, space, and mass. Magic isn't. It changes too much. It can shift between tangible and intangible. It can be here and there. It can be now and then. It can alter time, space, and mass at will, changing the history of an electron into something unrecognizable to our data systems."

"So, magic can't be a cause?"

"Not for our purposes, no. It's immeasurable. That's why when we look for evidence of magic, we don't look for the cause, we look for the absence of a cause. Don't look for the match or the candle. Look for the absence of either."

"Ugh! I think I'm getting a headache."

The other girl chuckles.

"I wouldn't think about it too much. Rhyme and reason are the least of arcane concern. Just check your theorems over; I'm sure you'll do better on the next paper." Wren looks at her sidelong. "Honestly though? It's all a load of crock. Any attempt to scientifically analyze magic is superfluous at best. If you want to understand something, you need to look at it from the perspective of the people who live with it, and technomancers don't live with witch magic."

Lily wakes with a start.

Wren Nocturne? She hasn't thought about Wren in years, at least not in a personal sense. Wren helped her with her schoolwork on more than a few occasions during the summit. Think quantum physics is harrowing on the brain? Try arcane physics. That's a whole 'nother ball game. Magic defies so much of what natural science establishes as law and order: witches defy gravity, lycans defy thermodynamics/ conservation of mass, and vampyres... Well, vampyres defy a lot of things. Chemically, they're more closely related to a virus than a human. It's really no wonder magic and science found themselves on opposite sides of a war.

Sebastian is turned away from her, sleeping half on his stomach and half on his side, his hip nudged into her thigh. He snores into his pillow, the little breathing strip on his nose doing absolutely nothing to assuage the sound other than making him look kind of cute. One of his students got him a pack of colorful strips as a teaching appreciation gift. It was supposed to be a gag gift since the kid's father was an old roommate of Sebastian's, but he kept them anyway, and tonight, he's sporting a pink strip with red polka dots.

Lily rolls to her other side, content to go back to sleep until her bladder makes itself known.

Oh, no. This is the dreaded moment. She needs to pee, and she is going to have to do it in the woods, in the middle of the night.

She lies on her back, exasperated and reluctant to acknowledge the cruel call of nature.

Damnit! Why couldn't they have just gone glamping like normal people? What are they? Heathens?! If there was ever proof evolution, industrialization, and innovation are moot endeavors, it is in the entire concept of camping trips. No one goes camping for real anymore, at least not sensible people, and bathrooms are a necessity, not a luxury.

She untangles herself from their double sleeping bag, careful not to let too much of their shared heat out, and crawls her way to the tent flap. The zipper is noisy compared to the chirps of crickets, but Sebastian doesn't stir, heavy sleeper he is. She's seen the man sleep through a hurricane, yet he always wakes when she is out of bed for too long.

Jeanine's tent is on the opposite side of the campfire from theirs. Javier and Derrick set theirs up a ways away for a bit of privacy, and Kyle's tent, a commando–style affair, lightweight and easy to hike with, is pitched between two trees across the clearing, KC sleeping in front. The little bot's light system broadcasts its snooze cycle via a steady pulsing wavelength, visually akin to a snore. The perfect location for a night sentry to position. Kyle may be a lot of things, but he and Sebastian were Eagle Scouts once upon a time. He knows his camping stuff.

The fire has long since burned down. Nothing but embers glow in the pit. It still holds a bit of warmth, though not nearly enough to stave off the chill of the night. Goosebumps prickle along her arms and legs, her pajamas too thin. She should have packed her flannels. Sebastian told her as much, but she was under the impression they would be camping somewhere in Aighneas, not somewhere just south of the damned pole.

Oh, she is not looking forward to having to pee in the open air. Thank goodness Javier and Derrick had the good sense to bring toilet paper. It's even biodegradable.

Holding her prize, the roll of paper fished out of Derrick's knapsack, to her chest inside her coat, she hurries her way into the trees until she feels she is a decent distance from the rest of camp. She turns back to look, and while she can see the glow of their nightsticks, she can't actually see their tents, which is exactly her goal. She'll see one of her companions coming her way before they see her; therefore, no unexpected visitors.

She takes a moment to orient herself, setting the toilet paper on a branch and picking a spot that doesn't have poison ivy growing anywhere. As she is organizing her clothing, the hair at the nape of her neck prickles.

She turns about to check if anyone is coming, but there's no one around. The grasshoppers sing in the starlight, and the wind rustles gently through the trees, a nocturnal symphony surrounding her punctuated by the hoot of an owl. Lily has never been afraid of the dark, and she's too old to believe in spooky campfire stories. So why does she have this creeping sensation she is being watched?

She shakes her head and takes care of her business, cleaning up as best as she can considering there isn't exactly a bathroom she can use. As much as she loves Sebastian, he is sadly mistaken to think just because she has a military background means she'll relish the opportunity to pee in a bush, but she can make do. No point complaining about it.

"Bbrrr." She shivers, stomping her feet and reorienting herself toward their camp when a rustling sound to her left draws her attention. She pauses at the sound of leaves crunching underfoot. And the sense of being watched intensifies.

Even with her enhanced vision, Lily can't see very well in the dark. Not directly anyway. She looks down, peering the direction of the noise out of the corner of her eye. Just beyond her little potty spot is a thick–trunked maple surrounded by slimmer evergreens. The leaves are thinning out from shifting seasons, the chill of the air clinging to the boughs of the tree in the tiniest of icicles even though the autumnal equinox is but two weeks come and gone. (What is the temperature, anyway? 35 degrees according to her system monitor. No wonder she thought she was going to freeze her butt off.) There is a patch of darkness between the branches, thicker yet more finite than the surrounding blackness. She squints at it, leaning forward and trying to decide if her mind is playing tricks on her. Maybe she should have gotten that nightvision modification after all. Or a more powerful flash-light in her utility kit, the one she has already provides barely more light than a glow stick and doesn't reach much farther than a radius of two feet around her.

Just as she is about to chalk it up to her overactive imagination, the patch of darkness shifts.

Is there an animal sitting in the tree? There must be. Probably a bird or a wild cat resting in the trees after its midnight hunt, but she can't quite make it out. Cats are certainly known to stare, and nighttime predators require an acute sense of sight. How else do you expect to catch a mouse on a moonless night? Not that those happen much in Deus, but Dei does go dark every so often, and once Koi reaches his new moon phase, he'll seem to disappear from the sky entirely for almost three weeks before the first slivers of the greater moon return. So just because she can't see the animal doesn't mean it can't see her.

She takes a step forward, leaning against a nearby tree as she goes up on her toes, trying to catch a glimpse of the creature in the tree.

A shriek rings in the distance, and Lily whirls around so fast, a tree branch whips her across the face, stinging something fierce along her left cheek, and when she touches the spot, her fingers come away damp.

Leaves crunch behind her.

She pivots, slipping on dew–slick grass. Her feet fly out from under her, the beam of her utility light going wide as a human foot disappears into the darkness followed by a long cow–like tail. Her scream, short but pitched, echoes through her whole body as she lands.

"Lily!"

It's Sebastian. The stars above her spin in a slow, blurry rotation. When she looks back to where she saw the flash of pale skin, there's nothing there.

"I'm here," she calls back, rolling onto her hands and knees. Ah, wire–cutters! Now she's covered in mud. At least she didn't land in the spot where she peed earlier. Then she would be covered in mud and her own piss.

"Are you alright?"

She makes her way to standing, trying in vain to pat the mud out of her pajama pants.

"I'm fine. Just—" A light shines in her face as Sebastian appears before her. "Just dirty."

He stifles a laugh with his fist.

She pouts.

"It's not funny, Sebastian!" she growls, shaking out her hair. Sprockets! She has twigs in her hair. Sebastian laughs harder. *Okay, maybe it is kind of funny...* She smacks him anyway. At least, he helps her pull the brambles out of her hair as he chortles.

"What were you doing out here?"

"I needed to pee, alright, and I tripped. Now my clothes are wet and muddy, I'm cold, and my boyfriend is laughing at me."

"I'm sorry, babe. You just look... Nevermind. You can borrow my clothes, unless of course you just want to sleep naked."

She can't see it in the dark, but she imagines his eyebrow is waggling.

"In your dreams, fly boy."

"Well, come back to bed so I can witness the most ethereal of sights as I float off to slumberland."

She smacks him again. "Flirt."

"It's not flirting if I'm being honest. Oh, baby—" His tone changes from lighthearted and teasing to instantly concerned. "You're bleeding."

He touches her cheek, and the sting reminds her why she fell in the first place.

"Something startled me, and I cut my cheek on a branch."

"Glad I packed an old–fashioned first aid kit then. Come on. Let's get you cleaned up."

"Don't you want to check out what it was?"

"It was probably just an animal, Lil. Nothing to get uppity about. Come on. You're shivering. Let's get you back in the tent."

Sebastian takes her under his arm and escorts her back to camp. He bandages her cheek, helps her out of her soiled clothes, and tucks her up against him in their sleeping bag. Despite her earlier quip, she forgoes clothing, draping herself in his skin instead. He fondles her breasts and tangles his fingers in the soft fuzz of her mound, dipping into her folds to circle her pearl. When he hardens behind her, she rolls him over and mounts him, spearing herself on his aching cock with a gasp.

She rides him to orgasm, and he tongues her open in turn. They catch their breath together, Lily's head pillowed on Sebastian's shoulder. Sebastian has a tattoo on his chest. It's been there since before they got together. A simple piece, it's just a unicorn's silhouette, no detailing, just a wash of rainbow colors, and as she traces her fingers over the tattoo, she forgets all about the too quiet night and the rustling of leaves in a windless wood. About muddied footsteps and moonless, starless skies.

She forgets that, as he was leading her back to the barely lit fire, Lily only looked back once. Just once to affirm to herself there was indeed nothing there despite the burn of inhuman eyes tingling up her back.

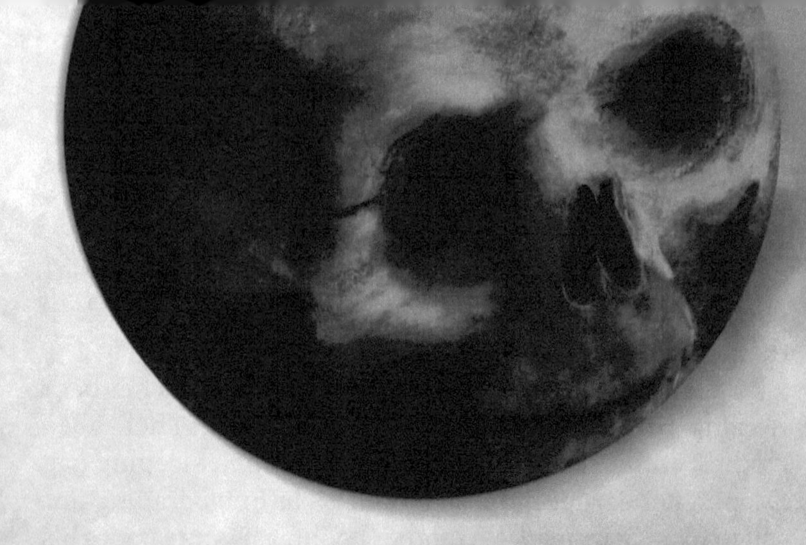

V

POISON GIRL

"Geez, I thought being in the mountains for the trials would be more whimsical. But it just rains all the time."

Wren shakes her hair out, tucking her hands under her head as she lays back on the towel she's spread over the grass.

"I mean, it is almost the Month of Storms. Its name isn't exactly arbitrary."

Their group of girls is sitting in the grass by the rock garden during their lunch break. It's the first sunny afternoon in days, and pretty much all the remaining trial participants are eager to get some sunshine. They found a good spot underneath one of the pine trees, and the shade is worth having to clear out all the fallen cones.

"Still, I'm getting so pasty pale being here," says Wren, rubbing more tanning oil into her chest.

She's hardly what Lily would consider pale. The girl's olive skin–tone might be a few shades lighter than it was a few weeks ago, but it's nothing compared to Lily's porcelain pink. Lily sits between Wren and Rhiannon, hiding under a floppy sunning hat while they lie in their spaghetti strap tops and shorts in a patch of sunlight, while Lydia, Selene, and Heather sit on the opposite side of the picnic blanket where the most shade is. Maybe she should move over to them before she ends up looking more like strawberry milk. Wren and Rhiannon wanted to sunbathe, and while Lily normally sits with the pair, she can already feel herself burning despite the sunblock she rubbed into her skin. Her dermal augmentations may filter out a large percentage of the UV rays, but they won't keep her skin from becoming lobster chic.

"I miss the beach," sighs Wren, laying back in the grass. "The water would be perfect for surfing by now. The waves are always the tallest in the spring."

"No, thank you," says Lily. "I burn like a ripe tomato in the sun."

"That's why you make a handsome boy rub lotion on your back," teases Selene from her cushy spot in the shade. "So you don't burn."

"It would take a battalion of boys to keep my skin from burning."

"Ew," icks Lydia. "Why would you give a testosterone-hyped boy an excuse to touch you?"

"Oh, I don't think Lily would mind the attention of our testosterone laden counterparts." Rhiannon smirks from under her sunglasses, the older girl's tawny brown skin already darkening to a cool coffee tone in the sunlight. "Isn't that right, Lily?"

Beside her, Wren exhales loudly. "Here comes the boy-talk again..."

"I'm not the one who's boy crazy, Rih."

"Mhmm, I'm not the one who spent the night in Lionheart's room last night."

Lily hits Rhiannon, aghast.

"Jerk! I told you that in confidence."

"Lily! You didn't!" exclaims Heather, aiming an electric fan at her face. It buzzes loudly on its highest setting to keep her cool

The blonde nods. "I did."

"Well, how was it?"

"It was fine, I guess. I don't really have anything to compare it to. It was my first time so..."

Wren sits up. "What! Was he at least careful?"

Lily turns to Wren in shock.

"Yeah. I–I mean, he didn't hurt me."

"My first time was terrible," says Selene. "The guy didn't know what he was doing at all. Lionheart seems much more capable. Good for you, Lily."

Heather heaves a dramatic sigh. "Oh, to be a lesbian and never have to suffer the ill–attentions of fumbling boys. You ever want a real orgasm, you let me know."

"Heather's a true ladykiller."

"What about you, Lydia? Have you ever, ya know?" asks Lily.

"No," says Lydia, the oldest of them at twenty–one. "I want to wait until marriage."

"Lydia has a partner back home," says Heather. "You told me you've been together for how long?"

"Since we were seventeen."

"Wow! Do you think they're the one?"

"I don't know. Mel is sweet, but with me doing the trials this year, who knows if it'll happen? If I graduate, I'll probably have to move somewhere else, and Mel is kind of focused on becoming a nurse which will take another four or five years of university."

"Maybe they'll move with you?"

"Maybe." Lydia shrugs. "What about you, Wren? Are any of the rumors true?"

Wren doesn't even open her eyes to answer. "No. I'm a virgin."

"No, you're not!"

"Yes, I am."

"But your brother punched Llywelyn in the face for saying you spent the night with him after the Apprentice Ball."

"*Che*! I wouldn't touch that *pendejo* with a 39-and-a-half-foot pole."

"So, you've really never—"

"Nope."

"But you're so popular?"

Wren laughs. "So? I'm supposed to sleep with someone just because they like me?" Heather looks away, cowed by the sarcasm in Wren's words.

"Are you waiting until marriage then?"

"Me? Don't be ridiculous, Lydia. I'm not marriage material. I pity any poor man or woman who would want me as a wife. Besides 'wife,' what a lackluster title... And the wedding vows! 'Til death do us part!' It's such a cliche, and no one actually means it anymore. The whole ceremony is just the start of an overdone stage play." Wren sits up, clears her throat, and begins to recite the traditional wedding vows in a nasally voice. "We gather here today to unite so–and–so and so–and–so in, ehem…" she pinches her nose closed, "oily ma–tree–moan–ie."

The girls all burst out laughing. Lily laughs so hard, the water she was just drinking sprays out of her nose, inciting the other girls to laugh even harder. As she buries her face in napkins and towels, she notices Kaito Miyazaki glaring at them from the other side of the zen garden. She hiccups when she notices his sights are spinning, and he looks very much annoyed by their behavior. Outbursts of laughter probably aren't considered the most courteous of sounds in a zen garden.

"Guys!" she hisses, smacking the girls closest to her and gesturing toward the prince. Heather, Rhiannon, Lydia, and Selene all pipe down, bowing their heads in deference to the prince, but Wren… Wren sits up taller and waves brightly at the stoic prince with her mechanical hand.

"Kaito–kun! Why don't you come join us? I packed some extra strawberries!"

The man's silvery gaze narrows at the girl. (It's so creepy how colorless his eyes are. She's never seen anyone with eyes like that.) How Wren doesn't just shrivel up like a raisin is far beyond Lily—that glare is so poisonous—but then he gets up and strides away without saying a word.

Wren cups her hands around her mouth and shouts at his retreating back. "If you change your mind."

The man gives her an annoyed harrumph and keeps walking, pointedly ignoring the Derivan girl, who merely giggles into her palm in response.

"Wren!" Lily proclaims, smacking the island girl in the shoulder.

"So scary!" shivers Lydia.

"Oh, please. He is so… Ah, I can't even!" Wren flops backward on the grass in a huff.

"Speaking of handsome men..." Heather hides her face behind her palm, girlish and pink-faced.

"Oh hush! Prince Kaito doesn't pay much mind to anyone except Lady Wren."

"Oh, please." The girl shakes her fingers at Rhiannon. "If by 'pay much mind to' you mean glare at me and then storm away *con un palo nuevo en el culo*, you're correct. The guy hates my guts."

"If you're so sure he hates you, why are you always bothering him?"

Wren shrugs. "He makes cute faces when he's angry."

Selene leans forward, a teasing smile on her face. "I think you like him."

"Yes, because I so thoroughly enjoy having holes glared into my head."

"Maybe he'll bring you flowers one of these days." Rhiannon twirls a tiny grass flower between her fingertips. "Roses are so romantic. Or maybe he'll bring you cherry blossoms. They're so pretty!"

Wren wrinkles her nose. "Eh, roses are overrated, and pink is not really my favorite color."

"Oh, and what kind of flowers would impress the illustrious Wren Nocturne?"

"My favorite are amethyst saltwater lilies. They are the most gorgeous shade of purple with blue centers. They grow in the shallows offshore at home, and at night when they bloom, they glow this really pretty blue-green color."

Rhiannon pulls up a picture of one on her comm unit, and Lily leans over to take a look at the pretty purple flower, opened up with dozens of pointed petals and framed by lily pads.

"Saltwater lilies. I mean they're pretty, but aren't they poisonous?"

"Exactly," says Wren, matter–of–factly. "Just like love. Beautiful but dangerous. My mother once read me a fairy tale about a sea nymph born from a lily. She fell in love with a handsome prince who in turn married her to save her from a witch's curse."

"Aww, that's so romantic."

"Not really. The prince lived far away from the sea, and without the freedom of the open water, the nymph withered away into nothing."

"That's awful! Why would you like a flower with a story like that linked to it?"

"It's just a story, Selene. It's not really true. Besides, the saltwater lily symbolizes love without chains or restrictions. Isn't that the way true love should be? Undefined by traditional boundaries and conventions."

While the other girls coo in agreement, Lily can't help but disagree. She's the kind of girl who reads fashion magazines and watches wedding reality shows. She imagines what her gown will look like, what her groom will say, the kind of flowers she'll have, the kind of life she'll have with him afterward, the children they'll raise.

She doesn't say anything then, but later that evening, when she is hanging out in Wren's dorm, she asks." But wouldn't you want to be with the person you love? That's what marriage is. The promise you'll be with someone always."

"Choosing to love someone and be with them is one thing. But marriage is a completely different thing, not always synonymous with love, unfortunately. The only reason I'm here is because my stepmother wants me to 'inspire a favorable match.' But I'll show her. When I go home as a technomancer, her dreams of selling me to the highest bidder will be sand in the sea."

"But what if you fell in love with someone? Wouldn't you want to be with them? Wouldn't you want them to be with you?"

"Not if it meant they would have to give up the things most important to them. As romantic as the notion of 'all you need is love' is, it's unrealistic. People need friends, family, their careers, their hobbies. No one person can make up for having to give up the most important things. That leads to resentment, and no relationship can survive true resentment. I would rather be apart from someone than force them into a life that may not make them happy."

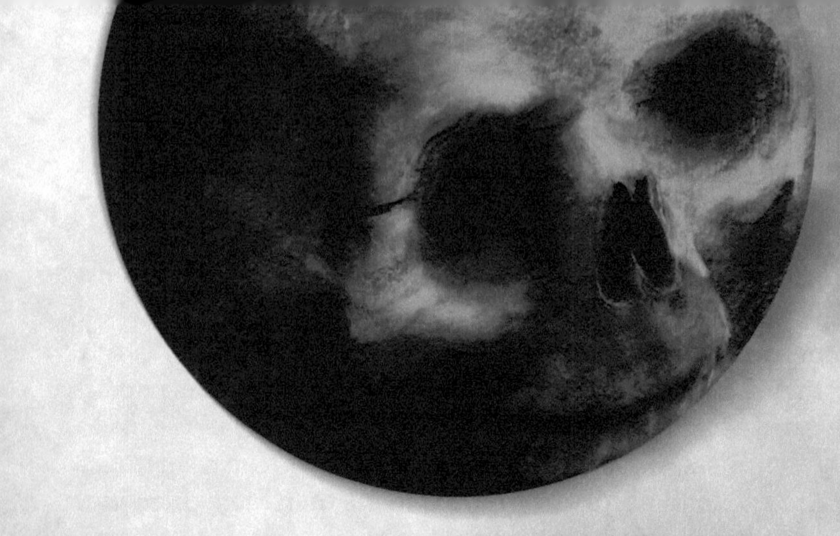

VI

RADIO STATIC

"Who the fuck took my axe?"

"No one took your axe, Kyle."

It's too early for this. The sun hasn't even risen yet and already there is yelling outside. Lily stretches out, still naked between the soft downy of the sleeping bags. Sebastian is gone. Up already, dealing with his brother.

"Then where is my fucking axe?"

Lily rolls her eyes and pulls on her pants. With a slide of the zipper, she slides herself into the dewy morning light, the smallest of icicles melting with the sunrise.

"Hey, Lily, you want some eggs?"

Derrick, wielding a cast iron skillet, hovers over a gently burning fire pit. He's fed some twigs and dried up leaves into the flame to make it just hot enough to cook over.

"You brought eggs."

"Powdered but I know the value of good spices. There's bacon, too, and I think Javier packed some energy bars."

Lily helps herself to a few strips of crispy bacon. It's a little blacker than she would like, but it's good and the crunch distracts from the argument still unfolding across the camp. Sebastian and his brother go back and forth, back and forth in their home language. Something Germanic spoken in the smaller countries between Seraphim and Aighneas. Sebastian once took Lily to visit his mom in New Jutland. She lived in one of those assisted living communities. All the old ladies spoke in this sweet dialect that made them sound like the kind of women who once traded stories around the dairy farm while milking the cows.

"Anybody know what they're saying?"

"No clue," answers Jeanine. "I only speak common."

Javier shrugs. "I know a bit of Hexen, which sounds similar, but I haven't a clue what they're saying."

"That's because Hexen is about as different from the Germanic languages as Hanasu is from Japanese or Derivan from Spanish. Similar enough to be recognizable but too far removed to provide any kind of true cross–fluency."

Lily is taking another bite of bacon when a pair of familiar hands clamp down on her shoulders.

"Happy Halloween!!"

She jumps. "Sebastian! You scared me."

"Well, 'tis the season for a good fright."

Kyle traipses over and abruptly stamps out the tiny fire. "Alright, banquet hall is closed. Pack up your shit and let's get going."

Derrick and Javier scramble to salvage the pots and pans from the man's boot while Jeanine tries to save the food from flying ash.

"Hey, what the hell, man?"

"I said we're going."

"Hey, take it easy. None of us took your damn axe."

Kyle huffs, then smiles his winning smile.

"I know. Sorry. It's just we're burning daylight, and we still have a ways to go before we get to the spot. If we don't get going, it'll be pitch black by the time we get there. Not exactly primetime for a photo op. I just—" He cuts himself off and threads flesh fingers through his hair. "I just want to make sure you all have a good time. It's Halloween after all. Hexennacht! The best holiday of the year. Let's not waste it over some over–salted eggs."

Derrick lifts a hand to his chest, aghast. "They are per-fectly salted, thank you very much, and you certainly had no problem scarfing them down a minute ago."

"They were over–salted," coos Javier.

Derrick harrumphs at his husband even as the smaller man tries to smooch a kiss onto the side of his face.

And just like that, the tension evaporates.

As she is helping Sebastian pack up their tent, Lily can't help but glance toward the poor splintered tree Kyle chopped up last night. A deep fissure, like a jagged scar cracked through the center of the poor maple, is the only remaining evidence of the axe previously embedded in the trunk. The wound is deep enough for Lily to fit her whole hand inside. It would've taken some serious muscle to pull that axe loose, and Derrick is the only unaugmented person in their group who could possibly manage it. Lily doesn't have the augmentations necessary for enhanced strength.

So, who took the axe? Or better yet: *what* took the axe?

They trek through the woods, Kyle forging his way forward despite his lack of wood–rending equipment. Javier, trudging along at the rear, stumbles for the nth time in as many minutes.

"Hey, Kyle, how much farther? I think the girls are getting tired."

Jeanine scoffs. "Speak for your own asthmatic self, Javi."

"I haven't had asthma since I was a teenager."

And as though to contradict himself, he coughs. A nice, long hacking fit that inspires Derrick to pull out his husband's inhaler.

"Mhmm, in the words of William Golding, 'Sucks to your Assmar!'"

Javier pouts at the proffered medicine but takes a big puff, scowling at his sister the whole time.

"Don't worry, scrawny legs," Kyle calls back over his shoulder. "We're almost there."

"And where is there?" asks Lily, side–eyeing her boyfriend. "Some great rock formation? An actual glamping site in the middle of nowhere with running water? Or is it just an empty clearing in the middle of the forest carved out by aliens? Huh! Sebastian, did you bring me here to abduct me? Are you taking me to your mothership and never taking me back home?"

Sebastian laughs, snaking an arm around her waist.

"You'll see. Don't worry. You'll love it!"

"I better love it, or you're going to be sleeping outside the tent tonight."

"I submit myself to your judgement, milady." He leans toward her face, but just as she closes her eyes, something scurries past her feet with a yowl. Startled, she jumps, her head slamming into Sebastian's chin. His teeth clank together, and he grabs for her arm as he careens to the side. They slam into a nearby tree as a fluffy, ringed tail disappears into the underbrush.

"Ow..."

She has a goose egg already forming on the top of her head, and Sebastian clutches at his chin, a thin line of blood trailing from his lip.

"Ah, fuck."

"Did you bite your lip?"

He spits some blood out of his mouth. "My tongue, yeah."

"Hey, you two okay?"

Kyle doubled back to check on them.

"Just an animal," Sebastian answers, rubbing the bruise already forming on his jaw. "Startled us."

"Did you see what it was?"

"A raccoon, I think. Didn't get a good look at it."

Kyle hums. "Well, hurry up. We're here."

He then walks off, leaving the couple behind.

"Your head okay?"

With an ache already swelling behind her eyes, Lily checks in with her internal systems to see if she has a concussion, but her vital signs read normal. Just a headache, then. Damn, Sebastian has a chin sharp enough to cut glass.

"Yeah, it's fine. I'm sorry you bit your tongue."

"Eh, it's just a tongue, but unfortunately that means tonight I won't be able to, you know..."

Oh, she's gonna smack that shit–eating grin off his face! "Perv."

"You love it."

"Fortunately, for you. Otherwise, I'd have to find a replacement for my injured boyfriend. Oh, wait, nevermind. I did pack my bullet. Guess you're off duty, buddy."

"I'll show you 'off duty.'"

He lunges for a retaliatory tickle. She squeals, dodging around waggling fingers, and races after their friends. The wind tousles her hair, the smell of the forest rich as she sprints through the trees, leaves crunching under her feet and the air cool in her lungs.

"You can't escape me." Laughter, deep and rich and far too happy to be menacing.

"Mhmm, just try to catch me, big boy."

She's faster than him, naturally. Her augmentations make it so she can run faster, harder, longer than any normal, but she isn't pushing herself. She isn't really even trying to get away. She wants to be caught. That primitive adrenaline of being hunted by a hunter you wouldn't mind being eaten by. Little Red Riding Hood and the Big Bad Wolf, a roleplay in the woods. Too bad her wolf now has an injured tongue.

Broad hands dig into her hips, knobbing around the bones of her pelvis and spinning her. Her backpack gets squished against a tree, her fingers winding around his neck. His face is wind–burned and pink, his breath puffing in short bursts of steam between them, and she leans up to steal the breath from his lips.

He tastes like toothpaste and the instant coffee he drank this morning, fresh but strong. Like a peppermint cappuccino even though pumpkin spice is all the rage this time of year. If she were home, she would have baked a jack–o–lantern pie: pumpkin puree, whipped together with spices, then spread through a pie crust. She likes to add a lattice of crust over the top in the shape of a toothy pumpkin face and bake it for about twenty minutes.

She wonders what the neighborhood children will dress up as this year. There will be the usual ghosts and witches and vampires, probably a few kiddos here and there dressed as their favorite hexen–slaying technomancer. Last year, a number of little girls dressed up as Morrigan Gewalt, the president of Aighneas and the current Primarch of the technomancer council. Even a few boys dressed up as the fearsome woman known as The Morrigan. Lots of kids loved dressing up as the Murasakan technomancers—their garb is just so unique compared to everyone else.

Lily had been planning to dress up as a fairy this year, something sweet and innocent so as not to scare the kids, even if Sebastian had been planning on going as a zombie or something equally undead. But then they decided on this camping trip. She meant to bring a mask with her for posterity's sake but forgot in the flurry of trying to pack the car.

Sebastian's mouth moves over hers, and unthinking, she presses forward with her tongue. The coppery tang of blood meets her taste buds. She jerks backward as he hisses.

"Oops! I forgot."

"You know for having a computer in your head, your memory sucks."

"It's not like I can make a neural checklist of every little thing."

"Even so—"

"Hey, Lily, you have to see this!"

Javier's call of her name draws her attention, and she slides around Sebastian and hurries along, stopping just short of running into Derrick's broad back.

"Whoa."

The clearing they've entered is anything but empty. The ruins of an old cottage rest on the far side of the clearing just inside the tree line. Neglect has left it in disrepair: ivy grows up the side, one of the windows hangs off its hinges, the door is cracked down the center, and leaves and dirt trail into the small home. She can even see the branches of a tree poking through the roof just past the crumbling chimney. There is a weed–infested garden, an abandoned tricycle, a deflated a deflated ball, and a rotting structure that looks like it might have once been a cat's climbing house.

All these things on their own are relatively benign. Homes are abandoned all the time, especially in a place as isolated as this. And there are no signs of death anywhere, no rancid scents, no flies, no bodies frozen in the ground. There's absolutely no reason for this place to put her on edge, so why does she feel like an intruder in a very private place?

Haunted...

This is a place where people once laughed and played and lived. Now left desolate, Time and Decay are the only residents here.

The aura of magic she has felt in the whole of the forest is heavier here. The kind of imprint left on a place that has been hearth and home to magic for a long time.

This is where Sebastian wanted to bring her? To an abandoned house in an enchanted forest for Halloween? It's romantic, she guesses, if she believed in that kind of thing. But why? When she turns to him in question, he just beams at her, proud for some unfathomable reason. She is clearly missing something.

"How is this place still standing?" asks Jeanine, striding toward the ruined home.

"Jeanine!" scolds Lily.

"What? It's just an old house. I want to see what's inside."

"Said the protagonist of every horror movie ever."

"Shut up, Derrick."

"I'm just saying this is the part where somebody either goes missing or the first body is found."

Kyle gives an uncharacteristic snicker.

Jeanine shoulders her way through the crooked door, flinching when dust and debris fall from the ceiling but then striding right on through into the dark confines of the cottage.

"Jeanine," growls Lily, trailing after the younger woman. "Don't touch anything!"

The inside of the house is as dilapidated as the outside and twice as disconcerting. In a dusty kitchenette, there's an overhead rack where the stringy remains of once carefully tended herbs hang limp and black, weeping from lack of care. There are pots and pans, tarnished with rust and crawling with insects on the stove. Was someone cooking when the calamity struck? But when she looks in the pots, there is no food, just a gelatinous fluid being feasted on by centipedes. Over the oven rests a wood–carved wheel with seasonal etchings decorating each notch.

Across from the kitchenette is a living space with a gnarled rug settled in the center, a rocking chair, and cushioned sofa. The cushions have been long ravaged by animals, tears and holes scratched into the fabric and the stuffing scattered on the ground. A bookcase stands mysteriously devoid of books, one of the shelves torn from its place. In echo to the tricycle outside, there are toys strewn about the floor: a set of soft building blocks, stuffed animals with patchy spots of faux fur and unravelling seams, a pair of pink child–sized slippers.

Most disconcerting though is the cauldron broken on its side in the fireplace and shattered crystals on the floor.

"This is a witch's cottage."

And witches mean ghosts.

"We shouldn't be in here—"

"Whoa…"

Jeanine's awestruck exclamation draws Lily's attention.

"Jeanine, I said not to touch anything!" she says, taking a wad of papers from the younger woman.

"They're just drawings."

Jeanine has dug around in one of the dresser drawers and unearthed what is indeed a collection of drawings stacked together haphazardly.

Lily leafs through the pictures, the crayon masterpieces of a toddler. There's a rough sketch of a cat, notable only by the whiskers, pointed ears, and a triangular pink nose, and two four-legged blobs, denoted as dogs by the scrawled "BARK" next to their noses. There are stick-like figures of people. Two women: one dark-skinned and tall holding a broomstick and the other yellow-haired and sitting by a tree, a tail waving behind her from under her dress. Pictures of butterflies and animals and another black-haired, green-eyed woman with music notes dancing around her head. Some of the drawings are even colored across composition paper, over musical scores handwritten by an adult hand.

"Eep!"

A noisy clatter followed by the shattering of glass. Lily looks up to see Jeanine sheepishly holding a now broken mirror, etched through with strange sigils and shapes, including a five-pointed star now cracked down the center and missing one and a half of its points. Lily doesn't like the look of the designs, but she doesn't remember enough from her arcane alphabet classes to know what they might signify.

"Really?"

"Sorry," replies Jeanine, dropping the cracked mirror on a moth–eaten sofa. "Guess that's seven years of bad luck for me."

The joke isn't funny. Not here. And Jeanine's wide grin just makes it worse.

"Please, don't touch anything."

"Aye, aye, captain!"

As Jeanine wanders into the back part of the house, Lily turns her attention back to the pictures in her hand.

There is a boxy figure of a man, tall next to a small child, with two sticks poking from his back. Next to the man's figure in purple crayon is written "TekNo MaAn." There are a few pictures of "tekno maan," one featuring him with the singing woman, another with the child in–between, the man and the singing woman holding onto either hand. But the last drawing... The last drawing in the stack gives her pause.

It's the singing woman by herself, the child's attempt to draw a portrait of her face. Bright–green eyes, dark curly hair, and pink lips drawn into a crooked smile. At her brow, in bright green crayon, three interlocking spirals sit, and it is this detail that makes Lily's fingers go numb, especially when considering at the corner of the page the word "MaMa" is written.

"You've got to be kidding me."

"Lily?"

Lily storms from the house, the pictures gripped tight in her fist as she makes her way toward Sebastian. He and Javier have their heads tucked together in a most conspiratorial way, and it only riles Lily's anger.

"Sebastian, you are going to tell me right now. Which forest are we in?"

"Whoa, Lily, hold on. I told you. This is Blackwood Forest. This is all part of the trip. Kyle mapped this all out for us."

"This is not Blackwood Forest, and I don't care if this is part of the trip or not. Now, you tell me where we are."

"Lily, calm down. What does it matter which forest we're in? It's just a forest. Kyle wouldn't have brought us here if it wasn't safe."

"Do you even realize whose house this is?"

Sebastian blinks owlishly at the building. "No. Am I supposed to?"

"That house belonged to the Songstress of Lorelei."

Sebastian turns to look at his brother. "What?"

"This is Lorelei Forest," says Kyle.

"What did you say?" squeaks Derrick.

"Lorelei Forest. You know, the haunted forest where the Songstress of Lorelei supposedly bit the bullet."

Javier and Derrick make a startled sound behind them, and Lily rounds on her boyfriend.

"Did you know about this!?"

"Lily, don't be mad at Bassy," calls Kyle. "He didn't know. I showed him the map but not the actual names of anything."

"You told me," says Sebastian, "this was an unexplored part of Blackwood."

"I lied because I didn't want to freak anyone out before we got here."

"You kept this a secret!" she shouts, rounding on the older man. Sebastian holds her back. "You brought us into a cursed forest, and you kept it a secret!"

"It's not cursed," Kyle spits back. "You said so yourself. It's just hexen tales."

"This is where she died! And you think—" A sob chokes its way out of Lily's throat. Sebastian folds her into his chest.

"Kyle, what the hell were you thinking bringing us here?"

His chest rumbles under her ear.

"You were the one talking about wanting to do something big for your girlfriend this weekend, and you mentioned she was into hexen shit, and my boss mentioned wanting to look to open up tours here, so I figured, hey! Why don't I bring my little bro, his girlfriend, and a couple of her friends to check out the tour? Depending on what you guys think, I'll be able to start booking people as early as next week."

"Wait a minute," says Javier. "Let me get this straight. You are planning to take money from people so you can lead them into the very forest where the Songstress of Lorelei killed herself."

"Why not? People love ghost tours, and who wouldn't want the chance to see the ghost of the Songstress of Lorelei? It's an untapped gold mine. And once we find the actual grounds where she kicked it—"

Lily rips her face out of Sebastian's shirt.

"We are not looking for the place where Wren Nocturne died!" shouts Lily. "Wren was—"

Wren was my friend! Lily nearly shouts it but bites her tongue before the words can leave her mouth.

"Look, Lily," says Kyle, putting on a charming smile nearly identical to his brother's. It looks wrong on his face. "I know you're upset, but I swear to you, I scouted this place out weeks ago. There aren't any real ghosts around here, at least not any hexen ghosts, so there isn't anything that will hurt us around here, and the Songstress hasn't so much as made a peep since her death. Bassy told me you were doing your research on her, so I thought you'd like it."

"You thought I would want to see the place where a woman was driven so mad by magic, she ended her own life."

"Okay, okay. You're the boss. We don't have to go to that spot."

Jeanine steps forward, a plying look on her face.

"Lily, your thesis is literally about the Songstress of Lorelei. Wouldn't it be cool to actually stay and investigate the last known place where she lived? The ghost story is just an added bonus."

She can't be serious. She wants to stay here. Lily can see it in her pleading expression. Disbelief, cold and cloying, rocks through her as she recognizes the same exact look on Javier, Derrick, and even Sebastian's face.

"You want to stay here."

"It's just a ghost story, Lily," says Javier, sinking into his hip.

"Ghost stories aren't just games around a campfire, Javi. They exist for a reason."

"We know that, but you heard my brother," Sebastian implores her. "Kyle says this place is perfectly safe. He's scouted the whole area."

"At night, too," adds Kyle.

"See, at night, as well, and nothing happened."

"Not on Halloween!"

He holds her by the upper arms, and god, he's lucky he's handsome; otherwise, she would be punching his nose in.

"Lily, baby, I understand you're scared—"

"I'm not scared."

"—but nothing is going to happen."

"We're too far in to make it back out before dark, anyway," says Kyle.

"Why don't we go ahead and set up camp?" provides Javier, looking at Derrick.

"Oh, maybe I can get the oven inside the house to work. I can cook a real spread for dinner."

Javier's eyes brighten, turning to Lily. "We can explore the surrounding area. You can take pictures, and then when you present your dissertation, you'll have awesome photographs no one has ever seen before. Hell, we can even sleep inside the house. Nothing like having a real roof overhead."

"No one is sleeping inside!"

No one would be setting foot inside of that house. Not if she can help it.

"And no pictures either."

Let the ghosts of the past rest in peace.

"Okay, shit, Lily. If I'd known you'd be a total bitch about this, I'd—"

Sebastian angles himself toward his brother. "Kyle, shut up."

Lily yanks herself from Sebastian's arms and runs, deaf to the panicked shouts of her name. Tears blur her eyes, she is so, so angry at all of them.

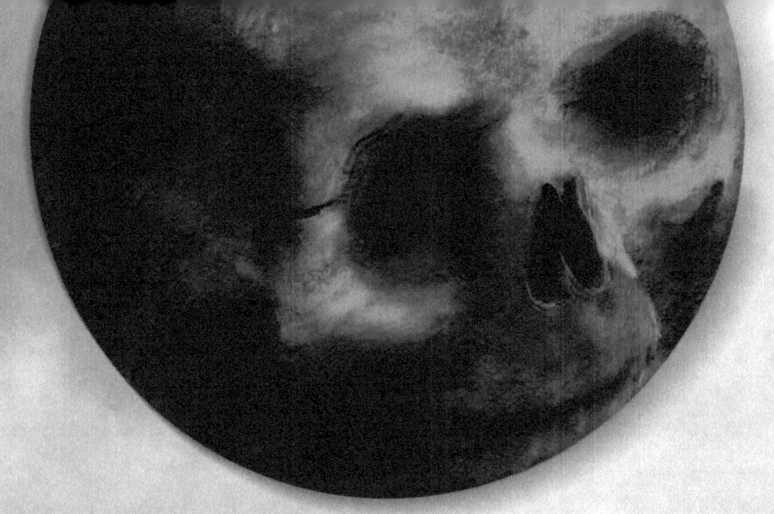

VII

FAIRY DANCE

She runs for what feels like hours but is probably just five or ten minutes. She can't hear anyone coming after her, but she can't hear much of anything right now anyway, the blood pounding in her ears, and she pays so little attention to her surroundings, it's a wonder she doesn't stumble her way into a ravine or river.

Shortness of breath forces an end to her run to nowhere. She pants, hands on her knees and a stitch in her side, trying to catch her breath. Curse her sorry lungs! She used to be able to run for hours on end. Now, in the wave of anxiety–driven adrenaline, her own body fights against itself, a constant push and pull between the tech systems that keep her alive and an overactive immune system that doesn't rec-ognize the difference between her own tissue and foreign invaders.

Counting through her breath cycles, her heart slowly returns to a reasonable beat, her muscles unclench, and her tech system whirrs to life, filtering out the excess CO_2 and flooding oxygen into her muscles before her system attacks itself. When her lungs fall in line once again, she lifts her head and takes a look around for the first time since she started running.

Kyle was right when he said it was getting too late to make it back out of the woods. The watercolor wash of sunset skirts over the treetops, reflecting a crystal–clear amethyst in an unending expanse of perfect glossy silver.

She's found a lake.

The water reflects the sky as clearly as mirror glass, unbroken and undisturbed, as pure as the legendary sword Excalibur given to King Arthur by The Lady of the Lake. When she was studying in the Abbey, the congressional capital of Aighneas, she took a course on old world litera-ture, some of the texts dating back as far as 2200 B.C. While Earthling humans believed the legends to be no more than myths, their ancestors, the pagans who forged Deus, knew better. See, the legend, as written by a human man, is a twisted rendition of the truth. Excalibur, having been the athame of the Lady of the Lake, was stolen from her by Arthur to devastating effect. It was another witch, Merlin, who took the blade back and returned it to its rightful owner. It came over with the witches when the gods carved out Deus for them. Rumor has it the king's blade is currently hidden in a vault deep under the ocean with a host of other pow-erful athames protected by the merfolk and only accessible to witches of the sovereign bloodline.

A fish breaks the surface to gobble up an insect, the splash so noisy in relation to the previous unbroken stillness that it echoes through the entire clearing. Ripples lap at the pebbles scattered along the shoreline, the watercress wave under the surface, and at the disturbance, a sparkle of fireflies take flight. They dance and flit along the shore, weaving in and out of the trees, getting bigger and brighter the closer they get to her until she realizes they're not fireflies at all.

They're fairies.

Real, glitter-dusting fairies, no bigger than the length of her pinkie. They waltz around the area in duets and trios, flickering and fluttering through different colors in a sparkling kaleidoscope. It's like sitting at the center of a living, breathing rainbow.

Such sights, as commonplace as they were before The Vanquishing, are rare these days. Magical beings of all kinds going into hiding—if they didn't die out completely—in the wake of an inordinate amount of magic being snuffed out in one fell swoop. It's cathartic, almost: knowing there are magics more powerful than science, and life's ability to persist is one of them. Thanos! The Vanquishing happened less than ten miles from this very spot, the city of Lorelei nothing but rubble where once was a neutral zone between hexen and human+.

How could she completely fail to realize which forest they were in? No wonder she flunked out of her technomancer trials.

"Hey."

Sebastian's voice carries across the clearing of fairies. The dancing fae scatter, flying upward in fright before descending back down as Sebastian approaches her. He's refreshed his cologne, the scent of sandalwood and leather embracing her cool and familiar. He's wearing Steel Noir, a scent Lionheart endorsed a few years back. As much as technomancers are warriors, some of them embrace the celebrity of being the elite of society. Selene has done quite a few modeling campaigns over the years, and Jamar even starred in a movie not too long ago, so can Lily really blame Lionheart for choosing to sit in on a commercial photoshoot or two? He's a handsome man, and with the current climate, technomancers aren't exactly racking in the paid missions. There aren't exactly enough hexen wreaking havoc to keep the technomancers busy.

Sebastian winds his arms around her, and Lily sinks into his embrace. His chin rests bony on her shoulder as he looks out over the water, more fairy lights blinking over the once again still surface. Even through the thick thermal coat she wears, she can feel his body heat. He's like a human furnace. In the summertime, she can barely stand cuddling for too long post–coitus—he runs so hot.

"I know you're mad at me, but I wanted to say I'm sorry. I didn't realize Kyle lied, and if I'd known the reason he chose this place, I would have told him to choose a different forest. I told him we wanted to go on a camping trip, not a ghost hunt."

Her shoulders sag. "I'm not mad. I'm just frustrated. You guys don't understand, and I just... nevermind."

"Tell me. I want to understand."

"I knew her, Sebastian. I knew Wren. She was... She was my classmate at the summit. She helped me on my assignments. Before Wren was the Songstress of Lorelei, she was a brilliant technomancer, and she... she was someone I would have called a friend."

"Oh, baby. I didn't know."

"I know you didn't know. I didn't tell you, and it's not exactly something any of us who knew her ever actually talk about. Heck, not even her own brother will say her name anymore. If it weren't for family records, you would forget the Vulcan of Deriva even had a half–sister."

Because that's what people do when they want to forget all about something. They shove it in the darkest corners of their closets, and they never mention it again, but if there was anyone who didn't deserve to be shoved in a box...

"Wren was the most bubbly, optimistic person I've ever met. She didn't take no for an answer and never let anything get her down. I–I don't understand how someone like that could take their own life."

"Hon, she went crazy. The reports said she suffered from magically induced psychosis. If she hadn't done it herself, the League would've had no choice but to put her down."

"Yeah, according to the League."

"What does that mean?" he asks, confused. Oh, she's put her foot into it now.

"The League is, well, the League. They only give information as is necessary for the safety of the public, and almost 100% of the time, they only give half of the full story."

Less than, if she's being honest.

"Is that why you're doing your dissertation on the rumors surrounding what happened?"

"Yes... and no. I don't know. I guess I just want to know what really happened."

"Lily, she was driven mad by magic fever. And the things people do during a mental breakdown? Well, it isn't them. Not really. The tribunal wrote a whole article on the dangers of magic sickness after it happened, and they rerun the article every year."

"You're probably right. I shouldn't think into it so much."

He turns her around, pulls her in until her breasts press flush against his chest. She's forgotten her gloves again. He breathes a long "haaaa" over her icy knuckles, warming them between his hands.

"Hey. I'm sorry about all this. I should've just told you. I may not have realized exactly where Kyle was taking us, but I knew it had something to do with hexen ghosts—but the Songstress herself!"

"It's fine, babe. Your intentions were good."

"You know what they say about the road to hell."

She chuckles. "I guess."

The glow of the fairy lights twinkle—starlight she can touch.

"This is what I was hoping we would see, though. It's rare enough to find fairies in the countryside. Good luck finding them in the city. You have to travel into the untouched parts of the world to see them."

"You mean into the dead zones where technology can't connect."

"Yes, into the dead zones where my girlfriend can't disappear into the network."

"It's not like I go anywhere when I'm connected, Sebastian."

"Maybe not physically, but you're like my students when we're reading a particularly riveting story. They disappear from the real world entirely, but that's the magic of storytelling. You can take anyone anywhere without ever leaving your home, and for the most part, it's totally legal. But with you, when you go into the network, you become someone else entirely. It's like you're more there than here. More outside yourself. I could watch you conduct your research for hours, you're so alive when in your element, but at the same time, I miss you terribly whenever you're in that other space."

Lily's chocolate–brown eyes averted down.

"I know it can be off–putting at times. I'm sorry—"

He takes her hand. "No, no, no. That's not what I'm saying, Lil. I love that you're augmented. I love that you're connected to this giant universe that I can't even comprehend. I love that you love being connected. I love how smart and fun and passionate you are. But most of all, I love you."

One of the more courageous fae titters forward. The little sprite dances around their heads, leaving sparkling halos of dust in its wake. It taps Lily on the shoulder before flitting away into the night. When she turns back to Sebastian, he's disappeared from her line of sight and dropped down onto one knee.

"Lily..."

Her breath catches in her heart.

"The last two years of my life have been the best I have ever lived. Meeting you, getting to know you, loving you has been the highlight of my life, and if you could humor this mere mortal of a man long enough to feel the same, then all I can do is ask..."

Sebastian pulls a small box from his coat pocket and opens it to reveal a simple silver band; inlaid at its center is a shimmering solitaire diamond.

"Lily Marie Esquire, will you marry me?"

Her heart hiccups as though struck by Cupid's arrow. Her tech systems register her as in distress, and she can see the light of the node on her wrist flickering like a flame in the wind.

"Yes, Sebastian. Yes, I'll marry you."

And she tackles him to the ground with a kiss.

The sound of a champagne cork popping echoes through the clearing, scattering the fairies dancing in the grass and sparking Lily away from her fiancé's lips. Kyle whoops as the fuzzy alcohol spills out onto the ground.

"Woohoo!! My lil bro is getting married!"

Beside him, Jeanine has her camera out; the flash goes off, catching Lily's smile.

"Congratulations!"

Javier and Derrick spin each other around as they race into the clearing to embrace both Sebastian and Lily in a hug.

"We won't be the only married fogies around here anymore. Let's see the ring. Is it as good as he said it would be?"

Lily turns to Sebastian in surprise. "You had all of this planned."

"Of course, I did. I wanted to make this special for you."

Kyle shakes the champagne bottle, aiming it up and spraying a rain of bubbly over all four of them.

"Now that we got that bit of business over with, let's fucking party! Happy Hexennacht, bitches!"

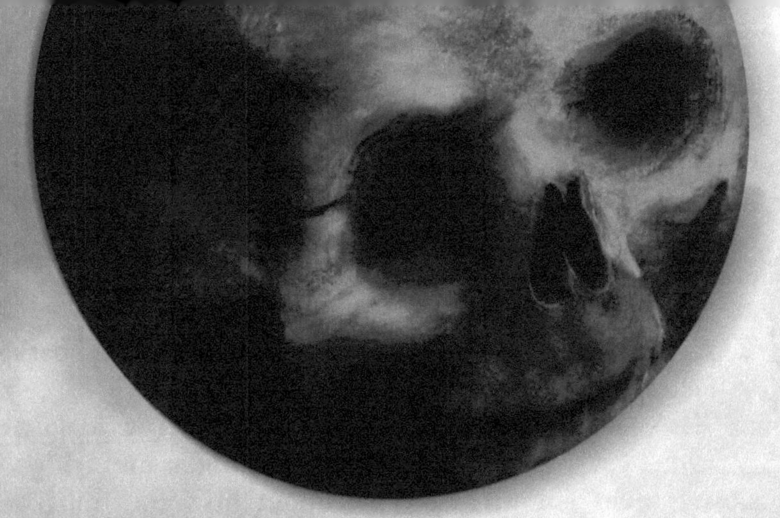

VIII

THE FOG DESCENDS

Booze flows like water around the campsite. Javier plays music from his phone through a pair of Bluetooth speakers. Sebastian and Derrick have gathered stray branches and leaves to make a decent fire. Javier even unearths a set of masks he brought with him. It feels like a true Halloween celebration, complete with frivolity, merriment, and even a "haunted" witch's hut to sleep next to—not that Lily appreciates them sleeping anywhere near it.

After Lily ran off, the others set up camp by the dilapidated cottage. It's a small comfort to know they've all taken her warning seriously, and none of them are planning to sleep in the small house; Lily accepts the small olive branch.

Kyle wears the mask of a jester and twirls a fox mask–wearing Jeanine around the fire while Sebastian sways Lily back and forth at the edge of the glow. The whiskey is warm in her belly, her thoughts fuzzy around the edges, Sebastian's hands cool on her heated skin and the ring on her finger even cooler.

The fairies have long since flitted away.

As they dance, she trails her fingers along the rigid bark of the trees.

"You've just made me the happiest man in the world, Lily."

"Don't get too jolly," she teases, winking at him with a sloshy smile. "I'm still mad at you about this whole thing."

"Guess I should have stuck with the usual ring-in-the-champagne-glass-at-a-restaurant shtick." He tugs her closer to the fire, guiding her to sit on one of the picnic blankets.

"I wouldn't say you had to go that mundane, but some-place with running water would have been nice."

"I promise I'll make it up to you."

She kisses him as he starts a one-handed massage on her neck. "I can't wait."

"I bet you can't. I'll have to pamper my fiancé."

And he plants a butterfly kiss at the nape of her neck.

"Anyone want to come swimming with me?" Jeanine calls.

The redhead shakes her head in answer while Javier squeaks in outrage. "Are you crazy! The water is gonna be freezing by now."

"Well, I'm going."

"Alright."

"I'll come with you," offers Kyle, following behind the girl. "Make sure nothing tries to drown her."

The jibe earns him a good-natured smack to the shoulder. Oh, Lord, she better not be fixing to have Jeanine as a sister-in-law.

But she'll worry about that later.

Sebastian's fingers work magic into the tense muscles of her shoulders, and her eyelids, weighted down by the day and the drink, fall shut.

"Lily..."

Whispers in the night, the sound of a fiddle playing over the water, and fairies dancing in the grass. She floats on an autumn breeze, light as a feather, unwilling to move, her bones stiff as a board on a pillow of mist.

"Lily..."

She drifts down the river toward the trill of the violin. Her own face stares back at her from the ripples of the water.

"Beware the river spirits, love. I hear they love to make a splash at parties."

A misty hand breaks the surface and reaches toward her face.

A scream frightens Lily awake. She doesn't even remember falling asleep. Around the campsite, the boys are all passed out as well. Kyle hugs a beer bottle, Javier hugs Derrick, and Sebastian is wrapped around her. But where is Jeanine? She went swimming, didn't she? But Kyle is back, so shouldn't she be back as well?

"Jeanine?" Lily untangles herself from her fiancé, loudly hushing for the other girl.

"Over here." The quietest of whispers responds, a voice that sounds like Jeanine but also doesn't.

"You alright?" she asks, moving toward the voice.

No answer comes.

There's a rustling sound in the bushes. The other girl's pack is still on the ground next to her tent. The pink backpack sits upright, untouched and unobtrusive. Jeanine's roll of toilet paper sits undisturbed atop her backpack.

Did she maybe go to the bathroom and forget her roll?

"Jeanine, you forgot the toilet paper."

She calls again to no answer, making her way to the edge of the camp with the roll of paper in hand.

It's much darker around the clearing than it should be. With the fire still lit, the shadows seem to stretch in the opposite direction of where they should.

As she steps past the radius of the campfire, her boot squishes into a wet spot on the ground. What the—? It hasn't rained. Why is there water on the ground? Maybe from when they went swimming?

"Jeanine?"

"Psst!"

"Just stay there. I'm coming."

Except when she reaches the tree line, a dark green crusted thing lunges at her chest. On trained instinct, she backhands the creature away with the metal inlaid part of her arm. It gives a human–like groan and disappears toward the lake, and she lands in a patch of damp earth.

"Jeanine, I swear if you—"

She wipes her hands on her jeans but instead of a dark brown smear of soil, she finds instead a ruddy red streak. Red has seeped into the ground all around her. A dark, viscous red disturbingly akin to the texture of blood.

"Jeanine!" she shouts, jumping to her feet. What the hell just attacked her?

"Lily? What's wrong?" Sebastian bolts awake at Lily's yell.

"There was this thing, Jeanine is missing, and I found blood."

"You found what?"

"Blood, Sebastian!"

Kyle, Javier, and Derrick jolt up.

"What's happening?"

"Fuck, when did we fall asleep?"

"Where's my sister?"

Upon finding his sister missing, Javier begins to hyperventilate.

"Weren't you with her?" asks Derrick, looking at Kyle.

"Well, yeah, but I don't remember coming back here."

"Lily, where is she?"

"I don't know. I woke up and she was gone and—"

"You woke up. How long have you been awake? Fuck, how long have we been asleep?"

"The last I checked it was 7 o'clock," says Derrick, checking his watch. "That's weird."

"What? What is, honey?"

"My watch is broken."

Derrick holds his arms up, and sure enough the analog watch on his wrist is completely busted. The glass of the face cracked, the hour hand limply spins around its anchor point.

"How did that happen?"

"Does anybody else have a watch?"

Kyle tugs his multitool from his belt and, glancing at it, frowns.

"Alright. Whoever is playing a joke needs to cut their shit."

"Whoa, Kyle chill. No one's pranking anyone."

"Then explain to me why my clock is fucked up, too."

"Lily, do you have the time?" asks Sebastian.

Lily pulls up her interface. Lines of code appear before her visuals, flashing to remind her she's out of network range, but she should still be able to check what time it is. Only when she swipes open her date/time screen, the numbers are all scrambled.

"I can't get a time read, either."

"Fuck!" Kyle's curse sends a flock of birds flying into the sky.

A distant scream.

"Jeanine!" Lily takes off, sprinting toward the sound.

"Lily, wait!"

She runs scans on her systems as she goes. Hawthorne branches, peppercorn bush, poison oak, northern sugar maple, pine... so much pine. Pine needles, pinecones, pine thorns, scraping across her face and arms as she blindly barrels through them. Her system beeps at her in alarm, and she stops mere inches from tumbling over the edge of an overcrop. Below her, about ten feet down, black water churns. The lake.

"Jeanine, where are you?!"

No answer comes.

"Lily!"

Behind her, she hears the men shouting for her. Crap, in her haste to get to Jeanine, she completely left them behind. Now she's alone. No Jeanine. No Sebastian. Nobody.

"Over here!"

"Don't move. We're coming your way."

"Okay!"

She can hear them coming through the brush. It shouldn't take them too long to reach her. There are two trees to her left woven around each other, a lover's embrace in a whispering forest. If she tilts her head, it almost looks like the trees have faces, their branches arms reaching to curl around one another. Helpless fancies.

Just beyond the peculiar pair, something pale flits past, milky white and quick as a fleeing rabbit.

"Jeanine, is that you?"

A giggle greets her in response. A sweet, tinkling sound like daisies dancing in the wind.

"Jeanine, this isn't funny!"

The giggling fades into a cadenced hum, notes that rise and fall with the sound of the rustling leaves. The sounds of the forest rest almost in deference to the melody. The wind stills, the insects quiet, and Lily holds her breath.

Hmm hm hmmm hm hm... Hmm hm hmmm hmm hm hm hm.

Haunting and beautiful and climbing up the octave in a steady ascension of full steps intertwined with dissonant halves.

A song hummed by an invisible songstress.

Beneath her feet, the ground seems to pulse, mist curling around her feet and rising to thicken around her.

WARNING: MAGIC DETECTED

The fog shimmers with it. Wild, untamed magic, similar to the glittering dust of the fairies, but this is different. More somehow. Thicker, penetrating, the harsh unyielding nature of rock and stone and wood compared to the ever–shifting wash of water.

Blades of grass prick at her ankles, and when she looks, the previously wilted brush thickens and lengthens, rising taller with plant growth.

"Who's there?"

Her feet crunch alarmingly as she steps forward. Unthinking, as though compelled, she makes her way toward the music, toward the enchantment, using the trees to guide her footsteps. The fog folds around her, dense but thin, light yet heavy, suffocating yet the only thing filling her lungs.

Çlevær uɲt mina...

A whisper on the wind.

Çlevær uɲt mina...

A harp on the water.

Çlevær uɲt mina... Come to me...

A woman in the mist.

Golden locks, braided in flowers and crowned in brambles, fall around her shoulders to cascade over the swell of her naked breasts. Her milky white skin gleams in the moons' light. The soft swell of her stomach, the full curve of her hips, the smooth meld of her buttocks into her thighs.

Venus! A living goddess in the middle of the woods singing an unearthly melody in a language Lily has never heard before, and she cannot look away.

The woman lifts her head. Eyes black as coal penetrate into her being. Reflected in those eyes is the quiet peace of a clock frozen in time.

"Lily, there you are."

And in the blink of an eye, the woman disappears.

"Sebastian."

Sebastian climbs his way over a fallen tree, Kyle close behind, Javier and Derrick pulling up the rear. Javier holds his side as he folds over, hands on his knees as he pants for breath.

"Can we not do that again?"

Lily looks back for the singing woman. She's gone. Vanished as easily as a dream.

"Are you alright?" asks Sebastian, his hand warm on her elbow.

Light burns her pupils as Kyle shines his flashlight into her face.

"I'm fine. We need to find Jeanine."

"It's pitch black out here. She can be anywhere. The farther we get from the camp, the more we risk getting lost ourselves. Better to wait until dawn and look for her when it's light out."

Javier coughs, trying and failing to speak before spitting on the ground, catching his voice as Derrick rubs his back.

"We can't just leave my sister in the forest alone."

"Baby, she probably just lost her way coming back from the loo. She's a smart girl; she'll know to stay put until morning when we can find her more easily."

"You call that scream getting lost?"

Derrick shrugs, looking at Javier. The man, hyperventilating, looks like he is about to have a panic attack. "I shouldn't have invited her to come."

"Jeanine is fine, babe."

"There was blood in the grass."

"Maybe she's on her period," scoffs Kyle.

"I'll give you a period," growls Lily, balling up a fist and thrusting it under Kyle's nose. What an asshole! "You were the last person with her!"

Derrick steps in between with much the same idea as Lily. Sebastian tries to cut them both off. Kyle directs his aggression toward Derrick, and in the scuffle, Lily gets shoved sideways into a tree. Kyle punches Derrick in the stomach who in turn uppercuts him on the chin. Kyle spits blood out of his mouth and elbows Derrick in the face.

"You wanna go, you fucking organic? Watch me rip your fucking head off!"

"Kyle! Derrick!"

Sebastian pulls Kyle around to try and break the two up while Javier tries to grab Derrick.

"Guys, stop it! I don't think—Ah!"

Yanked off his feet with a sickening crack, Javier lands on his back, glasses flying from his face as he disappears into the underbrush with a scream.

"Javi!"

Derrick chases after his husband, dragged along the ground by some incorporeal force.

"Derrick, wait!"

Sebastian, Lily, and Kyle give chase, following Derrick's shouts. Derrick's cry of Javier's name cuts off with a sound like an axe hitting a tree.

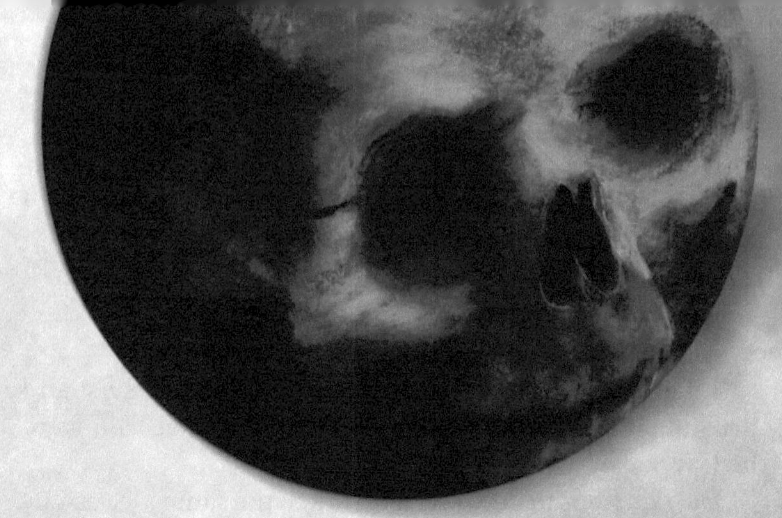

IX

SPOOKY SCARY SKELETONS

They find Kyle's axe, broken in two and lying in a patch of bloodied leaves and bloodstained grass ripped from the ground. Derrick and Javier are nowhere in sight, and when Lily calls their names, her own voice, echoing back through the trees, is all the answer she gets.

Sebastian rounds on his brother. "You said you'd been here before. You said it was safe."

"It is safe. It's just a forest."

"Then what the hell took Derrick, Javi, and Jeanine?"

"I don't know."

"You don't know! You said you'd spent the night here. You said you scouted the place for danger."

"I lied, okay? I lied! I haven't fucking been here. Who in their right mind would come into Lorelei Forest alone? Do I look suicidal to you?"

Who in their right mind would come into Lorelei Forest at all?!

Kyle laughs in his brother's face. Fury boils in Lily's belly. Augmentations alight, and Lily rounds on the man, uncaring of the fact that he's Sebastian's older brother.

"You brought us here blind." Her fist meets his chest, the node on the back of her hand burning an aggravated red. "And you didn't even have the decency to be honest about it. You think you can use us as your fucking guinea pigs!"

"Get the hell off of me before I test just how good your goddamn augmentations are."

Spit flies into Lily's face, and she balls her hand in his shirt, ready to spit in his eye.

"Hey, hey! That's enough, you two. Fighting each other isn't going to help anything." Sebastian steps in between the two augmented humans, completely uncaring for his safety. He pulls Lily off his brother by the hip and shoves Kyle backward, keeping a hold of him by his coat collar. "Now, we are going to figure out what the hell we're going to do. Jeanine, Javi, and Derrick are missing, and we don't have the equipment we need to find them. Lily, are you able to send a message?"

Lily huffs, righting her clothing from the manhandling. "No. I'm completely cut off from any network."

"What good is having a computer in your head if you can't use it?" Kyle complains.

"I don't know. What good is having a cell phone if you're going to secretly lure a group of people into the middle of a forest that is known as one of the most haunted places on earth and therefore out of network range?"

Cowed, Kyle backs off.

"So, we make our way back to the cars, and from there, we can get to the network. Call for help, so we can find Jeanine, Javier, and Derrick."

It's the most sensible thing to do, rather than run around in the dark, so with the plan set, they pack up the bare minimum of items to go. At least, it sounds like a good plan. The execution of it leaves much to be desired. When KC refuses to turn on at Kyle's command, they are forced to take even less gear in hand to head for the exit.

They get nowhere. Literally nowhere. The forest seems to shift and change around them, a labyrinthine biosphere, and they are at the center of it. Kyle has his compass out and insists they are heading the right direction, but her scanners read the same landmarks over and over again.

"Kyle, do you even know where you are going?"

"I'm telling you. It's this way."

"This is the third time I've seen that fallen tree in an hour."

"It can't be the same tree. We haven't made any turns, and the moons have been on our right this whole time."

"It's the same tree."

"Baby, Kyle's right. We haven't made any turns. I've been keeping an eye on the compass."

Falling quiet, Lily scowls and follows since that is apparently what is expected of her. She tracks the sky, watching the moons dance across the dome, or rather, watching the moons *not* dance across the dome. The minutes tick by and Koi and Dei remain ever stagnant in the sky. Suddenly she is made aware of just how quiet the forest has become.

"Guys?"

"Now what?" gruffs Kyle. Sebastian gives him a "Dude, chill" look.

"What is it, Lily?"

"Something is wrong."

"How horror–movie cliche of you..."

Kyle scoffs, already shaking his head as he keeps marching the same direction.

"I'm serious."

"I'm sure you are, sweetheart, but I know where I am. I told you. Why can't you just trust me?"

"Because this is the fourth time we've passed the same fallen tree, and you're not listening to me."

"It isn't the same fucking tree!"

"No, Kyle. I think it is."

Sebastian stares down at the fallen wood as though he was looking at a death sentence. He kneels down and pulls directly from the bark... one of his rainbow nose strips.

"I left this the last time we passed it."

"That's not possible."

"Kyle, I'm telling you, that's what I did."

"No! That's not possible!"

In a mad outburst, Kyle takes off running. Lily tries to chase after him, but Sebastian stops her as mere seconds later, Kyle runs back into them from the opposite direction he left. Hazel eyes wide with shock, the man heaves a breath, hands coming up to clench at his hair.

"What the fuck..."

"Kyle, calm down, man. We need to figure out what is going on—"

"What the fuck!!" He swings, narrowly missing Sebastian's face, to nail a tree dead center. "I'm going to tear apart these goddamn woods!"

"Kyle, don't!"

Kyle's mechanical fist meets the tree trunk, leaving a dent in the wood and punctuating his words as he strikes over and over and over again.

"I'm so..."

Punch!

"...sick of this..."

Punch!

"...goddamn forest!"

Punch!

He slams his fist into the wood over and over and over again until the tree topples sideways, collapsing into its neighbor with a shattering of wood and leaves.

"Kyle, stop it!"

The sound that spills from the man's mouth is bestial and primitive as he zeros in on the next tree, rearing a fist back with enough power to send a hole through the thick trunk. But before the hit can land, a branch swings out. *Thwack!* The branch catches him across the chest and tosses him backward as though he weighs no more than a miniature poodle.

"What the—"

The branches continue to swing wildly, Lily and Sebastian backing up even farther until the wood creaks back into place minus a few pockets of leaves.

"The forest is defending itself."

"But how can it—"

An inhuman trill echoes through the night, a cross between an owl's screech and a wolf's howl.

"What was that?"

Lily's scans sift through the analytic systems in her head looking for an explanation for the sound neither animal nor hexen.

"I don't know, but it isn't human."

"Whatever it is, I'm going to rip it in two."

Exhaust ports along the man's mechanical arms ripple with orange light. The machinery whirs and hisses as he charges up, ready to go after the next thing that moves.

"Kyle, calm down," says Lily. "We have no idea what it is."

"You stay out of this."

"Leave her alone, Kyle!"

Sebastian comes up behind his brother and grabs him by his mechanical arm.

"Sebastian!"

Kyle swings back, slamming Sebastian across the chest. There's a sick crunching sound as Sebastian's back hits a tree. Lily runs to Sebastian; he's unconscious.

"Oh, fuck! Bassy?"

His head lolls to the side in her hands, unresponsive.

"Bassy! I didn't mean to—Shit! Lily, is he going to be okay?"

"Shut up, Kyle!" Lily looks for Sebastian's pulse. His breathing is shallow, his heart rate disturbingly slow. "Sebastian. Sebastian, look at me. Open your eyes, baby."

Sebastian's lashes tremble as his eyes open, a weak flutter like the wings of a dying butterfly.

"Lily..."

Oh, thank god!

"Lily, it—it hurts."

"I know. I know it does, baby. I'm going to get you help. It's going to be okay."

But she can't make that promise herself. They have no more first aid supplies, no way of contacting help, so she composes an S.O.S. in her head and sends it.

MESSAGE DELIVERY FAILED

Try again.

DELIVERY FAILED

Again!

NETWORK CONNECTION UNAVAILABLE

Damn it! Keep trying!

A twig snaps to her right. Kyle's flashlight swings around to focus on the sound.

"Who's there? Who the fuck is there? Come out!"

"Kyle, stop it!"

A branch creaks to her left, and she jumps to her feet, one foot on either side of Sebastian's body. That was too close. Disconcertingly close. Lily's scanners are going crazy, identifying trees and roots and insects in microseconds but unable to pinpoint the source of the sound or catch the glimpse of a pale body darting through the darkness.

"I said come out, so I can rip your fucking head off!"

Hwroohwroo... Hwroohwroo...

The hooting call of an owl is the only reply he receives, and the quiet settles like a thick fog over the area. So still Lily holds her breath.

"I swear to God whoever the fuck is doing this I'll—Argh!"

Something jumps onto Kyle's back. Something humanoid and angry. Matted locks of hair whip from side to side as Kyle thrashes. Kyle's flashlight sails through the air, hitting a tree and dying.

"Kyle!"

Snarls and hisses punctuated by the man's screams.

"Get it off me!"

The creature's back is bark–like and rough, and Lily's fingernails scrape painfully against it as she tries to pull the creature off. A metal prong opens on her wrist, and she strikes the attacker across the back of the head, dislodging it and sending it racing into the woods before she can get a good look at it.

"What the hell was that! A ghost?!"

No. It couldn't have been a ghost. She'd touched it. Some sort of fae or hexen? She turns back to Sebastian only to find him gone.

"Sebastian?"

Lily scrambles to turn on the torch implant at her wrist. The LED bulb, no bigger than her pinkie nail, flickers on, washing the area in white light. The grass angrily rustles where he once laid, the indentation of his body still carved through the ground.

The leaves of a bush fold back into place. A furry tawny-colored tail disappears with a hiss.

"Sebastian!" Lily runs into the night after Sebastian, the beam of her flashlight burning from tree to tree. Why didn't she ever get night vision implants?

"Lily, wait!"

"Sebastian!"

A pitched shriek answers her.

"Don't you hurt him!"

The forest shifts around her despite the rigidness of the night, oppressive and penetrating to her. Creaking in the trees and screams in the night as the woods close in around her. A sharp branch cuts across her cheek. Her breath steams in the frigid air, turning to icicles before her eyes. It shouldn't be this cold. Not even this far north. Not when the solstice is still two months off.

Crack!

"Ahh!"

Pain alights in her ankle, and Lily tumbles heels over head into the dirt. She lands with a squelching sound, her hands sinking into the mud and leaf litter. The roots spring up. Jagged wood winds around her torso, tugging her deeper into the frozen ground. The damp of decay seeps into her

socks, and fire flares across her wrist as a red–tailed centi-
pede crawls over her skin.

She yanks herself out of their grip, pulling up grass and
decaying leaves.

"Lily, stop! You don't know where you're going."

Kyle chases after her.

"I have to save Sebastian!"

She keeps running, the air pumping into her lungs with
the aid of her O2 supplementary augmentation until the
bulk of a half–mechanical body tackles her from behind.
She falls with a shout, and she and Kyle go tumbling down
an incline.

"Listen to me, you little tramp. My brother wanted to
bring you out here to propose, and now he's missing."

A mechanical palm slaps her across the face.

"He's missing because of you, you prick! You hit him hard
enough to break his ribs. You might have killed him, and
now he's gone because you thought it would be a good idea
to go for a stupid ghost tour!"

She knees him in the stomach. He curses, rolling off her
as she gets her hands and feet under her. A boot flies into her
side. She catches his ankle and tugs him off his feet. He falls
to the ground, heavy as a boulder with a grunt. The bigger
they are... Metal fingers clamp down on her head and tug
her sideways.

"Your augmentations are trash, girlie." He bears down,
pressure building painfully in her head.

"Let go!"

"You're going to turn on that fucking computer in your
head and get someone out here to help me find my baby
brother. Do you understand me? I don't buy that bullshit
you're on about the network. I've seen technomancers work
from less."

"Argh! I'm not a technomancer!"

"You could've been!"

"That doesn't mean—"

A high-pitched squeal zips past her elbow into Kyle's eyes. Dust and glitter fly into Kyle's eyes. He lets her go with a roar of pain. Hwrooooo!

The blur of a great grey owl flashes across Kyle's head, talons flashing red in the moonlight.

"My eye!"

He collapses, clenching his face. Lily scrambles backward as growls rip through the trees. A meaty flank knocks her sideways, and the back of her skull meets a rock. Two wolves rush forward, lunging for Kyle. One of them, sharp teeth glinting white, bites down on the soft tender flesh of his throat. He gurgles as the other rips into his side.

She blinks, and Kyle's bloodied outline blurs. The two wolves become three and a half, and into her line of sight, a pale human figure steps forward. Tall, angular, walking on their toes like a gargoyle or feline. A tail flicks agitated behind them.

A blink of her eye, and the woman is before her, inhuman eyes glaring at her. Before Lily can react, the creature's hands close on her forearm, human but not human hands, nails dirtied and gnarled from the wilderness. She yanks her arm up and sharp teeth bite down, burying deep into the meat of her forearm. Fire ignites along the limb, boiling hot like acid spilled from a testing beaker.

And the stars blink out.

Lily's eyes open, heavy and crusted as though she has been sleeping for hours. The moons hang high in the sky, Dei—full as usual while Koi hangs in an upturned crescent—a Cheshire Cat grin. *We're All Mad Here.*

But where is "here"?

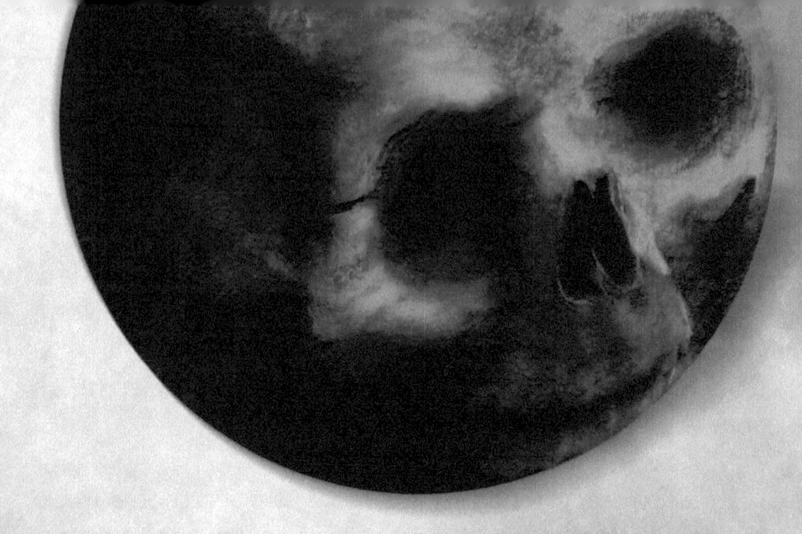

X

KISS, KISS, KISS

"I am assigning you a partnered task. You shall work in pairs on your final project. Either you both pass with full colors or you both fail. There is no one or the other. I fully expect you to assimilate yourselves with a participant from a different background and/or nation than you."

Finnick Lockcrafte is a burly old goat. Probably the most famous technomancer of his age for his prowess in slaying vampyres and werewolves, he is also the most antisocial person Lily has ever met, so receiving a group project from this man is, to put it mildly, unexpected.

To their credit, none of the participants groan. There are only a few murmured whispers of disdain, namely from the Derivan and Sekhmetian students. So close to the end of the theoretical portion of the Summit, they are, and everyone is ready for the final project, though none of them expected a partnered assignment to be the crux of their theoretical assessments.

The moment Lockcrafte says to disperse, she turns around to face Rhiannon and Lydia while Selene and Wren wander over from their seats closer to the Ebelean and Derivan participants respectively. And that's when Lily realizes they have a problem. From their group of friends, Heather has already been dismissed, and Wren, making her way over from beside her brother, seems to realize the situation as well.

There's an awkward moment when the five of them all look sheepishly between themselves because unfortunately 5 doesn't divide evenly by 2.

"Maybe one of you could work with my brother. I'm sure Xipilli wouldn't mind if—" Wren cuts herself off mid-sentence as her brother fist bumps Chike. "Never mind. The bromance continues between Xipilli and my future brother-in-law."

"What if we asked Irene?"

Except when Lily turns to find the girl, she's already partnered up with a girl from Ebele.

"Oh, look Lionheart's coming over."

The next few minutes that unfold are the most painstaking moments Lily has ever experienced. Her face warms, a blush rising into her cheeks as she averts her eyes.

"My lady, I'm sure we could finish this project with an all-nighter or two."

"Well, I..."

"What do you say, *mon cherie*?"

Only when she looks up, Lionheart isn't talking to her. He's talking to Wren.

Lily has never known what it feels like to be stabbed in the heart, and she might be being overdramatic, but this might be the closest she's ever come to that. But Wren isn't even looking at Lionheart. Despite his attempt to woo her with the usage of a Derivan endearment, she's staring past him.

One of the other girls has approached Kaito, seemingly to be his partner. He doesn't rebuke her, but he doesn't exactly seem accepting of her either. She sits down anyway, leaning into his space and setting her hand on his shoulder. Her hands squeeze the teen's shoulder in mimicry of a massage. At this point, the prince says something about pursuing a particularly complex theorem for the final presentation. It seems to deter her because she quickly retreats from the man's side, veering back to a group of giggling girls, leaving the Miyazaki teen alone once again.

"You think they'll make an exception for someone if no one wants to work with them?" Lydia whispers to Lily.

"Don't you mean if they don't want to work with anyone else?" inserts Selene with a laugh.

Wren rises from her seat.

"Sorry, Lionheart. I don't think you and I have the same definition of an all–nighter."

The boy stutters. "Well, hold on. I—"

Lionheart's jaw drops, stunned, as Wren angles around him, wishing the other girls good luck on their projects, and makes her way to the vacated seat next to Kaito.

"What is she doing? I thought he couldn't stand her."

"Maybe she wants to test the limits of her mortality for her final project."

Only instead of being rebuked like the last girl who approached Kaito, she settles into the seat across from him, activates her mechanical hand's holoscreen, and begins plotting something or other for the assignment. For his part, the prince doesn't say anything, simply turns his head toward her, activates his sights, and reaches out to make an adjustment on her holo.

"Xipilli is going to throw a fit," says Selene, stunned.

"Xipilli," starts Rhiannon, "is going to have a piece of my mind if he bothers his sister for her choice in partner."

Lionheart stands speechless for a long second. He must not be very practiced at handling rejection.

"So, uh, Lily. Would you like to be my partner?"

Lily starts at the boy's address. He gives her a winning smile—the same smile that convinced her to spend the night with him just a few days ago. She won't be fooled by it this time.

"Sorry, but Lydia and I are already working together."

The Murasaki girl, at the mention of her name, giggles.

"Oh yeah, sorry, Lionheart. This one's spoken for."

Lydia flings an arm around Lily's shoulders, and Lily learns something that day that she won't soon forget.

Boys suck.

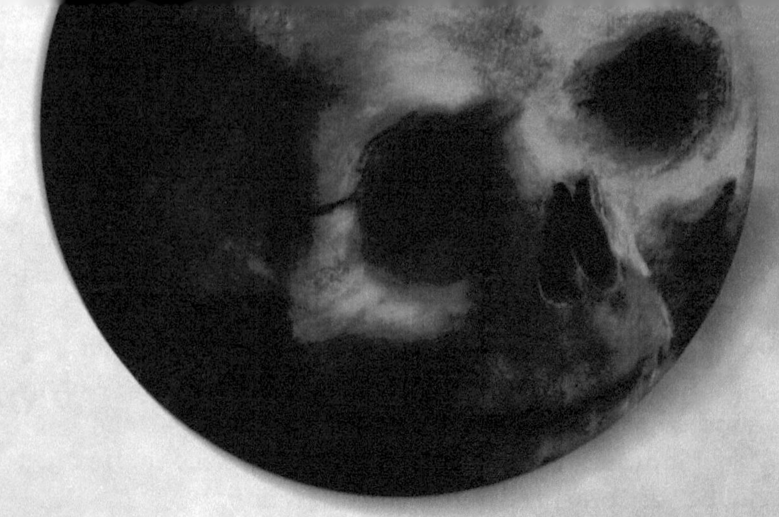

XI

DEAD ON ARRIVAL

The forest is gone, replaced instead by four walls, furniture, and the thin, naked trunk of a willow that stretches upward through the roof only to weep down around her. Lily lies on her back in a bed, a dusty, old double draped in gauzy netting, torn and yellowing with age. Blinking up at the half–broken circular canopy, where she expects to see ceiling and timber, there is instead a hole torn out by the tree growing through the center of the room. Starlight and moonbeams trickle through the incomplete blackness. Hanging from the canopy ring are several crystals, hung from ribbon and string as well as a child's necklace and a torn–up picture colored in crayons and markers.

Her fingers go numb as she realizes where "here" is. The cottage. In the back bedroom. In a bed not her own. A bed that once belonged to a witch. A very dead witch. She's been sleeping in the bed of a dead witch.

Jolting up with a shriek, she scrambles for the door, tripping over the hem of a long nightgown. What the hell? This isn't hers. It's threadbare and motheaten, like it hasn't been worn in years. Oh God! It hasn't been worn in years. Surely, this isn't *hers*! She woke up in Wren's bed wearing Wren's clothes. She gets up, the hem tearing, but just as she reaches the door, the wood slams shut, vines winding around the paneling, locking it in place. She pushes and pulls at the handle, but it isn't until she slams her shoulder into the rotting wood that she falls plain through it. Crawling to the front door, vines lash at her calves, thorns scratching into the meat of her shin. One of the spines pierce the center of one of the nodes on her leg. Electricity shocks through the plant, warding it away as she pulls herself backward by her elbows.

The vines wither and die at her feet, but the anguished cry of pain comes from behind her.

Out of the mist, a woman steps, naked but for the foliage woven around her torso. Like a creature from a fairy tale, she drifts over the mossy earth as intangible as the mist from whence she unfolded. Her hair is matted and tangled through with leaves, her skin milky pale, eyes like obsidian gems in her narrow face. Behind her flicks a long bovine tail of the purest white, and over her back ripples the roughened patterns of tree bark. In an instant of clarity, Lily realizes this creature is not merely of the forest. She is the forest. The woman's lips part, and she ducks her head between her knees as the sound that spills forth cripples her.

The ear–splitting falsetto of a huldra's scream.

A thorn pierces through her mind, wedging its way into the very center of Lily's skull. Mites dance up her arms, the bugs crawl under her skin, eat at her sinew, and from their fatted corpses, seedlings sprout. Seedlings which take root in her bones and marrow. The roots replace her skeleton and brambles her hair. Her skin becomes as rough and hard as tree bark and her voice becomes the rustling leaves.

The screaming stops.

Lily gasps, once again herself. Ripped from the hallucination, she feels her face and throat. No tree bark. Her hair is soft copper. Her body is flesh and blood and bone. Not plant matter. Not compost.

Lily's tech system is going on the fritz. Her internal servers whine at her to retreat, vacate, run away. But there is nowhere to run. This huldra will hunt her down and kill her. Kill all of them. Damnit, why did Kyle have to bring an axe into the woods?

The huldra watches her. The woman looks at Lily, crouched where she is on the ground, curled up with her hands over her ears. Carefully, Lily lifts her head and meets the woman, this queen of the forest, eye to eye.

"I'm sorry we came into your forest. I'm sorry we hurt your trees."

She looks at Lily with those eyes, like shark's eyes, cold and calculating. Her head cocks to one side like an owl or a hawk. Can she understand Lily? Does she even speak common? Does it matter? Her tech nodes flash in the dark, normally a cool pink, now red with distress.

The huldra trills a chirrup sound the whole forest vibrates to.

"Please, let my friends go, and I promise you we will never trespass on your forest again. It was a mistake for us to come here."

MESSAGE SENT

Something got through. Her S.O.S. went through. To whom? Which network did she connect to? Who cares! Hurry, whoever is seeing this message. Please, hurry!

The huldra hisses, stepping toward her.

She's going to kill her. She's going to kill all of them.

With her eyes screwed shut, she counts the creature's footsteps on the grass. 1... 2... light as a bunny and equally quiet. 3... 4... 5... Leaves crunch right beside her, and she bows her head down.

"Please, I'm so, so sorry."

The huldra leans down. Fingertips thread through her hair, cold and smelling of damp earth. They catch in the tangles behind her ear and slowly unravel the knots, almost careful, as though she is trying not to hurt her.

"I'll do whatever you want. Just please let us go."

The huldra's head tilts, her left ear coming to her left shoulder. Her fingers smell like dirt and leaf litter and drip with enough power to pull Lily's skull from her spine.

She closes her eyes and prays.

BrrBeep!

KC barrels her way across the clearing like a deus ex machina (No, a machina ex deus!) ramming into the fae's legs, throwing her off balance, and Lily races away from the creature into the forest. Her blind dash through the woods is interrupted only by the shiny chrome painting of KC's metal shell.

"KC, activate reconnaissance systems."

A responding series of chirps greet her. The drone is on high alert, searching for her missing friends, and Lily runs, following behind KC's taillight, blinking red in the darkness, not stopping until she nearly trips over the little bot as it comes to a sudden halt in front of a massive oak tree.

Its trunk is as thick as a dining room table, branches reaching up so high they disappear into the descending fog. The leaves shimmer golden in the dark, wild magic alive and pulsing through its branches, through the vines lacing up its trunk, and through its roots to bleed into the soil.

Still panting from her mad dash, Lily steps toward the tree. Her sensors go haywire as she sets a hand on the bark. This tree is old. Older than possibly even the bones of the first witches who migrated to Deus. Its unparalleled majesty is marred only by the charred, fire–blackened stain along its left side and the warding talismans hanging from the dead wood there. And at the base of this scar sit a handful of differently sized glass globes, all containing a single purple flower, the petals of which glow bioluminescent in the night light. Another kind of magic, a blending of earth and sea. Like a saltwater lily.

"Nngh!"

A groan draws her attention, and her gaze darts up to find a network of vines and brambles crisscrossing over deathly pale skin. Her breath hitches, and she climbs toward that patch of flesh, anchoring herself on a branch as thick around as a tire. Clawing at the bark and pulling up moss and brambles, her nails catch on the thick ridges and crack down the middle, but she keeps digging, keeps ripping into the tree until her fingers tangle in long black hair.

"Jeanine?"

A sleepy moan greets her.

"Oh God, Jeanine! I'm here. It's Lily. I'm here. I'm going to get you out of there."

But the brambles grow back too quickly, snaking over Jeanine's chest and face before Lily can free her. *Damnit!* So, she draws her utility knife from her belt.

"I'm sorry."

The blade stabs into the tree trunk, and the forest shudders around her. The smell of rain and compost, earth and mud, damp wood and ozone sloshes past her as she hacks into the thick wood until finally Jeanine's body falls limply from the wooded cavern into her arms.

"Jeanine, open your eyes. Can you hear me?"

A weak whimper is all the answer she gets, drowned out by the whistling of the wind. Lily unhooks the flashlight from the bioelectric charging port on her hip and clicks it to life. The beam traces over the wood.

"Javier... Derrick... Kyle..."

They're all here. All of them, coiled into the tree by plant matter, all of them ghastly pale, looking like ghosts themselves against the dark of the ancient oak. Javier is curled into his husband's side as though they were caught together. Kyle bears no markings of the wolf attack earlier. In fact, even his clothes are different, matching what he wore before everything started to go ass up. And lastly, scruffy facial hair, curly blond hair, and a chest decorated with a rainbow unicorn silhouette.

"...Sebastian."

Lily lays Jeanine down, cushioning her head with her jacket before getting up to cut Sebastian and the others from the tree. As she readies the blade, a pitched shriek rips through her synapse. Hands over her ears, she falls backward, landing on her back in the dirt.

He swims before her vision: Sebastian but not Sebastian. Sebastian, dead and rotting, surrounded by worms and roaches. Kyle, cold and still, mouth agape as a bat tugs out his tongue, mechanical arm broken and caked with rust. Jeanine, Javier, Derrick, pale, bloodless, fingers rigid with rigor mortis. Her own face, nose rotted away, eyes melted from her skull, a ghastly thing in a sylvan casket of thorns, a cadaver pillowed by autumn leaves.

"No!"

She crumples to her knees as thorns drill into her head. Or maybe they aren't thorns so much as they are worms—flesh-eaters feasting on her gooey white matter until all that's left is gelatinous slush. It feels like her skull is going to collapse on itself, sucked into a vacuum of her own dreams and desires until she is naught but baser, animalistic want.

"Stop it!!"

Crows take flight at her scream, and the silence that replaces their startled caws crackles with energy, like the aftershocks of an explosion or a bomb. The magic of the forest draws from her psyche, leaving her shivery and weak, her bones rattling like beads in a glass jar as she opens her eyes.

Kyle stands before her, blood dripping from his throat and arms, but it can't be Kyle. Kyle is buried in the trunk of the tree behind her.

The Kyle-shaped creature stoops down; its breath, putrid and smelling like rotting meat, ghosts over Lily's face. She gags on it, coughing up maggots as a clawed hand wraps around her throat.

"What are you?"

Its lips twist into a sharp-toothed grimace, revealing rows of pointed fangs sharp enough to rend her meat from her bones.

"What are you!"

The creature's maw opens to take a bite out of her when the huldra screams into its side, sending the other fae rolling off Lily. That's when she realizes this huldra is protecting her. This is the huldra's tree. She was protecting them all! The two creatures scuffle, ripping into each other with teeth and nails and magic. The shapeshifter, bigger and wider than the huldra, gains the upper hand, knocking the woman onto her back. Lily scrambles up, a stone in hand to bash the shifter's head in, but a ghostly claw wraps around her throat, lifting her off her feet in a magical hold.

The huldra cries out. The creature's face, now more impish than human, twists with rage. Lily's vision darkens, her oxygenation system keeping her respiratory system going despite the crushing force on her windpipe, but it won't last for long.

SYSTEM SHUTDOWN IMMINENT –
UNBLOCK AIRWAY

KC beeps erratically, throwing debris at the monster to no effect. She's going to die. She's going to die in this forest.

A blinding flash of violet floods her vision. The phantom hand disappears from her throat, a high–pitched shrill sounding from whatever the creature is. A shapeshifter of some kind? A hexen or a trickster fairy? She doesn't know. She doesn't care. All she cares about is the fact it now lies face down in the dirt with a katana buried in its back. A very familiar katana with state–of–the–art cabling connecting its hilt to its master.

Its master, who stands draped in pale gray and lavender at the edge of the clearing.

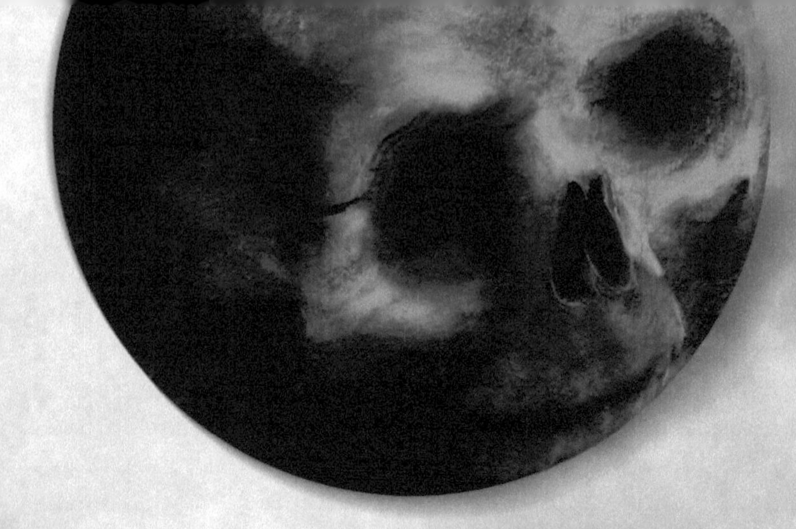

XII

The Kiss of Dawn

"Kaito?"

Kaito Miyazaki turns to her, his robes rustling in the wind. His sights spin in his eyes, a vibrant violet in the darkness.

"Miss Esquire," he says, pulling the blade from the body of her now dead attacker. At the formal address of her name, Lily remembers herself, folding into a bow appropriate to bestow a man of his rank and station. The crown prince of Murasaki no Yama, a technomancer hailed as one of the most powerful in the League. "I received your S.O.S. You should not have come into this forest."

She's lucky he was even within range to receive her transmission. She must have picked up his private network and her League permissions granted her emergency transmission.

"*Hveðrungr* don't take kindly to intruders who enter their forests without permission. You're lucky the huldra interfered."

Hveðrungr—The roarer. Of course! A trickster fae known for its shapeshifting abilities, often mistaken for doppelgangers. It probably took on Kyle's shape early on, so when the wolves attacked Kyle, they were actually attacking the *hveðrungr*. The wolves must answer to the huldra, the unspoken queen of the forest. Speaking of the fae, the huldra is gone, disappeared into the forest, no doubt to avoid coming face to sword with the prince.

"I've uploaded a route to your drone's servers. It will lead you out of the forest."

"I'm not leaving them."

From the trees, several adepts dressed in Murasaki colors of wine and burgundy filter into the area. One of them approaches the Miyazaki prince and bows.

"Be mindful of the forest. Harm nothing."

"Yes, your highness."

The adept moves toward the great tree as Kaito addresses her once more.

"My adepts will see to it your friends are taken care of. You should pack your things and leave."

"I understand what you're saying, your highness, but if it's all the same to you, I'll wait."

"Hm," he hums in acknowledgement.

"How were you in range to receive my transmission?"

What are you doing here, your highness?

Kaito looks at her with colorless gray eyes as his adepts begin to coax her friends down from the trees. The adepts don't take long, carefully extracting them from the tree as gingerly as possible, making sure no harm comes to the ancient oak. They are so cautious, the wildlife, countless birds and beasts who vacated the area during the ruckus of her fight with the *hveðrungr*, returns. Owls call to each other in the trees, the crickets take up their autumn song, and even a few thumb–sized fairies flit into the space, dusting over the transhumans as they work.

When they finally pull Sebastian from the bark, Lily hurries forward to check him over as they strap him into a gurney.

"Li–ly…"

He's awake, fingers lifting idly to touch her. *Oh, Sebastian…*

"Shh. Rest. They'll take care of you now." She looks to the nearest adept as he closes his eyes. "He has broken ribs. Please be careful."

"It's alright, ma'am. We've given him a stim. He should be just fine in a few hours."

"Thank you."

The *hveðrungr* is rolled into a body bag, and when the last of the adepts prepares to vacate the area, she bows to Kaito, reporting something to him in Hanasu. The prince acknowledges her with a tilt of his head and a polite dismissal before she pivots and makes to leave. Lily makes to follow with KC but pauses. Kaito remains unmoving.

The man stands still as a statue, gazing up to the sky.

Her internal clock activates. 3AM. The witching hour is at hand, the time when gloomtide reigns and even the most devout of technomancers have gone to bed. All except one, that is.

Instead of following the path out of the forest, Kaito turns to the great tree, drifting over the grass like a pale wraith, such a contrast to the deep, rich colors his adepts wear. Why does he not wear the same colors as his underlings?

"Are you coming, your highness?"

He doesn't answer her, turning instead to regard the charred patch of earth and wood. Lorelei Forest is a place where magic is richly embedded in everything else, yet here, there is a dead spot. It's almost like walking into a dead zone, but worse. Instead of just her augmentations lacking the ability to connect, her very person feels like it is missing something, like her essence is being pulled out and syphoned into nothingness.

She wonders if Kaito feels it too.

The prince kneels, his lavender robes blackening with dust and dirt. From his pack, he pulls a glass orb. Half full of water and decorated with colorful coral paints, in the center of the orb floats a single amethyst sea lily in full, bioluminescent bloom, a matching addition to the others already settled around the gnarled tree.

An amethyst sea lily... That was Wren's favorite flower, now set at the base of this tree by Kaito Miyazaki, a man long known to have had a relationship with the witch. A relationship rumored to have continued even after she defected from the League—even though such gossip was quickly squashed by the technomancer council and the man's own brother as soundly as a hammer could flatten a nail.

"This is where she died, isn't it?"

A stupid question, really. Why else would he be here? Kneeling in the dirt. Him, a prince, taking a weekend venture to arbitrarily bring flowers to a random tree, dress it as a grave, and make sure the spirits in the area are quelled enough to rest in peace. To make sure the spirit of his lost lover can rest in peace after dying in such a horrible manner.

"Is it true that Wren killed herself?"

The reports say as much, and they burned her body against a magical tree, probably in an effort to destroy its influence on the forest as well. They burned the witch but failed to fell the tree.

"I didn't know whether to believe it or not at first. Wren was always so sunny." Ever smiling, ever dreaming. She was the kind of person you knew would change the world, and she did. Lily just never expected she would change it like this. "You must have really lov—"

"Miss Esquire, if you please."

"Yes, my apologies. I'll leave you in peace."

With one last glance at the sigils painted across the shiny new talismans, Lily backs away from the man to follow KC, silently buzzing in the direction of the exit. By the time she sets foot on the dirt road, gaining sight once more of her fiancé's truck and the emergency transports fixing to take her friends to the nearest hospital, the sun is just beginning to peek over the horizon, filtering through the autumn leaves in a kaleidoscope of warm, tangy oranges and yellows.

She looks back just once.

In the light of dawn, Lily Esquire bids thanks to the huldra who kept her friends alive, goodbye to Kaito Miyazaki, goodbye to Lorelei Forest, and goodnight to the Songstress of Lorelei.

May she find the peace in death she couldn't find in life.

The huldra sits in the shadows at the edge of the clearing, watching as the adepts carry out the fools who encroached on her forest. The five of them will live, her sacred tree having kept them alive. The girl was nearly drowned by the *nøkken*, and the tall burly one is lucky the trolls didn't grind his bones to dust. A *draugr* almost sucked the life out of the skinny, glasses wearing one. The wannabe cyborg with the mechanical arm is in the worst shape, no big grievance in her book—he hurt her trees—but a trip to a League hospital will fix him right up. The *hveðrungr* got him and took on his shape, but Jessabelle's wolves ate at least a piece of the misaligned fae. She can never begrudge them a meal, and the technomancer's blade did the rest.

Now the forest quiets once more as the invasive species shows itself out. All but one of them anyway.

"Really, Prince. Every year, you come here and offer incense to the place she died. What are you expecting will happen? That she'll appear and give you a kiss from the other side of the veil?"

The man, silent as the makeshift grave erected for his lost love, cannot hear her. She is too far away from him. Not that she expects him to understand her anyway. She doesn't speak common or Hanasu, so the words she spits at him are the most loving of Eldritch, the only spoken language she knows, learned during her time with Jessabelle, the language of magic and beasts of the nether planes. The fae speak it a little. Kara, the huldra who fell in love with a witch, only speaks it because of Jessabelle.

But she's willing to wager, even if he could understand her, he would remain just as mute. Ever the stoic Kaito Miyazaki. The brooding warrior, forever mourning his lost love. Some people might call him steadfast. Her, on the other hand... she could puke. He's such a walking cliche.

"I suppose you're too smart to expect such things but really. It's been five years. Shouldn't you have found yourself some pretty little wife by now? Shouldn't you at least give your time to someone with a pulse?"

The huldra's words, though scathing, are not said in unkindness. He's not the only one who has lost a witch, after all.

The incense he burns is foul–smelling and poignant, harsh on her nose hairs, and it makes her eyes water, but she doesn't shriek at it. Once a year, every year since the raid that nearly destroyed her land, he comes without fail. Why he chooses this day rather than the anniversary of her death or perhaps even the woman's birthday is beyond her. But she supposes Hexennacht is an appropriate time to visit the closest thing to a grave for a witch who was never given the honor of a funeral.

But she supposes if she were going to suffer the presence of any human or posthuman in this case, this one is a reasonable choice. He is quiet and unobtrusive. He doesn't kill the animals under her charge or spoil the soil with garbage. He's always mindful of the trees, and on occasions like today, when fools wander into her midst in need of rescuing, he ensures the grounds are left pristine in the wake of the people under his command.

The prince kneels, holding vigil as the minutes pass on the witching hour. He doesn't speak or do anything outside of cleaning the grave and offering his brought flowers. Perhaps this is the reason she tolerates him: because the flowers complement her natural magic. The glowing blues, greens, and purples striking and cool against the golden shimmer of her tree. She knows they aren't really for her. They're for a dead witch, but she'll accept them anyway. It's not like the woman can claim the lilies for herself anyway.

Eventually though, he rises. He bows in her direction, saying something in a tongue she doesn't understand but understands implicitly.

"You think I watch over this place for your witch? Don't make me laugh!"

No, she does not guard this forest for any witch. She guards this forest from the humans not for the sanctity of any grave or cottage.

Humans are an invasive species. They plunder and pillage, and too many of them traipsing through her woods would kill the magic remaining in this place as surely as any nuclear bomb. An influx of people would have the animals scurrying off in fright at the mere sound of footsteps, birdsong would be drowned out by noise, and Gods forbid they set up any permanent settlement; the stink of sewage and waste would burn away the natural scent of earth and maple. A magic spell, beautiful and untouched, broken by too much humanity in one place. Not to mention the greater, darker truth...

Humans never arrive alone. With them come Death and Destruction, following behind like pets on a loose leash.

Destruction dogs humanity's footsteps, ever hungry for the best strips of meat, ringing the bell and waiting to be hand–fed its breakfast, and after Destruction follows Death, a starved shadowy thing scavenging for scraps.

Both had followed the Songstress of Lorelei, a techno-mancer–turned–witch. She never fed them herself. Never put food in their mouths, was as caring and careful of the forest as Jessabelle had been, yet still they panted after her, starving and rabid by the end, and look what happens when starving hounds are let off their leash.

"It's her fault Jessabelle is dead."

Even as she hisses the words, she knows they aren't true. Anger spitting lies. Wren was as responsible for Jessabelle's death as she is responsible for the sunrise, but...

Bitterness is sometimes a symptom of grief.

NURSERY RHYMES IN THE DARK

(A MIDWINTER TERROR)

While this tale does invoke a few fantasy and romance elements, this is at its heart a horror story. The content of this book may be disturbing to some readers. If any of the following topics are unsavory to you, proceed with caution: attempted/referenced infanticide, postpartum depression/psychosis, off-screen child death, deaths of animals including dogs, and the general horrors of war and childbirth.

The experiences of the main character in the story do not reflect or truly encompass the trials of motherhood. They are in no way meant to belittle or pass judgement on parents who choose a different means of raising their children. Every person's experience of parenthood is different and should be respected for that individual's story.

Many new mothers may experience symptoms of various postpartum disorders. If you or someone you know is struggling with such experiences as the intrusive thoughts portrayed in this novel, it is advised to seek professional medical care.

THE PSYCHOLOGY OF HORROR

In isolation is where ghosts haunt the living.

When we invite loneliness into our hearts,
we invite the demons in to possess us.

We fall to longing; we fall to the vampyre's bite.

In our rage, the werewolf's howl manifests.

We dance with the fae in our daydreams,
never knowing how close we are to the precipice.

Calling to monsters... that is what it means to live.

To live...

Ah, to live...

A word no witch dare wish.

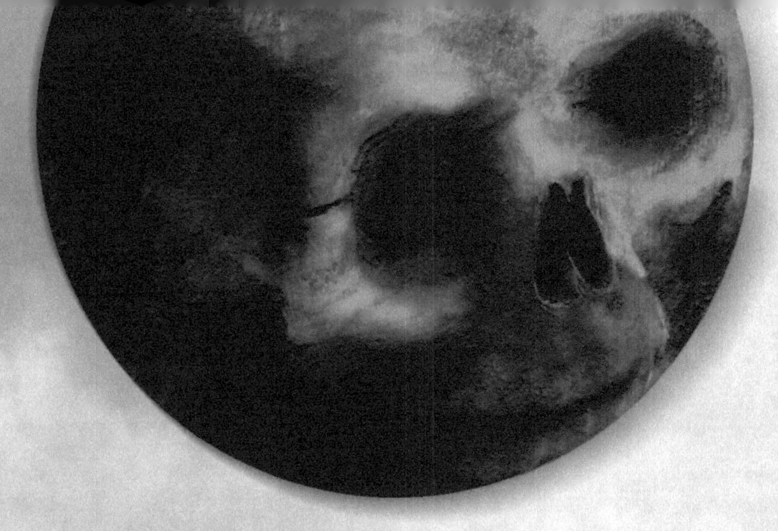

I

YOU ARE MY SUNSHINE

THE WASTES – DECEMBER 22ND, 1870 A.P. – THE
WINTER SOLSTICE

The fire yet burns, and morning is still many long hours away,
but for now, the largest toil of my life is over.

The fruit of my labor lies bundled up on my chest. The
tiny body snuggles into mine. With ten perfect fingers, ten
perfect toes, and a butterfly shaped birth mark in the small
of her back, she is perfect as can be.

Bark!

I smile tiredly at the canine resting her head on my thigh.
River's eyes look at me with uncertainty. In all my struggle,
my most loyal friend never left my side. The husky studies

the wriggling bundle in my arms with deep suspicion. Barely able to comprehend this sudden shift in my life, I can't imagine even she knows what to make of this new development. The bundle coos and stretches, and the dog inches forward, nosing the knit fabric of the swaddle. The tiniest of fists bonks the Siberian right on the snout.

"River, meet Astra."

River lifts a paw and sets it over the heart of my precious bundle.

My baby was born on the darkest night of the year, on a day the sun wouldn't dare to attempt to touch the mountain peaks. The winter solstice blankets the world and within it, the darkness comes alive.

My baby was born on this night, yet she is the brightest light in the whole world.

My baby's father was human+. He claimed he was a technomancer and had come to the Wastes to hunt and make a name for himself. There's always plenty of blood to spill in a place as hostile as this.

My home is as far south as you can go without scaling the mountains and crossing the border into Aighneas.

In name, Mountain View Villa may sound like a resort town, but it is not a place for your average human. It's cold, it's uncaring, and it's irradiated by magic and nuclear energy alike. Nothing works right here. The chaos is too saturated. One can skip a rock over a still lake, and instead of just rippling the surface, the pulse will echo through the very void that lies beneath the waking world. I've seen it myself.

The landscape folds in on itself and writhes like a snake in its death throes. That's how it is here: am I just touching a tree or is my ax going to trigger another avalanche later today? In the old world, philosophers once speculated that when a butterfly flapped its wings, a hurricane would blow through the other side of the world. Well, here if a butterfly flaps its wings at the wrong time, the hurricane will happen right underneath it.

That's probably why there aren't any butterflies in this part of the world anymore. It's certainly why there aren't any men.

With the exception of young man Thompson, there are no men in our village, and babies healthy enough to survive the womb are always assigned female at birth without fail. And Thompson was no exception to this second rule.

I would like to say that our village of women is as fierce and powerful as those ancient civilization like the Amazons and the Valkyries, but it would be a lie. We are not warriors, nor are we magic-weavers. We would hardly even constitute the standards of being noble human beings.

The women of Mountain View are the Disappointments of the once powerful hexen bloodlines. The hexen kings and queens from a time before technomancer reign. We are not witches, but the diluted magic in our bodies makes us not quite human either.

I guess that makes us wiccans. Or maybe some sort of mishmash of human and hexen that nobody wants to name because neither side cares enough to take ownership of us?

We are the in-betweens, the non-human that sits at the center of human and human+. We were rejected by humanity for our ties to witchcraft, but the hexen want nothing to do with us either. We are too mundane when we should've, by birthright, been fonts of magical might. Instead, we are clowns beholden to the curse of having power in our veins that will not allow us to yield it.

Our "magic" likes to laugh and giggle at the most inopportune times. I've always speculated that it is in some way linked to the mangled pathways that are the void waters around here. The radiation's interaction with the naturally occurring chaos in the void wreaks havoc on our bodies and minds.

I've seen Susan Cotton summon glorious boughs of holly and mistletoe one moment only for them to go up in flames the next. Janna, that miserable old goat, can't keep a proper shape to save her life. One day, she'll have horns sprouting from her head. The next, she'll be squawking about as a pink raven sporting a peacock tail. She once disappeared for three days and came back saying she had accidentally turned herself into a tree and didn't figure out how to change back until Julia Knot came up and tried to chop her down.

That's how all of us are. Magical beings with no control, never knowing what is going to happen the next time we so much as sneeze.

I, myself, feel like a radio broadcasting station trying to tune into the wrong frequency while the microphone is waterlogged, and the equipment is two hundred years old. I call my ability AIR Danica, and we only broadcast a daily morning show on the sixth day of the 3rd month, every other week, at all hours when someone is sleeping, dying, or pondering their midlife crisis. Such a broadcast will be immediately followed by a two-year-long intermission and a nightly rerun of the day's events. Does that make any sense to you? Because it makes zero sense to me.

Fine, I'll put it in layman's terms. I hear voices. No, not my own, thankfully. I'm not that kind of crazy. I just hear bits of thought from time to time—okay, a lot of the time.

Contrary to what you might think, I do not hear people who are nearby, nope, not at all. I hear from people thousands of miles away. I sometimes even wonder if I'm hearing aliens chattering on from a distant planet at times.

Do you know how worthless it is to hear a random stranger debating whether they should buy free-range eggs or grassfed eggs? It's utterly banal. Oh, even better was the day I heard someone literally think, *I was today-years-old when I realize that we check the eggs to make sure they aren't broken.*

The only good my "power" has ever done me is I once predicted a lightning storm thanks to the random musings of a meteorologist on the other side of the continent. Other than that, I get nothing from my "gift." If anything, it's a curse. Once everyone found out I was slightly telepathic, no one dared to speak to me for fear that they would accidentally think one of their deep dark secrets in my direction. Not that anyone has time to hold secrets around here.

Between the vampires and the bears, our lives are lived between a salt-circle and a shotgun. Just magical enough that putting a broom over the front door will keep out a malignant spirit about 75% of the time, but not quite magical enough to ward off the natural world, so we all carry a firearm or two to protect our animals and homesteads.

So, no, this is no place for a human. The technolyzed though, the human+, those who are half-machine, half-human, they come.

They come for glory and death, and occasionally, if they have the right parts, we use them as bulls.

Polar nights in the Wastes are said to be the remnant of a long-forgotten curse. People say that the ancients desolated the mountains of the far north so thoroughly that no mortal man could walk their slopes, and to my knowledge, it's true. No mortal man has ever stepped foot on the edge of our little village, if you could even call it that.

The fire is dimming. I worry that the wind howling outside will somehow force its way in and extinguish the flame.

Though it is nearly noon, the sun still has yet to rise. Were we farther south, we might be able to catch the barest of glimpses of the sun above the mountaintops in about an hour, but I don't expect such sights to grace my windows for another few weeks. The solstice night may be over for the rest of the world, but here in the Wastes, the coldest days are yet to come.

It is cold right now, and while Astra and I are wrapped and buried under a pile of blankets, I fear the chill will be the death of her. I've seen the headlines: "Newborn left to freeze to death in a stroller," "Another case of SIDS claims the life of Celebrity so-and-so's second child," and "Close your shutters parents: New strain of flu on the rise."

I should get up and tend to the fire. The solstice isn't over until the sun rises, and so many evil spirits wait for the Yule fires to peter out for the opportunity to sneak their way into the homes of unwitting mortals.

River's bark draws me from my pondering of the fire, and Astra stirs in my arms. Her little fists clench and unclench as she, once again, stretches her way out of the swaddle I had her in. The little escape artist has wormed her way out of no less than four swaddles in the few hours she has been earthside. Makes me anxious to see what kind of sticky situations she'll be able to get herself out of as she gets older.

"Come here, girl," I call River over to the armchair.

The dog trots her way up to me, tail wagging, happy for the attention.

"Are you hungry?"

The dog doesn't answer, but a little cry from my baby tells me the answer for her.

"I know you're hungry. Let's see what this mama has on offer."

I tug my gown aside, unclasping the ties that keep the garment together. Only a few short hours since becoming a mother and already nature takes hold to feed my young. My breasts are tender and full. If you've ever felt the sensation of having a blister full of puss, it's a lot like that, only instead of it being the result of an injury, this is just what is supposed to happen. My boobs feel like a pair of giant balloons attached to my chest. The only relief I will get must come from a tiny mouth only just learning how to suckle.

Astra hasn't perfected her latch yet. It's clumsy and over-eager. I wince as the gummy mouth clamps around my nipple, but within moments, Astra corrects her latch and the liquid gold flows from my bosom to her tummy. When I tried to hand-express, the colostrum I produced was thick and creamy, and I sighed in relief. It was a small victory, the goddess's nectar delivered to my babe via the conduit of my body. It's a pretty amazing thing.

I felt a distinct sense of pride at seeing those first droplets.

In a lot of ways, it was the first time my body had ever done anything the correct way without any fuss. Biology works in my favor when magic was never reliable. Though, as my mother would say, "Some magics are embedded in our DNA, and when they are called upon, they always per-form perfectly so long as our bodies are healthy and able to meet the need."

I can't help but roll my eyes at her. There is very strict science behind the female body's ability to raise and care for its spawn. There is no magic about DNA. She would disagree.

Maybe that's why I could never do magic. It's never felt real to me. Quite frankly, as far as I'm concerned, it isn't real. What has magic ever done for me other than to make my life worse?

What has science ever done for you other that poison your land?

My body tenses. The muscles of my back and neck seize up in fright as the whisper cascades over my psyche.

River whines, turning to the fireplace and barking.

The fire died, and I didn't even notice.

An icy wind flits through the house. River snarls at something I can't see. I bolt out of my chair, stiches be damned, and rush for the kindling, Astra tucked into my shoulder.

Foolish girl...

The whispers laugh at my footsteps. Astra begins to cry as River's barks rise in pitch. I need the matches. Where did I put them? The house is now so dark, I trip and stumble over the edge of the sofa and the leg of the table.

I shuffle into the kitchen, pain lancing through my whole body. The matches are in a drawer on the far left. I snatch them up and nearly empty the box of matches as I juggle them in one hand, but eventually I get it lit and race back to the fireplace.

You are not ready.

I fall to my knees and shove the tiny flame under the dried wood. It lights up with a sputter, but in a few short moments, the fire returns, and the cold wind evaporates out the windows.

I sit back on my bum. Astra yet cries, and I bounce her in my arms to get her to calm down.

River hasn't stopped barking, and up until now I've tuned her out in favor of solving the immediate problem, but now she is growling at something to my left. A strange smell greets my nose and I look down.

Astra's baby blanket has caught on fire!

I hurriedly unwrap her. Her little limbs flail and shiver with cold. My own hands burn on contact with the lit-up gossamer cloth. Without thinking, I throw the fabric into the fireplace. Deafened by my panic, I realize that Astra's cries have doubled, but when I check her little feet and hands, she is unharmed. I find no burns anywhere on her body and sigh in relief.

As I look into the fire, I can't help but mourn as Astra's name—so carefully embroidered into the fabric—is eaten up by the flames.

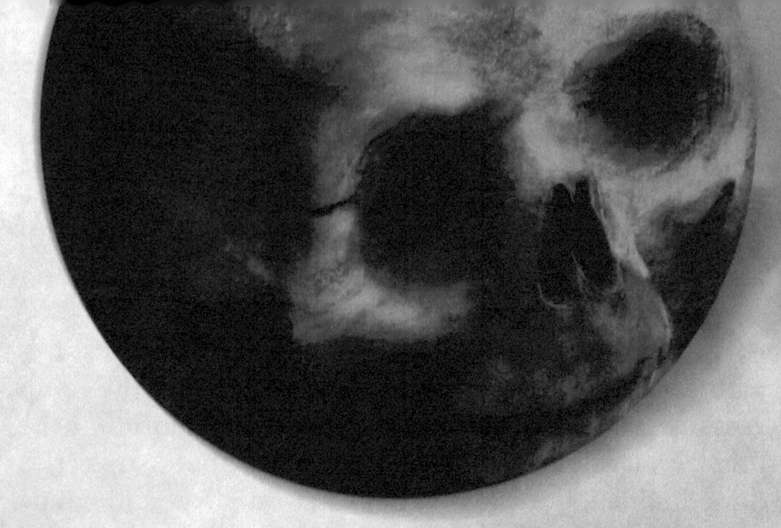

HUSH LITTLE BABY, DON'T SAY A WORD

There are so many mythical societies of women. We have the Amazons, fierce women warriors who lived their lives completely separate from men. Artemis and her hunters were sworn maidens who lived for the hunt and each other. The Valkyries, Odin's chosen warriors whose job was to spirit the souls of the worthy dead to Valhalla.

The League has no such equivalent.

Many would say that the Fireflies of Deus fit this societal mythos, but there are men and women within the various Firefly camps around the continent.

Beyond the border, though, is a society of women. We do not speak of them. They are not warriors. They are not hunters. They are not even magic-users. They are merely Disappointments. We mention them here because, as worthless as they are as Hexen, it is not advisable to go wandering into their village.

An Excerpt from *Hunting and Identifying Hexen* by Finnick Lockecraft, 1852 A.P.

There is a tradition in my family. All of the women are named for the stars. At least my mother calls it a tradition. I wouldn't know. Grandma died before I was born, so my mother is the only person I've ever known who is blood and kin.

She named me Danica because I was born the morning the sun returned to the north.

The climate here is tough, and we, the humans who live here, are just as gnarled and bitter. We are the descendants of witches, yet we are also the disappointments who could not so much as put out a candle with our magic.

My mother, Stella Hearthstone, hoped that because she had me with a half-elf that I would inherit some kind of control over any magical ability this place decided to manifest in me. Joke's on her. He was only an eighth elfish with not an ounce of magical talent in him. I'm as mundane as any normal human might be despite being 1/16th elf. Except for when I'm not mundane at all, in which case please give me a wide berth because I am not pleasant to be around when there are a dozen extra voices in my head.

Stella dumped him the moment she found out she was pregnant with me, bidding him begone as is the custom of our people. He disappeared to who-knows-where, and I've never exactly been in want of a father, so I cared too little to find out.

That is how children come to be in Mountain View. We keep the males around long enough to breed and then shove them to the curb. I didn't want to carry on in the tradition though. I didn't want to stay in Mountain View. I wanted my baby to have a father. Well, hopes and wishes amount to jack-diddly-squat in the Wastes.

It was the spring of my twenty-first year that David came into my life—a human+ stepping into the Wastes during a time when the sun holds power over the darkness. He wandered into our village at the end of spring, summer just beginning to bloom to life. At that time of year, the sun never sets, so the creatures of the night are at their weakest. I fell in love with the idea of him instantly.

I had hoped that David would whisk me away from this place. Carry me like a princess to the lower, milder climates of the world. Maybe he would even clear me to undergo techolyzation. If I were augmented, life would be so much easier. I've read whole textbooks about the benefits of augmentation: extended lifespans, delayed aging, even being able to record the events of your life as they happen. I could be stronger and/or prettier. I could be more charismatic, more intelligent.

Maybe the augmentations would even quiet the pathetic little storm of magic in me that whips up every so often.

"Danica, if it was but within my power, I would shake the world for you."

David was my ticket to such a life. If I could get him to fall in love with me, surely, he would save me from the horrid place. For a time, I was certain I had achieved just that. He started talking about taking me south and introducing me to his family. I didn't expect him to go off and die at the hands of a puny vampyre.

He didn't even realize I was pregnant when he went traipzing off.

So there I was, pregnant and alone—not much different on that front, really. Lots of women get left to raise a child on their own, especially when that is one of the given dogmas of our people. Every woman in Mountain View has had their children sans a male-parent, but at least a handful of them have their life partners around to be a secondary parent. But for those of us who don't choose that option, it's single-parenthood for the win. My mother had me on her own. So did my grandmother and my grandmother's grandmother, but it's always different when it happens to you.

David wasn't even a real technomancer. I found out later and laughed and laughed and laughed. He was just an adept trying to make a name for himself before the next round of trials. He was probably hoping that by getting a few hunts under his belt, he would be looked upon favorably by the council and qualify for ascension.

He was a fool.

That's not the way it works, but clearly, he never knew that. Because of his foolishness, he'll never know what it truly means to grow up. Just like Peter Pan, he died on some fairytale adventure, forever twenty. He'll never know greatness or hardship. He'll never know his true potential or if he really truly was just destined to be a loser. He'll just never know. Thus is the bliss of death-invoked ignorance.

He'll never know Astra either, too busy gallivanting off into the caves armed with every manner of weapon except a simple wooden stake.

I do hope Astra doesn't inherit his aptitude for sense of the most common variety.

My baby has been born into a frozen wasteland where so few of us yet remain. The birth was easy enough. I had a wonderful midwife, and the elves of the frozen woods, with all their years of knowledge and experience, send us gifted doctors to tend our hurts and ails.

It was everything that came after that I didn't expect.

I never tell my mother about the blanket. She doesn't even notice it's gone missing.

Throughout human history, many have heard the stories of witches stealing babies from their mothers' teet. She comes in many forms. Baba Yaga, Grylla, Yuki-onna, etc.

None of these witches made the voyage to Deus. Baba Yaga couldn't be bothered to leave her chicken-legged hut in the old world. The idea of moving away from the splendors of an already ignorant people just didn't appeal to her.

Grylla couldn't leave her Yule laddies. Who would take care of them if she left? And all of the unwanted children, who would take them under their wing if not her?

Yuki-onna, on the other hand, could not help but ask, who would torment the humans if she left? The answer to that question of course is simple: if all of the horrors lurking in the shadows disappeared, humans would have no problem tormenting each other.

Excerpt from "Second Coming:
The Pilgrimage to Deus"
By Moreen Hamilton 1845 Aventu Post

TWO WEEKS LATER

A blizzard shrieks in rage over our little village. Its anger is a welcome reprieve from the silence. I've not seen a single soul other than my mother since Astra was born. No one comes to visit. No one comes to help. I am to be given all the time in the world to bond with my baby. I've never suffered such a distinct loss of privacy and felt so alone at the same time.

I can hear Astra crying through the bathroom door. I hear her even over the sound of the shower bulleting down around my head. She's safe in her bassinet, displeased about being put down but safe. All I want is clarity. Just a few moments of quiet. A few moments of solitude. A few moments of not being needed.

I'm in the shower for far too long. The water goes cold.

I step out of the shower and look at myself in the mirror. My body is rife with the evidence of childbirth. At the peak of my pregnancy, Astra rode high. The women of the villiage would gush over how perfect my baby bump was, globular and perfectly round. My mother even said I was the spitting image of the mother goddess, heavy with child before the sun would be born from her waters.

Now, my tummy, devoid of a babe, is distended, a grotesque lump that sits under my heavy breasts. They too used to be "perfect." Now they hang, long as a harpy's and full of milk. The discomfort of being a milk cow is real. I always knew that I would want to breastfeed any babies that I had. It's customary when formula is so expensive and far away. I didn't expect it to come at such a high cost.

The pain of a clot. The swelling of my milk coming in. The chapping of my nipples as my hungry infant suckles greedily from them. The fevers... When the first fever hit after my milk came in, my mother came home to me passed out on the floor. I'd forgotten to eat. Hel, I'd forgotten to drink water. I was dehydrated and low on blood sugar.

That's the reality of caring for a newborn. It is no pain I would wish on an unwilling participant.

But I would do anything for Astra. She is so small. So precious. Even if I need moments away from her to maintain my own sense of self, she is my world.

By the time I am finished in the bathroom, my baby is inconsolable. River has her paws up on the edge of the bassinet, her wet nose nudging at the squirming bundle in its depths. She pads out of the way as I come around and pick Astra up as gently as I can, avoiding the rapidly waving fists she uses to further express her displeasure at being left alone.

"I'm sorry, little one. I needed to get clean. It's important for mama to take care of herself, too."

I let the towel drop to the floor as I settle in the rocking chair and allow her to latch onto my left breast. It's her favored side. On the floor, River curls up around my feet. Who needs socks when you have a warm furry body ready and willing to nestle around your feet?

As Astra suckles, my mind drifts. Did I remember to take out the trash? What am I going to cook for dinner? Should I try swaddling Astra in a different blanket tonight? She didn't seem to like the last one.

I don't notice when Astra drifts off to sleep, but at some point, her lips go slack and her head lolls deeper into my elbow. I look down into her peaceful face. My baby's breath is warm against my skin.

In this rare quiet moment—probably the quietest I have gotten since I brought my little star earthside two weeks ago—I gaze at this little creature my body helped me bring into this world. Fair-skinned with a tuff of pitch-black hair, she is perfect.

While she was born underweight, her cheeks have rounded out as she gains more substance. My milk has done her good. She is no longer the itty-bitty thing that the doctor fussed and fretted over. She even has a few of those oh-so pinchable baby rolls forming on her thighs and belly.

I shift in my seat, and for the briefest of moments, I get a glimpse of my starling's clear blue eyes. I hope they stay blue. Mother says there is no way they'll stay such a light shade. Apparently, no one in our family has had blue eyes since my great, great grandmother, but I can hold out for hope.

She drifts back to sleep, and I am tempted to follow her, so I shuffle my way out of the rocking chair. Ugh, just getting up hurts. River barks as I disturb her, but her tail wags happily as she follows me around the house despite how slowly I walk. Childbirth may be something my body was made to go through, but that doesn't make the process of growing and delivering a human being any easier.

My abdominal muscles have weakened, my joints have stiffened, and even now this process of feeding my child robs the calcium from my very bones. As I make my way from the nursery to my bedroom, I pass through the living room of our humble abode. Mother is late. It isn't surprising considering the weather. She is probably hunkering down at the shop until nature calms enough for her to safely trek her way through the newly fallen sheets of snow. It's a very real possibility that I won't see her until morning.

I hope the dogs are alright. I gave them plenty of bedding, and when I saw the weather coming in, I put an extra serving of piping hot slop for all of them. I glance outside the nearest window. I know the dogs are all hunkered down in the shed. I know I won't see them, but I'm hoping to see my mother's familiar lantern swaying along the path.

What I see instead stops my heart in my chest.

Inhuman eyes glow a dusty magenta in the darkness. They blink in my direction as I stand frozen in plain view of the window. The luminescent orbs circle the walkway then vanish, never having left my form. They're just gone as though they were never there.

I rush to the kitchen and grab the salt off the top of the stove. I fumble with the lid, ignoring the noises of protest Astra gives at being jostled, and pour a line of salt across the thresholds of the front and the back doors. As an extra measure, I grab the broom and lay it across the first stair, bristles facing east.

I hurry to up my bedroom and lock the door. More salt goes down in front of the two windowpanes before I run out of the precious ingredient.

Where I would normally settle Astra in her bassinet beside my bed, I don't dare to do so tonight. I tuck her into my chest, make sure the pillows and blankets are nowhere near her face, and curl my body around her.

River jumps up on the bed as normal, settling at my feet, but she does not curl up to sleep. Instead, she lays with her forelegs extended, her hind legs bunched beneath her, and her head upright, eyes trained toward the window and ready to spring at the slightest indication of danger. It's a small comfort but sleep does not come.

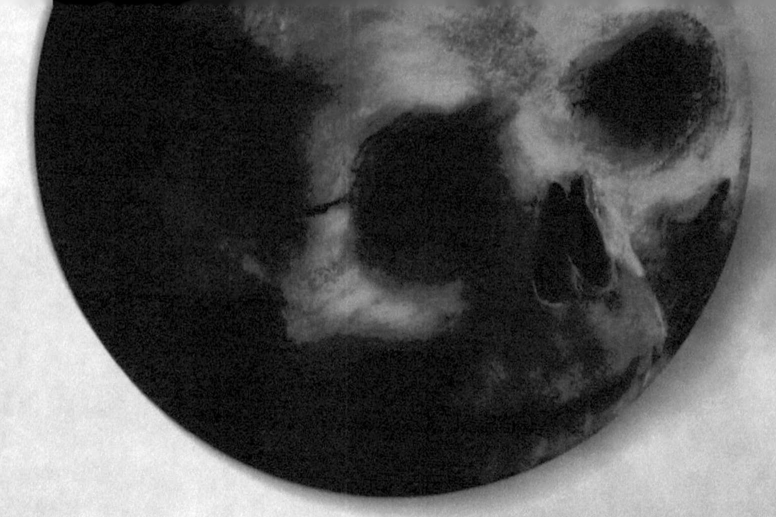

III

Mama's Gonna Buy You a Mockingbird

It is the nature of primates to sleep with their young. The infants are born so small and helpless that a babe left unattended for even a moment is an easy meal for even the most minor of inept predators.

So, sleep the way your infants want to sleep, girls, be that in the bassinet or at the breast. How could something so natural be restricted so strictly?

An excerpt from *Love from the Breast* by Mother Gothal, a wiccan midwife

Hours later, Mother arrives home in a tizzy. Her panic is enough to set River off. My loyal companion bolts from the bed and circles the woman's legs as she races through the door, knocking salt this way and that upon her entrance.

"Danica, Astra! Are you both alright?"

I haven't slept at all. How am I supposed to when I can see those eyes still tracking me in the darkness?

Astra stirs from sleep and cries. I can practically feel Stella slump in relief despite her being on the opposite side of the house. I shush my baby and roll her into the opposite breast. She suckles eagerly enough. I hope she'll nod back off to sleep without much of a fuss.

"We're here, mother. We are fine."

"Oh, my darling."

Stella appears in the doorway, my mother's face is tear-streaked and wind-burnt as though she ran here through the blizzard outside.

"Old Woman Rosette was screaming about a baby being taken."

My breath catches in my chest.

"What?"

"Ole Bonnie Jo and Old Woman Rosette were holed up with me in the shop when the weather turned nasty. You know that old hag is only half a seer on a good day, but she just happened to have a vision right there in the middle of the vegetable aisle. She just starts screaming her head off that 'Someone's taking the baby! Someone's taking the baby! Stop them!' So, I came as soon as I could."

I frown. "But Astra is the only baby in town."

"I know. That's why I'm so glad to find you both okay."

"Yes, Mama, we're fine," I say even as my heart pounds and the adrenaline rises once again in my body.

There was someone outside the house. There was someone outside *this* house, and I did everything I knew, used every old witch's tale I could think of, to keep a potential supernatural invader out of my home. I don't know if it worked as intended, but I am here. Mom is here. Astra is here. Everyone is safe.

"If it wasn't Astra that Rosette saw, who was it?"

In a community full of women, there are only so many small children around. As of right now, I can count them all on a single set of hands and still have a few fingers left over.

"No idea. With this storm, we likely won't know anything until tomorrow."

"But why would anyone steal a baby? There are so few here."

"Bonnie Jo thinks it's one of the vampyre grunts looking to gain favor with the queen. Says she's pretty sure the little thing will be returned home by the end of the week."

I can only hope Bonnie Jo is right, but a part of me doubts deeply.

The next morning, word arrives by raven from the town center. We find out that the missing baby was actually Joanna Johans' four-year-old daughter. Stella wasn't wrong to call Old Woman Rosette "half-a-seer." Just like the rest of us, any witchiness in her blood is so diluted that she is less of a witch and more of a witch-lite, but she is respected for her "talents" of foresight. Half of her visions are outright wrong. The other half are misnomers in some way or another. She once foresaw a flood that turned out to be a minor plumbing issue. There was another time when she saw the mayor having a heart attack of some sort. When asked later, Mayor Krestfield said she was suffering from just a bit of heartburn. Not terribly unlike, as in this situation, seeing a baby disappear when it was really a toddler. Also, she never sees anything ahead of when it happens. Her visions are that of the present, so fairly useless aside from being a live but highly inaccurate broadcast of current events. The particularly mean members of the community call her Bad News Rose.

That community, right now, is having a town meeting, and while I am loathe to leave the safety of my home, I must brave the cold and the dark.

Even in the darkness, if you want to survive out here, there are things that must be done. Firewood needs to be chopped, meat needs to be hunted down, snow needs to be shoveled, and news needs to be dispersed. When the power is down and all our broadcasting equipment is snowed in, the only way to do that is through a good ole-fashioned town meeting.

I have Astra strapped to my front as I go out to tend to the dogs. River, as my lead dog, gets the special privilege of coming and going from inside the house. She skips alongside Astra and me on our way to the dog shed. My team are all eager for breakfast. Grace, Bonnie, Kali, and Darleen are all huddled up together, licking and grooming each other the way girls do. Yehrik, Henry, and Lightfoot are playing a three-way tug-o-war with a large hunk of dried animal hide. Lilith, River's beta and second-in-command, oversees all of it with wise chocolaty brown eyes. She is the oldest of my pack; she likes to keep all the others in line. Though we've not run the sled since before Astra was born, I check on them every day, spending time with them to they are fed and happy. I want Astra to know them, and they were all eager to know her. Today is different though. Today, we run.

"Alright, team. Eat up! We've got a run on the calendar."

Every one of my dogs jumps up in excitement at the prospect of a run. They dig into their bowls with unbridled gusto, eating more ravenously than a pack of hyenas. But today's venture is not a supply run. Not in the way they are used to anyway.

While my people are not typically welcome south of the border, there are a few Aighnean businesses who will pass up the opportunity to make a few credits by trading with "them queer folk up north." Yay for capitalism and having resources that they couldn't possibly gain otherwise.

While we are lacking any substantial amount of currency like credits, dollars, or even gold, there is a far more valuable substance that we offer in trade to the League: aluminum, silicon, and copper.

Few countries have the same kind of endless reservoirs of natural metals as we do here. The radiation mixes with magic and hardens the skin of the earth. The result is a land rich with metal and mineral. We work together with the vampyres under the mountain. They give us the precious metals, and they take a cut of our earnings. Which is nothing to shake a tail feather at. The women of Mountain View are quite wealthy thanks to the land we live on. If only that land wasn't so poor in sustenance. If we want to eat anything other than potatoes or fish, we need to import it.

That's my job within the community. With my team of dogs, I'm the fastest musher around. The trip south normally takes anywhere between six or seven days to get there, but my personal best is a four and a half day run to the border. My mother said I was crazy to want to be a musher, but the moment I met River, I knew she was special. All I needed was a team to run behind her, and together we would claim greatness in all the lands of the north, and be lauded as heroine across the continent. We'd win some prize money, get our League citizenships, and kiss this frozen wasteland goodbye forever.

I was a fool.

Little did I know then, that while the League will let a wiccan like me race, they'll never let us inside their borders permanently, no matter how many times we might win.

Well, it was a young girl's hope, dashed to smithereens, but at least, the pay is good. I've amassed enough prize money to keep us afloat for at least a decade should work dry up, but that hasn't happened yet. With my team, we are the best modality of trade in and out of Mountain View. It makes my mother's shop prime real estate for anyone needing good supplies.

It's a good deal.

I've been on maternity leave, though, and it's time these dogs got a good run, though my trek today is not on a trade route. I merely wish to go into town to get the latest news on the storm and collect some reserves in case the power doesn't come back within a reasonable amount of time.

I wait patiently, aimlessly stroking their heads as they tuck in to their breakfast of slop: a trade-mixture of stew made from deer hoofs, hide, root vegetables, and various animal innards. They love the stuff more that life itself. Astra sleeps in her carrier, tucked in warm as a bug against my skin. She doesn't even bat her lashes when several of the dogs come up and give her little, hat-covered head a sniff.

"To set, pups!"

It's been nearly two months since I gave that command, yet they fall into their places as though I've hardly been gone a day. River, always the first to finish, barks in agreement, and within moments, my whole team of nine dogs have all lined up in formation in front of the sled. A few minutes more and all of them are hooked up to the gang-line ready to go on a run. Kali yips happily from her place as a wheel dog. Henry next to her tugs impatiently at his reins. In order behind them are Yehrik and Darleen, Bonnie and Grace—they're my twins; they must be next to each other--Lightfoot and Lilth and finally River. My team and I are the only sled team in Mountain View. That makes it our job to run supplies in and out of the village.

I settle Astra in a basket that I've strapped to the bed of the sled, making doubly sure that she is wrapped up tight in her swaddle and blankets. She makes a small fuss at being set down away from my breast, but she settles right in as I call "hike!" and the dogs pull us away. Within moments, she falls asleep to the steady lope of the sleigh.

The landscape is covered in snow and ice. The trees barely show any green at all. That's how densely the snow has fallen over their branches.

The tundra of the Wastes lends well to silence. There is a quiet here that I have never found anywhere else. David called it eerie. I find it a comfort, a frozen world, locked eternally in the embrace of winter. Even in the polar night, there is beauty in the purity of freshly fallen snow.

When the sun does come out, the view is spectacular. The beams reflect off the fallen snow like crystals peaking up from within the deepest parts of the earth. It's the best part of living this far north. In the lower parts of the continent, they have the privilege of taking the sun for granted. South of the Northern Meridian, the sun never leaves the land. Here in the Wastes, the sun disappears for three months of the year. It can seem like longer, too, with how moody the weather is.

This time of year, however, I don't start to see actual grass and soil until I cross into the mountainous peaks that mark the border between Aighneas and the Wastes.

It was on one such venture south that I met David. He was fascinated by the fact that I hailed from the Wastes. Such a pretty girl from such a dreary state. I couldn't help but laugh at the absurdity of his sentiment, but he made me smile.

I think he thought I would be able to guide him north, and I suppose I did eventually. I just didn't realize what he would accomplish by coming here which, in the grand scheme of things, ended up being nothing. David was killed by a vampyre just days after his arrival. He was a fool about it too. Everyone knows it is unwise to hunt a vampyre within the very cave systems that house the entire colony.

The vampyres lurk inside their mountain caves, coming out only to frighten the living and feed on our fears. They don't take our blood. Not anymore. In many ways, to do so would be to cull their livestock before the population has replenished. Instead, they take the occasional sip on our life-force and bask in our wintry nightmares. It is not enough to sustain them at full capacity, but hexen can't live in their full magical might these days anyway. With the witches all but extinct, the hexen masses have all but disintegrated. The few witches left hide in their hovels, never daring to show their face lest the League find and burn them, and the lycans and the vampyres do the same.

We run by the light of my lantern, the beam focused on River as she leads us through the dim polar night. I trust her wolflike-senses to guide us sure-footed into the town.

It isn't long before I reach the center of town where I find that most everyone has gathered. Huddled against the cold around a burning oil barrel, Mountain View gathers to give attention to our illustrious mayor. Camryn Krestfield, a mousy waif of a woman who inconsistently has the ability to sway people to do whatever she asks, has been the leader of our little community for nearly fifteen years. As she addresses everyone gathered, I can tell she is having a particularly off day when it comes to her persuasive nature.

"Everyone, please stay calm. With that blizzard passing through, we have more pressing—"

"What could be more pressing than a missing child?!"

Yeah, today, her gifts are definitely not working. The threat of a riot rustles through the crowd.

There is discussion of someone going to the caverns to speak to the vampyres. Bonnie Jo's thought has spread throughout the town, and it's the next most perfectly reasonable thing, but doubt sits heavy in my stomach. Eventually Joanna steps forward herself, a travel bag and weapon already strapped to her back.

"I'm going to the mountains to confront them myself. I'm not gonna let them take my little girl like this."

"Your girl is going to be fine, Joanna," says Camryn. "Just let the vampyres have their whatever-it-is-they-have. Little Emmy will be returned to you right as rain. The vampyres haven't taken nor hurt anyone in decades. Why would they start again now?"

"I'm not taking that risk."

"Don't be a fool, girl," says one of the other women. "If you march up there demanding blood, they'll be down here taking it themselves before dark."

"I'll come with you, Joanna," says Abigail Garret.

"Count me in, too."

"No, Ivory. We need to get the power going again in town. This whole place won't last long without some form of power."

"Oh, come off it, Camryn! There's plenty of firewood to go round. This is Joanna's girl we're talking about here. Since when do we forsake our little ones to the winter night?"

The mayor wilts. "Oh, very well. Go to the caves but get back here quickly. We need to get this place back up and running again."

There are grumbles of agreement, pats on the back, and various wishes of good luck as the group of women start to wander off in various directions.

"I don't think it's a vampyre," I say.

They all turn to look at me.

"Last night, there was something outside my house. It..." My throat clenches around my voice box. "It wasn't no vampyre trying to borrow a baby for a favor. It was..."

I freeze up, my voice locked in my throat. All of these older women turned toward me, looking at me with judgement and skepticism, it makes me want to disappear into the nearest snow bank.

"What was it, Danica?"

"I don't know what it was, but I'm pretty sure it wanted to hurt Astra and me."

"How do you know it wasn't a vampyre?"

"Vampyre eyes don't glimmer magenta in the night."

"Magenta!" laughs one of the elders. "What the hell kinda color is magenta! Ain't nothing with eyes that glow pink at nighttime!"

"That's what I saw."

They choose to ignore me.

The mayor turns to the women closest to her.

"I've seen this before. Post-partum paranoia. Poor dear needs to have her mother keep a closer eye on her, if you ask me."

"I'll be sure to send Lucifer to check on her. In the meantime, I say we get Stella down here to escort her home."

"Don't bother. My dogs will get me home just fine."

I turn to leave, Astra cradled in my arms. The child's mother goes with a handful of others to face the queen. I hope against hope that my instincts are wrong. I'm not worried for their safety. Vampyres may be terrifying to mere mortals, but we are the people of the Wastes. We've lived alongside them for generations. We know they can be reasoned with. Still, it is a pointless venture. They won't find the girl with the colony. I am almost certain of it.

While I'm in town, I take the time to help mother at the storefront. Astra does some tummy time while I help restock the shelves and take a stock of what I'll need to trade for the next time I head south. None of our stores are out, but something tells me I'll have to do a run soon.

No matter. That issue is a problem for future Danica. In the meantime, I make sure there is enough oil to keep the lanterns burning and set some wax to hang dry for some new candles. The only wax we have left, however, is gray. Not my favorite color for a candle, but it'll do well enough. Stella is the one who is superstitious about that kind of thing anyway. Me, I just light 'em and leave 'em. She especially hates it when I insist on blowing them out rather than using a proper snuffer.

"Scatters the good intentions," she says, and I would always respond with something along the lines of, "Yeah, well maybe it will send some bad ones down toward Karen Mulberry. Goddess knows she's in need of a karma check."

Eventually, I take my leave, tired of the number of customers who come in and glance in my direction as though

I had no right to be there. They think me queer in the head for my earlier display.

I saw Ms. Wolfston taking peeks at me through the canned goods shelves. A barrel of corn on the cobb is not nearly as good a hiding place as an actual corn field. Though, it is comical to see her trying to hide her shifty demeanor through a pair of corn ears.

Sara Janson comes in with her teenage daughter. The pair gossip worse than anyone else in town, and I can hear the way their whispers trail at my footsteps.

<She's only like two years older than me. That's what you get for chasing a dream to the south.>

The teenager doesn't realize that my head is an unfocused broadcasting station. Her thoughts ring clearly in my ears. Just to mess with her, I answer her unspoken comment with one of my own.

"I'd rather chase a futile dream than end up buried under ice and rock like some of these old biddies."

The teen blushes from the roots of her hair all the way to the edge of her turtleneck collar. Sara at least has the good sense to give her daughter a chiding look.

Let them think what they want.

It is impossibly darker by the time I have the dogs set up to run us back home. River is on edge. I can practically feel the tension rolling off her into the snow. I grab her jaw in both hands and scratch her ears as I talk to her.

"It's okay, girl. Just get us home where mama can make up a nice warm fire and serve up some food for all our bellies."

River yips in understanding.

As I'm double-checking that Astra's seat is secure, I hear a crunching in the snow behind me.

"They don't want you to be right."

It's Old Woman Rosette.

"Who? What?"

"Something's changed up in the mountains as of late. Something evil. They all feel it too, but none of them want to admit it."

"What are you talking about?"

"You take care of that baby, child. I fear they'll have to admit you're right sooner rather than later."

A shiver runs down my spine. Rosette, for all that everyone says she's a rusty old radio, has always creeped me out.

"I'll keep that in mind." I hurry into position on the sleigh, grab the guard rails, and shout, "Hike up, River! Hike!"

River takes off. Even though I don't turn back to check if the old senile woman is still there, I can feel her eyes on me the whole way out of town.

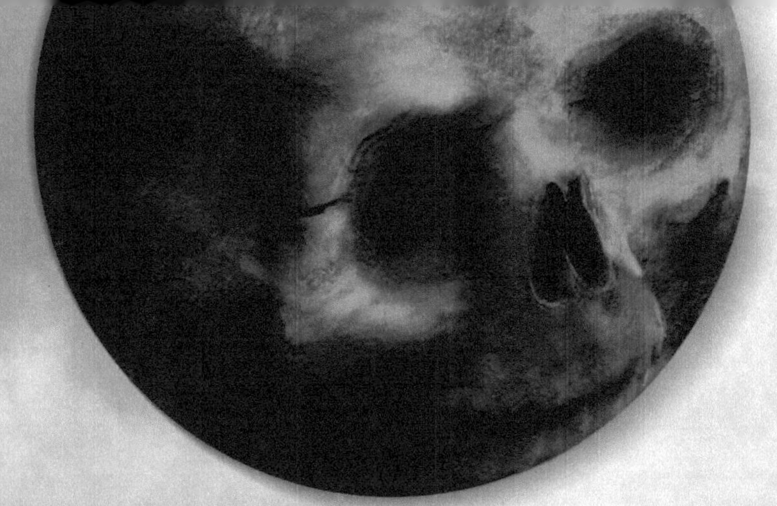

IV

ROCK-A-BYE, BABY, ON THE TREETOP

Twinkle, twinkle my north star.
How I wonder who you are.
Up above the world at night,
Like a diamond burning bright.

Twinkle, twinkle my north star,
How I wonder who you are.
Up above beyond the moon,
Guiding light, you are my boon.

Twinkle, twinkle my north star
How I wonder who you are.

One day soon, you'll fly away
With great wings, you'll make your way.

Twinkle, twinkle my north star
How I wonder who you are
But for now, you're safe and sound
In my arms here on the ground.

Twinkle, twinkle my north star
My sweet Astra, here you are.

Danica Hearthstone to her daughter.

The snow glows in the moonlight. Beneath the light of our dual moons, the world is lit in a soft lavender. Not a single sound breaks the silence. It is even quieter now than it was earlier.

True night descends on this northern wasteland, and with it, the snows begin anew. The wind whistles around us as we run. I hope I've bundled Astra warm enough in her basket. I can barely see more than five feet in front of me with how thick the blizzard is. Even as one who lives in this place, as one who has seen how dark the world can truly become, I can't help but feel like someone or something is watching. Out here in the middle of the tundra, there likely is something watching me: an owl prowling for a rabbit, wolves on the hunt, or a bobcat watching from a tree for its next unsuspecting meal to frolic by.

There are many things that watch the goings-on out here. And many of those things would leap at the opportunity to take an infant for a meal.

"Hike up, River!"

I push my dogs faster. We are minutes from home, and I cannot wait to cross the security of my gate and take refuge in my salt-sealed house.

A howl cuts through the wind behind us. Several of my dogs turn their heads toward the noise.

"Faster!" I shout as another answering howl comes from my right. I feel the first wolf before I see it. A brush of fur and teeth, and suddenly my dogs are tangled in their lines with a pair of wolves trying to yank them out of the harnesses.

The sled comes to a stuttering halt, knocking me and the sled sideways. Astra's basket stays tight to the bed, and my baby's wails ring out, louder than the fierceness of the elements around us. Knowing she is alive enough to cry, I reach for my shotgun.

"Bonnie! Grace! Away!"

I fire the weapon at the wolf that has its jaw around Bonnie's throat. My shot rings true, and the gigantic animal flails backward and away with a whimper. The second one, however, rounds on me. A beast of a wolf, all corded muscle and adrenaline, sprints straight toward me. I fire the shotgun again, but the kickback knocks me off balance. I land on my back with a hungry wolf launching itself atop of me.

Its jaws snap around the barrel of the shotgun. It gnaws at the metal, trying to work itself free to it can get its teeth in me.

"Get away, you devil!"

I kick the beast in the belly. It jumps and rolls away before leaping right back on top of me. Out of the corner of my eye, I see a third wolf running for the sled and my crying baby.

"Get off!"

I yank the gun back as hard as I can and jam the butt of it into the wolf's forehead. The animal rears back, stunned, and I hurry to the sled where I see River wrestling with the other wolf. She must have jumped in to defend Astra before the wolf could get to her. The dog is smaller than the wolf by at least 10 kilos but far more protective. She puts herself between the predator and Astra, snapping her teeth toward the larger wolf's underside.

"River! Get back!"

I peel out, launching myself behind my dog, and belly crawl to the basket with my baby inside. Astra is unhurt but screaming herself purple. I quickly untie the belts and braces that kept her safe, and curl her into my arms as the fight behind me rakes up in volume. With my baby tucked into the warmth of my fur coat, I put my back against the sled and pull a knife from my belt as River is shoved sideways by another wolf.

"Get back, you devils!" I shout, waving the blade in front of me. I whistle for my dogs. River and two others come to me. The rest, I can't see. Either they've scattered with the snap of the gang line or they're fighting their own battles. I don't know what to do, but I do know that I am willing to die before I let these wild dogs eat me, my dogs, or my baby. Even if that is my only choice...

My Gods, I'm going to die here. It's all I can think. *I'm going to die here.*

"Please, leave us alone!" I scream. I'm crying, frozen tears in a frozen wasteland.

A deep howl echoes through my very bones, but it is not a wolf's howl.

A giant animal, coming up to my shoulders on all fours, lands in front of me. Its pure white fur is almost impossible to see in the snowstorm raging about us. All I can hear over the storm is the sound of snarls and barks as the great creature launches itself at the wolves. Whimpers fill the air as the beast dominates the pack.

There is a whirlwind of activity. I cover my face, hunching over my infant as the beast turns toward me.

"Please... Please, spare us."

My dogs cower. River presses herself into my side, but she doesn't seem have her hackles rising. Something wet touches the bare skin of my cheek. I peek out from under the hood of my coat.

The golden eyes of a massive wolf stare at me.

<You should have better care not to take your young out into the open so early in life.>

A feminine voice speaks inside my head. I've never experienced such a thing outside of the occasionally telekinetic broadcast, and no one has ever spoken to me via this method.

"What are you?"

The edges of the wolf's shape blurs before my very eyes. The snow, as if summoned to her form, spirals around her. The gust disperses, and in place of the wolf is a woman wearing nothing but the snow itself. Her skin is the purest of sliver. Brambles of thorns and ferns dress her arms and legs. Heat rises to my face as I notice the pertness of her small breasts, offset by the full curve of her hips.

"You're... you're a were—"

"Wolf-folk is the preferred nomenclature, if you don't mind. Come. Let's get you and your pack home before this weather gets much worse."

The woman rises up onto her feet, extending a hand toward me. Whether by some strange magic or by the adrenaline-leaving my system, I don't know, but I swoon.

The colic is back. Astra has been crying and screaming for hours. I'm so tired. All I want to do is close my eyes and sleep. All she wants to do is nurse and nurse and nurse. My body, my mind, can't handle it anymore.

I take us to the bath. Maybe, just maybe a nice warm bath will calm the both of us down. Astra loves the bath. She splishes and splashes and plays with all her little toys.

Normally when I do this, my mother is here to help me in and out of the bathtub. She makes sure that I can clean myself as well as Astra, and keeps watch so I can close my eyes, but I think I've done this enough now that I don't think I have much to worry about.

I wash us both carefully. Astra is in her little baby bathtub—a half-cut barrel with a water pillow tucked inside to cushion her. I filled it only enough that the water comes about an inch or two up her body. Deep enough to play in. Shallow enough that if she somehow flopped over, her nose and face should stay above the waterline. She kicks her little legs, laughing and slapping the water like it was the best game in the world. For all I know, it probably is. I'm not exactly a good judge of that kind of thing anymore. I let myself lean against the edge of the tub and just close my eyes for a moment.

I can't help but smile as the sounds of her enjoyment as she plays and plays and plays.

I wake up to the sound of silence. The water is freezing cold.

Did my mom come home and take Astra out of the water?

"Mom!? Are you home!"

I lift my head up and look into Astra's tub.

My baby's head is under the water.

"Astra!!"

I shout as I bolt up and out of the tub. I hear a laugh, followed by a spitting sound and then a raspberry.

There she is. Sitting just like I last saw her, playing and kicking in her little bathtub. The water is still warm.

In a panic, I yank the plug out of the drain and remind myself to breathe. In, 2, 3, 4, 5, 6. Out, 5, 4, 3, 2, 1.

Wait... Why am I even in the water? The last thing I remember was being on the sled and the attack and then...

"Ah, you're awake."

A beautiful woman kneels on the floor mat, suds trailing up and down her forearms as she rinses the soap out of the bath sponge.

"You?"

"I put you in the water to warm you back up. Your baby has quite the love for splashing."

"How did you get into my house? I salted all of the entryways."

She laughs. "That's all well and good for evil spirits, but my kind won't sit there and count each grain of salt before we cross a salt-line. Come now. Let's get you both out of the bathtub."

The woman picks up my baby, and Astra, who always screams at being taken out of the bath, laughs. I sit there, stunned. My baby's first laugh and it comes from a stranger's touch.

"Who are you?" I ask finally after I am wrapped in a bathrobe and dry, my hair wrapped up in a towel lest my locks catch the chill in the air.

"Oh, I beg your pardon. I forget that humans are very sensitive about sharing their names with one another. My name is Naomi. You are?"

"Danica, and this is Astra."

"Yes, your little one told me her name. You've a bright little nugget here."

What? Astra isn't talking yet. How could she...

"What do you mean she told you her name?"

"Just that. She told me, in her own little way. The well of magic is strong in your offspring."

"That makes no sense. Magic doesn't work for my people. All of our abilities are caddy-wonk at best."

"Perhaps your womb has overcome the curse of the Wastes."

Che, not likely...

I pull out a set of warm pajamas for Astra and hand it to the lycan as she diapers my baby's pale, little bottom, adding a dollop of diaper rash cream in the process. The woman carefully, as though handling spun glass, wraps the infant in the clothes: one arm, then the other, one little foot into the onesie, then the other, followed by a careful zip of the zipper. She even has the presence of mind to use her forefinger as a guard to keep the zipper from catching on Astra's skin.

"Why did you save us?"

"This place is harsh enough without a new mother and her babe being eaten by wolves. But really though. You shouldn't have been out there, especially when you are still on your after-birth bleed."

I inhale sharply. I didn't even think about that. Every predator for miles around must have been able to smell me.

I'm a fool.

"So why did you save us?"

"I told you, your daughter called to me. Tis the duty of my people to answer a witch's call."

"My baby is no witch."

She looks at me quizzically with her unnatural golden eyes. "Perhaps not yet, but she will be."

"No, that's not possible. She can't be a witch."

"Possibility is a difficult thing to measure. I don't think even a mother's word has the ability to forbid her child from embracing their heart's path."

"Astra is not a witch. None of us are. It's impossible!"

"Is it?"

In the low light, the woman's eyes glint a sparkling magenta, and my stomach nearly lurches out my throat.

"It was you."

"What?"

I snatch Astra out of her arms and bodily shove her away from the changing table. "You were the one outside my house!" I yell. "You're stalking us!"

"I am not stalking you—"

"Get out!"

The lycan flinches but backs up. When she next speaks, her face twists into a spiteful sneer. "And you people wonder why the hexen call you Disappointments."

"We don't wonder about it at all. We know why we are Disappointments, and quite frankly, none of us care, so you can shove off back to whatever corner of the forest you crawled out of."

"How hospitable of you."

"I said, 'Get out'!"

"Alright, alright." She holds up her hands as though I was about to turn a gun on her. "I know my place, but if you find yourself in need again, just howl."

As if I was some animal...

As she steps out of the door, the woman looks back at me with sad eyes. "I'm not your enemy, Danica. I'm sorry I frightened you the other night." She turns and leaves, seeming to drift across the snow.

I shut the door on the lycan and pray for patience.

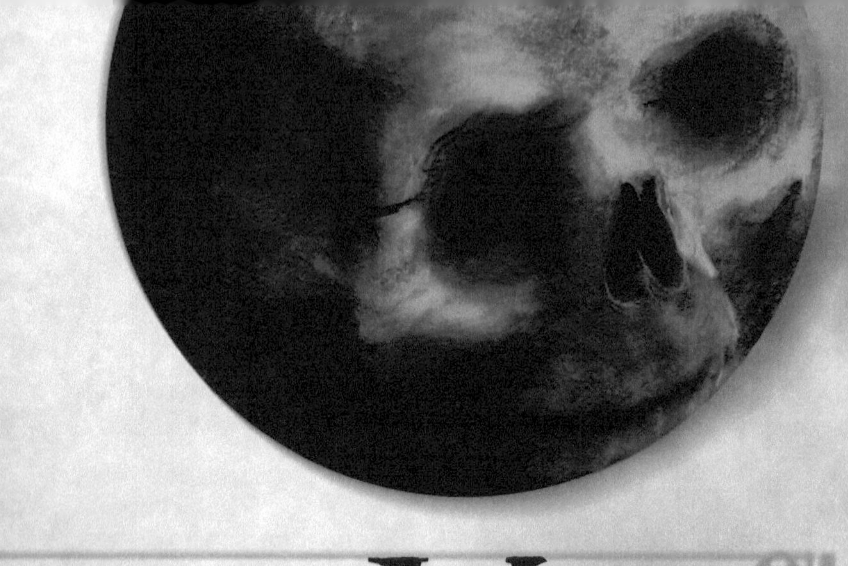

V

WHEN THE WIND BLOWS,
THE CRADLE WILL DROP

ONE WEEK LATER

One of my dogs dies of the wounds taken by the wolf pack. My sweet Bonnie, who'd never so much as barked at a stranger, took a nasty bite to the throat and shoulder. For a while, I thought she might make it, but then the infection set in. I had to put her down three days after the wolves attacked us. I was told it was the merciful decision.

I worry her sister, Grace, will go to meet her. She sits and mopes around the barn all day. I haven't been able to get her to eat even a bite of food since Bonnie's passing.

Something is off. I can feel it settling as deeply in my bones as the chill coming off the mountain.

Three days after the town meeting, Joanna, Ivory, and the others return from the caves empty-handed. The vampyres knew nothing about the missing girl, and they even allowed the women to search the caverns to their hearts' content. Nothing, not even any evidence of foul play. The only conclusion that can be drawn is that the vampyres are innocent.

Joanna is heartbroken. I cannot even imagine her pain and distress. Her child is gone, and we have no way of finding out where she has been taken.

I have half a mind to visit her in the village, but she takes the decision from me and comes to visit me instead.

Knock, knock, knock.

River starts barking instantly. She doesn't normally bark when someone is at the door. She must still be on edge from what happened last week.

"Oh, Joanna. I wasn't expecting you to come all the way out here."

The woman stands there, expectant. Behind me, Astra is playing on the floor. River growls. I shoot her a quick look, reminding her to be polite, before turning back to Joanna.

"So, what are you doing all the way out here?"

"I needed to speak to you about the thing you saw outside your house."

"What of it?" I feel like I'm forgetting something.

"Can I come in, first?"

Right, manners. I forgot those are thing people are supposed to offer one another.

"Of course. I mean, yes. Sorry."

River's growls intensify. I can't let her in with River acting like this.

"Just a second," I tell the other woman, grabbing River by the collar as I close the door. "You ridiculous animal. It's just Joanna. Where are your manners?"

I put the dog out the backdoor and return to let Joanna in, apologizing about the dog as I go. She gently steps into the house.

"Can I make you some tea or coffee?" I ask, remembering everything my mother ever taught me about hospitality and taking her coat to hang in the coat closet.

"Tea is fine."

I busy myself in the kitchen while Joanna settles herself in the living room. I shuffle through cabinets looking for a clean mug and our abysmal collection of teas, hoping against hope that we still had a bit of mum's favorite green jasmine tea or maybe we still have some of the black tea that we got from Aighneas six months ago. Unfortunately, I find we only have the earl grey left.

As I'm setting the kettle on the burn and cranking up the heat, Joanna calls out to me from the living room.

"I remember when Emily was this small. She was so cute but so time-consuming. I didn't think I would survive the newborn days, but weirdly enough, once we got past them, I missed them."

When I peek over the bar, I can see Joanna twiddling her fingers in front of Astra's face.

"Did Emily have colic at all?"

"Not really. Emily was a fairly easy baby. I really shouldn't ever have complained about raising a newborn. Now, the toddler years though... That was something else."

"Astra has colic a lot. Right now, I'm surprised she is okay with being set on the floor like this. Normally she would be screaming bloody murder at me."

"The hard times will pass."

The kettle starts to whistle. I'm quick to take it off the burner and pour it over the tea leaves. I inhale deep as the tea steeps. Earl grey may not be my favorite, but there is something lovely about a pot of fresh brewed tea. Once the timer goes off, I set up a tea tray and carry the spread out to my guest.

Once I've handed the woman her tea and settled across from her on the sofa, I ask Joanna to restate her question.

"What exactly did you see that night outside your door?" she asks.

Tension rockets up my entire body. I may not have known at the time what was stalking the woods outside my house, but I sure as Helheim know now. For some reason though, it doesn't feel right to tell her the truth. *I am not your enemy, Danica.* Golden irises, pale skin, and a body capable of transforming into a savage beast. I have not seen hide nor hair nor fur of Naomi since I sent her on her way. A part of me feels like I overreacted a bit. If I tell Joanna the truth, now, that a lycan was prowling outside my house, the town will launch a full-scale wolf hunt. I don't want that kind of blood on my hands.

So, I lie.

"I honestly couldn't tell you, Joanna. It was dark and the storm was coming in. All I saw were these twin magenta glows and a horrible feeling washed over me. I thought I could hear it talking to me, but you know how that is..."

"You heard it talking to you?!"

I nod. "In my head. I'm not telepathic, more like pseudo-telepathic, but I hear things from people every so often. I think... I think whatever it was tried to talk to me. It kept saying I wasn't ready. The last time—"

"This has happened before."

I swallow the bile from my throat.

"Astra was born on the Solstice, and I accidentally let the fire go out."

"Danica!"

"I know. I know. Something started calling through the cold, and I destroyed Astra's baby blanket trying to get the fire relit, but I don't think anything actually got in. When I saw that thing last week, I put salt-lines on all the doors and windows and just about broke the broom trying to hang it over the bedroom door. I think what I did worked because the next thing I knew it was morning and my mom was screaming at me to wake up because Old Woman Rosette had a premonition about a baby going missing."

Joanna's face darkens. "It wasn't a baby that went missing."

"I know. I'm so sorry, Joanna."

"It was my baby. My baby who I think wandered out of her bed and into the woods while I slept on, entirely unknowing of anything being wrong."

"It's not your fault."

"It is my fault. It can only *be* my fault."

I don't know what to say to that. I take a nervous sip of my tea and set my hand on Astra's belly. She is currently kicking a pair of balloons I tied to her ankles. She smiles every time they make a crinkling sound or catch on the light from the kitchen.

"I'm going to fix this."

"Joanna, you've already gone to the mountain colony. The vampyres had nothing to do with Emmy's disappearance. There's nothing you can do but wait."

"Yes, there is. There is always something that can be done."

Her tea sits untouched in her hand.

I sigh, leaving the woman to her thoughts while I take my empty cup of tea to the kitchen. As I run the water and rinse out the porcelain, I can't help but feel sorry for the woman. If it had been Astra, I don't know what I would do. Scream? Sure. Cry? Absolutely. Would I even be able to live with myself knowing that I couldn't protect my child?

I hear River start to bark again. I don't know what is with that dog. Since the moment Joanna arrived, she has been acting like a crazed chihuahua.

"Hey, is there anything I can get for you? The dogs need a run, and I'm thinking of heading into Aighneas soon for supplies, so—Joanna?"

As I round the corner, Joanna is nowhere to be found. Her coat has been taken off the rake, and the front door is wide open. Why would she leave the door open like that? I walk over to close it and stop cold halfway there. The two balloons I had tied to Astra's feet are now bumping along the ceiling. When I run forward to grab them, my baby is gone.

"Astra!"

She's taken my baby. Without a care for the cold, I race out of the house not even bothering to shove boots on my feet.

Joanna's cup of tea still sits steaming on the table.

"Joanna! Stop!" I yell as run into the snow. I see her running into the forest. She is holding Astra in her arms. I can hear my baby screaming in anger at being out in the cold. She isn't dressed warmly enough.

"Give me my baby!"

Barking greets me. The dogs. The dogs are faster than I am. I can't believe I'm about to do this.

"River!" I call. Already the husky is bounding across the tundra toward the tree line. I divert to the right and as quickly as I can I open the dog shed. My team, all seven of my remaining dogs, rush out. "Don't let her get away! Make sure she doesn't hurt Astra."

I don't know if my team understands what I am asking of them. They are sled dogs, not hunting dogs, but I'm desperate. I can only hope their instincts and River's leading barks will push them in the right direction.

I follow my pack into the forest. The broken twigs and thorns of the underbrush cut and whack at my legs. My hair is torn from my scalp as it catches on low hanging branches. I don't care. I keep running.

I have no way of knowing which way she's gone. I follow my dogs as they follow her.

Ahead of me, there is a hard thud followed by a whine. The next thing I know, I'm tripping over something warm. It's one of my dogs, Kali—the fastest member of the pack. There is blood sprayed all over the snow. Steams spirals up from where she has been gutted.

"Oh goddess. Please, don't let this happen."

I pick myself up and push on.

I hear howls echoing through the forest around me. Wolves? My dogs? I can't tell, but I do catch sight of Joanna's fiery red hair.

"Joanna!" I shriek. "Stop! Give me my baby!"

Naturally, she doesn't stop. She keeps running. If I only knew where she was going.

Two of my dogs are gaining on her though. I can see them: Darleen and Henry catching up to her. They attack from either side trying to trip her.

"Be careful with Astra!"

Their strike hits and Joanna goes tumbling down a ravine. Astra's cries intensify as the woman holding her falls down the incline.

<I'm coming, baby>, I think to her, hoping against hope that some part of the message makes its way through and soothes her. <I'm coming, I swear it! I won't let her take you.>

I follow Joanna over the edge of the ravine. I am suddenly and horribly reminded of my bare feet as the rocks slice through them. The sharp, stinging pain throws off my stride, and I tumble head over heels down the incline to land in a heap against a thick pine tree.

As I suck air back into my emptied lungs, I hear hard footsteps running past. I lift my head in time to see Joanna race by. I can't hear Astra crying anymore.

"Stop!" I yell.

At the sound of my voice, I hear the wails start up again. My poor sweet baby, she's alive. <I'm coming, my sweet star.>

I force myself to my feet and give chase. I'm so close. I'm gaining on her, using everything in my body to catch up to her. At my side, River continues to bark and growl. I don't know where my other dogs are. Lost in the forest? Caught by some animal? I don't know. I can't think about that right now.

My answer comes anyway.

Up ahead, in a snow-riddled clearing, something is buzzing. I can hear it penetrating my head worse than an out-of-tune violin. It rings through my skull, shaking it to pieces and trying to split it in two. My gods, if this is torture to me, I can't imagine what it's doing to my dogs. I almost stop, tears streaking through the mud on my face, but I keep going with my hands clamped over my ears.

"Joanna. Stop this! Stop this and we can talk! I can help you find Emmy."

"You can't help me!"

She runs into the clearing, and as I round the corner of the ravine, I see the source of the noise. A great circle of blackness sits at the center of the glade. It pulses with life. The edges seem to cut through the space. Around it, I can see the void waters rippling in anger like the water of the lake just before a great storm.

Joanna runs straight for it, her footfalls never hesitating, and I realize, this is where she was running to. This is where she was going.

Magic! Someone, some witch is helping Joanna with magic! A witch wants my baby!

"I'm sorry, Danica. I have to do this. For Emmy."

"You don't have to do this! Joanna!"

"I'm sorry." She steps into the portal.

"No!" I howl, but Joanna disappears as I trip over an exposed root.

"Astraaaaaaaa!" I scream and scream and scream until the world around me fades into a blizzard.

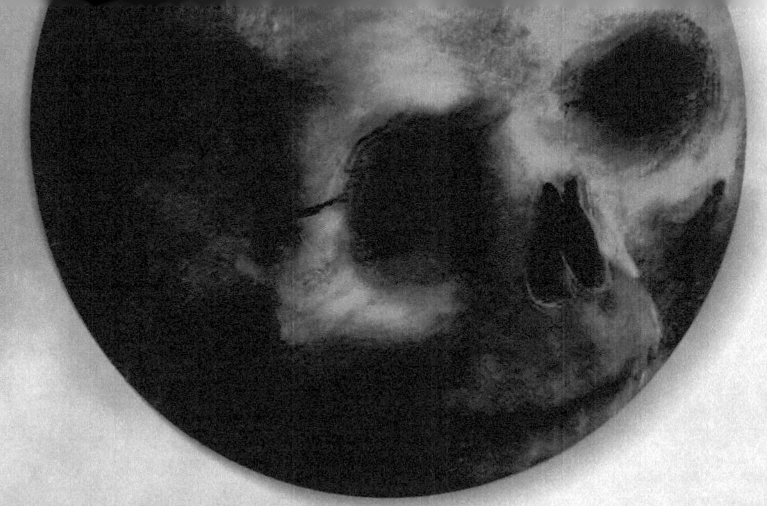

VI

HICKORY, DICKORY, DOCK

Have you known the Great White Silence,
not a snow-gemmed twig aquiver?
(Eternal truths that shame our soothing lies).
Have you broken trail on snowshoes?
Mushed your huskies up the river,
Dared the unknown, led the way, and clutched the prize?
Have you marked the map's void spaces,
mingled with the mongrel races,
Felt the savage strength of brute in every thew?
And though grim as hell the worst is,
Can you round it off with curses?
Then hearken to the Wild—it's wanting you.

Let us journey to a lonely land I know.
There's a whisper on the night-wind,
There's a star agleam to guide us,
And the Wild is calling, calling... let us go.

An excerpt from "The Call of the Wild"
A poem by Robert W. Service circa 1930-1945 C.E.

Wood pops as the fire cackles, louder than even the highest pitched radio. Water drips, drips, drips onto the stones, a metronome for an unseen musician. Somewhere farther away, the wind blows the snow this way and that way. The sound of snow falling on the ground, so subtle a song that only someone who is just as quiet could possibly hear it. Over that peaceful tune is the raucous whistling of the wind as it filters through the tunnels.

My head hurts something fierce, but the fire is warm, and the blanket around me feels like it has been made from the softest wool.

A baby cries...

"Astra, please stop."

"In time, dear. In time."

"My baby!"

I wake up with a jolt. My aching body protests violently at the mistreatment the motion evokes. I want to throw up. I do throw up, rolling sideways before I choke on my own bile.

"Some decision-making skills you have. Running out of the house and into the forest without even a pair of boots on. You're lucky you didn't snap your ankles in two."

I open my eyes to find the beautiful woman sitting there, tending the fire. Naomi, the lycan who I kicked out of my home after she saved our lives. Beside her lie River and four of my dogs: Darleen, Henry, Lightfoot, and Lilith. What happened to the others?

I remember Kali lying dead, her body steaming in the snow. "But what of Yehrik and Grace?"

"Your animals are loyal to a fault. They performed quite valiantly, protecting your unconscious body until I arrived."

"How did you find me?"

"I wasn't looking for you, but I was too late to keep the witchling from being taken through the portal."

The witchling? No...

"Astra! Where is my baby?"

"That woman who you invited into your home is a right piece of work. I think she knows who has taken her child and she is hoping she can trade your baby for her own."

"What do you mean? Why would anyone want to kidnap any child of ours anyway?"

Naomi's face darkens. "Latent magic is a powerful ingredient. It would not be the first time someone decided to harness it."

"What do you mean?" My voice quivers.

"There are rituals. Forbidden and impossible to perform that I believe she is wanting to attempt."

My imagination runs wild. I have heard of the kinds of things witches do with infants. Horrible things, ritual sacrifice designed to harness the innocent lifeforce and ascribe it to the practitioner. I imagine every horror movie I've ever seen about the Christian Satan, Baba Yaga, and Gryla, and my empty stomach tries to make it way up and out.

"No, she can't have Astra. She can't do that to my baby. Astra is my baby. She's—" A sob chokes off the rest of my sentence. "My baby's gone..."

"No," coos Naomi. "Not gone. Not yet. She is just out of reach for the moment. I can still feel her. It isn't too late."

"What do you mean, you can feel her?"

"Your little one's call still echoes in my head. I'm going to go find her once I've dropped you back off at your house."

"No, I'm coming with you."

Naomi frowns. "You can barely walk. You stay out in the cold any longer, and you'll catch your death."

"Astra is my life." I all but shout the words. "If you say you think you can find her, then I am going with you. I am going to get her back." My breath comes harder than it should. My chest, heaving with exertion and fury, feels tight like I can't draw a full breath.

"Alright, then. You'd best get changed then."

"Changed?"

The lycan raises her brow and thrusts her chin toward the far end of the space. It's the first time I've drawn my gaze away from Naomi and the fire. I realize that I'm not in a cave at all. The walls are a crisp white, glazed with ice and snow. Tapestries hang from the ceiling to help direct the smoke of the fire toward the hole in the roof. I am settled in a makeshift cot of furs and pelts. There is small wardrobe and a cabinet. Various cookery lines the wall, and around the mouth of the chimney hang several smoked fish and strips of dried meat. This lycan has made a temporary home out of the elements. It's an igloo.

I've never been in one before. I've never even seen one in real life, just in picture books.

"How long have you been living here?"

She doesn't answer my question, merely strokes the fire and tosses me a strip of meat. It smells divine.

"You can't run around in the wildernesses of the Wastes in nothing but a house coat and pajama pants. My clothes will probably be a bit big on you, but it's better than nothing, and I have a spare pair of boots. As soon as you're ready, we are leaving. There is little time to waste."

I have lived my whole life believing that the truth was an easy enough thing to see. The truth could be measured and observed. Facts were paramount to everything, and there was nothing in the world that could change cold, hard truth.

I was so wrong.

Truth hides behind a veil of deception.

The forest is full of lies. As I tread my way through the underbrush behind Naomi's surefooted steps, I can't help but wonder how I never noticed all of the strange things that live in the woods that surround my home.

For the first time, I see the forest as it really is.

The animals, those are the same as usual. Deer that may or may not have suffered the effects of radiation, having dual tails or deformed skulls and what not. The squirrels hide up in their trees, taking no heed of the owls that would scoop them up in a heartbeat were it nighttime. We even pass by a snoozing bobcat, sunning itself in a small patch of light.

The animals are not the problem.

The revelation lies in the unseen folk. Nisse scurry along the trail, diving into their little mushroom homes before they can be trampled by our passing footsteps. At one point, one of them pokes River with a stick, and my lead dog barks a chase through the woods until it dives into an underground burrow. I even see a sprinkling of dust in the air. Tiny things, barely-there at the edge of my vision. They hover between the trees and knock about behind my head.

At some point, just before we come to the edge of the forest, I see a human-sized being, half-man and half-goat, traipsing through the trees. I catch but a glimpse of it before it is gone, disappeared as though into thin air (or maybe into cold bark).

The instance sends a chill down my spine. I've never seen these kinds of creatures so close, and here they are a mere stone's throw away from my home.

"I thought the Wastes were abandoned by the fae folk."

"You can see them now, can you?"

"You mean they've been here the whole time?"

Naomi nods. "Perhaps knocking about in the woods broke through some of those stalwart wards in your blood."

I frown. What does she mean by that? Wards in my blood. How could there be wards in my blood? She continues on before I can voice the question.

"The fair folk did indeed leave in number after the collapse of the hexen rebellions, but there is so much of magic that refuses to be dispersed. Just like the Ukrainian peoples of Chernobyl, the fae here refuse to leave the land that has forever been their home just because some humans say the air is toxic to them."

"But why would they do that? Don't they see how decrepit this place is?"

"Why do you and your fellow non-witches stay in Mountain View, then? Your magic is unstable, and the land is hostile to your very presence. Yet you remain? Why is that?"

I wanted to get out of this frozen wasteland. I don't bother to share that with the lycan. Desires and dreams don't matter when reality wakes you up by dousing you in ice-cold water. Maybe there is resounding note of truth lingering in the idea of wards sewn into our blood.

"I think we are cursed. No one leaves Mountain View alive. Not even those of us who so desperately want to go."

Naomi hums in acknowledgement. "Well, perhaps the fae are chained to their homes as you are to your village."

I have nothing to say to that, so I leave it. So long as they leave us be, I have nothing to complain about.

It was decided before we left that my sled dogs would help us travel much faster than if we go on foot, and with little time to spare, I don't mind taking the trek back to my home. I only hope a few more of my surviving dogs have found their way back home. I can't live with myself if I failed them too.

The house looks just as I left it. Snow-covered rooftop, ice-drenched shingles, and I can even see the glow of the kitchen light I left on in my haste to chase after my child's kidnapper. I can't believe that just hours ago my child was kidnapped from right inside this place that I thought was a safe haven.

I don't bother going inside. There is nothing for me there.

Six of my dogs—River, Lightfoot, Yehrik, Lilith, Henry, and Darleen—are accounted for. Grace, I fear, never found her way back home after the mess of yesterday's events. She is either lost in the woods or she's ended up as a meal for one of the larger predators in the area.

With six remaining, it's a small team to be running a sled, but with just Naomi's and my combined weight to pull, they can manage it. At the very least, they will be faster than me on foot, and Naomi can't exactly wolf out if she is having to tug me along with her.

We load up with just enough gear to keep warm and fill our bellies. Just as I'm getting ready to command River to mush, a frantic voice calls out from across the property.

"No! Danica, don't!"

It's my mother.

Stella races her way toward us, arms waving frantically in the air as she runs.

"Stop!"

I realize belatedly that she is trying to stop us. But why?

I can't pay a mind to it.

"Hah!" I shout to River and she jolts forward, all of my dogs following. In the bed of the sled, Naomi barely rustles as we take off into the forest. A silent finger points the way.

It is not long before my mother's pain-stricken cries die on the wind.

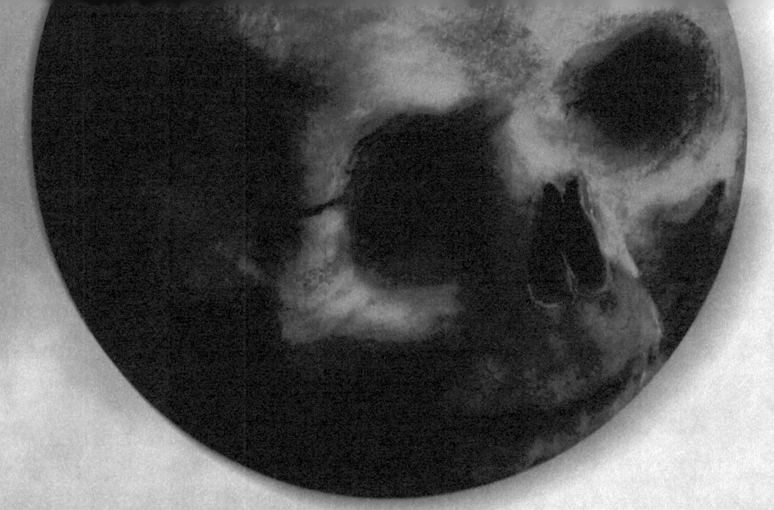

VII

THE MOUSE RAN
UP THE CLOCK

It is said that a troll can smell a Christian's blood from a mile away. They crave it, horribly. The blood of the people who cost them the easy meals that used to be left out for them. There are some who would say they have the same affinity for hexen. After all, if it weren't for the witches and their brood, trolls would have free run of the countryside.

An excerpt from *In the Forests of Deus:*
where the old ones sleep
By C.S. Hawthorne - Monster Hunter, 1776 A.P.

There are certain unspoken rules that you have to follow when you live so far north. For instance, in the dead of winter, when the sun doesn't rise, it is often considered a fool's choice to head into the forest. There is no sunrise here. There is no sunset. Only night. And right now, even the moons have vacated the sky, their beams too weak to penetrate the clouds. The world is covered in shadow.

We run into the darkness.

We run for so long, the forest becomes a strange place. I can't recognize any landmarks or trees. In the small beam of my flashlight, I'll catch sight of a fallen log or a unique looking rock formation. I try to commit them to memory for the journey home. This is a place so far from Mountain View, it is unlikely anyone has ever been this deep into the forest and returned to put it on a map.

I've never been this far away from the village. I imagine this is what the space explorers feel like when walking onto an alien planet. There is something darker, more primitive about these woods, like time forgot to pass, so everthing has been allowed to grow unchecked. The forest thickens; the trees curl and coil tighter and tighter around one another. It becomes harder and harder to find a path forward that the sled can manage, but River makes do. She keeps her nose to the ground and trots along at a steady pace.

Joanna is beyond this point. The portal she took, Naomi is certain she used it to bypass the horrors of the forest. A quicker modality of travel to achieve her goal.

I feel like time is trying to suffocate me. I don't know if I can take this much longer.

"How much farther?" I ask my lycan companion. She never answers. It makes me feel like a child asking their parents, *"Are we there yet? Are we there yet? Are we there yet?"* The feeling does not, however, discourage me from asking.

Every so often, Naomi lopes off in wolf form into the surrounding wilderness. I assume she is scouting ahead. Each time she returns, she directs me to alter our course ever so slightly. I always listen. This is her domain, not mine and not my dogs.

When she limps back on two legs, bruised and bloody from one such escapade, however, I stop the sled.

"What's wrong?"

"Kill the torch."

"But I can't see without the flashlight."

"I said kill it. We are being followed."

"By who?"

She shakes her head. "Not by who. By what?"

I didn't realize humans had hackles that could rise, but with that singular statement, mine go up. All of the sudden, the forest is too quiet. There are no animal sounds, no rustling in the trees, not even the stray scurrying of a squirrel. It is as though the wind has hushed for fear of whatever stalks us.

"What is it?" I whisper.

"Something big. I've been trying to angle us away from it, but it's found us."

In the distance, a tree falls over, the sound of a thousand splinters creaking and cracking before the inevitable thud that signals the trees demise. I can feel it shake the earth beneath my boots.

"Tell the dogs to run as fast as they can. I'll navigate us through the dark. We can't stay here."

She climbs into the bed of the sled, and I call out to River. The dogs take off as fast as they can.

It isn't fast enough.

A loud roar echoes through the darkness behind us. More trees fall in deference to the weight of a horrid creature plowing through them. I don't dare look back, not that keeping my eyes forward does much good. Other than the snow and ice on the ground, I can barely see the white patches of fur on my dogs and that's about it.

As though to make up for my blindness, my hearing kicks into overdrive, and I can hear the stomping of giant footsteps. And the smell... Oh the smell that invades my nostrils is like that of putrid eggs doused in mustard. It's the smell of spoiled garbage and rotten fruit. I nearly gag as I yell again.

"Run, River! Don't stop for anything!"

River runs. All of the dogs run. Their breath makes icicles on the air, but it isn't enough. As fast as they are, they can't outrun something so large. The stomps come closer. The sled quakes and hops in response until a foot as long as the sled touches down right next to us. The foot didn't even connect with the sled, but the impact of the giant appendage against the earth sends us careening sideways.

I hear my dogs barking and howling in fear and panic. The gang lines tangle as they are knocked over. I am thrown sideways. My ribs connect with a nearby tree. Stars dance before my vision as I fight to draw a breath.

Where is Naomi? I can't see her.

"Lilith, Lightfoot, Henry," I call for my dogs nearest to me. "Get away from there!"

I scramble forward to unhitch them from the sled so they can run, but a huge hand scoops downward and snatches River right up. Her harness drags me and the other dogs up with her.

"River!" I shout as the dog whines in the big hand's grasp. I look up to find the most repulsive face staring down at us. A huge bulbous nose surrounded by a squashed chin and eyes. There is hair, so much hair, on this huge head. Its ears stick out at odd angles, droopy but pointed at the tips like an elf whose had his ears pulled downward too many times.

It's a goddamned troll.

The creature carries us up and toward its face where its mouth opens. Teeth the size of boulders fill its mouth, each one covered in a dark substance that I can only imagine would be bloody red in daylight.

It wants to eat us.

It is trying to eat all of us.

Like Hel am I going to let it eat my dogs.

Holding on for dear life, I reach up as far as I can and start to climb up my team. The dogs thrash and panic in the troll's grasp. A part of me wants to just scream and let go, but River's pained howls drive me forward. This troll cannot have River. Through sheer willpower, I make my way up until the latch that connects the rest of the team to River is just right there. I reach until it feels like my shoulder is about to pop out of the socket, and I grab for the length of cord. Winding my legs in the cable, I pull myself up until I have a hold on River's leash.

"I'm sorry, guys," I whisper, and then I release the latch. The rest of my team falls to the forest floor. I wince as their furry bodies fall through branches of trees before they land, but I know it's for the best. They'll have a better chance on the ground that dangling in the air like a noodle of dog chow. I just pray they land safely in the snow.

Now for River. I'm not going to let this fiend eat her.

Having lost the bulk of his would-be meal, the troll pauses as though trying to figure out why he is holding fewer animals. He sees me and narrows his eyes. They are yellow, like piss and puke, and they gleam with fury.

He roars at me. The force of the yell swings me sideways, and my stomach lurches at the reek of the troll's breath. The stench of steamed garbage and days old cow dung mixes with the dead stink of decay—like rotten fruit that's been melted in month-old milk.

Without thinking, I kick at the creature, nailing it right in the nose. The strike cuts the beast off mid-shout. He stares at me in disbelief. His tiny troll mind struggles to make sense of the fact that a mosquito just essentially bit him on the snout. I want to laugh for a second until he does exactly what someone might do after being bit by a mosquito—he tries to fling us away.

I scream, dangling as I am off the end of River's harness. No carnival in the world could have prepared me for that gravity spin. The skin of my hands rips as I hold on for dear life. My own blood spills down the line.

Swinging through the tree line, I reach out and grab a broken branch. I turn the sharp end up and jam it as hard as I can into the tender space between the troll's fingers. His grip loosens just enough to let River whip her head around and bury her teeth in the troll's wrist.

The troll yelps. He lets go, and River and I freefall.

With my dog in my arms, we plummet from an even higher point above the ground than when I let loose the rest of my team. I close my eyes. It's over. There is no way I can survive a fall from this high. I brace for death, and hope that it will come quickly.

A body makes contact with mine. Two solid arms frame my waist, and when the falling stops, it is with a gentle landing, rather than a violent crash. Naomi puts me down, and River bounds out of my grip.

"River, no!"

A commotion explodes to life right in front of me, but I can't see well enough to know what's happening. A long length of black darkens the snow. I scramble for it, my fallen flashlight. I juggle it in my torn-up hands and flick it on.

Someone has unharnessed my team from the gang line, and my dogs are using its length to trip the troll. They run in circles around its ankles, the rope in their mouths, winding and winding until the line goes taunt. The troll tries to take a step. All the dogs bear down on their haunches, and the troll loses its balance.

"That's it, doggies. Get him off his feet."

I look up to see a great white wolf barreling up the troll's back. It's Naomi, growling a battle cry around something in her mouth. The werewolf leaps from the troll's shoulder. Her claws find purchase on the troll's nose, and without further fanfare, Naomi rams a long length of wood straight into the troll's eye.

The scream it emits shakes the entire forest. Blind, it backs up straight toward the cliff's edge.

"River, get back!" I yell, and my dogs, my beautiful, wonderful, smart dogs, untangle themselves from ruined gang line, and race toward me. In moments, I am surrounded by fur, and just a few heartbeats later, the troll disappears over the edge.

It takes me two heartbeats to realize that Naomi went over the cliff with the troll.

"Naomi! Naomi! Where are you?"

"Over here," a gravelly voice answers.

Oh, thank the gods. I rush over to the edge, squash down the nausea that threatens to spill my stomach from looking down into the ravine, and see her huddled on a ledge just below.

She's okay, I remind myself as I lower some rope down to pull her up. When her feet touch flat ground, I can't help but throw my arms around her in a hug.

"You saved us."

The lycan laughs deep in her belly. "I don't know, little star. That was some pretty impressive acrobatics you pulled off. I thought for a minute you and your dogs were going to be troll food for sure."

"Thanks," I say, heat rising to my cheeks.

Fingertips brush ever so gently across my cheekbone. The touch is so feather-light, I wonder if I hallucinated it, but when I look up into Naomi's crystal-clear gaze, her hand is just returning to her side.

"I should be thanking you. The troll would have killed me were it not for your dogs. Not to mention, you swept me off the edge of a cliff."

An invisible thread stretches between us. It grows taut and spirals like a heartstring on a cello. I feel it vibrating as though some unseen entity has just strummed this strange connection between us. It reverberates through my bones, into the sinew of my joints, and rests in the meaty part of my muscles. I remember, aimlessly, that the heart is little more than a muscle, pumping away to keep the blood flowing through the rest of my body.

Naomi's face has gotten closer somehow, but I don't remember moving. I couldn't possibly move, not with how enchanting her eyes are.

Rowwrroo

The yapping of one of my dogs breaks the strand. I look away, certain that I am imagining the subtle glow across Naomi's cheeks.

"We should check on your dogs. Not to mention your hands need treatment."

"Right," I whisper as she flits past me toward where the animals are huddled. She doesn't touch me, yet still I can feel her heat sink into my skin.

I stand, frozen and staring out into the sky, unable to move yet willing my body into action. I take a breath, and it feels like I am breathing for the first time in my entire life.

What, by Deus, was that?

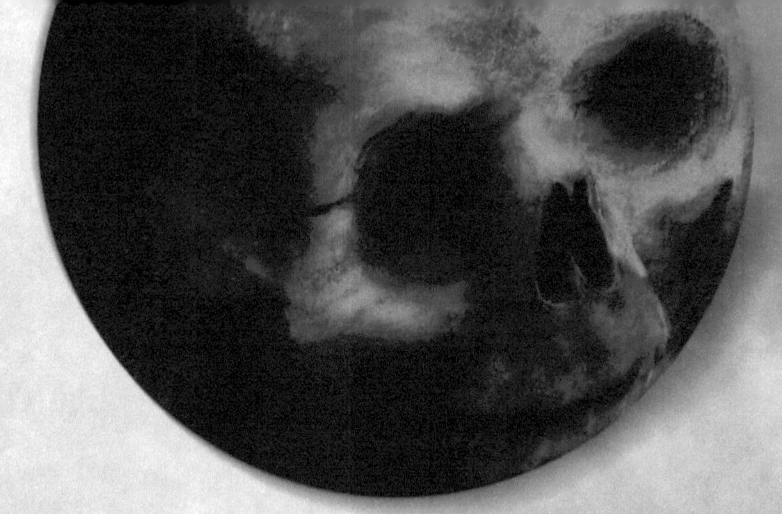

VIII

LONDON BRIDGE IS FALLING DOWN

It was too much to hope that all my dogs landed safely on the ground. We find Darleen hanging from one of the pine trees the troll broke, her body impaled on the jagged spike of the remaining tree trunk. Oh, my sweet, strong Darleen. She was one of my toughest dogs, not very fast but always determined to get the job done, and she never missed the opportunity for some steaming slop at the end of the day.

Naomi helps me bury her body while my remaining five dogs huddle together. They stare at the raised patch of snow as though holding a eulogy for their fallen comrade.

There is a lot to be said for working dogs. Loyal to a fault and determined to get the job done, there is no dog like a working dog. My mother never liked dogs much. Even after I got River and the others, she was skeptical about their value. We'd argued for weeks about whether or not they would be worth the expense. After this, I would say that each of my dogs has earned their weight in gold and then some.

The lycan, after we have finished laying the soil over Danica's broken body, proposes we stop to set up a fire. "We can eat and rest for a few hours before we continue on."

"No," I say, already forcing my way through the underbrush. "Astra doesn't have that much time."

"You must eat, Danica."

I don't want to eat. I don't want to stop. It's bad enough we were put off schedule by the troll's attack. The sooner I have my baby back in my arms the better.

"Danica," Naomi's voice is insistent. I manage to force out three more paces before her hands catch me around the shoulders, "when Astra is back with her mother, she is going to want milk. If you do not eat, if you do not drink, you will have nothing to offer her. Besides, I'm sure your body is telling you it needs a release."

My whole body sags. At the mention of milk, the discomfort that has been building in my chest takes center stage. My breasts feel tight and close to bursting. If I don't stop to at least take care of that, I will end up in a world of hurt. Mastitis, clots, infections... the last thing I need is to be incapacitated by my boobs.

Release indeed. I need to pump.

"Alright, we'll stop."

Naomi sets me down on a nearby boulder and goes to work starting the fire. She expertly wields the flint, and before long, a roaring fire rises out of the kindling she pieced together from dried leaves and branches.

She puts something to boil in a pot over the flames and then makes her way over to me.

"Your hands," she says, both hands raised in askance. Confusion drifts through my being for a moment before I look down at my palms. Looking at my threadbare gloves, I remember. My hands are so numb from the cold, I'd forgotten that in my desperate need to keep from being thrown to the forest floor, I had ripped my palms open on the harness.

She is offering to tend to my hands. A part of me wants to refuse, keep my injuries to myself so I can suffer as penance for losing Astra. It's irrational and self-destructive, the kind of thing my doctor warned me might happen postpartum. (It makes no sense how the process of bringing a life into the world can stray us down the path of insanity.) Instead of giving into the intrusive thought, I place my icy-cold hands into hers. It's the only logical thing to do.

She gingerly removes the shredded gloves. The sight is grotesque. Deep lacerations rest like canyons at the center of my palms. The flesh at the center segment of my fingers was cut nearly to the bones. Actually, scratch that, I can see pale white peeking through the tattered sinew of my right pointer finger.

Naomi winces as she assesses the damage before she gets up to grab the kettle she hung over the fire.

"Your hands are freezing."

I nod. They've been exposed to subzero air for nearly an hour. "I can't really feel anything right now. They're pretty much numb."

She hums, sagely. "I need to clean the wounds. The water isn't terribly hot, but it's warm enough that the feeling is going to come back to your nerves." She pulls a piece of clean wood from her pocket. There are dents in it, places for someone's teeth. "Needless to say..."

"This is going to hurt," I finish for her, taking the gag. "That's okay. Let's do it."

I place the wood between my teeth and bite down. On my nod, Naomi pours the steaming water over my wounds, and the pain ignites like a fire through the appendages. Torn nerve endings, which should by rights have been completely severed, scream to life as the heat reignites them. My whole body jolts. It takes every ounce of my strength and determination to keep from screaming.

As though in response, the air quivers. The void waters react to my spasms of pain. Somewhere farther into the forest, I hear the snapping of branches followed by the dull thud of a tree falling to the ground.

Naomi glances mutely in that direction but keeps the flow of water steady.

"Just a little more," she hushes. Sensation returns to my extremities as the heat invites the blood back into my hands. Within moments, the bleeding starts again. Scarlet stains the snow below me, but Naomi is quick to start bandaging the injuries. Her touch is quick but gentle. I try to focus on the softness of her fingertips as she twists my hands this way and that.

The closest I have ever come to being tended like this was by my midwife. There had been a problem with my placenta, and she didn't want to risk inversion happening, so she had had to reach in and tug my placenta free. I've never been in so much pain in my entire life. As I lay there, bleeding from the trials of birth and aching from drawing new life from the waters of creation, my midwife stitched me back together and applied the gauze that would keep my lower bits in place while I healed. But that touch was clinical, executed with cold accuracy to prevent further damage. It was impersonal, a job to be done.

This is different. There is care in Naomi's touch. Her fingers skate over and under my hands, cool relief spreading as such rubs a disinfecting salve into the injuries. The pain dies down as she winds the bandages around and between my fingers.

When she is done with one of my hands, she grabs a strange-looking vial from out of her bag and hands it to me. "Drink this," she says. "It will help you heal faster."

The liquid inside seems more gelatinous than fluid. It slugs around the vial as I twirl it in my bandaged hand. I don't know if the concoction is just catching the light as I move it or if the potion is somehow glowing of its own accord.

"What is it?"

"It's a healing draught. Made by the last witch to oversee our pack. It's meant to help us heal after a rough fight or conflict. Really good for mending lacerations like this."

"Why didn't you give it to me earlier?!" There's an edge of frustration to my voice that I don't mean to allow in there, but couldn't she have given it to me before she poured hot water over my nearly frostbitten hands?

Naomi looks at me blandly. "Well, do you want your skin to heal over all the splinters and bacteria that was probably just waiting to fester in those wounds?"

I wince. That certainly makes sense.

"Now that everything is cleaned up, it should be safe for you to take."

"Okay, but how old is it?" Do potions expire? I haven't any idea.

"It's a bit old, but potions don't exactly have a shelf life. Worst that will happen is you'll gag a little, but it won't hurt you."

Well, fuck it, I think and swallow the whole thing down. There wasn't much of it really, maybe a mouthful and a half.

It goes down with a tingling feeling akin to drinking a strong spirit. Almost immediately, the discomfort in my hands fades away, making my chest all the more uncomfortable. I reach under my shirt to rub a breast. With the barest of touches, a small stream of milk squirts into my hand.

"You need release. I will leave you to your privacy while I tend to dinner."

I mentally scoff. Release indeed. I need to pump.

Thankfully, my hand-pump wasn't damaged by the sled being turned over. There is an empty bottle along with it that I screw into place before I go to town. I yield a solid two and a half ounces of milk from each breast. A good offering for Astra once we find her.

I look over to where Naomi tends the fire. She is spinning a skewer of meat over the flames, and it smells absolutely divine, but the question that has been niggling at the back of my mind ever since I first encountered the lycan bubbles up without my say so.

"I still don't quite understand why you are helping me find Astra."

Naomi turns to look at me, and I blush.

"I mean, not that I mind. I just… don't take this the wrong way, but I've never heard of a hexen putting their neck out for anyone other than their own circle of kith and kin."

Naomi nods. "No offense taken," she says, angling herself so she can look at me while she continues cooking our dinner. "Danica, what exactly do you know about lycans?"

"I know there are two types of lycans in Deus: the Koi and the Dei. One for each of the moons that hang in our sky, but I'd be hard-pressed to tell you anything about them."

Naomi hums in appreciation.

"I am the white wolf of the Dei tribe of New Chernobyl. You know that Dei is the lesser moon of Deus. Due to this, many people believe us to be inferior to the Koi lycans. While it is true that we are smaller, we are hardly any less powerful than they. Our moon is ever present in the sky which means we can shift any time we want. Koi lycans can only shift when their moon is full which only happens every few months."

"Okay, that still doesn't explain why you are here."

"I'm getting to that..." Naomi swallows so hard I can see the sinew of her throat moving over the action. "Our people are dying. Since magic left the world, the young ones... they cannot make their first shift. They die horrible, painful deaths, caught between their wolfish forms and their human forms."

"Why can't they change? What is stopping them?"

"The great massacres of witches have ridden the continent bereft of the magic that shaped our people into what they are. Without witch magic, lycans would not exist, and without the aid of hexen magic, we are dying. Only one in every four teens will survive the shift, and that is if they even make it to adolescence to begin with.

"I have spent nearly a decade searching for a witch who could restore hope to our kind. I had nearly given up hope of ever finding a witch with the power of change and metamorphosis until I heard your baby's call nearly four months ago."

"But Astra is only two months old."

"Your infant called to me from the womb, Danica. Your child is more than a miracle. She is fated to be. She is the hope that will save the Dei packs from extinction."

"Do the Koi lycans not have the same issue?"

Naomi scoffs.

"Koi lycans are a disease made from a witch's hatred," she growls as she aggressively yanks the freshly cooked meat from the spit. "Diseases are made to reproduce without boundary. It is an irony, indeed. While we must care for and nurture our young into lycanhood, Koi lycans need only bite as many humans as they can get their jaws around. Most of them will die for the same reasons our children die, the strain of the shift too weak in their bodies to turnover, but when your method of reproduction involves violence over affection, you tend to have more success just for the sheer volume of influence you can impact. The only thing that prevents them from just rampaging across the continent is the fact that Koi is only full once every five or six months. Not to mention the technomancers hunt them relentlessly every opportunity they get."

It makes sense in a sick sort of way. Humans are nothing if not numerous. I never thought about the fact that if a freshly bitten prospective dies during the shift, what's to keep a lycan from just biting someone else? Nothing! Except, of course, the local adepts and/or technomancers who may or may not be in the area.

"I didn't realize your people were so negatively affected by how few witches were left in the world."

She sets a plate of food in front of me. "Our entire existence relies on witch magic. It is why we are called hexen, after all."

We eat in a comfortable silence. The meat is flavored with some salt and pepper, and it's a bit tough to chew, but I make my way through it like a wolverine. I feel kind of foolish for my earlier behavior toward Naomi. The way I kicked her out of my house, the way I have been distrustful of her...

"Naomi," I whisper. She looks up at me with those golden eyes, the magenta glint once more in their depths. "I'm sorry. I-I think I misjudged you terribly."

The lycan smiles. "Don't worry about it, Danica. You are not the first human to do so, and you won't be the last."

We finish our food without another word. It's nice, I think, to sit and enjoy the quiet of the forest with someone else for once. I should've guessed that this would very likely be the last respite we would get on our journey.

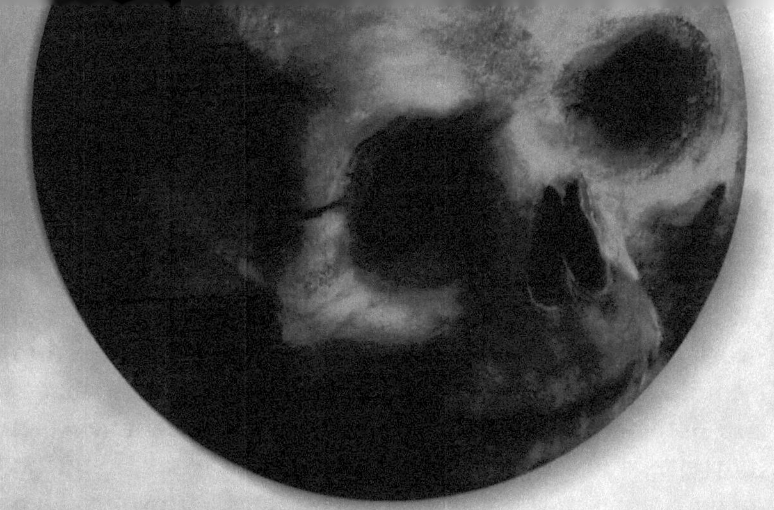

IX

FALLING DOWN, FALLING DOWN

I stood in the water for so long, my body went numb from the waist down. From the waist up, I stood equally unfeeling. Not even the infant crying in my arms could shake me from my trance. I didn't realize I'd stepped deeper into the water until Jessabelle snatched the days-old baby from my arms and hauled me to the shore.

From the diary of
Wren Nocturne
1862 A.P.

We rise when the fire dies.

The sled is a busted-up wreck from our encounter with the troll. With the amount of splintered and broken boards, it takes an hour to salvage the bed before we can keep going. At least, the rails and the musher's standing post are still workable after a few repairs. If I survive this, I'll need to rebuild a new one from scratch. Naomi and I save what is left of the rations and the supplies, dividing them between ourselves and the dogs' harnesses. It's going to take longer to make progress along the path, but my dogs, as downtrodden as they are, remain up to the task.

We are solidly in the mountains now. I've never been claustrophobic, but there is just something about a sheet of rock climbing up beyond your visual field that triggers an incredibly primal fear inside you. All along the path, the mountain ridges loom on either side of us, sharp juts of rock which could, at any moment, succumb to gravity. I've seen the remnants of rockslides. It's amazing how they can consume a roadway with utterly terrifying precision.

"The vampyres tread these paths often. There should be little to fear from rockslides."

Naomi points out the metal nets blanketing the mountainside. I don't know how she knew exactly what was going through my head. Perhaps, I'm broadcasting my thoughts across my face, or maybe it's true that wolves can smell fear. I choose not to question it and just look at what she is pointing at instead.

It's hard to see them at first, but when I point my flashlight to the rock, I can see the steel poles jutting out of the mountain's face. Laced between each pole is finely woven netting designed to catch and release fallen rocks. Despite the reassurance, I can't shake the paranoia that I am either about to plummet to my death or be crushed beneath chunks of falling mountain.

We have miles of this left to go. I don't know if I can keep myself from panicking that long.

A mile later, and the terrain on our left drops out. Great! A wall of rock on one side and a sudden drop on the other. To be honest, I don't know which is worse. My fear of falling kicks into overdrive. I don't know where it was when I was dangling from a troll's clutches yesterday, but it rears its ugly head now.

In the darkness, I have no choice but to rely on River's acute senses. With the steep drop and the winding curves of the path, my torch is useless, the beam falling on open air. She should know where we are going, and she should also have enough awareness of the territory around us to keep us from going over the edge of the cliff, but the loss of control is still unsettling.

The mountains shift and change the farther and longer we run. Naomi and I take shifts driving vs. resting in the sled's bed. I feel like when Naomi holds the reigns, we somehow travel faster and farther. Despite the fact that this is my team and my sled, she insists on driving longer. I cave to her insistence. After all, she is a lycan. Her senses are just as good if not better than my canine team. It's fine by me.

I am in the sled, dozing when I hear her call my name. "Danica, wake up."

My eyes, sleep still clinging to my lashes, refuse to open. I blink several times before I can finally force them open. The first thing I notice is that we are stopped. My dogs are curled up in their harnesses, taking a breather. The trees that surround us are a strange black. Most of the pine trees surrounding Mountain View are plush with needles and cones and wildlife. The ones here, however many miles we are away from my home, seem dead. The needles are sparse, no animals walk their branches, and not even the wind seems capable of bending their boughs. I can see the sky peeking through each branch like the forest has given up any chance of filling out enough to prevent the sky from touching the earth.

Not only that. A terrible silence lingers in the air. The icy quiet chills me more than any snow drift I could have ever fallen into. Naomi steps off the sled bearings and trudges through the snow toward a spot of clear trees.

"The moons are out. Come and look."

After a quick stretch, I rise from the sled. The snow is piled thick here. I trudge my way to where Naomi stands, using the other woman's slightly larger tracks as a means to get there with as little difficulty as possible.

When I finally reach her, I realize what has made her so somber. A mountain lake stretches out as far as my search-light can reach, and its surface is frozen solid. The ice is so crystal-clear, I can see the moons' reflections staring back at me. Koi, a bare sliver in the sky, for once is overshadowed by Dei, ever full, ever bright.

Dei is volcanic. Its surface is covered in molten lava. That's why it's always full. The constant eruptions make it glow an orange-red in the sky. It is so prominent the entire landscape is painted in a dull red. It's not the first time I've seen a night like this, doused in red and eerie to see, but there is just something desolate about looking at the frozen water while it is painted such a color.

Blood and moonlight... This is a bad omen.

In the back of my mind, the map of the Wastes taunts me. I know this patch of water. This too long, too deep, and too cold stretch of water spans the length of two seas: Spøkels Lake. So named for its ghostly history.

"What's wrong?"

"This is the way we need to go."

"Across the lake? No one crosses Spøkels. Not if they want to avoid drowning."

"We have no choice. We need to cross."

"Can't we go around?"

"It would take too long. Going around would add a day and half to our journey. Astra does not have that kind of time."

"But how—"

River barks, and dread fills my heart. My lead dog is telling me the answer. I turn to find River and the others have already pulled the sled to the water's frozen edge. River's paws pad anxiously on the snow-crusted beach, but she looks at me, her eyes big and pleading. Readiness shines within them.

I turn to Naomi.

"You realize this is suicide, right? We have no way of knowing if the ice is thick enough to hold us, let alone if it is frozen all the way through."

"Unfortunately, we do not have the luxury of choice."

Before I command my dogs onto the ice, I feed them. I find what's left of the rations and I make sure they get the best pickings. I need them strong if we are to have any hope of making it across the great lake. Once they're fed and watered, we're off.

For the first two hours or so, everything seems just fine. The wind burns against my face. With nothing to buffer the angry element, we are exposed in the worst possible way. Naomi has wolfed out, running alongside River to pull us faster over the frozen water. I have my coat and scarf pulled tight over my face and still my nose goes numb. My hands, bandaged and bound in my gloves, still throb. The magically healed wounds pulse with phantom pain against the cold, but they refuse to lose feeling.

It's uncomfortable, it's painful, it's a slow death from exposure running through this wind, but I don't care. The ice holds. Thank the gods, the ice holds. The wind may bring a slow death, but if that ice breaks... people don't realize how fast water that cold can kill. It hits you like a thousand needles piercing into your skin and injects you with ice. The air in your lungs crystallizes, your organs slug to a stop, and lastly, your heart literally bursts as the blood flowing through it becomes ice. So, I thank every god I can think of who might be within earshot because the ice is holding. The ice holds and for a time, the fear in my chest loosens into something resembling hope.

We are so far out, I can no longer see the shoreline. I haven't been able to see it for at least an hour. We are in the dead center of the Spøkels with nowhere to go but forward. It should be impossible what I hear next. The sound that greets me from the darkness shouldn't exist, but I hear it, nonetheless.

A baby's cry pierces through the noise of the wind. It is so quiet, a barely-there sound, yet it surrounds me. A whimpering wail so loud it reaches my core.

My attention, which had been entirely on my dogs and Naomi before, whips around. I circle my flashlight in a 360-degree swing.

"Astra!"

Naomi's ear twitches at my call, but she urges River on. An immediate fury swells from the pit of my stomach.

"Stop! We need to stop!"

My dogs stumble. Half of them attempt to follow the command, coming to a skidding halt on the ice. The other half fall to their knees as the dogs they are harnessed to yank them backward. Naomi howls in protest, but I jerk the reigns again, trying to get them all to stop.

"Astra," I scream, stepping off the foot rails. A series of dull thuds echo in the back of my mind as I run out on the ice toward the sound.

"Danica, stop!" I hardly register Naomi's voice. "That's not Astra!" But it has to be. Who else could it be? I can't just sit here and listen to her. I keep running until a slick patch of ice sends me stumbling down.

My chin knocks on the ice. The teeth of my lower jaw snap up into my upper teeth, feeling like I just cracked all of the enamel to pieces. Blood spills from the split in my chin, steaming in the snow, but I don't care. I fight to get traction under my feet then take off again; only as I run, I realize the cries of the infant are no longer coming from a single direction.

They are all around me. I don't know where to go.

"Astra?" I call, looking frantically around. Everywhere I look, I see only crimson moon-touched ice. Ice that is as deep red as freshly spilled blood.

"New mother, still shedding your creation blood," a voice calls out of the darkness. "You are unworthy."

"Show yourself!" I shout.

"I am everywhere." I can't tell where the voice is coming from: my left, my right, in front of me, behind me. In a lot of ways, it feels like the rasping evil echoes in my own mind. No, in my heart.

"Where is my baby?"

"Don't fight it, girl. You and I know the truth. You've thought it yourself. How easy it is to snuff out such a helpless life."

I remember. Less than healthy nights just letting my baby scream. Scattered, terrible thoughts of quieting her in *any way* that I could after every single thing I tried failed to placate her. *Stop crying, please. Just please stop crying.* I begged my own baby to stop. To be quiet. Anything. I didn't realize what I was doing until I caught myself hovering over Astra with a pillow in my hand.I was horrified with myself.

"You were right, you know. If you'd gone through with it... It would be more merciful than raising her in such an ugly world."

I crumble to my knees.

"I didn't want to kill my baby. I-I just..."

Before me, a woman appears shrouded in bloodred shadows. She is old and young at once. She wears a hood on her face and a cowl over her mouth. The mask she wears reminds me of a human skull.

At her side dangles a strange metal instrument. It looks like a pair of tongs but larger and curved. The handle is wrapped in what looks to be old leather, and the metal pieces that should grasp something are extremely curved. One of the tongs looks to be a pair of widely forked spokes bound together with a strip of leather. The other is a long, rounded strip of metal.

There is something about the tool that sends shivers up and down my spine. I might be imagining it, but there is a haze of darkness writhing around the instrument. It drips evil. An instrument that serves only the purpose of pain and suffering.

"There are so many women just like you. They lose themselves in the face of motherhood, so they slay the enemy which sought to destroy them."

"But they are innocent. No baby comes into this world to torment their mother."

"Don't they? What about those who are born against the will of the mother? Aren't they the enemy?"

"It is not the child's fault. It wasn't Astra's fault that I couldn't handle it."

"But it doesn't change the fact that you couldn't. You still cannot. You are too weak. Rid yourself of this burden. Walk away. Leave the child to me before you cause the worst."

The figure raises the tool and points it directly at me. Before I can react, a streak of black lightning strikes my heart.

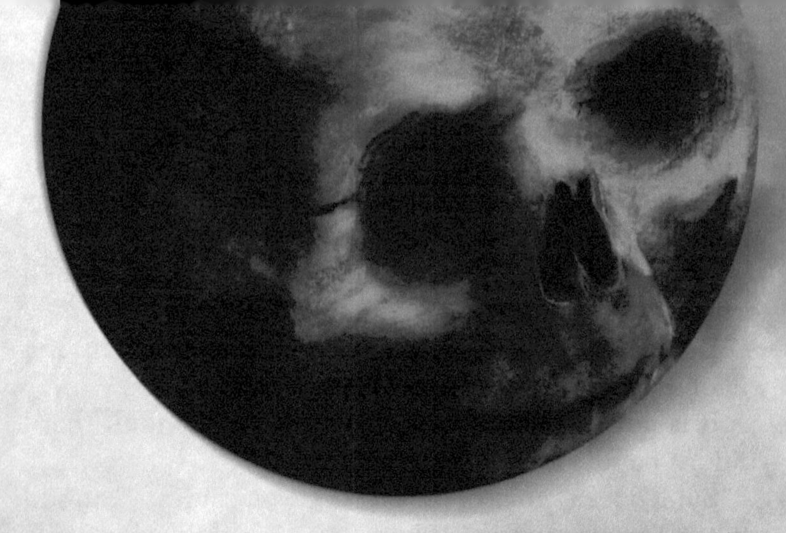

X

MY FAIR LADY

When I wake, I am not in my body. I can tell I am still in the Wastes, but the land looks different. Less sickly and more vibrant with life. The trees are greener and full to bursting with needles and wildlife. The ground even seems healthier like the nutrients haven't yet been burned away by radiation poisoning.

I hover above the ground, so high I feel dizzy looking up and seeing a cloud hovering just above my head. It is winter in this strange out-of-body place. The Spøkels is frozen over, but the scenery, as bursting with life as it may be, is not pleasant to look at.

Men tear each other to pieces. I've heard the term blood-bath—I've never truly thought about the implication behind it. The battle taking place below me rages, blood spilling in rivers over the frozen ground. I would worry the steaming life blood might very well melt the ice no matter how cold it may be.

The scene shifts, and the horrors that pass my eyes make me want to stop breathing. Babies drowned in cold water, children left to starve in the streets, women crucified and hanged as witches... My vision is flooded with a campaign of evils. Ships succumb to the fury of an ocean storm. Hurricanes lay waste to the landscape, felling homes and destroying the floodgates. Nature is volatile, but man is crueler.

Another strike of lightning pulls me out of these horrors and into a single-room house. The house is old, a run-down, beachside cabin left to sway on the dock that makes up its foundation. Dried herbs decorate the walls, shelves sit full of thick tomes, jars, and boxes of ingredients, and a cauldron hangs over the fireplace. I am not one to so readily give in to stereotype, but this certainly looks like a witch's home. And in the center of the room are the witch herself with another. I yearn to cry out, but I am nailed to the ceiling, unable to interfere yet unable to look away from the grizzly scene below.

A woman screams in agony, a hunched figure before her. She lies prone, her body fighting against her will, as she labors to bring a new life into the world.

"It's alright, dear," hums the witch. "You're almost there."

The twisted figure hovers between the woman's legs. She sits, tattoos decorating her hands, in a shroud of darkness. Her words are poisonous, and they inject venom into the pained woman's body as effectively as a needle.

"Just let me take care of it, dear. You've done enough."

"I don't want to hurt my baby."

"I know you don't, darling, but your body has betrayed you. There is no other way forward."

The midwife pulls out a strange instrument. In an instant, I realize exactly what that instrument is: a pair of sinister-looking forceps. I watch in horror as she pushes it into the laboring mother-to-be.

Neither the mother nor the baby draw breath past the midwife's ministrations.

I see myself next: the fireplace, my new baby, the burning blanket. It all floods before me like a black and white horror film. I am seeing my body from above the ground through a flatscreen on the ground.

"Danica!"

Naomi's call dispels the ghost, and the suffocating feeling trying to sink me under dissipates. When I turn around, Naomi is there, running my dogs and the sled toward me. Her eyes are wide with fear and surprise.

"That's a villdød, Danica. A dead witch. She's evil. Don't listen to her."

"A villdød?" I ask, dazed as she pulls up beside me.

"It means wild dead. It's a term used for witches who have died and come back as undead. She's an evil spirit, Danica. Get away from her."

"Why is she here?"

"This is where I died, young one. The ancient ones, they did not agree with my philosophy, so they drowned me in the same waters where I brought mercy to my charges."

"You killed them. That's not mercy!"

"It is mercy enough. No matter. They sank below my waters anyway. My lake has been the last resting place of so many burdened souls. It is why no one crosses my waters. Any who do meet their end at my will."

My hands come to either side of my head, trying desperately to muffle her voice.

"Don't listen to her, Danica! She is trying to get you to give in to despair."

The witch's voice shifts from without to within, echoing in my head as loud as the beat of my heart in my chest.

<*You are so tired.*>

"Stop it!" I scream. My hands press so hard into my head that I can hear my how blood rushing in my ears. It is not loud enough to drown out the voice.

<*You are weak. You can't save your baby.*>

"Danica!"

"I can't get her to stop."

"Danica, move!"

My eyes snap open. The vengeful spirit is less than a foot in front of me. The forceps, rusty and glinting red in the moonlight, are raised high over her head like an ax ready to be brought down over my head. I dive out of the way and land hard on the ice.

<*You will never save your baby. You are doomed to fail.*>

Gnarled fingers flex in the air, slim, spidery fingers with skin and muscle flaking off the bones. Black magic lashes at me.

I'm on my side, staring in horror as the gruesome energy streaks toward me. Below me a dull thud echoes beneath the ice. I feel it shake though my bones as a loud barking pulls me from my fear.

Bark, bark, bark!

River body-slams the walking corpse. On her heels are my other remaining dogs, now freed from their harness.

Lightfoot and Yehrik tears at the witch's cloak while Henry and Lilith snap at her legs. River, oh my River, launches herself at the witch's face, tackling her to the ice.

"Danica, we have to move."

Naomi's hands are solid on my shoulders, the first comforting touch I feel like I've had in ages. How long was I under the witch's spell? How much time has been wasted?

"Ahh! Curse you, you mongrels!"

The witch kicks Henry in the chest. My dog goes rolling sideways with a loud whine. He lands on his side. I rise to help him, but before I can get on my feel, dark hands reach up through the ice below his body and drag him below. The ice reforms after swallowing him whole.

"Henry!"

Laughter screams from deep within the wind. It is not the laugh of a singular entity. It is the laughter of a collective.

"They wake! My darling children! They wake and they will drag you into the deep."

The witch gloats as though she planned it this way the whole time.

All around us, shadows rustle into existence. Of varying sizes and shapes, some I suspect to be the souls of the battle-slain, the larger bulkier ones that exude menace. The slimmer, slighter spirits, must be the souls who died in childbirth. However many, I suspect, took their own lives in post-partum despair. The smallest though are the most numerous. Drenched in pain and regret, they hover barely separate from the ice from whence they rose. These are the innocents. The small ones who were unwanted. Infants given and left to die in the arms of this witch. Forever restless, these lives that were snuffed out too soon with so little time under the sun. The aura that weeps from their shadows is enough to make me want to curl up and cry myself to death.

I know what these are: draugr, the spirits of unrest who died at sea or in this case, the spirits who have died on the Spøkels.

The undead close in around us. The closest ghosts reach for us with sharpened pieces of soul. Yehrik, my red-flecked Siberian, turns away from the witch and angles toward the ghosts. His body passes through their forms as easily as mist, but on the other end of his charge, my dog goes limp, his essence ripped from his corpse.

"Yehrik. Oh, Yehrik…"

In a shuffle of red-tingled snow, I hear the ice open and claim a second dog.

"Danica, there's no time," Naomi growls into my ear. "We have to run. Now."

The draugr come after us. Their combined fury seeks to drown us, pull us beneath the ice just as they did Henry and Yehrik.

"I will take everything from you. You and your babe will serve me for eternity."

"Never!" I scream. Naomi goes wolf beside me. "River, heel. Lilith, Lightfoot, to me!" I call for my dogs. I can't lose them to these creatures. I draw my dagger from my boot and charge the witch, Naomi right at my side.

I leap at the vildod, the blade raised high and reflecting crimson in the moonlight. I refuse to die here, on this frozen wasteland with naught but the bloodied moon as a witness.

Blood and moonlight. Crimson in the glare of the moon.

My body moves without my say so. I jump into the air, something within me, something primal and long forgotten, wakes in the blood that runs through my veins. The blood of my ancestors drifts to the surface, and I am no longer human. I am no longer a Disappointment. Supernatural strength floods my legs. I jump higher and farther than I have ever jumped before, my muscles flooded with certainty that my aim will be true, and it is.

My feet touchdown on the chest of the vildod, and my blade plants itself between the skeletal seam of her forehead.

"Ahhhhhhhh!"

The midwife bursts into a scream of inky blackness. Her form discorporates. Whatever magic gave her corporeal form disintegrates, leaving her nothing but dust and shadow. All that is left behind is the pair of forceps, her gruesome athame.

Naomi, once again human-shaped, picks up the instrument. It glows like a blacklight, an aggressive violet that seems to ward off the draugr and neflim.

"Come, we must flee this place."

She doesn't have to tell me twice. River, Lightfoot, and Lilith are quick into their harnesses, and before I can even urge them on, River takes off run. Neither Naomi nor I ride on the sled. I run with my dogs, pushing the sled forward as they pull. Naomi races alongside on all fours. It is amazing to me how quickly she able to shift back and forth. I guess that is the gift of being a Dei lycan. With a moon that is ever present, Naomi's wolf lurks forever beneath the surface ready to burst forth. What that means for her more feral nature, I haven't a guess, nor do I want to contemplate it at a time like this.

Naomi keeps the witch's athame in her jaws, the light paving a path forward for us through the countless spirits that stalk our escape.

Desperation floods my whole being. I keep my eyes on the horizon just hoping and praying that the shoreline will make itself known. My legs pump harder and longer than I have ever had to run before. My lungs strain against the cold. I can feel the coughing fit bubbling up from my chest, but I squelch it down. I can't stop, not even to catch my breath.

In the dull red light of the moon, I have to keep hope alive. I have to trick myself into believing the shore is just a few more feet in front of me.

But then the ice cracks.

If you've ever heard the sound of ice breaking, you know how horrible it is. It's the same sound I heard when I slid across the ice after being batted away by the undead witch. A dull thudding beneath my feet followed by a watery fizz, it's the sound of death. Like a bullet going off in the distance, only I can feel the rumble of it beneath my feet.

"Hike up, River! Keep going, girl. Get us across!"

For a moment, I am one with River. Her heart becomes my own. Her breath sinks into my own lungs. I have no idea what bring this on, but it is the last thing that keeps me from panicking.

All around us, the ice breaks. Angry whooshes of water fly into the air, drenching us in mist and cold. The water freezes on contact with the sled, tiny icicles that slide off only to disappear in the ice at our feet.

We race against our doom, but you can't outrun ice. It comes for you faster than your senses can comprehend. Most people won't believe it until they've seen it, but even though it can sit unchanging for eons, ice, like rock, breaks within the blink of an eye and often with an explosion.

Ahead of us, the ice breaks and a fissure the size of a small stream opens up.

River veers away from it just in time to keep her, Lilith, and Lightfoot from taking a dip in the water. However, the angle of the swerve is too sharp, and the sled goes careening into the water.

I let go and stumble away from the rail before the sled can drag me in with it. The two separate plains of ice crash into one another. The sled and our supplies with it disappear beneath.

No time to mourn the loss because my dogs are still attached to it.

I rush to my dogs. All three of scramble for purchase in the ice, their claws leaving indentations in the ice to little effect.

Naomi is there already, River's harness between her teeth as she attempts to keep the three out of the water. Her breath steams on the air.

Before I can even doubt the decision, I pull the dagger again and slash at the part of the harness attached to the sled. I hack and hack and hack until the cord unravels, letting Lightfoot and Lilith loose. The violence of it, however, causes the cable to snap back on itself, flinging out and hitting Naomi square in the face.

The lycan goes down. The only thing that keeps her from being dragged off by the draugr is the athame still glowing at her feet on the ice.

I gather all of them in my arms. I rest Naomi's head in my lap. The she-wolf is bleeding. My dogs, I huddle them around my seated form, the athame held aloft in my hands trying in vain to ward away the restless spirits who want to drown us. River licks my cheek while Lightfoot whimpers into my shoulder. Lilith, my sweet Lilith, whines nudging Naomi's limp body with her nose.

My poor babies. They've survived so much. They've come so far with me and done so much for me, and this is how I repay them. I've led them to their deaths.

We are going to die here.

I am crying. Tears stream down my face. All around us, the draugr close in. Spirits of the drowned, spirits of the slain, spirits of innocent lives snuffed out by the hands of women who should have protected them most.

"Don't do this," I plead. "Please, don't do this."

The souls of the dead close in on us. My dogs, my last remaining three dogs, whimper as I cradle Naomi's prone form in my lap.

"I am not one of those women. I am not a child-killer. I am a mother, and all I want is my baby back."

The screeching gets louder and louder. I can barely think. I can barely even breathe from the intensity of it.

<Surrender to us, weakling. Give in. You haven't any other choice.>

"Stop it."

My voice comes out ragged and desperate.

"St-stop it!"

I croak like an ugly toad, but I push more strength into my demand.

"I said STOP IT!"

Ahead of us, I see it. The slightest beacon of hope on this dark day.

A small sailboard, like a gondola with a jib attached to a central mast, floats through the ice. Standing at the prow, a hunched and hooded figure strokes the water with an extended pole. At the fore of the boat, a great lantern glows, its light warm and yellow, the tiniest of suns in the eternal darkness of winter.

The draugr flee at the lamplight. Even the wind calms and the ice ceases its breaking.

My tears spill faster and harder. I am more terrified now than before. What if this being simply wants to kill us? What if this is a false hope? What if...

My questions vanish as I catch sight of the person rowing the boat. In the warm light of the lantern, the figure's face comes easily into view. A wizened face, features that on any other face would seem grotesque. Liver spots line his face, his beard reaches always the way to the deck of his boat, but his eyes are warm. They twinkle with mirth and look at me with unfathomable kindness.

"Your people may not have much by way of magic, but today, the gods have answered your prayers, Danica."

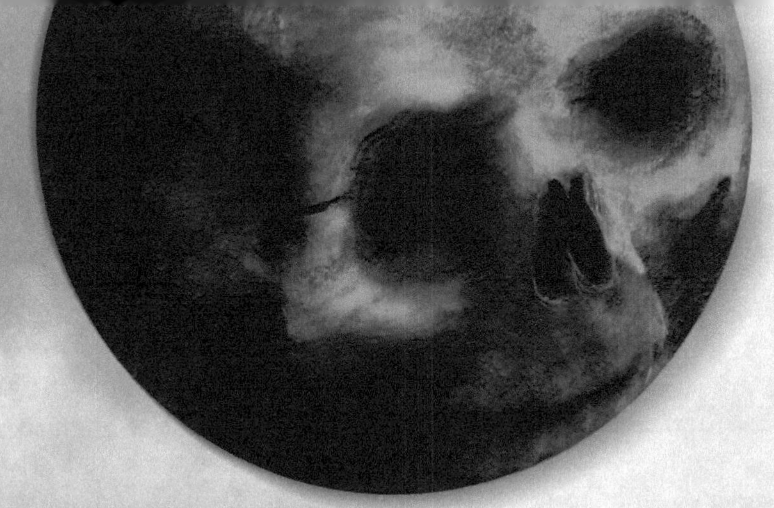

XI

Jack, Be Nimble.
Jack, Be Quick

When I saw the sailboat approaching, I never would have guessed that all five of us could fit aboard. I don't know if some trick of magic or simply my over-active imagination caused the discrepancy, but we all fit just fine.

The boatman shuffles us all onto the gondola, and he pushes us on our way. Using his oar, he seems to almost banish the ice from our path. By now, the water laps freely at the belly of our boat. It won't be long before all the ice has dispersed into the water or out to sea.

"How did you..."

The question dies on my lips. I don't know what I want to ask. How did he find us? Why did he find us? Who is he? How is his boat not ten feet below the surface right now?

"I am a guardian of travelers, my dear. I answer your calls for help because yours is a journey of great importance."

I frown.

"I want to rescue my daughter. I understand how that is important to me, but how is this important enough to catch the eye of..." I trail off. I still don't know who he is. Is he a spirit of some sort? A witch? A god? No, he can't be a god. The gods died long ago, slain by science. "Who are you anyway? What are you?"

"Shh..." He brings a finger to his lips and lets the note fall over me. "Names have power this far from the sun. Rest, weary traveler, for I mean you no harm."

My eyelids grow heavy. My body is spent on adrenaline. I can practically feel my veins vibrating from how rapidly my heart has been beating for the last, however many ... minutes, hours. How long has it been since we set foot on the Spøkels in this foolhardy attempt to make up time?

"Just rest, young Danica. Your journey is yet a long way from over."

His words fall over me like a blanket. I feel warm and safe. Even if I wanted to, I couldn't have fought against this lullaby.

"When you wake, you will have to be ready, for the hardest part is yet to come."

I know I am dreaming before I even recognize what I am dreaming about.

"I think I've fallen for you, Dani-girl."

Astra is sleeping. I've just finished rocking her. My bare feet pad along the hardwood of the floor as I carry her to her crib. As I lower her to the bedding, a pair of strong, semi-mechanical arms encircle my waist. A sharp, metallic musk engulfs me. I wrinkle my nose at the scent, but I know to whom it belongs: it's David. He's behind me, his arms wrapped around my midsection, too tight on my tender parts. He's never known his strength, something which can be quite titillating in the bedroom but unsettling any-where else.

"You've done good, Dani. Our daughter is just perfect."

"David? What are you doing here?"

He smiles a boyish grin at me. David isn't terribly tall. He's only about three or four inches taller than me, but being wrapped in his embrace again sends tingles up and down my spine.

"What do you mean what am I doing here, Dani-girl? This is our house. I brought you here, remember? After I killed that vamp and we found out you were pregnant. I'm a man of my word, ya know."

"But... but you died."

David laughs, heartily, throwing his head back. His tan-gled, sunny blond locks fly out in all directions.

"What are you talking about, starlight? I didn't die."

His head returns to look at me, and all of the festivity disappears from his face.

"You're the one that died."

Astra begins crying. Bile rises into my mouth, the sickly taste nearly making me barf right in his face. When David kisses me, the taste of copper joins the putridity of my last meal. My hands push against his chest, and I force my head way back, breaking the kiss and splitting my lip on the teeth that had been trying to gnaw on my lower lip.

"What's the matter, Dani? Aren't you happy to see me?"

Blood trails from the corner of his mouth. There are fang marks on either side of his throat and a deep laceration through the apex of his shoulder. His hands, blue, decaying things that smell like rotten meat, reach for me and grab my biceps.

I slap him across the face.

The blow shakes the entire house, and before my eyes, he dissolves into dream mist.

Astra's cries intensify, nearly drowning everything else out.

I turn, tears streaking my face, to pick her up, but she is gone. The crib is empty.

"Astra!" I call. My baby is gone, and my heart drops into my stomach.

I swivel my head this way and that looking, frantically for anything, any hint of where my child could have been taken. Joanna's face swims before my eyes. The house crumbles to bits around me, replaced with the biting cold of winter.

"Astra!"

"I have her, Danica." A calm voice slices through my frightened calls. Soothing and full of gentle care, the voice comes with a warm touch and a scent that reminds me of campfires and the outdoors.

"Naomi..."

"We're right here, love."

And there she is. Naomi is standing in a small room, painted in sweet pastels. A mobile featuring a veritable menagerie of colorful animals glitters and jingles from the ceiling. The soft chimes of a music box fill the air, playing "Twinkle, Twinkle Little Star." The space smells like baby powder and clean laundry.

In the lycan's arms is my daughter. My baby girl babbles and laughs, but she is no longer the tiny newborn that I set out to find on this quest. She is months older with control over her head, awareness just blossoming from her little eyes to capture the space around her. Tiny hands swat at the spinning animals above her head.

"We are right here, Danica. And here we will always be."

A magnetism of sorts draws me into the room. My bare feet drag through plush carpet. I accidentally kick aside a squeaky stuffed animal, but before I know it, I am wrapping my own arms around Naomi's waist.

I lift myself to meet her lips. The other woman is taller than me by a good foot, but she stoops to meet me. We kiss, long and sweet, and so wonderfully right.

Ideally, I notice the brush of soft fur against my calves and knees, River bounding around us, her happy barks sound like happiness.

"If we want this future, Danica," Naomi breathes against my lips, "you have to wake up and take it."

I wake up to dog slobber.

A warm, wet tongue laps up and down my cheeks, steamy breath wafting over my skin the way I would expect a heater/humidifier to blow in my face back home. Neither of these are a problem. It's the smell that wakes me fully. Dog breath is not the most pleasant thing to get a whiff of first thing in the morning.

I wink my eyes open to see a long pale nose shoved right into my forehead.

"Lightfoot, get off." I push the cold wet snout away with a cough. "My gods, you seriously need a dental treat."

The dog whines as if knowing I just accused him of having bad breath, but he backs away, giving me back my space so I can look around.

We aren't in the boat anymore. I can't even see the shore. We must be quite a ways from it.

I hear a sniffle to my right and look down to find Naomi still sleeping beside me. My cheeks get warm as I remember the dream kiss I just woke from. Gotta love irrational visions gifted to us from our subconscious.

Snow falls all around us, but I'm still plenty warm, thanks to the blanket someone threw over us and the three dogs that have been laying on top of us for who knows how long.

"Naomi. Naomi, wake up."

Despite how gently I nudge her shoulder, the lycan snaps awake as though the world were shaking underneath her.

"What happened? Where are we?"

"You got hit in the head while we were on the water."

"The lake? You mean..." Naomi's already pale face goes ghostly white. I would think she was dead were it not for the heat of her body radiating against me. "How did we get here? I thought for sure we were going to die."

"I'm not sure, exactly. There was..." I trail off. How do I explain what happened? I don't even know who that guy was or how he somehow managed to get us here. "Someone saved us. I think he left us here. He... he was very old and he said something about the gods."

"A spirit of the lake. He must have been a potomas or a nokken. He didn't hurt you."

I shake my head.

"You're lucky. Most water spirits will drown mortals just for the sake of getting a good laugh."

"I think he was thankful that we got rid of the vildod that has been haunting the water." I don't know what inspires me to say as much, but once I've puked the idea out, I know in my heart that it's true. Personally, I wouldn't like it if an undead witch was haunting my house. The spirit, whoever he was, said he was answering my prayers. I don't know whether to be scared stiff that he heard me or to just go about my business hoping that he won't come knocking later hoping to call on a debt I unwittingly agreed to by accepting his help.

"Any idea what direction we need to go in now?"

Naomi looks around. Her nose even swivels from side to side as she sniffs the air.

"Whatever reason the potomus had to help us, he did us a great favor. We are close. Much closer than we were before."

"You can tell that much by just sniffing the air."

Naomi nods.

"Your baby's scent was here not too long ago. We are gaining on the kidnapper."

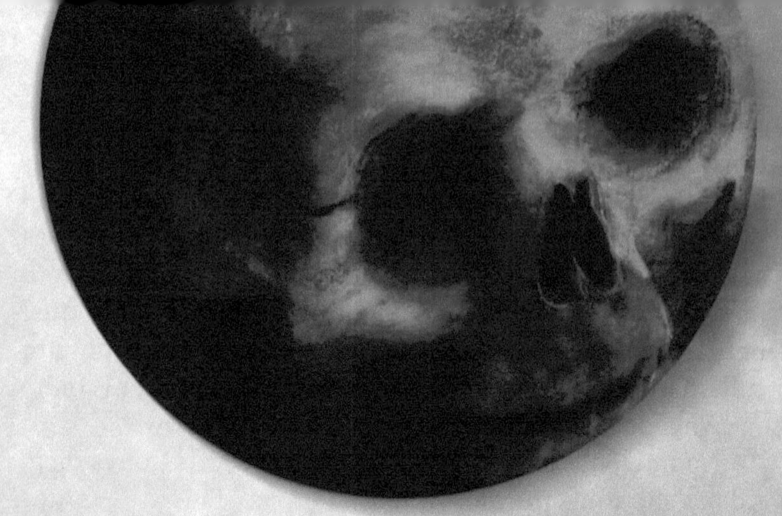

XII

JACK, JUMP OVER THE CANDLESTICK

I don't know what frightens me more: the knowledge that my child was snatched from me right under my nose or the idea that I will soon confront the woman who has attempted to steal away my most precious treasure. Honestly, I don't know what I'm going to do when I see her. I've lost so much on this journey: my dogs, my livelihood... my innocence.

My gods, if anything has happened to Astra. If we are too late...

"Everything is going to be fine, Danica."

I look over at Naomi. I can tell she is in pain. The lycan is hunched over herself against chill of the wind. It's hard to imagine a lycan being cold, but I suppose in her human-form, she is just as bare to the elements as I am.

"Thanks, by the way."

Naomi angles her head toward me. I dare not look her in the face, though. I don't know what I'll see.

"I only mean… It's just that—Well, I know you didn't have to bring me along or even keep that troll from eating me. Nor did you have to rescue me from the midwife, and just… I wanted to say thank you for all of those things. You've taken better care of me the last few days than…" I don't finish the thought. How can I tell her she's done more for me than everyone I've ever had in my life, including my own mother?

"I'm not only here for Astra, Danica."

Naomi's fingertips brush the exposed skin just beneath my chin as she encourages me to lift my gaze. My brown eyes meet the clearest of blues. I never realized just how pale her eyes are. I feel like they could freeze me in place, and I would opt to never move a single muscle again.

"I am here for you too, Danica. I always will be."

I frown, not understanding.

"I've known you for less than two weeks. And yet, I feel I've been linked to you my whole life."

"Humans care very little for fate, and those that do believe in it often seek to change it or mold it to their will. They never get the answer they seek, and they often fall in the battle against it in some of the most gruesome ways."

A flicker of cold brushes against my cheek. When I hold out my hand to investigate, more flecks of ice brush against my palm. It's snowing. The gentlest snowfall we've had in a long while tumbles from the sky in neat, sweet flurries.

"I suppose citing all of those old Greek tragedies would be moot, considering we are discussing a thing as fickle as destiny."

Naomi chuckles.

"You don't have to believe in it. Like I said, most humans don't, but fate has a way of getting its way whether its three little old ladies knitting the largest sweater ever made or an old blind man lugging around the thickest tome ever written."

Both of those references go completely over my head which prompts me to ask my next, rather rude question.

"How old are you exactly?"

Naomi's laugh sounds more like a bark. "Too young, according some of my people, but I'm practically an old woman according to others."

"How many years?"

"I am twenty-two years old."

I blink. "I'm twenty-one. That's not super young."

"You are 21 in a race of being that live to be 40 or 50 at the most. I am 22 in a race of beings that live to be up to 200 years old. Many of the elders still consider me a pup. Comparatively, I would say you are probably more in line with being a full-fledged member of your community than I."

That isn't comforting.

"So you're saying I am the adult here." *Well, shit! Aren't we lucky we haven't died yet!*

"Yes and no. Once we accomplish our first shift, our rite of passage, as it were, is complete, and we are considered adults in the eyes of the pack. Now does that make us respected figures in the community? No. This quest is my way of proving to the pack that I ready to embrace my role as the white wolf."

"Is that supposed to be a special thing?"

"White wolves are rare. In each generation, it is said that only one will be born. The white wolf is supposed to guide and support younglings through their first change. My pack has not had a white wolf in three generations, not since the technomancers took power."

"So your pack hasn't had anyone to help the young ones shift."

"Correct. It's bad enough that the witch magic that sustains us has been so badly weakened. It even worse now that the League has burned the remaining witches to ash."

I wince.

I'd heard of such practices. Not too many years ago, the most powerful witch of the southern continent apparently lit herself on fire as a way to prevent the technomancers from lighting her up themselves. She'd apparently gone mad after a recent dispute left her childless and without allies to support her. She made a great show of taking out nearly half of the League's current roster of technomancers though.

"So you are the first white wolf to be born in your pack in however many years? Doesn't that mean you should be tucked away for safe keeping?"

"That's exactly what the elders wanted for me. They even set up my parents with a beautiful house and garden to insure I was kept safe and sound."

"So what's the but?"

"I kept hearing the call. Your call, Danica. Yours and Astra's." Naomi steps closer into my space. "There is a legend from the ancient times. The first lycan to be born was a white wolf. A witch king fell deeply in love with his personal bodyguard. The bodyguard was a master animal handler and his most faithful companion was a dire wolf that he had found and raised from a pup. One moonlit night, the king took his lover for a picnic at the palace edge. An assassin appeared. The bodyguard and his loyal wolf stepped in. He slayed the king's attacker, but in the process, he and the wolf were poisoned by a very specific toxin that lined the assassin's weapons. I'm sure you're familiar with monkshood."

"Wolfsbane," I whisper. "That's the other name for it."

Naomi nods.

"The witch king couldn't bear to let his lover die, so he morphed the poison into a blessing. In order to save his lover's life, the witch wove a spell that joined the pair. The bodyguard and his dire wolf became one and the same. Every Dei lycan is descended from this first lycan, and we live to find balance between our wolfish selves and our human selves, and for many of us, love is a large part of that fight."

"I still don't understand what that has to do with me."

"Love, Danica, is not a happenstance. It is fated, determined by the gods of old and extending into eternity for all who are fortunate enough to experience it."

I snort. "Well, that's a load of crock."

Naomi blinks at me.

"Everyone at the village uses destiny as some sort of explanation for why we are Disappointments. Everyone says we are the result of what happens when someone tries to defy their own destiny. Well, I think it's a bunch of bullshit. There's no such thing as fate. People use destiny as an excuse for their sad, miserable existence because it's convenient. Nobody actually believes in it. The idea that the Fates care enough about people's love lives to weave them together... I'm sorry but the idea is laughable."

As I end my tirade, I realize that Naomi has stopped walking.

"Naomi?"

"Just because you've only seen the negative side of a coin doesn't mean the coin can't be flipped. This isn't some double-sided coin I'm trying to toss. I'm not trying to trick you. I just..." Naomi's voice trails off.

My thoughts backpedal as I realize how dismissive everything I just said must have sounded. "Naomi, I didn't mean—"

A stick snaps to my right. I look over in time to see a small shadow rush past. A menacing feeling drifts over my psyche.

"Noami, look out!"

Before she can move, a body half Naomi's size manages to knock her over. The creature moves so quickly, I can't get a good glimpse of it. I draw my knife and rush forward to help her, but before I can get very far, two more creatures appear out of the woods and attack Lightfoot and Lilith.

"Run, Danica! Run!" Naomi cries as she disappears into the underbrush.

"Naomi!"

"Run!" I hear her call one last time, fainter as she is taken into the woods. I hear barking behind me. When I turn around, Lightfoot and Lilith are gone too. Only River wrestles with our attackers.

"River!" I shout, rushing forward and kicking the creature away. It yelps. I see a dirt-encrusted, bark-like body and a conical head disappear into a nearby bush. Before I can even think, growls chorus through the night, and for once in my life, I follow directions.

I run.

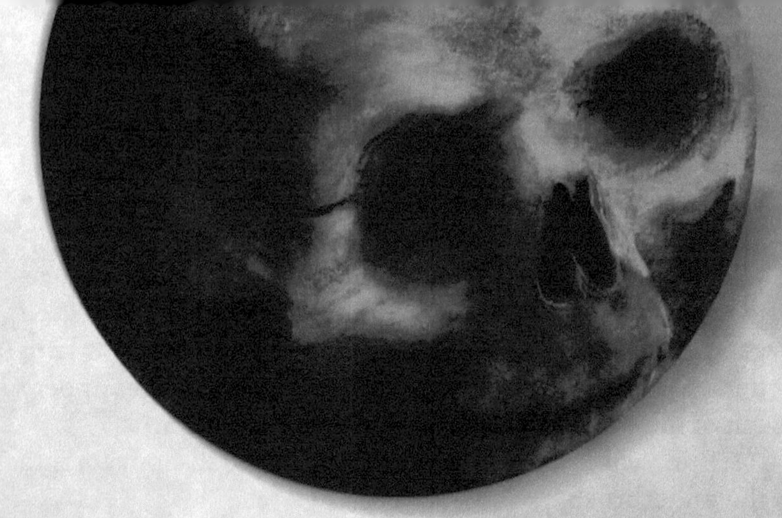

XIII

THE DISH RAN AWAY WITH THE SPOON

I run blind through the forest. River's white tail bounds back and forth before me. I follow the dog as best as I can. If I lose River's trail, I'll be completely lost. Alone and lost with no way of knowing which direction to go.

The hair on the back of my neck stands on end. Every time I hear one of those things growl or shift in the trees, I suppress a scream from rising out of my throat. First a giant troll, then the midwife, now whatever these horrid little things are. I had no idea the forests of the Wastes were so treacherous, but suddenly Old Woman Rosie's warnings of never straying from the beaten path seem like much better advice than my pigheaded self ever thought before.

We run up the mountain path, the incline rapidly getting steeper and stepper. My thighs cramp and creak with every step. I can barely draw a breath, it hurts so badly. My lungs burn from the exertion. Every exhale forms icicles in the air, and every inhale I choke down feels like I am swallowing ice cubes. Any more of this and the frost in the air is going to freeze the air in my body.

River takes a sharp turn to the right. In my attempt to turn with her, I lose my footing. Landing hard on my side, I skid along the ice, grasping at anything that can stop my momentum. I finally just jam my knife into the ground. Not a second too late either as the ground disappears from under my feet and ankles. A chance glance back tells me I am mere feet away from plummeting over a sharp edge.

If I'd had any food in my stomach, it would have come up right then and there.

I scratch my way back onto the mountain to find River standing at the mouth of a cave. My dog barks at me as though to say *hurry up, hurry up!*

In my near tumble over the side of the mountain, I forgot the more immediate danger. I turn my flashlight on and see them, small forms on the ground with beady eyes and gnashing sharp teeth. Barely indistinguishable from the ground, they look like rocks or pieces of wood rippling across the snow.

Bark! Bark!

I get it into gear, racing toward River. I don't know if they will stop chasing us once we get into the cave, but it's better than staying out here in their element. I dive blindly into the cavern, and I don't stop until the last twinkle of light fades from view.

I thought it was dark before. The sunless north, devoid of the light of our brightest star, is often thought of as the darkest, most terrifying place to reside. That darkness has nothing on this: the underground.

I've never been spelunking, myself, and I automatically know why when the claustrophobia creeps up my spine and decides to live at the base of my skull. I can't even see the walls yet I can feel them closing in on me.

River pads along beside me. We've gone from trying to go up the mountain to now going inside the mountain. It is a descent I never imagined I would make in my life. The smell of damp and dark. I didn't know darkness had a scent until now, but there is no other way to describe it. Cold air mixing with underground water and the stale droppings of nocturnal life. There's a dusty musk to it as well. The scene of footsteps treading through a space for the first time in ages.

Speaking of footsteps, the ground beneath my feet seems to shudder in a strange rhythm. Ba-Boom, Ba-Dum, Ba-Boom. I don't know where the sound is coming from, but it resonates all the way into my bones.

I feel like I am walking into the pit of some strange rock concert.

I'm not an avid hiker or even that much of an outdoor-adventure type of person, but I'm fairly certain there is a certain lack of equipment that is about to make this trek into the mountain very, very dangerous, but I am surprised yet again when as we reach a somewhat level ground, the cave seems like less of a cave and more like a corridor.

Torchlight brightens the space. Turning off my flashlight, I can see clearly for the first time since we lost the stars, and the view that greets me is beyond believable.

Humans used to write books about elves and dwarves and any number of strange mythical beings. I've always wondered if those fables were based on any actual fact, but walking into this mountain hall, I can't help but think there must be some merit to such fantasies.

The stone floor has been paved and laid out with the plushest looking carpet I have ever laid eyes on. My gods, it even smells different. Instead of the cave and the musk of animals, I can smell clean wood and freshly laundered linens. There is a distinctive lack of the entropic smell I'd grown accustomed to in the cave.

Artwork lines the walls—paintings of animals and landscapes coupled with the portraits of women. As I walk through, I begin to suspect they are all different aspects of the same woman. Different hair colors paired with different styles of dress. Some of them are dressed to go hunting. In others, she wears fine clothes and jewelry. Crowns which sparkle like icy diamonds even decorate her head in a few of the portraits. No matter her visage though, she has the same face and expression: a haughty smile.

Furs and sculptures decorate each side of the hall. One sculpture depicts a naked woman being waited on by four collared men. She is giant next to the men, at least three times their size. She lays on a dais while the men crowd the floor around her. Hoarfrost patterns decorate her skin. Her hair is shaped as though the wind is whipping it through a blizzard. And her face, her face is the finest I've ever seen. Smooth curves and perfectly symmetrical, whether that is the artist's correction or a true depiction, I couldn't say, but her beauty is marred by the cruel smile gracing her lips.

The men offer her grapes and goblets of drink and—I cringe—something that looks suspiciously like human fingers, tiny human fingers. I avert my eyes and pretend I didn't see such artwork.

I don't see any doors or turns, so I can only assume the way forward is, well, forward.

My footsteps echo along the walls. It isn't quiet per se, but noise down here is very different from noise on the surface. The sound kind of bounces around. Off the walls, off the paintings lining each side, even off my own body.

It's strange and unsettling.

Eventually, we come to a cavern so large, the torches don't shine bright enough to reveal the entire expanse to my dull human eyesight.

Stone pillars rise into the abyss. If there is a ceiling up there somewhere, my mortal eyes are not powerful enough to even conceive of it. I didn't think we had ventured that far down, but it is a mountain after all. We weren't exactly on the highest peak when we dove into its heart.

The heart of the mountain...

My gods, its heart is beating under my feet.

Mama!

On the next pulse, the word ricochets through the very fibers of my soul. The echo is followed by the sharp sound of crying.

"Astra?" I whisper. Disbelief makes me hesitate. Is it real this time?

Another cry, even louder than the last. Before I can react, River bounds forward.

"Astra!" It must be. It has to be! My lungs still ache from running through the woods, but it doesn't matter. I can hear my baby. The phantom sensation of holding her in my arms pushes me forward. I can imagine it now, holding my baby in my arms, smelling her hair and the sweet scent of clean soap, the orange-scented shampoo my mother made for her. I want to feel her little hands squeezing my face and hair. Whenever she nurses, she likes to pinch and squeeze my mouth and chin, sometimes even my other nipple. I yearn for those things now. All I want is my baby back in my arms.

I want it so badly, I am willing to kill for it.

"Quiet, you horrible little thing!"

A new voice shouts at my baby. It echoes off the walls, loud and frightful. The cries quiet, and my heart stops, but it is only for a moment. My baby resumes, her voice louder and more determined for attention. The sound of her voice is like a defibrillator, restarting my own heartbeat before I can finish my cardiac arrest.

"Don't you touch my baby!"

I don't take in my surroundings. I don't process anything I pass, not the images on the walls, not even the fire burning on either side. It's like my senses all shut off until I see her, and with her, I find the greatest horror I have ever experienced.

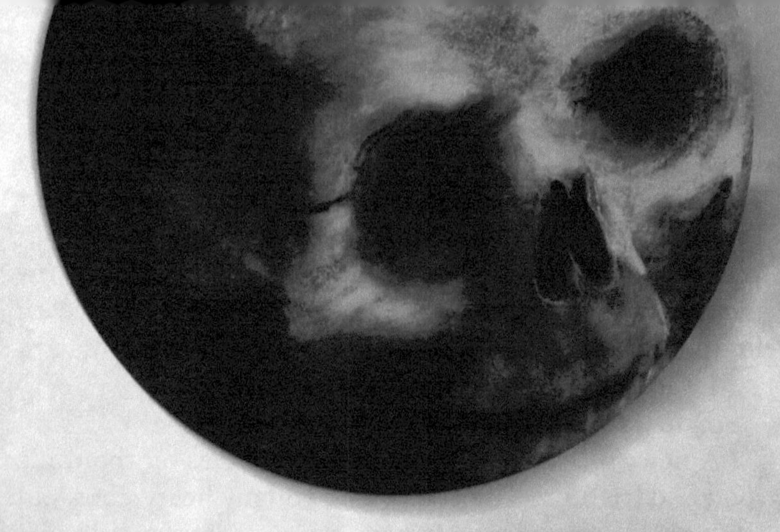

XIV

OLD MOTHER HUBBARD WENT TO THE CUPBOARD

My mother used to tell me a lot of different stories as a child. Some of them were purely fantasy: stories about mermaids turning into seafoam and princesses losing their slippers or falling asleep for thousands of years. Some of the stories were a little scarier. I always hated the one about the girl in the red cape that got eaten by a wolf. There was another one about the old hag who spread disease and famine. If she had a rake, a few people might survive her plague. If she had a broom, not a soul would survive her pestilence.

I won't lie. I was a scaredy-cat of a child. I was afraid of the dark, I was afraid of spiders, heck, for a while I was even afraid of looking out the window for fear that I would find something staring back at me. The stories always frightened me. But there was something my mother would always say afterward: "Stories are stories, Danica, and stories can't hurt you." At least, that's what she always said when I didn't want to sleep with the lights off.

There was always one in particular that frightened me.

Long, long ago, in a time when the gods still walked the earth, a giantess ruled from her mountain throne. In her youth, the giantess was kind and friendly. She gave blessings to the villagers who tended the lands around her mountain and even went out of her way to ensure that her servants lived comfortable lives.

She would take walks through the forest, greeting the animals and caring for broken or injured trees. In the wintertime, she would strike away the worst blizzards and weave a thin blanket of snow to spread across the land.

The giantess's name was Skabine.

But something changed.

When her father, the mountain king, passed away, Skabine was made queen of the mountain. At first, she handled the responsibility well. She kept peace for her people and continued to maintain the easy lifestyle her people had come to love and appreciate.

Five years into her reign, a giant came to call. The suitor's name is unknown and unimportant, but he was handsome and brave, and Skabine could not help but fall in love with him. The two were married in the spring, and for a time, Skabine was happy with her new consort. The couple was even ecstatic to announce a new heir on the way.

The queen's pregnancy was difficult, and as a result, she had to step away from her duties, leaving her consort responsible for her queendom.

During this time, the consort showed his true colors. In his greed, he raised taxes on the people. He put the servants to work for long hours at pitiful wages. He even attacked the nearby villages, demanding tribute each month lest they invite his full wrath. When one of the villages failed to offer an appropriate tribute, he laid waste to the entire town. When he was through, not a single survivor remained.

Naturally, as happens, whispers of rebellions began to spread. People made moves to take down the giant and destroy everyone in league with him.

Meanwhile, the queen was told none of this. She was so sickly, not even her nursemaid dared to tell her of her husband's deeds. The midwife feared how hopeless the situation was saying she would lose either her baby or her life if she tried to carry the pregnancy to term, but she would not lose hope, for the queen had already bonded with the tiny giant growing in her womb. How could something with such strong kicks not be given a chance to breathe for the first time?

On the day the queen went into labor, the consort declared war on her people. Her consort was struck down, his arrogance proving his downfall. The queen suffered through her labor entirely unknowing that her entire world was falling apart around her. But she cared nothing about it because in the small hours of the morning, the doctor put her precious baby into her arms. He was perfect. Everything she could have hoped for. So enchanted by her new life as a mom, she didn't even think to wonder where her servants were.

Days later, the angry villagers force their way into the mountain.

The queen is entirely overcome, and she is helpless to keep these people, whom she spent her whole life protecting, from destroying the one thing that matters most to her. The mortals tied her down and made her watch as they tossed her little boy's limp body around like a beach ball.

In her grief and her rage, the mountain queen let out a huge burst of magic. For the first time in decades, a blizzard blasted across the entire countryside. Anyone outside froze upon coming in contact with the blast of freezing air. The people within the mountain found themselves snowed in with the angry giantess, and when Skabine broke her bonds, she ripped every person present to shreds. Some she merely pulled to pieces. Others she devoured whole. The last few, she played with the way they played with her son.

When the blood was spilled and the souls bound to Helheim, Skabine sat on her forsaken throne and wept.

The legend goes on to say that the giantess would come down from her mountain every one hundred and fifty years looking for the blood of the innocent to quelch her hunger. Her servants would steal children from their mother's arms, and if they were the descendants of the ones who killed her babe, she would eat them. To the children of the nonviolent, she showed slightly more mercy by letting them voyage to the far lands before the cruelties of this world could taint their innocence.

Her hatred tainted the whole of the land. Her midwife began hurting her charges, drowning them soon after birth. The elves of the woods became sinister and bloodthirsty. The trolls of the forest collected prizes to present to their queen. The Wastes themselves became frigid and inhospitable.

The story ends when the witches of the Wastes pour their magic together in order to putting the giantess to sleep.

Either way, the ghosts made as a result of her revenge haunted my dreams for years.

I never expected to stare that very legend in the eye.

Seated on a throne larger than even the tallest skyscraper I've ever seen sat a giantess. David took me to a museum in Aighneas once, and I remembered seeing a beautiful medieval gown on display. Encased in a glass, airtight case, it was a stunning shade of emerald green, with rhinestones and lace inlaid into the bodice and the various ruffles of the skirt. The dress the giantess wears reminds me of that same dress, only this one hasn't been sitting devoid of the elements for however many centuries. It is tattered and torn, off-color and stained. The stones have lost their shine, and the lace looks more like cobwebs. The giantess's long hair lays tangled around her head and chest. In the dim lighting, I can't really tell the color, but the locks are somewhere between a dull red and a dark, brassy brown.

But her face, sunken and gaunt, is nothing but skin stretched over bone. I'm reminded of a Halloween or Samhain decoration. Even her nose seems to have crumbled away. Looking at the hollow cold of her unseeing eyes, I know I am looking at the mountain queen who so many years ago had her baby taken from her.

"Please, your majesty. Please give me back my daughter." A familiar voice curls in my ear, and for a moment, my own grief and rage rise to the surface.

At the giantess's feet, a familiar figure kneels, hunched over herself and crying. It's Joanna.

"You dare demand a boon from me."

The sheer force of the queen's voice nearly knocks me off my feet. It echoes off the walls and hits me like a blast of freezing cold air. The giantess's breath doesn't steam in the chill. Instead, it drops the temperature lower.

"Please, the midwife—"

"The midwife told you to bring me another child of the bastards that destroyed my hope. Instead, you bring me a witchling."

"This is no witch, your majesty. She is a child of my village. The most recent Disappointment. There is no way she is magical."

A giant fist slams against the arm of the throne. Joanna falls backward. Out of her arms, a bundle of blankets rolls. My eyes widen as Astra's little body, flailing in anger, comes to a stop on the cold stone. Her screams double, no longer muffled by the swaddle.

"Astra!"

My feet move before my brain can even think. In no time, I am across the throne room, scooping up my baby into my arms and holding her to my chest.

"Astra. Oh, Astra, my darling. Mama's here. Mama came to find you."

"Danica?" Joanna looks up at me as though I might stab her in the face. "How?"

River blasts past me, barking and growling. She barrels into the woman who kidnapped Astra, attacking her with all the vehemence of a dog protecting its owner.

When Joanna starts screaming, my heart unfolds. Joanna's screams make me call my dog to a stop. "River, heel!" The husky stops immediately, but Joanna doesn't get up. I worry, for a moment, that enough damage was done to keep her down, but then her head lifts.

"Danica, how did you get here? How did you follow me?"

I don't answer, countering instead with my own question. "Why did you do it, Joanna? Why did you take my baby?"

"I had no choice. My own daughter was taken. I had to get her back."

"So you would trade my daughter's life for yours!"

"Yes."

"Danica, don't talk to her!"

Naomi's voice coming from the ceiling startles me. When I look up, I see her, Lightfoot, and Lilith bound and hanging from a hook right above our heads.

"Naomi! You're okay!"

"Eh, I think 'okay' is a relative term."

"Silence!" Skabine's voice booms across the room.

Astra screams.

"Shhh, little one. I'm here. Hushhhh."

But the cold of the room is too much. Her little lips are turning purple. Uncaring of my own comfort, I unzip my jacket, tuck her against my body, and wrap her as tightly in the thick down as I can.

"Please, let us go. We mean you no ill will. If you'll just let Naomi, the dogs, Astra, and me go, you'll never see us again, I swear it."

Skabine laughs.

"You come into my realm and take the offering gifted to me."

"My baby is not an offering!"

"Yet she was brought to me for exactly that reason."

"Where is Joanna's daughter? You were a mother once. Please, give her back her daughter. Surely, you have enough of a heart to—"

"My heart was murdered by your kind. It wasn't enough for them to slay the one who had done them wrong. They had to inflict as much misery and damage as they could. I devoured them for their crimes, and still I hunger for revenge. I cannot and I will not bring back the one who is descended from those monsters."

"Please, give me my daughter," cries Joanna.

"Your daughter is dead, girl. Best move on and do what you humans do best and make another one."

"You cruel, horrible—"

Moving faster than I ever could have imagined a being of her size moving, the giantess brings her scepter down, crushing Joanna with a sickening crunch. I nearly retch at the sight of her broken body lying on the ground. A gust of frost blasts past me and snatches Astra from my arms. Some invisible entity carries her up, toward the giantess, suspended by the arms of my coat.

She begins to cry as fingers the size of my lost sled turn her this way and that.

"Perhaps I will keep the witchling, after all. I would be worthwhile to have a witch under my employ once again. The villdød was getting irksome."

"No!" shouts Naomi, but white noise floods my ears. Having Astra back in my arms just to have her snatched away again... something breaks in my core.unfolds. Joanna's

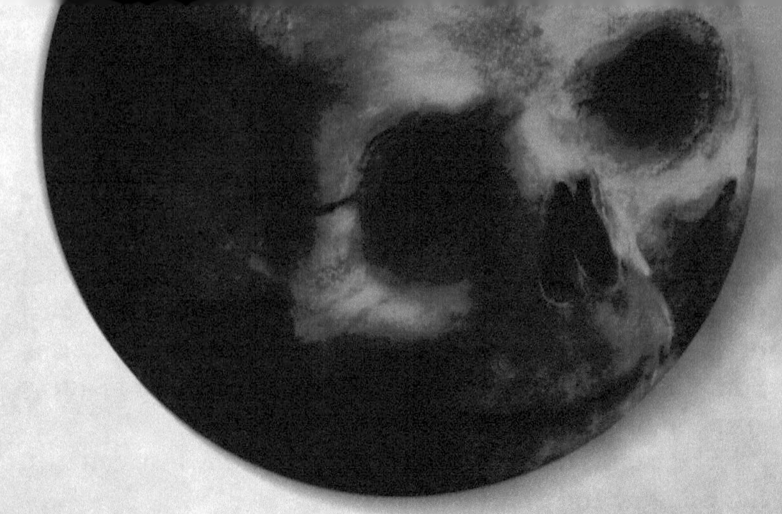

XV

KNICK, KNACK
PATTY WHACK

"You can't. She is my baby."

"I will do what I well please, human."

The scepter rises again, and I dive to the side before Joanna's fate becomes my own. River starts barking and running around the room trying to draw the giantess's attention. My insides burn. Shards of glass wedge their way into the clogged pathways of my essence and rip open new tunnels. Like a radio finding the right frequency, whispers buzz to life in my mind.

<Her weakness is her strongest need. If you want to leave here alive, you need to make her see.>

"Danica, get us down from here."

The scepter comes down again, barely missing me. I can't overcome a giant on my own. I need to find a way to get Naomi down.

During all of this, Astra's cries worsen. She screams and wriggles, and the makeshift swing made from my jacket tilts precariously from side to side. My goddess, what if she falls!

"Quiet, child! Enough of this racket!"

The giantess flicks a finger toward Astra, and my baby's cries go silent. From my vantage point on the ground, it looks like frost is forming around the jacket.

No! Has she frozen my baby?

<Help me> I project in my head to whomever tried to talk to me before. <Help me save them. Help me save my baby.>

<We cannot, young star.> The voice that answers sounds like a collective rather than a singularity. Hundreds, no, thousands of voices all tied up together to form one consciousness. <We too are chained.>

<How?>

<We are the Echoes of the past.>

<You mean you are ghosts?I ask.>

<No, we are the Echoes of magic left behind to guard this place.>

Oh, great, I think. I'm talking to a leftover magic spell. How much crazier can this whole thing get?

<When the magic died, our power was weakened, allowing the queen to wake. She has enslaved us. We bend to her will because the witches that formed us are no more. We linger as her slaves waiting for a chance to pull the mountain queen's prison back together, so this suffering will happen no longer.>

Maintaining focus on a conversation happening in my head is really hard. On my way to the wall, I knock over a bust. It clatters to the ground. The scepter comes down again where the statue broke.

Cave-dwelling creatures are often blind. Many of them evolve to get rid of their eyes entirely. This giantess has been trapped inside her mountain for over a thousand years. She hasn't seen the light of day in just as long. It would make sense for her to have lost her sense of sight.

I stop running. The queen attacked Joanna right after she had shouted at her. She tried to squish me after I demanded Astra back. Then she struck where the statue hit the ground.

She is attacking based on sound, not sight.

Bending to pick up a piece of broken tile, I toss it as far away from me as I can. As I predicted, when it hits the ground, the scepter comes down again. Now that I know how to avoid her, I have time to figure out a solution to the next problem. I need to get Naomi and the dogs down.

It would be ideal if there was a rope tether somewhere on the ground that I could release, but this is a giant's realm that we're talking about. Who would have need of such a device when you're able to touch the ceiling just by standing up?

An idea forms in my head. I wish I could communicate it to Naomi. I wish so hard that the glass in my veins slips further along. I gasp. It feels like water is flowing through me, chilling me to the bone but warming me at the same time. Such a wonderful sensation. It's like realizing that I've never been truly warm. My whole life, I've just been packing on layers and layers of clothing to stave off the worst of the chill. How could I have not known such a feeling existed?

<Danica, is that... You're in my head.>

My eyes widen. She can hear me. Naomi can hear me in her own head, and I can hear her.

<You need to make her cut you down. I'm going to try and get her to drop the scepter. When she does, she'll resort to the sword. Use your voice to get her to slice the rope above your head.>

As I relay the plan to Naomi, I tiptoe my way over to the throne. There are intricate carvings all along the seat, plenty for rock climbing. Just a few feet of the ground and my muscles protest loudly. I'm not built for this kind of thing. The little rock climbing I've done has been with the help of my dogs, pushing a sled up a steep incline.

There is no incline here, just a perfect 90 degree scale up a wall.

"You can't hide forever," says the giantess. "Or have you given up your hope like I did? Don't worry. At least, your infant will be cared for. The mountain spirits are quite good at tending to the young and helpless."

I grit my teeth, pulling and pushing my body up another foot. I keep praying to any entity that will listen that the call goes through. Air Danica is newly broadcasting. I can't be sure how effective the transmitter is at the moment, but Naomi is quiet, which is all the blessing I need.

I grab a handhold around a jewel that has been crusted into the side panel of the throne, and in my haste to pull myself up, I dislodge the aged upholstery. I nearly scream as all of my body weight goes into my non-dominant hand.

The gemstone clatters to the ground, and for a moment, I fear I am about to be squished. Sure enough, the scepter appears over the edge of the arm, but loud barking draws the scepter away from me. When I peek over the edge, I can see River running around in circles, trying to distract the giantess from me. When the scepter comes down, my heart stops as River disappears from my view.

"River!" I cry out unthinking. In that same instant, the butterfly effect triggers. The scepter's impact causes the ripples of void to convulse, and an unseen force knocks me sideways. The throne's carvings shift and change, my handholds disappearing as more are created. I plummet two feet down before a spike suddenly protrudes from the side of the arm-rest. I land on my stomach and curl around the protrusion for dear life.

A bark bids me open my eyes, and a sigh punches out of my chest as River reappears a moment later. The scepter came down right in front of her, but she stopped short before she could actually be crushed.

Before the relief can actually have any kind of impact, I remember that there is a 30-foot-tall giantess currently swinging a scepter in my direction. In a mad dash to get out of the way, I push off my little ledge with all my might, a sensation not unlike what it looks like to see a squirrel jump from one tree trunk to another, and I catch hold and scramble upward as fast as my arms and legs can take me.

I hear a deafening slam behind me, but I don't stop and look back until I can curl my arms over the flat edge of the throne.

In her attempt to hit me, she lost hold of her scepter. She curses under her breath, frost drifting from her mouth with every abyssal word she utters.

"My, my!" Naomi heckles, sounding more like a hyena than a wolf. "I hadn't any idea, her majesty knew such language!"

"I've heard fouler things from the mouths of mortals."

"Nevertheless, it is unbecoming for one such as yourself to degrade yourself to such ugliness."

"You dare call me ugly! I used to keep your kind as pets, young wolf. It was always such a pity when they got too old, too violent, and too untrainable."

"What? Were you afraid we'd bite you?"

"You did bite, I'm afraid. That's what lycans do. They bite even the hands that feed them. Even the hands that love them, they bite."

The sound of metal sliding from its sheath rings through the room. The blade flies. The whistling of it cutting the air flings my hair across my face.

I watch in horror as Naomi and the dogs fall from ceiling until before my eyes, the woman who has helped me every step of the way here transforms from woman to beast. I've never actually seen Naomi shift. It's always just kind of happened behind my back, out of my eyesight. Seeing it happen as she falls from the ceiling, I feel like I should be horror-stricken by the visual. Her spine elongates, her jaw lengthens, and her hands and feet curl into paws. Fur sprouts across her face. Her bones seem to break and reform. I don't know what happens to her clothes; I don't think my mind would be able to comprehend it even if I did happen to realize the answer. Muscles stretch and reform until a great white wolf spins through the air to land on all fours on the ground.

Naomi's paws touch the ground, and a mighty howl is unleashed. It echoes around the cavern, shaking the stalactites and the carved columns as though they were made of jelly. Lightfoot and Lilith, as though thriving off her aura, land upright as well, and they join her chorus.

Then something unexpected happens.

"Stop that racket! I said, stop it!"

The queen goes mad. She begins madly clawing at her ears. She screams in pain as the howling becomes louder and louder.

Now is my chance.

I pull myself all the way up onto the throne. Astra is hovering there, quiet as the grave despite all the noise. With the giantess thrashing not too far from me in her throne, chunks of rock and granite fall around the room. There is no time. This is my only chance. My feet find traction on the torn, upholstery surface of the throne's arm, and I run. I run straight to the end of the armrest. Astra is so close. I have to get to her. I have to jump. I need to make the jump. What happens after doesn't matter. I need to get my baby.

I take the leap and pray for enough faith to make it.

<Naomi,> I call in my head. *<I don't know if you can hear this but... Take care of Astra.>*

My arms close around my swaddled daughter, and I pull her in tight and angle my back downward as we freefall to the ground. I hold her to my chest, peeking in-between the folds of the coat to see her. She is freezing cold, but her chest rises and falls. The chilly silence the giantess encased her in breaks when I reach my hand in to stroke her cheek.

"I'm so sorry, Astra," I whisper to her. My tears streak down my face and land on hers. The salty, warm water serves to defrost her faster, and she starts crying again. "I know, sweetheart. I know."

I don't know if I am going to die, but if I do, I know in my heart that Naomi will take care of Astra. Any second now, the floor will rise to meet me. My body may shatter to pieces, but it will act as a pillow for Astra. I only hope she isn't hurt badly.

I close my eyes, and my body jolts on impact.

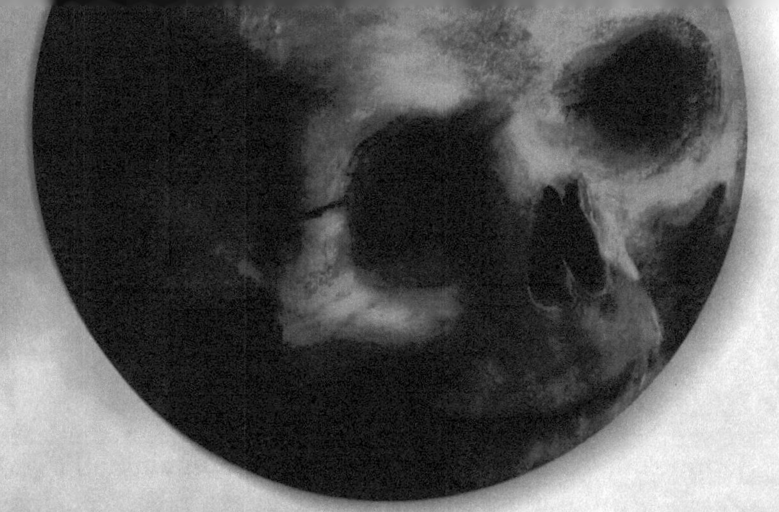

XVI

MY ONLY SUNSHINE

I don't die. I don't even break.

It takes me half a second to realize that I have not hit the floor at all. Instead, I am riding on the plush, furry back of a great wolf. On either side of us run River, Lightfoot, and Lilith. My dogs. My dogs are still with me. My pack, as fractured and torn apart as they were by this ordeal, is still a pack.

"Naomi."

<You're not dying on me yet, Danica. Not today, not tomorrow, not anytime soon.>

I turn onto my front, straddling Naomi's back. Holding Astra in one arm and finding a good purchase with the other around Naomi's neck, I pull aside my shirt and snuggle Astra in. How long has it been since she last nursed? She must be starving. As it is, I don't like how weakly she is moving in my arms. I guide her mouth to my breast. Relief floods my being as she latches, the connection as strong as ever.

<Rest, Danica. Leave the rest to me.

For once in my life, I listen.>

Naomi runs us all the way out of the mountain hall as it crumbles around us. Behind us, the queen rages, causing more and more of her palace prison to crumble to bits around her. Naomi doesn't stop running until we near the mouth of the cave that River and I entered through. And not a moment too soon either, because the moment we exit the glamourous hallway tunnel, the roof caves in, leaving the mountain queen trapped once again under the mountain. Hopefully, this time, it's a permanent prison.

A part of me sends a prayer to the Echoes who spoke to me in the mountain hall. I hope they reclaim their purpose.

At my bosom, Astra becomes warm again, her belly filling for the first time in days. She even burbles happily when she looks for the opposite breast.

<We did it.>

I hear Naomi's voice in my head, but I respond verbally. "It's over. The whole thing is over."

<Joanna didn't make it.>

I shake my head and say nothing. I can't say that I regret saving Astra. I pity the woman for the loss of her daughter, but in the same breath, she took my own daughter from me to bargain her own be returned to her. A foolish bargain—there's no way to bring the dead back to life. The dead belong dead.

I insist on getting off. We're all dog-tired. She shouldn't have to carry us any longer than she must. When my feet touch the ground, Naomi shifts back to her womanly form. I should probably avert my eyes, but after watching her transform into her wolfish form, I wanted to see the change happen in the opposite direction. Her fur shortens until creamy pale skin glows in the dark, her long hair grows back out to its full length, and her bones and muscles all rearrange themselves to reflect human anatomy. When she is done shifting, she looks at me with eyes so blue I worry that one day I'll drown in them.

"So, telepathy, huh?" she asks, starting the walk topside.

I don't know how it is possible. I've heard that trauma can act as an impetus for magical awakenings. I just didn't think it was possible for a Disappointment to achieve such a thing. We are, after all, cursed.

No, not cursed, just docile. We became so subservient to the ways of the world we lost our power over it. So strong was our belief in our own failure, that we manifested it in our reality.

"I guess that's the right term for it. I always just called myself a radio station without a firm channel."

"You're definitely on all frequencies now."

I laugh, a true joyful laughter that seems so far removed from everything we've just gone through. My gods, it feels like I haven't laughed in years.

Astra suckles happily at my breast, gurgling as she guzzles the milk down as fast as her tiny mouth can manage. I try not to jostle her as much as possible as we make our way through the caverns.

"How is our little one?" asks Naomi.

I smile.

"So unbelievably strong. I can't believe she's here." As I look at her face, I notice the faintest of glows under her chin. I adjust her little body to take a look, and my eyes nearly fall out of my head. There, right over where her voice box would be, a strange mark blazes to life in a breathtaking shade of magenta. It is a butterfly—metamorphosis, a symbol of change. "I guess, there really is some sort of magic alive inside her."

"It's alive inside you, too."

It didn't used to be, and I honestly don't know how I feel about it now. Am I a witch, now? Will I be able to do other things? Or am I just Air Danica, broadcasting all your private thoughts across the Wastes 24/7?

I decide to put the question out of my mind. That'll be a problem for future Danica. For right now, I have everything I need right here.

"Now what?" I ask. "What do we do? Are you..." I hesitate, heat flooding into my face. "Are you sticking around?"

Naomi swallows, her eyes peering down at Astra and me.

"Well, if you'll have me. I would like to stick around." My eyes go wide, and Naomi's cheeks redden. "I mean, of course, to make sure Astra is safe until she comes properly into her powers."

She turns her head away from me, and I laugh again.

"I'm sure I can figure out a sleeping space for you."

I slip my hand into hers, and with a soft adjustment, Naomi laces her fingers with mine. It feels, strangely, right. Righter than anything has ever felt before...

Bark! Bark!

With an excited bark, River bounds ahead, Lilith and Lightfoot on her heels. As we round the corner stepping into the mouth of the cave, a warm, long-lost light kisses my face. I can't help but smile.

The sun is rising; the fluttering wings of butterflies have returned to the Wastes.

FIN

Danica, Astra, and Naomi
will return in Book 4 of the
Nocturne Symphony: Berceuse.

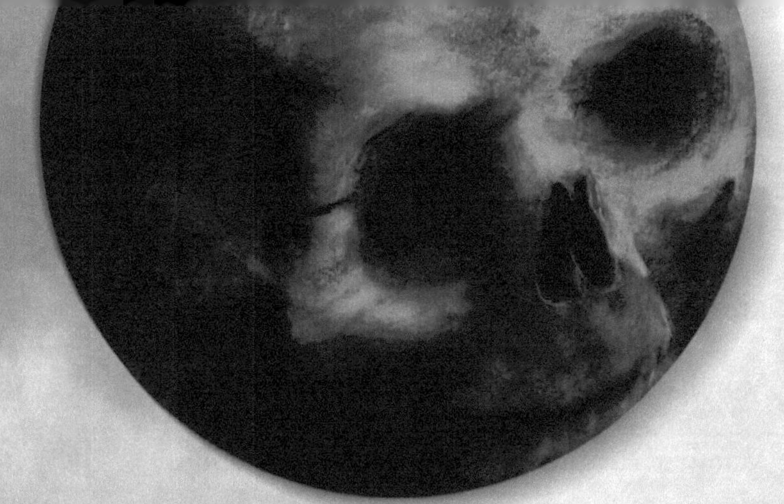

INDEX

Month of Falling	Autumn Equinox
Month of Darkness	Hexennacht (Halloween)
Month of Harvest	
Month of Cold	Firefly Hearth Festival
Month of Hearths	Midwinter Celebrations

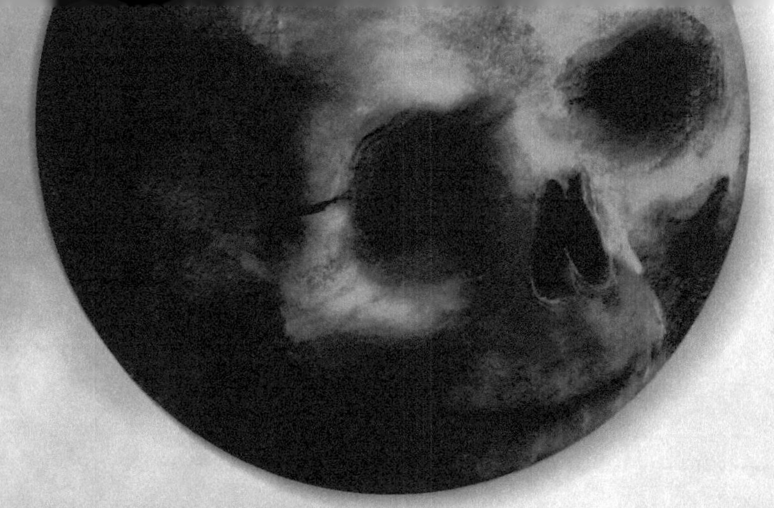

GLOSSARY OF TERMS

Adept – An augmented person equipped with military–grade technology. Certified to hunt and track hexen.

Aighneas – Largest League country on the west side of the continent. Known for their military, diesel fuel technology, and tank–like machines, Aighneas is similar in culture to the European Union, Canada, and The United States.

Cyborg – An augmented person possessing a set minimum of technological enhancements, or a human+ possessing enhancements essential to their ability to live (i.e. respiratory life support, mechanical hearts, spinal augmentations to prevent paralysis).

Deus Ex Machina – Latin – God in the Machine – A story-telling trope in which the author introduces a god or savior–like element to pull their protagonists out of trouble.

Draugr – An undead creature similar to a revenant or vampire in Scandinavian Folklore. Considered ghosts with corporeal forms, draugr are bloodthirsty and dangerous to humans.

Fae – Fairy Folk – Magical creatures that pre–date witchcraft in Deus. The Fae generate their own wild magic and live independently of witches. (Examples of Fae in Deus: Pixies, Nymphs, Huldra, Mermaids, Trolls.)

Hexen – The Spell Folk – Magic users and creatures reliant or resultant of witchcraft. (Examples of Hexen: Witches, Werewolves, Vampyres, Goblins.)

Huldra – A fae, forest guardian originating in Scandinavian Folklore. Huldra are characterized by their cow–like tails, tree–bark backs, and their alluring charms. Said to seduce unsuspecting humans into the woods, sometimes to devour them, other times to reward them, Huldra do not take kindly to trespassers, especially if said trespasser causes damage to their forest.

Human+ – A person who accepted technology into their existence via a permanent integration. This can be as medi-ocre an augmentation as a cochlear implant or as extensive as a prosthetic limb or neural net.

Nøkken – A water spirit originating in Scandinavian Folklore. The Nøkken is said to entertain humans at their shores, enchanting them with a harp or violin. Typically, they are considered benign to humans who are respectful of their waters, but more sinister tales say the Nøkken is an omen of drowning or that the creature is responsible for the drown-ings themself.

Technomancer – A League–certified human+ capable of channeling energy through their technology. Technomancers are specially trained and equipped to hunt and kill dangerous fae, hexen, undead, and other magical creatures. Their augmentations are top–of–the–line and require an immense amount of discipline to maintain and control.

Witch – A practitioner of witchcraft, the act of molding and utilizing wild magic to effect change in the outer world. Witches in Deus achieve their powers and abilities through a mixture of blood–inheritance and practical study and are considered the most dangerous of beings as the practice of unrestricted magics can lead to psychological breakdown and magic fever.

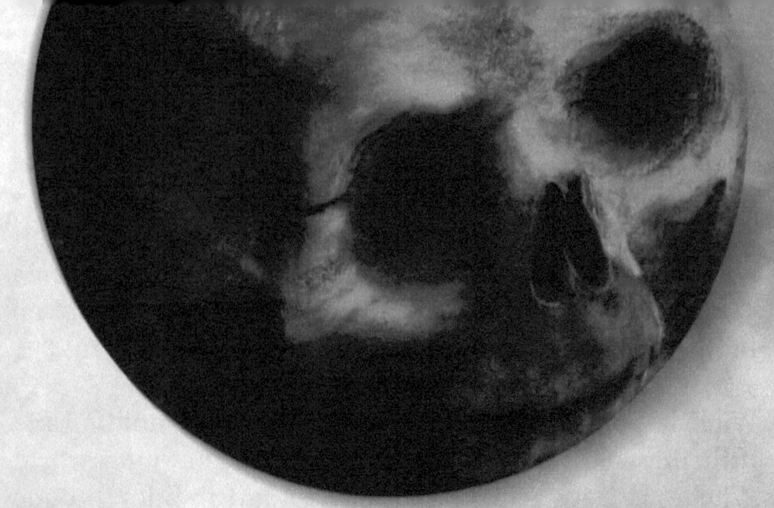

CHARACTER LIST BY STORY

Summer Helsdottir (Hexen) – Summoning Witch. Married Donarick Thames in secret.

Montwyatte (Technomancer) – Archibald's right-hand man. A cyborgean brute known for his hostility and aggression.

Donarick J. Thames (Adept) – Son of Pontiflex Catalan. Enters into a whirlwind romance with Summer Helsdottir.

Yggfret Bloodfang (Hexen) – The Goblin King. A powerful witch and leader of the Hexen who join Seraphim's forces during the war.

Monsieur Géant (Hexen) – A half-giant witch boasting superhuman strength.

Xochtli (Hexen) – The bruja of the Mojavan Desert.

Howard P. Thames – Pontiflex Catalan of Seraphim – Religious leader of Seraphim and father to Donarick Thames.

Archibald Llywelyn – General of Seraphim – Father of Oswald Llywelyn.

Atzi Moctezumo – Princess of Deriva – Eldest daughter of Tlanextli and wife of Chike Nagi. Mother of Zenza Nagi.

Wren Nocturne – The youngest child of Tlanextli Moctezumo – 247th Trials Graduate – Known Alias: The Songstress of Lorelei.

Chike Nagi – Crown Prince of Ebele – 247th Trials Graduate – Husband of Atzi Moctezumo and Father to Zenza Nagi

Chiamaka Nagi – Princess of Ebele – Younger sister to Chike Nagi and Zenza's paternal aunt.

Rameses Sahra – Pharaoh of Sekhmeti – Father of Jamar Sahra. First Primarch of The League.

Morrigan "The Morrigan" Gewalt – President of Aighneas. Elected Primarch after the death of Rameses.

FALSETTO IN THE WOODS

Lily Esquire – An augmented young woman who failed the technomancer trials due to physical disability. She is presently working toward her doctor's degree in Folklore.

Sebastian – Lily's boyfriend. He is a regular human lacking augmentations of any sort.

Kyle – Sebastian's older brother. He is more than a little misogynistic. Tricks them all into the woods on the premise that he has already scoped out a "Safe" area for them to camp.

Javier – One of Lily's friends from school, he is incredibly paranoid and hates anything frightening. Has a terrible fear of ghosts. He is terrified of anything ghostly. He loves to knit to deal with his stress.

Derrick – Javier's husband. A body builder and personal trainer, Derrick looks like a rough and tumble type, but he's really a big teddy bear at heart and a total nerd.

Jeanine – Javier's little sister and gothic sorority girl extraordinaire.

Wren Nocturne – The Songstress of Lorelei. A witch who committed "Suicide" after the League tracked her down for the various crimes she committed. She was Lily's friend at the trials.

Kaito Miyazaki – Technomancer and prince of Murasaki no Yama. He is considered one of the greatest technomancers of the present era for his intelligence, his skill, and his tactical ability.

NURSERY RHYMES IN THE DARK

Danica Sheepsong - A new mother struggling with Postpartum Depression and Postpartum Psychosis. Has mild telepathic abilities but can't channel or broadcast with any consistency. When her child is kidnapped, she undergoes a transformative quest to rescue her and learns things about herself and her abilities that she never would have thought possible.

Astra - Danica's newborn daughter

Stella - Danica's mother. Tries to be helpful but really doesn't know the first thing about being there for her daughter.

David - Astra's birth father. A failed adept who got himself killed trying to hunt down a vampyre.

Naomi (The White Wolf or varulven) - a lycan summoned by Astra to help protect her and her mother against an attack of wolves.

Camryn - The Town Mayor. She has the power of persuasion but only sometimes.

Joanna - Another woman in the town. When her own daughter is taken, she kidnaps Astra in the hope of trading the baby's life for her daughter's.

Emily (Emmy) - Joanna's daughter. Wandered into the forest curious about a song she was hearing in the night.

Old Woman Rosie - A failed mystic. She has premonitions, but they only serve to tell her things about the present and/or are often misinterpretations of the events that are to come to pass.

The Spirit of the Northern Sound - Answers Danica's prayers for a rescue after the encounter with the vildod. He ferries Danica, Naomi, and the three remaining dogs nearly to the mouth of the cave where Astra has been taken.

The Queen of Winter (Skad) - a giantess. With the disappearance of witch magic in the world, the spell that kept her slumbering in the mountain has worn off. She is now awake and ravenous for sacrifice. Her minions are as follows:

Vildod (Jordmor Haxa) - a murderous midwife. She is a wild-dead, a witch who was killed centuries ago for stealing babies from their cribs and sacrificing them to the gods.

The Elves (Nissen) - These creatures, as much as we want to believe them to be beautiful creatures of J.R.R. Tolkien's world, are not to be trifled with. Before the queen's awakening, they were peaceful enough, but as the forest is distorted by the Queen's presence, the elves become something more primal, reducing themselves to their previous tendencies of hunting and killing any who enter their forest.

DANICA'S DOGS:

River

Lilith

Kali - Dies trying to rescue Astra.

Darleen - Dies after falling from the troll's grasp, impaled on a tree branch.

Henry - Taken by the draugr.

Grace - Goes missing after the chase after Joanna.

Lightfoot

Bonnie - Killed by the wolf pack.

Yehrik - Killed by the midwife.

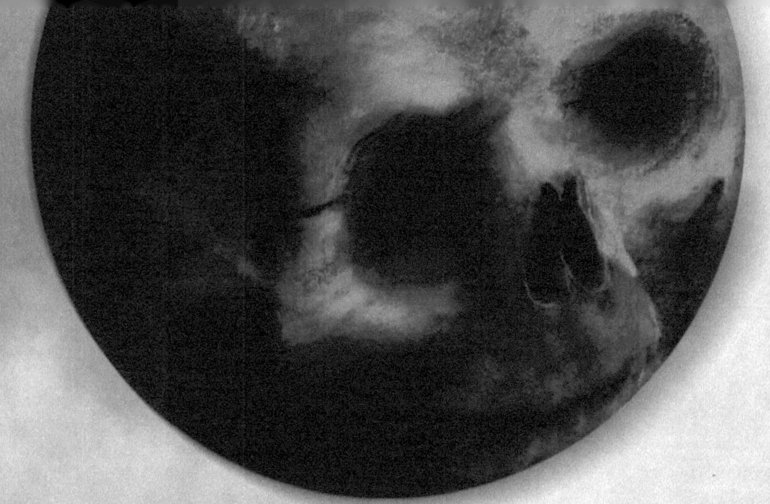

BOOK CLUB QUESTIONS

1. How would you say each of the stories in this anthology relate to one another?

2. If you could give advice to any of the three women, who would it be and what would you tell her?

3. How does the setting impact each story?

4. How did it impact you to read about the trials some of them went through?

5. How does the world of Deus reflect or mirror our reality? What is similar? What is different?

6. Why do you think Donarick changed so much after becoming a technomancer?

7. How could Lily have better handled the situation with Kyle?

8. Danica is experiencing Post Partum Depression throughout the story. What advice might you give her in order to deal with that?

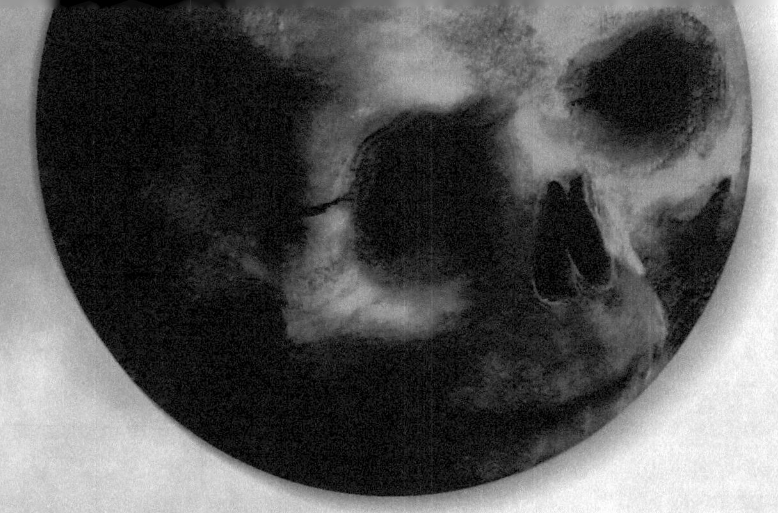

ABOUT THE AUTHOR

LYRA R. SAENZ is a writer of Science Fiction/Fantasy. A romantic at heart with a love for supernatural horror, they believe that while happy endings don't come easily, they do come, even if it means excising your ex into a glass jar.

Born and raised in South Texas, Lyra is a multicultural, eyeliner-wielding member of the LGBTQ+ community, an animal-lover, and a cynic of all things political. They presently haunt the Denver area with their amazingly supportive partner, their tiny toddler, and their feline-shaped void, Violet. Lyra grew up bouncing between their Chicano and Scandinavian heritages, never feeling like they never really fit in one world or the other.

Despite growing up on enchiladas and lefsa, they'll never turn down an offering of sushi or pho. And while their friends were getting boyfriends and girlfriends, they were too busy crushing on dreamy anime and manhwa characters to bother with real people. So, with one foot on either side of the border and their head full of East-Asian pop culture, Lyra started creating their own worlds.

A lover of all things witchy, paranormal, and ghostly with a side of Victorian–futurism, cyberpunk, and posthumanism, Lyra imagines worlds where the IT tech is a werewolf, and the coffee machine has a fairy living inside it, but the androids love to take walks down the forest trail and host the occasional bonfire. When they aren't lost somewhere between an inkwell and a notebook, they can be found acting as a throne for the real queen of the household: their cat, and her royal majesty demands snuggles constantly. Or, on calmer days, they'll sit and listen to her partner play video games while they unsuccessfully knit and/or binge their latest international tv show.

Discover more at
4HorsemenPublications.com

10% off using HORSEMEN10

www.ingramcontent.com/pod-product-compliance
Lightning Source LLC
Chambersburg PA
CBHW020225010826
48973CB00006B/1373